Praise for Alexis Daria

Praise for *Dance with Me*

"Yes, it's an absolutely sizzling romance! But, at heart, it's a book that explores creativity as a vibrant, personal, and urgent human activity... *Dance with Me* is another great book from Alexis Daria. You'll fall in love with Dimitri and Natasha, and like me, you'll be fervently hoping that there are more books coming soon from this talented author."

—JenReadsRomance

"Despite the glamour of the show business setting, Daria focuses on the difficulty of pursuing a dream despite financial instability, which is especially intense in the world of dance, where a wrong step can result in career-ending injury. But dance also frees Dimitri and Natasha to enjoy their intense connection without fear and provides a way for them to become something more than their public personas. The passion Daria has for this world is palpable in every word of *Dance with Me,* and one hopes she has many more love stories to tell within it."

—*BookPage*

"[Natasha and Dimitri's story] wasn't just about learning to accept love and to give love, it was also about taking risks in their professional lives as well…and finding their passion and following it… The true strength in this book lies in their adorable, if reluctant, romance. They were so sexy together, I LOVED the dancing scenes."

—Lenore, Celebrity Readers

"*Dance With Me* is a sexy, character-driven, romance that will tug at your heart… I cannot wait to read more from this author, and based on this book alone, she's going to keep on delivering solid romantic stories with interesting and complex characters."

—Geri, Dirty Girl Romance

Praise for *Take the Lead*

2018 RITA® Award Winner for Best First Book

Named one of the Best Romance Novels of 2017 by
The Washington Post and *Entertainment Weekly*

"Believable, emotional, and hot—everything you want from a story about dance partners!"

—Jasmine Guillory, *New York Times* bestselling author

"A sparkling debut . . . Daria's story of this behind-the-scenes romance is a perfect ten."

— Entertainment Weekly

"Vibrantly written."

— The Washington Post

"Their dancing is joyful, sexy, and mimics the trust and intimacy they develop as partners and lovers. This perfect romance will dance its way into the reader's heart."

— Kirkus Review (starred review)

"The structure of the competition keeps the pages flying, and Daria does a fantastic job making the thrilling dance routines jump and twirl off the page. . . .this whirlwind romance scores a 10 out of 10."

— Publishers Weekly (starred review)

"As the chemistry sizzles...Daria brings humor and colorful detail to each scene."

— Booklist

DANCE WITH ME

Also by Alexis Daria

Take the Lead

Dance with Me

Dance All Night (novella)

You Had Me at Hola

A Lot Like Adios

Along Came Amor

The Holiday Hookup List (novella)

Only Santas in the Building (novella)

What the Hex (novella)

Amor Actually: A Holiday Romance Anthology

DANCE WITH ME

THE DANCE OFF

ALEXIS DARIA

To Mom and Dad.
Thanks for everything.

Chapter One

Three years ago

Natasha Díaz cursed under her breath as she peered down the hallway. What had Donna said? Room B? D? Natasha couldn't remember where the producer had told her to go, and now she was all turned around.

The Dance Off's headquarters in Los Angeles was large and labyrinthine. Poster-sized photos of couples from previous seasons lined the long corridors. Natasha stopped in front of a picture featuring Kevin Ray. Kevin was arguably the most popular dancer on the show, which paired ballroom pros with semi-famous celebrities in a televised dance competition.

Someday, Natasha's picture would hang on these walls. She hadn't met her celebrity partner yet, and she was savoring the days until she did. Once they started rehearsing, it would be a whirlwind of work and stress. But she was more excited than anything else.

Even though this was Natasha's first season, she'd previously been a featured dancer on the network's sister show, *Everybody Dance Now*, so the producers at *The Dance Off* were starting her as a pro. Under normal circumstances, Natasha would've had to do time as a backup dancer to gain audience recognition. Her best friend, Gina Morales, had been tagged to choreograph some upcoming episodes of *Everybody*, so Gina wasn't going to join *The Dance Off* until the following season.

Natasha sighed as she passed the door for Room A. It was weird being here without Gina. They'd been nearly inseparable since they were fourteen, two Puerto Rican girls from the Bronx for whom dance was life. Gina was ambitious and organized, whereas Natasha usually got into some kind of trouble if left to her own devices.

Case in point: if Gina were there, Natasha wouldn't be lost at this very moment.

Determined not to be late on her very first day, Natasha marched up to Room B and grasped the doorknob. She'd stick her head in, and if this wasn't the right room, she'd apologize and try the next. No harm, no foul. Maybe someone could point her in the right direction.

But when she stepped inside, she knew immediately that she'd made a mistake. There was no chattering group of dancers, no busy producers or PAs, no camera crew capturing the first-day-of-school-level excitement of the pre-season.

Instead, her eyes landed on a sole figure backlit by the long row of windows. The glare of the California sun burned his dark silhouette into her retinas. If she closed her eyes, she'd see the afterimage of him behind her lids. Tall. Broad shoulders. Trim hips. Long legs. Impeccable posture.

But then he turned around, and at the sight of his profile, her heart slammed into her throat and threatened to choke her.

Holy shit. She knew *exactly* who he was.

Dimitri Kovalenko. One of the judges on *The Dance Off*. World-renowned choreographer. Star of the cult classic *Aliens Don't Dance*.

And teenage Natasha's celebrity crush.

Dimitri Kovalenko. Here, in the flesh.

And striding right toward her, like a panther stalking its prey

—and she was his next meal. Before Natasha could open her mouth to apologize or explain or even breathe, a song began to play, a 90s R&B slow jam with a thick, pulsing beat. Dimitri grabbed her hand and pulled her against his chest. His eyes were dark but distant, as if he'd been lost in thought when she stumbled upon him. His forbidding brows drew down, making him look severe and so fucking hot, she thought she might melt. Her fingers itched to twine themselves in his thick brown hair, and his cologne wrapped around her, luring her in. It reminded her of the expensive scents advertised in the thick fashion magazines her mother had sometimes brought home from the hair salon once the stack in the waiting area got too tall—something woodsy and alluring, but not overpowering.

Her heart pounded, but her breathing stayed even. She didn't question what Dimitri was doing with her. Her body knew what to do.

She let him lead.

He guided her with commanding touches. Not just his hands, but everywhere their bodies connected. Fingers, feet, hip, shoulder—she moved with him, surrendering completely. He spun her out, tugged her back, and caught her on his hip. Her hair, still loose, flipped over her head and covered his shoulder and neck.

Underlying the music were the sounds of their breathing, of their sneakers on the shiny floor, of fabric shifting over their skin.

They swayed together, leading into a low lift, before beginning a sensuous salsa across the floor. They moved so fast, it felt like flying. Her feet barely touched the ground.

But she wouldn't fall. He wouldn't let her. He was in complete control.

Still, every time he pulled her close, fire raced along her nerves. Her chest felt tight, her skin sensitive. It hungered for his touch, waiting for the next hint of direction.

Seconds ticked past, but she had no idea how long they'd

been dancing. The fiery intensity in his eyes filled her vision, and she lost track of all else.

She forgot this was the wrong room.

Finally, Dimitri flung her into an ending pose. Her hands braced against his solid chest. Their eyes locked. He held her by the hip and shoulder, his grip firm and unyielding, yet also somehow…protective.

Their harsh breaths mingled as he dropped his forehead to hers. It wasn't a particularly long or taxing dance, but an unmistakable heat flared between them, and Natasha knew he felt it, too.

His gaze dropped to her parted lips. They were dry. She licked them.

His eyes snapped back up to hers.

"What's your name?" His voice was deep, like a growl or a grumble. He had a reputation for being the cranky judge, and she steeled herself to answer without stumbling over the word.

"Natasha."

His grin was quick, his teeth flashing against his trim, dark beard. He repeated it, giving the syllables a roll, an accent. "*Natasha.*"

The back of her neck prickled, and she wished he'd say it again. Her name sounded delicious in his mouth.

"You know who I am?" he asked, still grinning.

If anyone else had said that to her, she would've rolled her eyes. But for some reason, his cockiness made her want to tear her clothes off. "Yes."

"Good." He leaned in even closer, their lips now just a whisper apart. Her mouth longed for him to close the gap. "Spend the night with me."

Holy fuck. Had she died? Was this Heaven?

She swallowed and said again, "Yes."

He nodded, releasing her and taking a step back. "Go. You're probably expected somewhere."

The dismissal was abrupt, but he was right. She was

supposed to be meeting her fellow castmates, not dirty dancing with one of the judges. She took a few steps toward the door and grabbed her bag. She didn't even remember dropping it. Once Dimitri had taken her hand, she was in his thrall.

"Wait." Before she could leave, he strode forward and took the bag from her. Digging his hand inside, he pulled out her phone. "Unlock it." She did so without question and waited while he sent himself a text from her phone.

"Nine," he said, dropping it back into the bag.

She gulped. Nine was late, and she was expected back here early the next morning.

But she didn't care. A night with Dimitri Kovalenko would be worth any price.

He caught her chin in his hand, and with a look that threatened to burn her up from the inside out, he stroked his thumb over her lower lip. "See you then…Tasha."

Her reply trembled out on a shaky breath. "Yes."

When his hand dropped, she turned and dashed from the room.

And the second she was in the hall, she remembered where she was supposed to be. Not Room B. Room *E*.

And now she was late.

Chapter Two

Present day

Being a professional dancer on TV wasn't all false lashes, sequined spandex, and vamping for the camera. The reality involved long hours of rehearsal, weekly live performances, and the delicate management of big personalities. Yet after spending the day racing all over LA from one gig to the next—with way too much time stuck in traffic—Natasha Díaz missed *The Dance Off*'s headquarters with its tiny breakroom, spotty air conditioning, and unflattering fluorescent lighting. Most of all, she missed the simplicity of having only one job.

The Dance Off filmed two seasons a year, each lasting three months. While the show paid well, money still seemed to slip through Natasha's fingers as easily as it had when she'd been a teenage waitress in the Bronx. And now, after a string of unexpected expenses, she'd been forced to take on as many jobs as she could fit into the summer off-season, everything from yoga to spin to something called "Soulsa."

But she was doing it. Living on her own for the first time in her life. Covering the full rent for the two-bedroom apartment in

West Hollywood that she used to share with her best friend. And driving an eight-year-old, new-to-her blue Prius.

Buying a car hadn't been on Natasha's to-do list, especially after she'd just paid off and closed all her credit cards as part of her New Year's resolution to get out of debt. She was proud of herself for actually having the funds, thanks to a recurring role on the teen comedy series *Drama Club*. Never mind that at twenty-seven she was a decade older than her character. Give her a high ponytail and a backpack, and she could easily pass for a high school mean girl.

It didn't matter that her checking account was nearly wiped out and she spent most nights collapsing into bed exhausted— and alone. She only had to hold out for a few more weeks. Once season fifteen of *The Dance Off* started filming, she'd be fine.

So instead of dancing, clubbing, or drinking, her new nightly routine consisted of going straight home after teaching evening dance classes and private sessions. There, she popped out her contacts and washed off approximately a pound of makeup before slapping on a cheap sheet mask. People expected a celebrity instructor, and she had to look the part, even though she'd been forced to cancel all her regular beauty treatments. Being a woman in Hollywood was fucking expensive. Then she curled up in bed to read.

At the moment, she was making her way through *Jane Eyre* again. Natasha loved a period drama, and it was comforting to read about someone whose love life was more toxic than her own. After all, Natasha had never hooked up with anyone who kept their wife locked in an attic.

At least, not that she was aware of.

Right as she was dozing off, her phone buzzed on the nightstand. Blinking blearily behind her glasses, she glanced at the screen.

A text from Dimitri Kovalenko stared back at her.

Come over.

She exhaled harshly, disgusted by his audacity even as she

slid out of bed, suddenly wide awake and moving on autopilot. In the bathroom, she put her contacts back in. She'd straightened her long, curly hair the day before, so all she had to do now was unwrap her silk scarf and run a brush through the dark tresses.

Her better judgment kicked in as she was rifling through her closet.

You're tired. You have work early tomorrow. The pendejo hasn't called you since the season ended. You told Gina you're done with him.

Scowling, Natasha yanked an expensive and totally impractical black spandex-and-lace catsuit off a hanger. Her common sense sounded suspiciously like her mother.

But that irritating little voice was right. This was a bad idea.

The last time Natasha had slept with Dimitri, they'd been so drunk, the sex had been so good, and he'd murmured so many delicious phrases in multiple languages about how much he wanted her, that a stupid flicker of hope, never fully extinguished, flared brighter inside her chest. But the next morning, he'd been unbearably nonchalant about the whole thing.

"We should do that again soon," he'd said, coming up behind her while she was dabbing moisturizer onto her face. Then he'd smacked her ass and smirked at her in the mirror. "*If* you can fit me into your busy schedule."

Her hands clenched on the fabric as she recalled the hot flash of anger that had seared through her. *The fucking asshole.* Okay, yes, she'd been messing around with Jackson Garcia, a TV actor and one of *The Dance Off's* celebrity contestants last season. But she knew for a fact that Dimitri had gotten cozy with another participant, Olympic figure skater and total bruja Lauren D'Angelo. And Dimitri was one of the show's judges!

Pot meet kettle, motherfucker.

She'd left his house and hadn't said a word to him after that. They'd seen each other from afar during the season finale, but Natasha had avoided Dimitri backstage. Since then, he'd maintained radio silence.

Until now.

Come over.

Would it kill him to phrase it as a question? It'd serve his ass right if she ignored him.

As if Dimitri could sense she was considering it, the phone buzzed with another text.

This time, only one word.

Now.

Arrogant jerk. Did he really think she was going to drop everything and race to his side?

Except she was already changing into a pair of lace panties. Because who was she kidding? He never asked, and she never said no. Only in the darkest recesses of her thoughts could she admit that even after three years of his nonsense, she still wanted him more than she'd ever wanted anyone in her entire life. More than charismatic young actors like Jackson García or Rocky Lim, or any of the other guys she'd fucked in this industry. More than any of the men who, if she let them, would worship the ground she walked on.

Instead, she wanted Dimitri, the one person who'd never give her the validation she so desperately sought. It was fucked up, but she couldn't help herself.

It was the only kind of love she knew.

In the back of her mind, she imagined Jane Eyre mocking her. *Who's toxic now, bitch?*

Pushing away the image, Natasha swiped on mascara and red lipstick before slipping into the bodysuit and a pair of four-inch designer heels. In these shoes, she'd be taller than Dimitri, but she wouldn't be wearing them for long. Striking a pose for her full-length mirror, she admired the results. She looked like a dominatrix, but it was only for show.

They both knew who was really in control.

Grabbing her phone, she typed back, *On my way,* and then she was out the door, heading to the man who held a tiny piece of her heart. Every time she was with him, she hoped to steal it back. Instead, she always ended up giving him a little more.

And the asshole didn't even know it.

Chapter Three

Three years ago

Natasha pulled into Dimitri's driveway at 9:07. It was the exact number of minutes late she'd been to the correct rehearsal room after he'd waylaid her in Room B.

A little petty, sure, but she didn't want to come off as *too* eager.

Even if she was jumping out of her skin at the thought of touching him again.

She flipped down the mirror and decided against reapplying her lipstick. If things went how she suspected they would, it'd just end up all over him.

The front door of the Spanish-style house opened. Dimitri leaned against the jamb, silhouetted by the light within.

The rush of desire brought on by their dance reignited in Natasha's veins. She grabbed her purse and bolted from the car.

As she strolled toward him, she told herself to play it cool. It wasn't like this was her first time meeting a guy for sex, although she didn't usually feel quite so jittery. He was hot, sure, but she barely knew him.

Except that wasn't entirely true. She'd been low-key obsessed with him in high school. She knew he was thirty-two years old, and that he'd been born in Ukraine and had grown up in Brooklyn. She'd used her babysitting money to buy *Aliens Don't Dance* on DVD the day it came out, and she'd clipped his magazine interviews and kept them in a folder to reread. It had been one of her biggest regrets that she hadn't saved enough for a ticket to see his Broadway show before it closed.

But that was knowing his career. She didn't know the feel of his lips on hers. His tongue between her teeth, his hands under her clothes, his body against her bare skin.

Dancing with him had given her a taste, but she wanted more. She wanted *everything*.

And even then, she feared it wouldn't be enough.

It scared her a bit, the depth of her desire for him, but she also didn't care. She'd give this man everything just to keep this feeling going.

Because as much as she wanted him, she got the sense that his want equaled hers.

It was there in the quirk of his lips, the hunger in his eyes, the deceptively casual angle of his body as he lounged against the doorframe. The light from inside the house bent around him in a way that highlighted those little details. He was far from the first man to look at her like this, but his intensity was stronger than she'd ever experienced.

And she craved it.

When she reached the door, he didn't even let her get across the threshold before he cupped her face with both hands and laid his mouth on hers.

Madre de Dios…

The kiss was *perfect*. His lips were soft, his beard scratchy, his tongue hot, but not sticky. Arousal swept through her as his tongue swiped against hers, making her hyperaware of her body, his hands, his mouth. All of her attention laser-focused on the points where they touched.

And she still wanted more.

She raised her hands to his shoulders, and it was like her touch broke something in him. He grabbed her waist and hauled her into the house, slamming the door behind them.

From that point on, a wildness overtook them. His mouth came back to hers. His hands skimmed over her body, and her clothing melted from her skin. She wasn't nearly so elegant, yanking at his buttons and shoving his shirt off his shoulders. He laughed when she attacked the fastenings on his pants and she muttered, "Shut up," which only made him laugh harder.

When they were both down to their underwear, she wrapped her arms around his shoulders and kissed him again. It wasn't hard to reach his mouth—he only had a few inches on her. He hitched his hands under her thighs and lifted her. He wasn't built like a typical dancer. He was thick and broad, and Natasha, well, she was still built like a ballerina.

Aside from the subtle boob job she'd finally gotten.

He carried her into his bedroom while she kissed his face, his neck, his shoulders.

"Natasha..." he whispered against her lips, and for a second, she was surprised he remembered her name. Then he toppled them onto his enormous bed, and she wasn't thinking about anything anymore except his hands and mouth on her skin.

The next few hours were an insatiable maelstrom of panting, begging, and orgasms. She came so many times, she didn't know which way was up. She tried to return the favor, grabbing for his cock every chance she got, but he just laughed and distracted her again. When he was finally inside her, she was so wrung out, all she could do was hold on for the ride.

Sex with a dancer was a fluid choreography of limbs and positions. Dimitri twisted her around like a pretzel, but every-thing felt good with him. As with their dance, she surrendered control, trusting him with her body, with her pleasure.

She could tell when he was getting close. He stopped shifting her around so much, and he gathered her closer in his arms as he pounded into her. Their eyes locked, and she wanted to look away. It was too raw, too real. But she forced herself to hold his gaze. There was something in it she wanted more of, but she didn't know what. Her muscles clenched, his cock still lighting her up from inside, even though she'd thought she was done. Gasping, mewling cries fell from her lips, and she gripped his sweat-slickened shoulders with fingers that had nearly gone numb.

He brought his hand between them, and a second before he touched her clit, he growled her name.

"Natasha."

"Oh, *God.*" She ground the words out just as the orgasm roared through her, finally giving her the strength to squeeze her eyes shut.

His hand gripped her jaw, and she looked at him just in time to see his own eyes close, his face tightening as he gritted his teeth and groaned. His hips moved in short, hard thrusts, sending aftershocks through her body, and she held him in her arms as he came.

When it was over, they both sank into the bed. He was still on top of her, their legs twisted around. She couldn't figure out how to untangle herself, and it seemed like too much trouble anyway. He tucked his head into the curve of her neck and let out a deep sigh.

Natasha stared at the ceiling, trying to collect her scattered thoughts, when Dimitri's hand fell away from her chin. She expected him to get up, but instead, his fingers stroked her hair.

The tenderness in the gesture, and the gentle pulls against her scalp, sent leisurely tingles across her skin and down to her toes. What was he doing?

It was too much. She leaned to the side, giving him the hint that she wanted to get up, but he only tightened his grip on her. Just for a second, long enough for her to know he didn't want to let go, before he released her.

Why?

She grabbed a handful of tissues from the box on the bedside table and thrust them at him so he could dispose of the condom, then shut herself in the toilet stall in his impressive en suite bathroom.

She needed a few minutes away from him. Already, her body longed to return to the bed for more snuggles, but her mind wasn't ready for such closeness.

This was just a hook-up. A one-night stand. She'd done this plenty of times.

So why did tonight feel different?

When she passed through the bedroom again, it was with the intention of leaving. She must have misread his actions. There was no way he'd want her to stick around. And frankly, after all they'd just done, she needed time alone to process.

That, and time to forget, to convince herself that sex with Dimitri hadn't been as magical and mind-blowing as it really was. She couldn't afford to get addicted to this guy.

Natasha had a bad habit of wanting more from the people least likely to give it.

But he snagged her wrist as she passed the bed.

"Where are you going?" he grumbled, his voice husky. "I'm not done with you."

Once again, she went where he directed her, sinking back onto the bed with him. He pulled her close, nuzzling his face into her neck, and she let him.

Who was she kidding?

She'd let this man do *anything*.

Chapter Four

Present day

The next day, Natasha was plagued by a single question.

Why the fuck had she worn lace panties?

Yes, Dimitri had gone absolutely wild when he'd seen them, dragging them off her with his teeth, but after teaching five dance and fitness classes, Natasha had major regrets.

She hadn't meant to spend the entire night with him. But he'd been so ravenous, so determined to make her come as many times as possible—six, possibly a new record—that she'd been utterly laid to waste by the time they were done. When her alarm went off three hours later, she barely had enough time to jump into his shower and rush off to teach an early morning yoga class. The smell of his soap tormented her all day, as if the sweet ache between her legs wasn't already a constant reminder of him.

And, of course, there were no underwear to be found in the gym bag she kept in her trunk. Hell, she was lucky the bag had been there at all, considering this was a new car. Her choice had been the lacy bikini briefs or going commando, and with as much action as her pussy had gotten the night before, she'd decided spending the day sans panties would be worse. Now, after leading two back-to-back spin classes, that choice was up for debate. She was positive there was some chafing going on down there.

All she wanted was a shower, a pair of plain cotton bikini briefs, and a nap, in that order. When her last clients of the day—a couple preparing for their wedding dance—canceled their private lesson, Natasha could've wept with relief. She headed straight home, fantasizing about drawing the blackout shades against the afternoon sunlight and sinking into her luxurious memory foam mattress.

But apparently, a simple fucking nap was too much to ask for.

As she staggered into her room, ready to strip naked and jump in the shower, she stopped short.

A fine layer of white dust coated everything in the room. A wet, moldy odor filled the air, and the trickle of running water drew her attention to the en suite bathroom. With a heavy sense of foreboding, she strode forward and slapped on the bathroom light.

Her heart sank.

Of course, she thought. *Just what I fucking need.*

Chapter Five

Her bathroom ceiling was gone.

Well, not *gone*, exactly. But instead of being where a ceiling was *supposed* to be, broken pieces of wet plaster filled the tub and covered the floor, vanity, and toilet. Water was everywhere, including—oh shit, *her closet*.

The closet was just on the other side of the wall from the tub. Natasha shoved the sliding door open and stared in genuine horror at her beloved wardrobe.

Her clothes.

Her purses.

Her *shoes*.

Tears welled in her eyes.

During her five years in LA, she'd amassed a considerable collection of beautiful outfits. They were her pride and joy. Some people had kids or pets. Natasha had *style*.

And now it was all ruined.

This was what she got for wanting the master bedroom. When she and Gina had moved in, Natasha insisted she was cool with paying more for the bigger room and private bath. For someone who'd spent the first twenty years of her life sleeping in a corner of the living room separated by bookshelves, an en suite had seemed like a dream come true. Never mind that she'd had to look up what "en suite" meant after reading the rental listing.

Now, that private bathroom had turned into a nightmare.

She pressed her fingertips to the corners of her eyes, dabbing away the gathering moisture. She needed to calm down and figure out what to do next. Taking a deep breath, she immediately coughed from the plaster dust lingering in the air.

First order of business: get the hell out of here.

She headed into the living room and shut the bedroom door behind her. Now that she knew to look for it, she could see that plaster dust covered everything out here too. She pulled out her phone and called the management company. No one picked up, but she left a message explaining the situation as calmly as she could. Then she sent a text to the building's super.

Since a hollow whooshing sound still came from the pipes, Natasha jogged upstairs to knock on her neighbor's door. No reply. She was on a first-name basis with the people who lived on either side of her, but that was it. Whoever lived above her had moved in only two months before—she'd heard the noise from the movers—but other than that, she had no idea who lived there.

No use dwelling on it. They had to come back sometime.

In her own apartment, she opened all the windows and got to work emptying her closet into three piles: laundry, dry cleaning, and ruined beyond repair.

As she worked, she gave herself a pep talk. Okay, this was bad, but not horrible. The apartment had another bathroom off the hallway, and a second bedroom, vacant now that Gina had moved out. Natasha could stay there while her own room underwent repairs. Or maybe the management company would finally reply to her emails asking if there was a one-bedroom available.

A small part of her regretted turning down Gina's offer to pay rent through the end of the lease, but it had been high time Natasha stopped leaning on her friend for support. She was twenty-seven years old, old enough to stand on her own two feet. Plus, she didn't want to deal with learning the quirks of a new roommate.

She'd just retrieved the detergent from under the kitchen sink when someone knocked on her door. It was Manny, the building's super, a wiry Venezuelan man with honey-brown skin and a ready smile.

"Hola, Manny," she said, switching to Spanish. And even though she was on the verge of hysteria, she politely asked about his children.

It was their dynamic; when their paths crossed, they chatted in Spanish—he asked about *The Dance Off*, and she inquired after his two kids—and he came to her assistance quickly when she needed something.

As Manny told her about his twelve-year-old son's computer camp, she ushered him into her bedroom and gestured at the water still pouring in.

Manny stood with his hands on his hips, staring at the ceiling —or at least, the place where the ceiling used to be. With a weary sigh, he removed a giant key ring from his belt and left to turn off the water.

Natasha began to move things out of the bedroom while she waited.

It was a while before Manny returned, and it wasn't with good news—a pipe had burst, and he'd had to shut the water off in the entire building. No, he didn't know when she'd be able to do laundry, and he didn't think her moving into Gina's old room or an empty one-bedroom apartment would work.

"¿Por qué?" she asked, trying to ignore the prickling sensation on the back of her neck when he cringed. Whatever Manny was about to say, this was going to get worse.

"Hay un problema en el edificio con…insectos…"

A problem with "insects" in the building? The prickles spread down her back as Manny explained that the apartment upstairs, along with a few other units in the building, had experienced an "infestation."

Yikes. Maybe that was why the management company hadn't responded to her requests to move into a different unit.

Natasha started to ask what kind of "insect," then cut herself off. Only one kind of bug struck this kind of terror into the hearts of building superintendents, and it wasn't roaches.

Just the thought made her skin crawl. There was no way she could stay here during repairs. She wouldn't be able to sleep a wink.

Manny said she could leave her furniture in the apartment while the exterminator and contractors worked. However, he recommended she wrap everything in plastic first, to protect it from potential bugs and construction debris. When repairs were done, she could move back in. But in the meantime, she still had to pay rent.

She thanked Manny and held it together until he left. The second her apartment door closed, despair washed over her.

She was going to have to move out. Immediately. Chest tight, she eyed the piles of clothing, wondering how fast the bugs she didn't want to think about could move through a hole in the ceiling. A chill went down her spine.

If only Gina were here. Gina would take care of everything, and their lives wouldn't even skip a beat. All of this would be a minor nuisance, flattened by the force of Gina's efficiency.

Natasha shook off the urge to call her best friend. No, she could do this. She could be an adult and handle challenges on her own.

What would Gina do?

Research. Gina always started by informing herself about the topic at hand. When they'd learned ballroom dance styles, Gina had made them color-coded study guides and playlists.

Natasha typed the dreaded word—"bedbugs"—into her phone's browser. The photos that popped up made her gag. But apparently, if she washed and dried on hot, she could salvage most of her clothing. The more delicate items had to get to the dry cleaner immediately, which would cost a fortune, but it was worth it to save her wardrobe.

There. Adulting wasn't so hard.

Except she still didn't have a place to live.

And she had a whole apartment to pack up.

And she was exhausted.

Stupid Dimitri and his late-night texts. Stupid *her* for craving his inconsistent attention instead of ignoring him.

Ugh. Enough wallowing. She had a ton of shit to do before she could even think about sleeping.

At least she had a new car to curl up in, if it came to that.

Natasha cringed and sent up a prayer to whatever deity might be listening. *Please don't let it come to that.*

———

AN HOUR LATER, Manny stopped by to tell her the water in the building was back on. Natasha grabbed the first two piles of clothes and hustled to the laundry room on her floor.

While the washers ran, she vacuumed and wiped down all the surfaces in her apartment. The next step was to wrap the furniture in plastic and move it into Gina's old bedroom.

What a fucking chore. Her eyes and throat burned from exhaustion and plaster dust. She took a break to swap out her contacts for the red-framed glasses she wore at night.

Her phone rang while she was loading the dryers. Dimitri's handsome face flashed on the screen, cropped from a selfie they'd taken one night while naked in his pool. She answered out of habit, then silently cursed herself. She didn't have time for him. Holding the phone to her ear with her shoulder, she grabbed a handful of wet socks that had fallen to the floor.

"What is it?" she snapped, then winced. She'd never spoken to him that way before.

"Tasha?" His deep voice tickled her ear. She should've put him on speaker. "Is everything okay?"

She let out a hysterical giggle, which seemed to shatter the last vestiges of her composure. "Okay? No, nothing is okay." And even though he was the last person she should confide in, she couldn't stop everything from tumbling out. "My bathroom ceiling fell in, there's a leak in my bedroom, and my building has an infestation. I have to pack everything up and find somewhere else to stay, and I'm only running on three hours of sleep because I spent all night with *you*. So, no, I'm not okay. And I don't have time for whatever sexcapades you have planned, so just...call whatever girl is next on your list. I'm busy."

And then she hung up on him, which she'd also never done before. Then, because she felt the urge to call him back and apologize, she slapped her phone facedown on top of the dryer and continued shoving wet clothes inside.

It was ridiculous to spill her guts to him and even more ridiculous to worry about the effect her snippy words would have. After all, she was trying to keep her distance from him—and doing a terrible job of it, considering her behavior last night. Maybe this would finally push him away and give her some breathing room. He was the last person she wanted right now.

Mentirosa.

Natasha closed her eyes and sighed. She *was* a fucking liar. She wanted Dimitri with her every breath.

Even if all he'd ever do was break her heart.

She closed the laundry room door behind her and headed back to her apartment.

She was halfway through vacuuming the living room rug—*again*—when the stress and exhaustion from the day crashed down on her.

This zero-commitment, on-and-off shit she had going with Dimitri was putting her through the wringer. No sleep plus a day of teaching had left her physically drained. And now, faced with the prospect of being broke and homeless, she was done. So fucking done.

Tears burst through the flimsy emotional dam she'd constructed and streamed down her cheeks. This sucked. Everything sucked. And she had no idea what to do.

She'd been in tough spots before, had made hard decisions she hoped to never have to make again. Life had shown her early on that she could only rely on herself, but over the past few years, thanks to Gina and *The Dance Off*, things had been pretty great. She had a steady gig working as a dancer and enough money to live the kind of lifestyle she'd always dreamed of.

And then Gina found true love and moved out.

Natasha shoved her fingers under her glasses to swipe her gritty, tired eyes.

She was happy for Gina. Truly. Cynical though she may be, Natasha still believed in love, and Gina, of all people, deserved a happily-ever-after.

Even so, she *missed* Gina. Gina had been her best friend since they were fourteen. They'd done everything together—high school, starting a dance career, moving to Los Angeles—mostly thanks to Gina's limitless drive and superior executive functioning skills.

But then Gina and her celebrity partner, the Alaskan survivalist Stone Nielson, had fallen in love while paired together on the previous season of *The Dance Off*. Their win had opened more career doors for them, and Gina had returned to New York City, leaving a hole in Natasha's life the size of…well, the size of the hole in her bathroom ceiling.

Fuck. She had to get out of here.

Natasha turned on the vacuum again and mentally ran through her options. Gina would send money if Natasha asked, which was exactly why she wouldn't. Aside from Gina, Lori Kim and Kevin Ray were Natasha's closest friends from *The Dance Off*, but Lori's roommates were awful, and Kevin was weird about having people in his house. As often as the three of them hung out, they never went to Kevin's place, even though his home was the biggest and nicest. Mila Ivanova or Rhianne Davis, two other dancers from the show, might let her stay with them, although just the thought of asking made Natasha want to shrivel up in embarrassment.

Well, it looked like she'd be sleeping in her car and using the showers at the gym. Wouldn't be the first time.

A heavy knock cut into her thoughts, audible over the roar of the vacuum. Natasha shut it off and wiped her cheeks with the back of her hand before she called, "Entra." It didn't matter if Manny saw her like this—she had a good reason to cry, and he knew it.

The door opened.

It wasn't Manny.

Chapter Six

Three years ago

The early morning light was misty and gray when Natasha attempted to slip from the bed. Still half-asleep, Dimitri tightened his hold on her wrist and grunted a wordless command into the pillows.

"I have to get ready for work." Her voice was a low murmur in the dark. As much as he wanted to pull her back into the circle of his arms, he let her go. Her lips touched his one last time, then she was gone.

Her warmth lingered on his sheets, taunting him. Dimitri burrowed into the pillow she'd used, breathing in the scent of her shampoo, something tangy and sweet. He wished he could go back to sleep and dream that she was still there. Instead, he was awake and confronted with an unwanted mess of emotions.

Holy hell. What the fuck was all that?

Thanks to the ease of their dance at the studio, he'd suspected that sex with Natasha would be good. Great. Phenomenal, even. But he hadn't counted on wanting her so bad.

No, actually, that was a fucking lie. From the second they'd started moving together in the rehearsal room, he'd known.

Dancing with Natasha was like the best kind of dream, the kind you didn't want to wake up from because everything was so magical and perfect, and you knew the real world wasn't like that. Except she was real. And now they'd fucked, and Dimitri had hoped it would be like waking up, but it wasn't. He was still dreaming.

And it scared the shit out of him.

He scrubbed his hands over his face and flipped over onto his back. He hadn't fucking asked for this, for a woman to walk into his life and turn him upside down. Hell, he didn't even know her.

And he had to keep it that way. It would make it easier to pretend he didn't already want her again.

Hormones. That's all this was. Hormones, a pretty face, an amazing body, incredible responsiveness—

Fuck.

He hauled himself out of bed and went to take a cold shower. And over the next few days, he managed to convince himself that his night with Natasha had been a fluke, a momentary lapse into sentimentality. Good sex. Not great, not phenomenal. Just good.

The restaurant he owned kept him busy, and *The Dance Off* hadn't needed anything from him, so he didn't see Natasha again until a few days later.

And yeah, he knew he should have at least texted her. The fact that he hadn't made him feel like a dick. But it wasn't like he hadn't tried. He'd started to type out several messages, then deleted them all before hitting send. From inanities like, "Hey, how's it going?" to commands like, "Come over." Even a few dirty things, like, "I can't stop thinking about the way you taste," and lies like, "This isn't going to work." He was a fucking mess.

But she hadn't contacted him either. And he was losing his mind wondering what she was thinking.

It wasn't just him, right? It had to have felt different for her, too. Shit, maybe it hadn't. Maybe he'd been pining for someone who hadn't given him a second thought.

Wouldn't be the first time.

So, he told himself she was just another woman. And he was just another man.

Until he saw her.

She was in the small breakroom at *The Dance Off*'s headquarters. Dimitri paused in the doorway, on his way to get…something. He'd immediately forgotten what. The scent of her shampoo wrapped around him, drawing his attention like a giant cartoon hand. She was laughing at something Kevin Ray was saying, loud and genuine, her head tipped back, and her eyes crinkled with mirth. And Dimitri knew he'd been fooling himself.

It wasn't smart, but he went over and interrupted her conversation with Kevin, all but barking her name.

"Natasha."

She spun around, eyes wide, lips parted on an inhale. Her gaze swept him up and down, and Dimitri didn't think he imagined the heat flickering there.

"Yes?" The word was breathy. Either from surprise, or maybe she was more affected by him than she wanted to let on.

He hoped it was the latter.

Kevin greeted him with an affable smile. "Hey, Dimitri, what's up?"

Dimitri tapped fists with the other man, but didn't say anything, instead turning back to Natasha.

"Can I talk to you for a minute in the hall?"

Something crossed Kevin's face as his light eyes darted between them, but Dimitri didn't pay him any mind. Kevin might be hot shit around *The Dance Off*, but Dimitri knew better than most how quickly a rising star could flame out.

Natasha's mouth tightened, but all she said was, "Okay."

And when Dimitri put his arm around her, she let him lead her out.

He couldn't have said why that felt like a victory, but it did.

Chapter Seven

Present day

Natasha stumbled backward over the vacuum cord as Dimitri strode into her apartment, a sexy tornado ready to sweep up panties and common sense alike, obliterating both to smithereens. Masculine energy crackled in every step of his fluid dancer's walk, highlighted by his casual gray trousers and tight navy blue polo. It was open at the neck and revealed the glint of a thin gold chain. He froze when he spotted her, his dark gaze tracking over her tear-streaked cheeks.

No. No, he couldn't see her looking like this. Like an utter fucking disaster. What was he even doing here?

Before she could gather the wherewithal to ask, his usually stern expression tipped toward concern. "Tasha? What's going on?"

As if his broad frame and commanding presence weren't overwhelming enough, his voice, normally loud and forceful, was softer than she'd ever heard it. He stepped toward her, and she trembled, both wanting his touch and fearing it. *Don't be nice to me,* she wanted to beg. *I'm too raw already. I can't take it.*

His warm hands clasped her shoulders in a solid grip, and

the scent of his cologne surrounded her. After three years, it was as familiar and comforting as the remembered aromas of her great-grandmother's cooking, lulling her into a false sense of security.

She swallowed hard, wishing she could lean on him. Just for a moment, just to know what it would feel like to have someone there to catch her if she fell.

But that someone wasn't, and never would be, Dimitri.

He leaned in now, probably to kiss her. Somehow, Natasha found the strength to press her hand to his chest to hold him back. Something flashed across his features—hurt? No, it had to be annoyance. She'd never denied him before. But she steeled her resolve. If he kissed her now, it would break her, and she had to stay strong if she was going to figure out the mess she was in.

Natasha lifted her chin and tried to sound like someone who had their shit together. "What do you want, Dimitri? I told you, I don't have time for you right now." She'd meant to make the words harsh, but they came out weary.

He stepped back and took in the garbage bags stuffed with clothing and the smaller pieces of her bedroom furniture crowded into the kitchen. "You said you weren't okay. What happened?"

She gestured toward the door to her room, which she'd shut to limit the amount of dust in the rest of the apartment. "Go look in my bedroom."

He wiggled his eyebrows. "My favorite place."

She let out an exasperated sigh. "Just go look." She kept her eyes averted as he opened her bedroom door and went in. The man had a fantastic ass, but now was not the time to admire it. She turned the vacuum back on and ran it over the carpet again, just to keep her hands busy.

A few moments later, he returned. At his pointed look, she shut the vacuum off.

"Your bathroom ceiling is gone."

"Yes, thank you. I noticed."

He didn't comment on her heavy sarcasm. "What about Gina's room? Can't you stay in there while it's being fixed?"

Natasha prayed for patience. "Like I said on the phone, there's some kind of infestation in the building. I have to wrap everything up and leave."

He glanced around, like the chaos in the apartment suddenly made more sense. "That's not good."

No shit, Sherlock. She kept that thought to herself.

"Do you have renter's insurance?" he asked.

"What's that?"

His lips pressed together, and he exhaled audibly through his nose. "Never mind."

She shoved the vacuum into the corner with more force than necessary. "Why are you here, Dimitri?"

He quit his perusal of the room and grinned widely. "I came to help."

She stared at him. "With what?"

He propped his hands on his lean hips. "Whatever you need. Cleaning, packing, moving stuff. Where do you want me to bring everything?"

Her chest tightened at the direct question, the one that had been on her mind since Manny delivered the news. "I...I don't know."

His brows creased. "What do you mean? Where are you going to stay?"

"I don't know!" She gestured wildly at the mess around her as the words came tumbling out, powered by stress and anxiety. "I'm screwed. I can't live here, but I don't have the money to stay in a hotel or the time to search for another apartment. But if I don't figure it out before the next season starts filming, I'll have to quit *The Dance Off* and move back home to the Bronx to live with my mother—and honestly, I'd sooner sleep in my car, which is my current plan. So, unless you can snap your fingers and conjure up a place for me to live, you might as well leave, because there's nothing you can do to help."

The motherfucker actually had the nerve to laugh. She rolled her eyes and wound the vacuum cord in its holder.

"Tasha."

She suppressed her annoyance. "What?"

"Is that all you need? A place to stay?"

Is that all? Jerk. "Yeah, that's what I need."

"You can stay with me."

Natasha went still, her hand frozen on the vacuum. "What did you say?"

"You can stay with me, at my place."

He couldn't be serious. Stay with Dimitri? That was a recipe for disaster. But where else could she go? She swallowed hard and closed her eyes. "Do you mean that?"

"Would I offer if I didn't?"

He wouldn't. He was an asshole most of the time, but he wasn't cruel. She straightened, biting her lip as she thought it over. On the one hand, it was an easy solution. If she let the building keep her deposit, she wouldn't have to pay for storage for her furniture. Staying with Dimitri would be a hell of a lot cheaper than a hotel or moving into the first open apartment she could find. She could save a little money and take her time finding a new place.

Not too much time, though. Dimitri was bad for her.

At least he was up-front about his womanizing. He'd once told her to call first before coming over to make sure he was alone. So, while she didn't expect more from him, damn it, sometimes she wanted more. She didn't know what that might be, exactly, but something she could hold close when she was alone at night, to remind herself that she mattered to someone.

She couldn't tell him any of that, so she instead voiced the one concern that might make him reconsider. "It's a conflict of interest."

"It definitely isn't a conflict of *my* interests."

She ignored his suggestive grin. "You're a judge on *The Dance Off*. I'm one of the dancers."

He waved away her objection. "No one cares about that. Besides, we're not filming right now. Who's going to know?"

Natasha didn't have his confidence. The set of a reality TV show was a lot like high school. Everyone was messing around with each other, and nothing stayed secret for long.

Plus, there was a difference between casually hooking up and *living together*.

She tossed out another question, mostly to see what he'd say. "What about all the other women you bring home? Isn't having me there going to cramp your style?"

He snorted. "I'm sure they won't mind sharing my bed with you."

"I didn't say *I* would be sharing your bed, either." God, that would be too much like truly moving in with him, as opposed to using his house as a temporary living space while she got her shit sorted out.

"Why not?" At her withering glare, he held up his hands. "All right, all right. You can use the guest room."

Not the answer she was looking for. He hadn't said, *Of course I won't bring any other women home while you're there.* Still, she wasn't likely to receive any other offers tonight. Desperate times and all that.

Besides, it was only for a little while.

"Okay." She ignored his beaming smile and held up a finger. "On one condition."

He shrugged, his arrogant confidence both infuriating and sexy. "Whatever you want."

Her pulse beat faster in her throat. She couldn't believe she was going to say this to him, but it was necessary, both for her career and her emotional well-being. If she was going to live with him, she needed boundaries.

"No sex."

His expressive brows shot up. "What?"

"We can't have sex. Not while I'm living with you. I mean, staying with you. Temporarily."

His jaw worked as he considered her words, then he shrugged. "Sure."

His agreement came too quickly, and it wasn't like him not to argue, but she had no other options.

True to his word, he helped her finish packing up the apartment. Even though he made a show of digging through her lingerie drawer and holding her lacy underthings to his nose with an exaggerated expression of rapture, the task was faster and less stressful with him around. Dimitri ran to the hardware store for supplies, they sealed the furniture in plastic, and finally, there was nothing left to do but drive to his place in Beverly Hills.

This was a setback, but Natasha would get through it. All she had to do was save money and find a new apartment before the next season of *The Dance Off* started filming.

And try her damnedest to protect her heart in the meantime.

Chapter Eight

After Natasha had hung up on him, Dimitri had grabbed his keys and driven over without a second's thought. Tasha was always collected, composed. Hard to read. He'd never heard her sound like that, like she was unraveling, and he hadn't questioned the immediate urge to go to her. When he'd walked in and seen her with red-rimmed eyes, her light brown cheeks ashen with fatigue, panic had gripped him, along with a desperate need to help her. The solution had been so simple, he'd had to laugh. She'd stay with him, of course. As if he'd let her sleep in her car when he had a whole empty house.

His younger brother, Nikolai, had moved out a few months ago. After growing up surrounded by relatives, including cousins, aunts, and uncles who were always coming and going, Dimitri found living alone unnerving. Houses were meant to be filled with people.

Besides, he liked having Natasha in his space. She never stayed long, and she never left a trace. But each time, he found himself wanting more.

Sometimes the depth of his want for her scared him, and he ran in the other direction. Weeks or months would pass before he called her again.

Other times, that desire made him want to chase her down. He'd invite her over for a weekend, or claim to be in her neighborhood, or go to a club when he knew she'd be there.

When he asked for her, she always said yes. But he always had to do the asking. She never sought him out, never pursued him.

They both slept with other people. It was part of this casual, no-commitment thing they had going on. He hated it, but he hadn't been able to see a way out.

Now, he'd solved two problems. The chance to develop a new dynamic with Natasha, and someone to fill the empty space in his home.

The perfect solution.

Except…

She'd said no sex.

If he put himself in her shoes, he understood where the stipulation came from. It might not look good if their bosses knew they were living together, what with him being a judge. But it was the off-season. No one had to know.

Despite his easy agreement, he knew they were kidding themselves. They were never able to stay away from each other for long. He didn't see how this would be any different.

He turned the Porsche down his street, quiet and lined with tall palm trees, then pulled into the curving driveway. Damn, he still had to fix the gate. Something he could have had his assistant do if he hadn't fired the guy for being too tentative. Dimitri had turned around one too many times to find him standing quietly behind him, like he was scared to interrupt. It was fucking creepy. And despite his reputation on TV, Dimitri wasn't a monster. Just loud, and maybe a bit too forceful when expressing his thoughts and opinions. He couldn't work with someone who was terrified to talk to him.

So, the gate was still broken.

At the end of the drive, Dimitri clicked the remote for the garage. He'd grown up in Brooklyn on a street lined with hundred-year-old limestone row houses. The exterior of the sprawling one-story was more Spanish style than he preferred, but the red clay roof tiles and white stucco were growing on him. Behind him, Natasha parked in the driveway, like she usually did. But when he got out, he grabbed one of the other remotes and opened the middle spot, which had been Nik's, indicating she should park there. His SUV occupied the third spot.

Once she'd pulled into the garage and shut the car off, he opened her door and offered her a hand to step out. She took the assistance, but behind her glasses, those dark, heavy-lidded eyes held wariness, like she didn't trust his help. He'd be lying if he said it didn't hurt, but he didn't comment on it. He had to accept that he hadn't done enough to earn her trust. Moving her into his home provided the perfect opportunity to gauge her feelings.

"New car?" he asked, eying the Prius. He hadn't noticed it last night.

She gave the vehicle a sideways glance. "Yeah."

"That's exciting."

"More like unexpected and expensive."

She opened the trunk and they collected her meager belongings to carry inside. She'd had to leave a lot behind, and some of it had been dropped off at the dry cleaners on the way to his house.

At the threshold, she paused and cleared her throat. "You said you had a spare bedroom?"

He wanted her in his bed, like always, but he was willing to play this out. "Yeah, this way."

At Nik's door, she pulled back, her brow creased. "Isn't this your brother's room?"

"It was." He pushed the door open and carried her bags inside, where he set them under the window. "He got a spot on the national tour of that *Seize the Night* musical and moved out. Says he'll get his own place when the tour is over." It made sense, but Dimitri couldn't help feeling like Nikolai had left him behind, a betrayal of sorts. He gestured around the room. "Some of Nik's stuff is still in the closet, but there should be space for you to hang things up, and I think the drawers are empty."

"Thanks." She lingered in the doorway.

Her hesitation jabbed at his nerves, made his voice sharp. "What are you, a vampire? Waiting for an invitation? Come in."

Her lips flattened into a line, and she rolled her eyes toward the ceiling. With a deliberate step, she entered the room and dumped her belongings on top of the dresser. "Better?" she snapped.

It wasn't, but he liked the bite in her voice. It was preferable to the cool, reserved demeanor she usually showed him, or the frantic worry when he'd called her earlier. And while he didn't like settling her in here, it didn't matter where her stuff was. Sooner or later, she'd be back in his bed.

And maybe this time, she'd stay.

"Come on, I'll give you the tour."

"*Tour?*" She turned away from where she had started to line up a series of bottles on the dresser, eyes wide and tone incredulous.

"Yeah. I'll show you the rest of the house." He took her hand and pulled her from the room. She didn't resist, but the stunned look didn't leave her face.

"Macho."

He stopped at the sound of his nickname on her lips. He loved that she had one for him, something she didn't call anyone else.

She stared at him like he was crazy. "I've been here before. I was here *this morning*, in fact. I don't need a tour."

"That was different," he said. "That's when you were just—"

Her eyebrows shot up, and she crossed her arms. "When I was just what?"

He was digging a hole for himself, but he couldn't stop his mouth. "You were just going to my bedroom." And the sofa. And the dining table. And the pool. And— "There are some rooms you haven't seen. I want you to feel at home here."

Her eyes narrowed, but she went with him.

Dimitri felt like kicking himself. How was it that he'd never bothered to show her around before? The first time she'd come over, he'd worried about appearing clingy, coming on too strong. But somehow, that night had created a pattern, one where they fucked a lot and spoke little, at least, not with words. Their bodies, on the other hand, spoke volumes. Now, he had to face the fact that he'd done something wrong that night, and if he wanted something different with her now, he had to correct it.

Starting with a tour of the fucking house.

He pointed out the hall bathroom, which would be hers to use. Then the kitchen, gym, TV lounge, and his office.

He spotted a short stack of papers on his desk and paused.

It was his contract for season fifteen of *The Dance Off*. He'd demanded they send him a printed copy. He hadn't signed it yet, hadn't decided if he was going to or not. Now that he'd seen it, the pressure weighed on him. *Sign me*, it said. *Give up on your dreams. You know they're never going to come true.*

He couldn't take it another second. "Hold on," he said brusquely, and stalked into the room to flip the papers over. When he came back and shut the door behind him, Natasha gave him a quizzical look that bordered on hurt.

"I'm not going to snoop around your office," she said in a quiet voice.

"That's not—" Crap, he'd made her think he had something he didn't want her to see. "I know. But you can. It's okay." He was making a mess of this. But he didn't want to bring up the show or his contract, or the reasons why he hadn't signed it yet. He had to get her to the next room before he made it worse. "There's something else I want you to see. You're going to like this."

"I've heard that one before," she muttered as she followed him down the hall.

He barked out a surprised laugh. "Don't give me any ideas."

Her snicker eased the tightness in his shoulders.

"Here we are." He opened the door with a flourish, stepping back so she could get a good look inside.

The expression on her face made up for the previous awkwardness. Dark eyes rounded, and those pretty lips parted in awe. She entered the room on her own and turned in a circle to take it all in.

"You have a private dance studio?" The wonder in her voice warmed him, and he followed her in.

"Doesn't everybody?" He checked out their reflections in the wall of mirrors she shot him a smirk, he added, "You can use this anytime you want."

"Thank you." She ran her hand along the barre on the opposite wall. "I will."

Unable to resist, he drew closer to her. And because it had been ages since he'd danced with her, and even longer since they'd danced without anyone's eyes on them, he took her hand from the polished wood and pulled her into a spin.

When they danced, nothing stood between them. He led, she followed, and he lost track of everything but the movement of her body and keeping them in rhythm. He'd done the competition circuit for years, had danced with countless women during that time, but never anyone like Natasha. She got him like no one else did. Ever since she'd walked into his rehearsal room by accident and he'd pulled her in to try out the number he was choreographing, he'd known.

He wanted to dance with her forever.

But before he could approach her about that, he had to figure out what was actually behind this "no sex" rule. They needed to move forward, not backward.

When he tugged her into his arms, she landed against his chest. With one hand on her back and her body pressed to his, he caught the undulation of her spine as she finished the move. It was part of the dance, sure, but he knew her movements and her body well enough to catch the telltale extras. The slight arch of her back, the short thrust of her hips, the sharp intake of breath verging on a moan.

She was turned on.

His body pulsed and hardened. He slid his hand up between her shoulder blades and tilted his head down.

With a gasp, Natasha shoved against his chest. On instinct, his arms tightened around her, ensuring she kept her balance. She squirmed in his grip, and when he released her, she backed away toward the door.

"Let's get something straight," she said in a low voice at odds with the heat in her gaze and the slow way she licked her lips. "We're not roommates with benefits, okay? I thought I made that clear."

"Yeah, sure." For now. "You're my guest. I want you to feel comfortable here."

She narrowed her eyes like she didn't believe him. "Thanks for the tour. I'm going to unpack." She hurried from the room, leaving him standing alone in the studio with only his reflection for company.

Dimitri scrubbed a hand over his face and trudged back to his office. Well, that had been a fucking disaster. Instead of bringing them closer together, he'd managed to insult her and put her on guard. Not just today, but by neglecting to give her a tour in the past. How had he never noticed that she'd only seen the spaces where they'd fucked? Why hadn't he shown her the rest of his *home*?

He sat in his desk chair and leaned back as far as it would allow, staring at the ceiling like it would give him some answers.

In the recesses of his mind lived a tiny, flickering hope that they would someday figure out how to talk to each other, and then they could see how deep their connection ran.

But what if sex was all they had? Or great dance chemistry?

Both his common sense and his instincts told him that if she could read him so well that she could anticipate his every move and desire, then there was a very good chance they could have something real. They'd always managed to communicate without words. He'd thought that was a good thing, and as dancers, it was. But if he wanted more than the occasional fuck, maybe they needed to learn how to…well, *talk* to each other.

God, why was that so fucking scary?

The contract on his desk caught his eye, mocking him. Those papers, stamped with *The Dance Off*'s logo, represented his failure to take risks and produce his own projects, and his reliance on the entertainment industry grind to keep him in the spotlight.

Hell, maybe his focus on Natasha was simply a further indication that he was lonely and looking for a distraction.

No. Deep down, he carried an undeniable certainty that they were right for each other. Yet in three years, she'd never shown any sign that she wanted more from him.

She was in his house now. He'd get to the bottom of it and find out what she really wanted. They were good together in bed. She didn't hide anything there, didn't hold back in her pleasure. They'd start with that, and once he was past her guards, he'd find out what else she was hiding.

But for now, he'd give her space. Let her unpack and settle in. Even though he wanted to help, he stayed in his office instead, ignoring the contract and pulling up a spreadsheet of wine orders on his laptop.

Show business was a fickle beast, and dance careers didn't last forever. Nothing did. He'd learned from experience that the best move was to diversify his interests, and he went for low risk with maximum reward.

The restaurant had been a sure bet. Everything had lined up perfectly to make it happen, but he hadn't gone public as the owner until Krasavitsa was a clear success. It turned out he was good at running a restaurant. Of all his side ventures, it was the one he was most involved with and brought him the greatest fulfillment.

But it wasn't dancing.

His eyes wandered over to the bookcase in the corner and the massive three-ring binder gathering metaphorical dust.

Not real dust. Trina, his housekeeper, would never allow it.

An email popped up from one of the vineyards he did business with. Putting the binder, the contract, and Natasha out of his head, he got to work.

Half an hour later, his phone buzzed with a call.

"You're up late," he said by way of greeting. "It's almost midnight over there."

"Yeah, but I knew you'd answer." His cousin Alex sounded tired. "What are you doing?"

Dimitri closed his laptop and played with a pile of paperclips on the desk, pushing them into ever-changing designs and patterns. "Going over wine lists."

"Aren't you glad I forced you to take that sommelier class?"

Dimitri grunted. His cousin had not only pushed him into taking the wine class, but Alex had also facilitated the purchase and opening of the restaurant. Putting the phone on speaker, Dimitri leaned back in his chair. "I know you didn't call from New Jersey in the middle of the night to discuss wine. What's going on?"

Alex was silent for a long beat. Dimitri abandoned the paperclips and sat up straight. Alex always hesitated before admitting something Dimitri didn't want to hear.

The line was quiet for so long, Dimitri worried the call had cut out. "Sasha?" he said, using Alex's family nickname.

"I have news, Dima," Alex finally said, using Dimitri's own nickname.

"Tell me."

"Marina's pregnant. We're having a baby."

Dimitri blew out a breath. "Don't scare me like that. I thought you were calling to tell me something bad. That's great news. Pozdravlyayu."

"Spasibo."

Dimitri switched to Russian. "Why don't you sound more excited?"

Alex sighed. "I am. I'm thrilled. A little tired, because there have already been doctor appointments, and Marina's had bad morning sickness. By the way, don't mention this to anyone else in the family. I'm only telling you."

That was suspicious. "Why haven't you told your parents yet?"

"We will, but we want a little time before they start smothering us."

"I'm flattered you chose to share the news with me first, but why?"

"Two reasons. One, we want you to be the godfather."

Warmth sparked in Dimitri's chest. His cousin's child, still just a little bean, would soon be connected to him, too. He swallowed hard.

"That's…yeah, of course. Of course, I'll be the godfather."

"Thanks. And the second reason…"

Shit, Dimitri had forgotten there was a second reason, and he'd fallen victim to Alex's stalling tactics.

"This puts us on a deadline."

Dimitri wrinkled his brow and glanced at the contract pushed to the corner of his desk. "A deadline for what?"

"If we're going to produce another stage show, it has to be now. I want to be around more once the baby's born. I can't be flying to LA whenever you need me, or spending all my time in Manhattan. I've got a wife and a home in New Jersey, a kid to prepare for, and my own practice to run. If we're going to do this, it has to be now."

It was Dimitri's turn to fall silent. He sucked in a breath through his nose and leaned his head on his hands. "When is the baby due?"

"Early March."

Shit. They were already midway through July. That was hardly any time at all.

"Look, I know you're sitting on a ton of ideas. If we go all-in for the next seven months or so—"

"It'll be a risk. Especially to rush it."

"It will always be a risk, but that doesn't mean we shouldn't do it. Think about it and get back to me, okay? I'm going to bed. I just wanted to let you know."

"Thanks. And again, congratulations. I'm honored you asked me to be the godfather."

"Who else would I ask? Ivan?"

They both laughed. Their youngest cousin was nineteen and always busy playing video games for his "followers." Dimitri didn't fully understand what that meant, but he supplied Ivan with camera equipment all the same.

"You sure you didn't just throw the godfather thing in to keep me from getting upset about this deadline?"

"You'll never know."

The call ended, and Dimitri stared at the phone for a minute. Then he picked it up and dashed off a text to his agent.

When is the contract due?

The reply was almost immediate. The man lived with his phone in his hand.

In a few weeks. Why? You got the copy I sent you, right?

Yeah, just checking.

After placing the phone carefully on the desk, Dimitri slid the contract over. Grabbing a pen, he scrawled his messy signature across the line but hesitated before dating it. Instead, he shoved the whole thing into the bottom drawer. When he slammed it shut, his phone buzzed, and he jumped.

The restaurant. He picked up immediately. "Dima."

He listened while Carlito, the manager, rattled off the latest emergency. With a sigh, Dimitri pushed to his feet.

"I'll be right there."

He spared the desk drawer a glance before leaving the office and heading to Natasha's room.

He stopped short in the middle of the hallway. Natasha's

room. Not Nik's room, which it had been for years, and which he had still thought of it as until…

An hour ago.

Already, his mind was making her a permanent fixture in his home, in his life. Of course, she didn't view it that way. "Temporary," she'd said.

They'd see about that. He didn't see how she could want to return to that tiny box of an apartment, and he had no intention of letting it be her best long-term option. Not when he had all this space here, just waiting for her to fill it.

Chapter Nine

This wouldn't be a long stay. Maybe a week, max, until she got paid for all the gigs she was working. In fact, Natasha would start a search for available apartments tonight. Maybe if she were lucky, she'd find a place that didn't require a security deposit.

Yeah, right. And maybe her delinquent fairy godmother would swoop in to save her.

Still, there was no point living out of suitcases. Tired as she was, Natasha unpacked her clothing into the empty drawers—or at least, the clothing she'd managed to salvage. Mostly gym wear and casual attire that could survive being put through a hot dryer.

As for her shoes…she couldn't even think about them. If she did, she'd cry. Again.

Ignoring her reflection in the large rectangular mirror above the dresser, she tucked away the last of her garments. She didn't need to see the dark circles under her eyes to know she was exhausted.

Screw it. She'd look up apartments tomorrow. Sleep beckoned, although knowing Dimitri was down the hall would probably keep her up.

He'd acted so strangely during their "tour." Most of the time, his vibe alternated between sexual fiend and arrogant flirt, but today, he'd been more like an eager puppy.

It threw her off. Dimitri was difficult enough to handle when he was trying to get in her pants, but this happy host version of him was even more suspicious.

And yet here she was, moving into his house with no assurances and no clear sense of where they stood.

A knock sounded on the bedroom door, and her fingers stilled on the neatly folded pile of gym clothes. If she opened the door, he'd be standing right there, too close. If she were going to live here and stick to her rule, they needed to keep their distance. So even though it was rude, she raised her voice and called out, "Yeah?"

The door muffled his deep voice. "Problem at the restaurant. I have to go out." A pause. "Will you be okay?"

She let out a relieved breath. "Yes."

"I'll see you when I get home."

Not if she could help it.

What the hell was she doing here, playing house with him, acting like they could be roommates? Even the sound of his voice through a door gave her a thrill, his simple farewell affecting her like a promise.

Be strong.

She cleared her throat. "See you later."

The house was big, but quiet. She put her ear to the bedroom door until she heard the garage open, then she stepped into the hallway and out into the living room. Moments later, the sound of the engine faded as he drove away.

She exhaled deeply, letting her shoulders slump. Alone at last.

It was weird being in Dimitri's house when she wasn't drunk or horny. This time, she was desperate in a totally different way.

The living room sofa mocked her, reminding her of all the nights they'd fucked on it. She wandered past the dining table with its seven chairs. Once, there'd been eight. She still wasn't sure how they'd broken one, but maybe it was a sign not to bang on top of tables.

She hurried back to the bedroom—Nik's bedroom? Her bedroom? No, *the* bedroom. It wasn't hers. But at least it held no memories. She collected an armful of toiletries and carried them to the hall bathroom, arranging her bottles in a line on the counter.

The most intriguing room in the house was the dance studio, but even that now held a memory. Dancing with him was irresistible, something she'd dreamed of long before they'd met, when she was just a teenager watching him on the movie screen. The rush of a rollercoaster, but with the security of knowing he wouldn't let her fall.

The first time they'd danced, his body had made promises the rest of him couldn't, or wouldn't, keep. *Trust me. Let me lead. I've got you.* But those were just pretty lies.

Sometimes it seemed like he knew her body better than she did. When he'd pulled her against him, the thrill of the dance, her delight at the room, his warmth, his scent—all combined to set her body pulsing. It had taken all her strength of will to push him away.

No sex, she'd told him. And she was sticking to it.

Even if it killed her.

Her phone buzzed with a text. Natasha swiped it on to see a selfie from Gina. Gina's arm was hooked around Stone's neck, and a beautiful landscape of water, mountains, and pine trees stretched out behind them. Gina had added the caption, *Look who's hiking!*

After winning the previous season, Gina had accepted a starring role on Broadway, and Stone had gone with her. They were now splitting their time between New York and Los Angeles for work and spending breaks at their new home in Alaska.

Natasha smiled in spite of herself, but a pang of jealousy

shimmered underneath the glee at hearing from her best friend and seeing her so happy.

Natasha typed back, *I see you, nature girl!* with a line of heart emojis.

It had been an exhausting day, and Natasha was more than ready for sleep. After showering, she rationed out tiny amounts from her dwindling supply of expensive skincare products that she couldn't afford to replace. Then she climbed under the covers, intending to read for a bit. The bed was comfortable, but it was strange being alone in a bed that wasn't hers. The sheets and pillows held a light lavender scent, and she wondered who did Dimitri's laundry. She couldn't picture him doing it himself.

She shook her head to banish the thought. Better not to think about him in domestic terms at all.

She'd just cracked open *Jane Eyre* when her phone rang. Natasha reached for it, but the name flashing on the screen made her snatch her hand back.

Esmeralda Díaz.

Her mother. The last person Natasha ever wanted to talk to, especially when she was so out of sorts.

Some fucked up combination of guilt, codependency, and self-sabotage made her answer. With a sigh, Natasha leaned back into the pillows and said, "Hola, Mami."

"Mira, nena."

Natasha rolled her eyes. Her mother still called her "girl," even though Natasha was now twenty-seven years old. And Esmeralda usually said it like a curse.

She'd never once called Natasha "mija"—*my daughter*. But at least Abuela had.

Esmeralda continued to rattle on in Spanish, skipping the pleasantries and getting right to the point.

"One of my friends from the salon wants to see the show. We're flying out for the premiere. Get us tickets."

Pinching the bridge of her nose, Natasha fought for calm. She'd been offering her mother tickets to her performances since she'd started working in television. Now Esmeralda was finally coming, but only because her friend was a fan of *The Dance Off*. It figured. Esmeralda didn't even watch the show.

"You have enough space in your apartment for us to stay with you?"

You'd know if you ever bothered to visit, Natasha thought. And before she could stop herself, she said, "Sí, tengo un dormitorio segundo."

The second the words were out of her mouth, Natasha smacked her forehead.

"Bueno." Her mother said it like it was all settled. "See you next month. Hasta luego."

"Bye." Natasha dropped the phone on the bed and rubbed her eyes. What the hell had possessed her to agree to letting her mother stay with her in an apartment that was currently off-limits? Temporary insanity? Short-term memory loss? It was like she'd forgotten her home was currently in shambles, her bank account nearly empty, and she was staying with a man who could most accurately be termed a fuck buddy.

Of course, her mother would pick *now* to finally visit.

But she couldn't tell Esmeralda the truth. The woman would go nuts, shouting at her about her life choices, with a strong, underlying current of her favorite phrase: *I told you so.* She'd been saying it Natasha's whole life, ever since she'd shown a natural aptitude for dance and an interest in pursuing it as a career.

You'll never make it as a dancer.

She had, though. She'd gotten jobs as a working dancer on not one, but two major network TV shows. *The Dance Off* was always in the top ten for ratings, and before that, Natasha had been on *Everybody Dance Now*. While *The Dance Off* paired professional dancers with celebrity partners, *EDN* focused on pairing dancers from different backgrounds and styles. After Natasha and Gina moved to LA, Gina had gotten them an audition, and they'd joined *Everybody Dance Now* together.

Natasha made enough to live in Los Angeles, where she enjoyed more luxury than she ever had while growing up in the Bronx in a two-bedroom apartment occupied by two old people and a teenage mother whose daughter slept in a partitioned-off area of the living room.

This is your home. And when all that dance porquería doesn't work out, I'm the one who'll take you back in. Remember that.

Natasha shook off the memory of her mother's words. She'd come a long way. Being able to afford a good apartment on her own was going to be the final step. Except now it was ruined.

If only she'd saved more…

If only she'd put off paying down her credit cards and canceling them…

If only her car hadn't died right when it did…

If only the ceiling hadn't collapsed, or the building not been infested with bedbugs…

Any one of those things, if removed from the equation, would have left her stable. Secure. Able to cling to the outward signs of success.

But all combined, the events of the last couple of months had reduced her to living in the spare bedroom of a man she couldn't even call a friend, with only a pile of tank tops, yoga pants, and denim shorts to her name. At least Los Angeles weather was predictable enough in summer that she didn't need much.

Maybe it was better this way. If she didn't have access to her killer wardrobe, she'd be less tempted to go out partying, which she couldn't afford to do anyway. And besides, she didn't have the time. She'd lost track of how many gigs she was working now, teaching classes at various gyms and dance schools, from spin to pole dance, from elderly aerobics to kiddie ballet. Her schedule was nuts.

One thing was for certain: Esmeralda could *not* find out that Natasha was living with Dimitri.

When her phone buzzed again, Natasha checked it with dread. But it wasn't her mother calling back to berate her about who knew what. It was her group text with Kevin Ray and Lori Kim, two other pros from *The Dance Off*.

Lori texted first. *Who's coming to Club Picante tonight???* It was followed by the dancing lady emoji.

Kevin's reply flashed on the screen. *I'm in!*

Natasha grimaced as a wave of longing threatened to swamp her. She wanted to say yes, to go out drinking and dancing with her friends. Kevin and Lori were a blast, and since Gina moved out, Natasha had been spending way too much time alone. She wasn't used to it.

But it was time to act like a responsible adult.

Before she could answer, Lori's next text popped up. *Pre-game drinks at Natasha's?*

Oh, hell no. They couldn't know she was staying with Dimitri, either. Not only would it be dangerous for her job, but then they would know about her utter failure to take care of herself.

Besides, Kevin didn't like Dimitri. His green eyes narrowed whenever they were out partying, and Dimitri showed up to sweep her away. It wasn't jealousy—Kevin had never shown the slightest bit of interest in her beyond friendship—but the few times she'd gotten drunk and whined about Dimitri's lack of commitment, Kevin spent the rest of the night scowling.

She quickly typed a reply. Sorry, guys. Not tonight. Got work early tomorrow.

Before she could see their answers, she put her phone on silent and practically threw it onto the bedside table.

She set the book aside, as well. Reading had lost its appeal.

She settled back into the pillows, staring up at the unfamiliar ceiling in the dark.

Temporary. This was only temporary. Then she'd get back on her feet, back in her own place, back to being a success. No one had to know about this little lapse.

No one would know she was a failure.

Chapter Ten

Twenty-one years ago

After months of practice and earning a lead role in the ballet recital, the show was over, and Natasha hadn't made a single mistake. She'd been *perfect*. She knew it, and everyone else said so, even Mr. Richie, the teacher in charge of the ballet program. For the first time ever, she'd done something *perfectly*.

Mami would have to be proud of her now.

The thought gave Natasha a funny, wiggly sensation in her stomach, the kind she felt right before jumping off the top of the jungle gym. She was scared, but excited, too.

Abuela had told her that Mami was always proud of her, but because she wanted Natasha to do her best, Mami pointed out what could be done better. "Needs improvement," like it said on Natasha's report card for math class. Mami was just showing her where she needed to improve. That was all.

But tonight, she didn't need improvement, and she'd done better than satisfactory. She had been *excellent*. If she got a report card grade for dance—and part of her wished that were the case, since it was the thing she was best at—it would be an "E."

She rushed backstage with everyone else. She wanted to stop and chat with Aja, her friend whose mother picked them up from dance and brought Natasha home, since they lived in the same building. But Natasha was so excited to see her mother's reaction, she didn't talk to anybody except to grin and say "thank you" and "gracias" when they told her how great she was.

For the first time, she *knew* she was great.

She changed quickly in the room backstage that had been set up for the girls. She was in such a rush, she took off her costume but left on the pink tights. Instead, she pulled her shorts, T-shirt, and sneakers on over them. She left her hair in its high, tight bun, and grinned at herself in the mirror. Mami had done her hair, so it was neat and perfect. Mami was so good at doing hair, though she usually complained about how hard Natasha's was to deal with. "Like your father's," she always said. Natasha didn't know that for sure, since she'd never even seen a photo of him. But Mami let her wear dark blue eyeliner and red lipstick for the performance, which made her feel pretty and special, even though her front teeth were only half grown in.

She grabbed her bag, then doubled back to make sure she hadn't left anything behind. She was always getting yelled at for forgetting things, and she didn't want to do anything to make her mom upset. Not tonight, when everything was going so perfectly.

When she burst into the gym from backstage, it was chaos. Kids were running everywhere, chairs took up most of the floor space, and adults were standing around talking, making it hard for Natasha to spot her mom.

In her head, she imagined Mami waiting with open arms, a smile on her face, and a bouquet of flowers. Just like in Natasha's favorite Friday night sitcom, *Home Is Where the Heart Is*. Mami would scoop her up and kiss her and say, "Oh, I'm so proud of you." That's what the dad did on the show when Melissa, the oldest daughter, overcame her stage fright for the school play.

That's how Natasha wanted it to happen, but she knew real life wasn't like TV. Even if her mom only hugged her and said, "Muy bien, nena," that would be enough.

But she didn't see Mami. There were more people telling her "good job" and "congratulations!" But she only wanted to hear from her mom.

To Natasha's right, Aja was greeted by her parents with a red rose wrapped in clear plastic cellophane. Natasha ran into the crowd, searching for her mom before Aja's family could speak to her.

Finally, Natasha spotted her. Mami was sitting on one of the folding chairs near the door. Her legs were crossed, her hands were tight on the purse in her lap, and her foot jiggled. She was alone, not talking to any of the other parents or teachers.

Now was her chance. Natasha raced over, skidding to a halt with a big smile splitting her face.

Mami's eyes flicked down at her legs. "Why are you still wearing your tights?" she asked in Spanish. "If you rip them, I'll have to spend money I don't have on a new pair."

Natasha's heart sank. She knew she should have taken them off. Before Mami could say anything else, Natasha jumped right in and asked, "Mami, did you see me? Did you see me dancing the lead part?"

Mami's brow creased in a scowl and she got to her feet. "Por supuesto." She held out a hand, empty of flowers or chocolate. "Vámanos."

Natasha held her ground. Maybe she hadn't been clear enough. "What did you think? Are you proud of me?"

Mami's face hardened. "Why are you asking such silly questions?" she snapped in Spanish. "Stop wasting time. I have to take you home and then I'm going out."

That funny, wiggly feeling was back, but worse. Natasha's throat tightened and her eyes got hot. Pressing her lips together, she didn't say another word. She just took her mother's hand and let Mami lead them out of the gym.

Chapter Eleven

Present day

The next morning, Natasha woke to a text from the owners of the West Hollywood branch of Spin Cycle, where she taught an early morning spin class that paired positive affirmations with rocking club beats. A gas leak on the block meant the building was closed.

With her first gig of the day canceled, Natasha closed her eyes and snuggled into the pillow.

And couldn't go back to sleep.

Her body tensed, ears pitched to pick up any sounds of movement from the rest of the house. She rolled over in the bed that didn't feel or smell like hers, mildly surprised that Dimitri hadn't crept under the covers with her in the middle of the night. She hadn't heard him come home—home, as in *his* home, not hers—and she knew from nights spent with him that he wasn't an early riser.

Worse, she had to pee. But what if he was up, and she ran into him in the hallway? She'd done the awkward morning thing with him plenty of times before—so many, in fact, it was no longer awkward to grab a spare toothbrush from under his sink

—but this was different, and not only because she'd brought all of her toiletries with her.

The reality of staying in Dimitri's home as a guest sank in with stunning clarity. There was no way this wasn't going to be weird.

Before her bladder burst, she got up and eased the bedroom door open, then tiptoed into the hallway. At the entrance to the hall bathroom, she paused to eye Dimitri's bedroom door, which was ajar. She swallowed, debating whether it was better to go about her business quietly, or shut his door so she didn't wake him. The carpet under her bare feet was thick and plush, completely unlike the scarred hardwood floors in the old prewar apartment where she'd grown up. By the time she was eighteen, she'd known every creak and crack in her great-grandparents' home.

This was a fairly new house in Beverly Hills. She could take a chance.

She reached his room without making a sound, but standing in Dimitri's doorway afforded her a perfect view of the man himself sprawled in the enormous California King-sized bed she knew so well. His wide chest was bared to the edge of his ribcage, where the blankets covered the rest of his goods. Thick arms wrapped around a squishy pillow, his face hidden in its folds. The scent of his cologne, something woodsy undercut with citrus, beckoned her in.

Natasha bit her lip. The sight of him, half-dressed and twisted in the covers, sent a low thrum of pleasure vibrating through her body. The way he held the pillow was how he held her, caged in his arms, his face buried in her hair. He'd once said the smell of her fig shampoo helped him fall asleep.

With great care, she grasped the knob and pulled the door shut, blocking him from view before she did something stupid, like climb into bed with him.

Since she had a little extra time, she carried her camera and laptop to the dance studio on the other end of the house. Yes, she should search for apartments, but her multitude of summer jobs didn't leave her a lot of time or energy to dance for the fun of it. The spin class especially wore her out, and she couldn't find it in her to be upset that it had been canceled, even though it paid well.

Dimitri's studio had a couple of stools in the corner, so she used them as tables to set up her equipment. Both the camera and laptop had been splurges, but they allowed her to film herself in high quality and edit the footage in ways she couldn't with only a phone. As much as she enjoyed the variety of gigs she was able to take on, she missed choreographing routines for real dancers.

The Dance Off was a crapshoot. You never knew if your celeb that season was going to be up to the challenge or not. Dwayne Alonzo, her most recent partner, had been a football player with a huge fan following. As a dancer, however, he'd had more energy than skill, and his footwork left much to be desired. She'd choreographed routines that played to his strengths, both literal and figurative. Lots of lifts and hip action, with uncomplicated steps his big, blunt athlete's feet could handle. They'd made it to the seventh episode before being eliminated.

Turning athletes and actors and anyone else who fell under the umbrella of "celebrity" into dancers was a challenge, for sure, but she'd be lying if she said she wasn't feeling creatively stifled.

Since she had access to this beautiful, empty, *free* rehearsal space, it would be a crime not to take advantage of it.

With the studio door shut and Dimitri dead asleep at the other end of the house, she did a quick warmup. Then she turned on the camera and the music—a slow, haunting melody with soulful lyrics about a woman who'd loved the wrong man —and began to move. The music and motion, as always, swept everything else away.

When she danced, it was the closest she came to knowing peace.

Chapter Twelve

Three years ago

Consumed by a mix of anticipation and apprehension, Natasha followed Dimitri out of the breakroom and into the empty hallway. She hadn't heard from him since she'd left his bed a few days earlier. While it was normally the kind of thing she'd shrug off, she hadn't been able to stop thinking about him. When he'd suddenly appeared behind her, looming gorgeously, a sense of elation had zinged through her, along with no small degree of arousal.

Now, standing alone with him, she tried to guess what he might say to her. Was he going to make a move on her? Tell her it had all been a mistake? Make her sign an NDA?

"Tasha." Dimitri's accent thickened when he said her name, and it gave her a thrill. She loved her name in his mouth, and he said "Tasha" how she preferred, with a thick "T," like the Spanish way, not a sharp "T" like in English.

"You're going to dance with me in the season nine premiere," Dimitri continued.

Natasha's thoughts stuttered to a halt.

Esperate. Work? This man had pulled her aside, after days of radio silence following an incredible one-night stand, to talk about *work*?

Oh, it's like that, is it? she thought. They were just going to pretend they were casual coworkers who hadn't been intimate with every inch of each other's bodies. Fine.

She bit back a sigh. Actually, it was for the best. She should be glad he was being professional.

Except she *wasn't* glad. She'd wanted him to declare he hadn't had a moment's peace since she'd left and beg her to give him another chance.

Ugh, she was a mess. Damn her inner romantic.

And then there was the way he'd spoken to her. "You're going to dance with me in the premiere," not "do you want to" or "will you." It was on the tip of her tongue to reply sarcastically with: "Oh, am I? Am I *going* to dance with you?"

But the fact was, even though he hadn't phrased it like a question, the answer was still a resounding yes. Turning down the opportunity to dance with Dimitri Kovalenko in the premiere episode of her first season on *The Dance Off* would be monumentally stupid. It was unheard of for him to pick a rookie like her and not one of the more seasoned pros.

"I'm a hard teacher," he went on before she mustered up a reply. His tone held a note of warning. "I don't indulge tantrums or laziness. If you're my partner, you have to anticipate everything, put up with my moods, and don't expect compliments. I don't give praise to people for doing what they're supposed to be doing."

She kept her expression blank as she nodded, ignoring the chill that ran up her spine.

She'd heard these words before. Back when she was twenty and mourning the loss of her beloved great-grandmother. Natasha had broken down and shouted at her mother that just once, would it kill her to say Natasha was doing a good job? Mami had gotten angry, yelling back that she wouldn't pat her daughter on the back for doing what she should be doing anyway.

This was the same situation. Yes, it made sense for Natasha to dance with Dimitri. On a career level, it was a great move. It would rocket her into the spotlight in her first episode—hell, in the first dance of the night. Dimitri was a judge, not a competing pro, and he was world-famous.

But on a deeper level, Natasha recognized what she was doing. This man sparked all kinds of needs in her, including the need for validation. The notion that he'd singled her out only made her want more attention. That he was so hard to please, and so stingy with compliments, fueled her desire to try to win them.

She knew this was a dark road. Christ, he'd just told her he didn't deliver praise.

But some part of Natasha had long ago invented this twisted logic that if she could manage to gain approval from someone who didn't give it freely, then maybe it would mean she was finally good enough.

Being near Dimitri made her heart pound. He absorbed all her attention, gave her jitters and flutters. She knew this unhealthy desire for approval was part of her attraction to him. But she was powerless to stop it.

He reached for her. "Dance with me, Tasha."

Without a second's hesitation, she took his hand.

<h1 style="text-align:center">Chapter Thirteen</h1>

____

Present day

The first thing Dimitri did when he woke up was check on Natasha. He knocked softly on the closed door, and when he didn't hear a reply, an intense surge of anticipation pushed him to grasp the knob and ease it open, despite feeling like the worst kind of host.

His hopes instantly deflated. Light streamed in through the open curtains. The bed was neatly made—something Nik had *never* done while living here—and empty. Dimitri took a deep breath. The room was already starting to smell like her, something sweet with a hint of ginger.

When he checked the garage, her car was still parked inside.

He walked back into the kitchen with a scowl on his face and his hands on his hips. Where the hell was she?

From the other side of the house, he caught the strains of music and grinned. Just as he'd suspected, she hadn't been able to withstand the lure of the studio. Once a fourth bedroom, it was his favorite space in the house, though he hardly used it these days.

He pushed open the studio door slowly and quietly. He'd

have to thank Trina, his housekeeper, for keeping the hinges oiled. Not that Natasha would have heard over the music. She was fully absorbed, her eyes half-closed as she pirouetted across the floor in a pair of worn pointe shoes. Her long dark curls were contained in a high bun, accentuating her sharp cheekbones and the elegant column of her neck.

As the music soared, so did she in a series of grand jetes. Her limbs cut through the air with grace and strength, and her arabesque was a thing of beauty.

It had been a long time, but he remembered the moves, learned at his mother's knee in her own ballet studio in Brooklyn. He'd learned to walk, then run, then plié. Ballet had been first for him. The other styles had come later.

In between the classical ballet moves, Natasha incorporated hip hop and jazz moves, along with steps from Latin dances, like bachata and tango. The fusion was seamless and executed with mastery and emotion.

He leaned against the doorjamb, overwhelmed by the sight of her. Natasha was always beautiful. Not just her body and her face. Not just the way she smiled, flirted, and sassed—even though it drove him wild. But when she danced? She awoke something in him he wasn't ready to name. Something deep and encompassing, making him feel settled and terrified all at the same time. More than anything, though, it made him want to be with her. He couldn't resist her when she danced.

The song came to an end and started again. Her chest rose as she took a deep breath and launched back into the routine.

When the song began a third time, Dimitri joined her.

He came up behind her on bare feet and took her in his arms. She jolted and her eyes flew open wide, but she didn't say anything. It was just like the first time they'd danced, and every other time since. He let the music flow through him, communicating in a way he couldn't explain and didn't question.

It wasn't perfect. He hadn't watched her long enough to learn the full choreography. But he followed her example, blending ballet with moves from other dance styles. Like always, it was magic.

The brush of their bodies, his hands on her skin, her weight in his arms. His own body, still tired from a late night and waking earlier than he was used to, thrummed with the restless energy she brought out in him. Passion—for her, for the dance— lit in his veins.

Cool and aloof as she was off the dance floor, when they came together like this, she couldn't hide herself. The glimpses were enough to make him crave more—more of her body, sure, but also a peek behind her sexy smirk and bedroom eyes. He wanted to know *her*, the secret Natasha she hid from the world, the Natasha who came out when she danced.

That Natasha touched his heart, bringing him to his knees in a way no one ever had, or, he feared, ever would again. If he had to use their incredible sexual chemistry to get past her walls, he would. And if he had to use dance to ignite the fire between them, he'd do that, too.

Even as it threatened to consume him.

When the song ended and started over, they didn't stop moving. This time, though, they danced closer. Their touches lingered. His hands gripped tighter, and her body arched more sinuously. They abandoned the choreography in favor of twining around each other's bodies to the beat of the music. The singer's rich, smoky voice wrapped them in a spell of harmony and desire.

Dimitri brought Natasha in from a spin, holding her back against his chest. She was en pointe, and he was barefoot. Her throat was *right there*, left exposed by the teeny tank top and her upswept hair.

Heart pounding, he pressed his mouth to her skin and dragged kisses up her neck, savoring her gasp as he tasted and teased the sensitive spot below her ear.

Drunk on the biting ginger scent of her, he spun her in his arms until she was facing him. Her eyes flew to his, heavy-lidded and filled with hunger. His gaze latched onto her lips, parted and wet. As he lowered his head to hers, the awareness in her expression turned to anticipation. Triumph sang through him as her mouth trembled and pursed to meet his. With his body heavy and throbbing, urging him to go fast, he took it slow and brushed a kiss to the corner of her mouth.

She released a soft moan.

"Hey, Dima!"

Dimitri jerked at the sound of his brother's voice.

Chapter Fourteen

Three years ago

When the first group rehearsal for the opening number ended, Dimitri shot Natasha a searing look.

Don't you dare fucking leave, that look said. After a slight nod of acknowledgment, she hung back while the others filed out of the rehearsal room.

Once they were finally alone, Dimitri couldn't stop himself from touching her. It had been agony to hold back in front of everyone, so he'd let it all out in the dance, and the others had remarked upon their amazing chemistry. *You don't know the half of it,* he'd thought, but suffered their compliments with his usual conceit. "Of course we have chemistry," he'd joked. "I mean, look at me." They'd laughed, but part of him wondered if they thought he meant it. But he couldn't say, "Look at *her.*" Even though she was absolutely stunning in simple indigo leggings and a white sports bra.

Now, he palmed the nape of her neck, his pulse thumping when she tilted her head back, leaning into his touch.

"You should come over again." His words were tinged with a desperate growl he couldn't control.

She looked up at him from under her lashes, and the corners of her red-painted lips curved. He wanted to wipe her lipstick off with his tongue.

"Maybe I will."

She was playing coy, flirting with him. It should have pleased him, but instead, it left him uncomfortable.

No, it wasn't her flirting that made him uncomfortable—it was his reaction. His urges. He wanted to drop to the floor and beg her to come home with him and never leave. The last few days, teased by her memory, had been hell.

But as beautifully as they danced together, he'd only met her that week. After their one night together, he knew she was into him. There was no faking that level of connection. She was the most responsive woman he'd ever been with, perfect in the ballroom and the bedroom. And today, she'd flirted and ensnared him with heated, lingering looks.

But she didn't talk to him. She didn't laugh with him. Dimitri had watched her with Kevin, and even though the two of them had also just met this week, they got on like old friends. There didn't seem to be anything sexual there—Dimitri had kept a close eye on them, and in all the years he'd known Kevin, he'd never seen the other man seriously flirt with someone—but Dimitri had been jealous all the same.

He blamed that jealousy for what he said next.

"Call first, to make sure I'm alone."

He meant his brother, Nik, who lived with him, but when Natasha's smile dropped and her eyes widened, Dimitri knew how she'd taken it. Maybe he'd even meant for her to take it that way.

And because sometimes he was an asshole, and he was scared of how much he wanted her, he didn't explain and let her think he was referring to other women.

He waited for her to make some sharp retort, but she didn't say anything. She just turned her face away from him. His hand was still on the back of her neck, so he kneaded the muscles there.

It was a dirty move, one he knew she couldn't resist. As dancers, they pushed their bodies to the limit, and sometimes beyond. And after the day they'd had, she wouldn't be able to turn down a massage.

Sure enough, she released a soft groan, and her head fell forward. Dimitri moved behind her, working her traps with both hands now, his thumbs tracing alongside the bumps of her spine under the racerback of her sports bra. And then, because he couldn't fucking help himself, he leaned down and dragged his tongue up the side of her neck.

Her body arched into his touch, and a moan escaped her lips.

Fuck it.

He spun her around, ready to kiss her and beg her to come over, when someone knocked on the door. Natasha immediately stepped away from him, and Dimitri dropped his hands. A second later, Kevin stuck his head in.

"Hey, Tash, you coming?"

"Yeah." Her voice sounded bright and normal. She jogged over to the mirrors, grabbed her bag, and exited the room without a backward glance.

Dimitri scowled at the door as it closed behind her, then slowly made his way to his own gym bag. Okay, he'd said something shitty to her. But it hadn't seemed to bother her, not in the way it would've bothered other women he'd known. Natasha hadn't reprimanded him, or demanded an explanation, or left in a huff, even though she would have had every reason to do any of those things.

If she had, maybe he would have tried to explain what he really meant.

Instead, she hadn't said anything. She'd let him touch her and appeared eager for more. But then she'd walked out like it had meant nothing. Like *he* meant nothing.

Was that it? Dimitri shouldered his bag and headed out to the parking lot. Had their amazing night together meant nothing to her? Why else would she brush off his comment, but still let him touch her?

Hell, maybe she was enduring his attention because he was a judge. That would be fucking terrible, but he didn't think that was the case. The way she looked at him…no, it wasn't that.

Maybe it was just a given that this was something casual. That was usually what he had with women, but they typically made their expectations clear, through word or deed. Natasha seemed to have…none. Like she didn't care what they did, or didn't do. Like it didn't matter to her either way.

He climbed into the driver's seat of his SUV and tossed his bag onto the passenger seat.

Before starting the engine, he rubbed a hand down his face and sighed. It sucked to admit it, but he wanted her more than she wanted him. And unless she gave him some kind of sign… then this was what they'd do. He'd play it cool. Take what she was willing to give.

And convince himself it was enough.

Chapter Fifteen

Present day

The surprise and shock of his brother's voice yanked Dimitri's attention toward the door. In the confusion, he loosened his grip on Natasha, only to realize she wasn't holding on to him. By reflex, he shot out a hand to grab her, but he hadn't counted on her own sense of balance kicking in. His attempt to catch her turned into a shove, and she stumbled backward, her eyes wide with shock.

Oh *shit*. She thought he'd *pushed* her. He reached for her again. "Natasha, I'm—"

"Dima, you home?" Nik's shout interrupted the apology on Dimitri's lips, and Natasha nearly tripped over her pointe shoes as she scrambled to gather her computer equipment and get away.

Dimitri ground his teeth and ran his hands through his hair. His brother had the *worst* fucking timing. "It's just Nikolai," he said, following Natasha out. "I didn't mean—"

"Yeah. Okay." Natasha's voice was breathy as she darted through the center of the house that held the main living space, running away from him before he could explain.

From the front door, Nikolai gave them a puzzled look, and Dimitri could guess how it seemed. The two of them coming out of the studio with him in nothing but sweatpants and Natasha in shorts and a leotard with her arms full of tech, pointe shoes slapping the floor as she hurried back to her room—fuck, to *Nik's* room. Where he probably expected to stay.

A grin split Nik's face. "Oh, hey, Tash. Nice to see you."

"Hey, Nik." She ducked her head and sent him a wave.

Dimitri stuck his hands in his pockets to keep from throwing something. Nik and Natasha knew each other from the times Nik had filled in as an extra on *The Dance Off*—and from the mornings when they'd crossed paths in this very house. While it was nice not to have to make awkward introductions, something about their easy greeting set him on edge.

"We were dancing," Dimitri said, and for reasons he didn't want to examine, his tone sounded defensive.

Nik raised his eyebrows and pressed his lips together to hide a grin. "Oh yeah?"

"Gotta get ready for work." With a polite nod, Natasha locked herself in the bedroom.

Nik shouldered his duffel bag. "I'm going to resist making a Goldilocks joke," he said in a stage whisper. "But just barely."

"Idi v banyu," Dimitri snapped, but the mild insult only made Nik laugh.

Scowling, Dimitri padded barefoot into the kitchen. He needed coffee if he was going to get himself under control and deal with his baby brother. He switched to Russian for the conversation, in case Natasha could hear them. "What are you doing here?"

"Unexpected break in the schedule. Figured I'd come back for a few days rather than stick around in Phoenix. Didn't realize you'd given away my room." Nik dumped his bags next to the barstools at the kitchen counter, then hopped onto one of them. "You know what? I can't resist." In a high, singsong voice, he said in English, "Someone's been sleeping in *my* bed!"

Dimitri threw a dishtowel at his face. "Durak."

Nik caught it and switched back to Russian. "The real question is, why isn't she in *your* bed? Hey, make me some, too."

Dimitri grumbled, but he got down the cups and began to grind the beans.

Dimitri's shoulder blades itched. He could feel his brother watching him, just waiting for the moment to make another joke.

He wasn't in the mood for Nik's teasing. He was tired, horny, and—thanks to Nik's timing—no closer to deciphering Natasha's mysteries or convincing her to abandon her "no sex" rule.

The grinder stopped, and in the ensuing quiet, the sound of the bedroom door opening was loud. A moment later, Natasha appeared in the arched kitchen doorway. She had changed into yoga pants, sneakers, and a loose off-the-shoulder top in teal green. Her face was bare of makeup, but her cheeks were flushed. She looked amazing.

"You're making espresso?" she asked, sniffing the air.

"Yeah, I was making you some." Dimitri ignored his brother's dirty look. It was worth it to see the small smile curving Natasha's lips.

"Actually, do you mind if I do it? You have such a great espresso machine, I was hoping to try it out," she said.

"Make me some?" Nik pleaded.

She winked at him. "I got you."

Dimitri moved out of the way and watched Natasha work at the counter. Her movements were precise and economical, yet everything was done with grace. She made the espresso shots and poured them into latte cups, then steamed the milk with the wand he never used. The whirring sound filled the room.

Nik pitched his voice over it. "Where are you off to, Tash?"

She kept her eyes on the task at hand as she answered. "I have a few Pilates classes to teach, and two auditions."

When Nik's eyebrows popped up, Dimitri realized his had done the same. "Auditions for what?" Nik asked.

"A couple TV spots," she said, shrugging. "Nothing big. Just trying to fill up my summer with work, you know?"

"Have you ever done a national tour? I'm touring with *Seize the Night* right now."

She shook her head and shut off the wand, wiping it down before she poured the milk. "I wouldn't want to travel that much. I like having a home base." Her gaze flicked to Dimitri and away.

Dimitri could understand that. It was hard enough being in Los Angeles, away from his parents and extended family. Nik had made it easier, but now he was gone, too.

Well, except for right this moment, when Dimitri wished his brother were anywhere but here.

Maybe it had been hard for Natasha, too. First, being away from New York, then with Gina leaving, and now, losing access to her apartment.

The way she poured the milk into the mug distracted him. "Hey, are you—" He stopped and laughed. "Where'd you learn to do that?"

Natasha pulled back the pitcher and admired the little white heart in the foam. A pleased smile played on her lips. "I used to work at a restaurant with an espresso machine at the bar. We practiced latte art when business was slow. It never gets old."

He pointed to the heart. "Is that for—"

She snatched the cup away and carried it over to Nik.

"Aww, I got a heart!" Nik's phone was already in his hand, so he snapped a picture. "Tash, you're a woman of many talents."

When she came back to the counter, Dimitri crossed his arms over his chest. "Why can't I have a heart?"

She stared at him from the corner of her eye. "Are you admitting you don't already have one?"

"Very funny."

Across the kitchen, Nik sipped, then gave Natasha a thumbs-up. "Excellent brew, sestra."

After Natasha had picked up the second cup in one hand and

the milk pitcher in the other, Dimitri shot his brother a glare. What the hell was Nik doing, calling Natasha *sister*?

Her moves with the milk caught his attention again and Dimitri watched, mesmerized. She tilted the cup as she poured, carefully turning it as she shook the pitcher lightly, pouring from farther away, then closer as the image began to appear. Even lines formed on top of the coffee, curving around and becoming a beautifully detailed leaf.

"There," she said, setting the cup on a saucer and nudging it toward him. "That's for you."

Dimitri stared at the leaf. It was so pretty, so perfect. "I don't want to drink it," he blurted out.

At her soft, offended gasp, he hurried to finish his thought. "It looks too nice, I mean. I don't want to ruin it." Damn, he was always saying the wrong thing around her.

Nik took a picture of Dimitri's cup, then filmed Natasha pouring her own. She made a design that looked like a heart coming out of a flower, as if it were the easiest thing in the world.

"Cheers," she said, smiling into the camera as she raised the cup to her lips.

Dimitri sipped his own as he watched. If he kissed her now, she'd taste darkly sweet, like espresso and milk.

"I didn't know you could do that," he said as she drained her cup.

"You never asked." She set her empty cup in the sink. "Will one of you clean up? I don't want to be late for work."

"He'll do it," Nik answered for Dimitri. "Don't be late because of us."

"Thanks, Nik." She tilted her head and they gave each other a quick, impersonal kiss on the cheek. But when her gaze shot to Dimitri's, her dark eyes turned wary.

The realization that she wasn't going to kiss him goodbye was like a kick in the gut. She'd kissed his brother like it was nothing, but for Dimitri, a simple goodbye kiss was too awkward. It shouldn't piss him off—after all, it was his own damn fault—but it did.

"Um, I have to get going," she said, not really looking at either of them. "See you later, D. Bye, Nik." And then she was gone.

Dimitri sipped his latte and waited. It wasn't long before Nik leaped to fill the silence, slipping back into English now that they were alone. Nik hadn't spent his formative years in Ukraine, like Dimitri had, so while Nik was technically fluent in Russian, he was more comfortable speaking English.

"Dude." Nik gestured toward the doorway, as if Natasha were still there. "What are you doing?"

Tamping down on the urge to yell, Dimitri kept his gaze on his cup and his voice level. "She had an emergency and needed a place to stay. I offered."

Nik blinked. "You *offered*?" Then he burst into laughter and nearly fell off his chair. "Wait a second. You offered to let a woman you're—"

"Watch it," Dimitri growled.

"Listen, this isn't the first time you've kicked me out of here so Natasha could come over. It's just the first time she's staying in *my* bedroom. What's the deal? Are you guys roommates now instead of...whatever you were?"

Dimitri drained the rest of his cup and stuck it in the sink. "No."

"So, you guys are still..."

"Blyat." Dimitri crossed his arms in frustration. "No, we're not that either."

Nik leaned his elbows back on the counter, making himself comfortable. "So... more than that?"

Rolling his eyes, Dimitri stomped over to the fridge and started pulling out stuff to make a protein shake. He didn't particularly want one, but he needed to move, to burn off the excess energy ignited by his dance with Natasha and his brother's penetrating line of questioning. He slammed the carton of milk on the counter and muttered, "No, damn it, we're not."

For now.

His brother held his hands up in mock surrender. "Calm down. I'm just trying to get a handle on the situation. I've never known you to hang around with a woman you weren't...you know."

That was because Dimitri *didn't*. Still, it rankled to have it pointed out so matter-of-factly. "I don't need to explain myself. She's a guest, and you'll be nice to her."

Nik squinted at him. "I'm always nice to her. You, on the other hand, are kind of a dick."

Dimitri didn't answer. It was true, he'd said some shitty things to her. Often, he didn't think about how they'd sound until they were already out of his mouth, and being around her twisted him up, made him impulsive and foolish.

But he'd never claimed to be nice. He had a reputation for having a short temper. As a choreographer, he was demanding and expected perfection. That didn't mean he didn't feel... No, he wouldn't go there, not now. Nik was too perceptive.

Dimitri grabbed a handful of ice cubes from the freezer and dumped them in the blender before turning it on. The loud whirr of the motor filled the kitchen, prohibiting conversation. But the second it turned off, Nik spoke again, his tone thoughtful.

"You once said you wouldn't live with a woman unless you planned to marry her."

Dimitri shut his eyes. Shit, he had said that, hadn't he? After Juliette Jacobs had laughed in his face over a decade ago, Dimitri had vowed never to live with a woman unless he was sure it was the real deal, that they had a future together.

Now, Dimitri shrugged, trying to act nonchalant. "What's your point?"

Nik stared at him, his brown eyes, a shade lighter than Dimitri's own, filled with disbelief. "You're planning to *marry* Natasha?"

"No." Although now that Nik mentioned it, the concept didn't sound as untenable as it might have a few years ago. That alone should have made Dimitri shit his pants, but instead, he just filed it away as something to think about.

His brother wasn't done grilling him. "So, you didn't mean it when you said that?"

"I did." Dimitri intended to use this time alone with Natasha to see if they had a connection beyond sex and dancing. For that, Nik had to leave. "Get a hotel."

Nik huffed. "Yeah, I already figured that out. I'm just waiting for you to make me a shake."

An hour later, Nik left, and Dimitri sat at his desk. His conversation—if it could be called that—with his brother had shed light on the strangeness of his situation with Natasha. They'd been locked in this stagnant dynamic for three years. Enough was enough. He picked up his phone, intending to text her and ask if she'd be home for dinner, when strains of Tchaikovsky rang out—his mother.

He picked up. "*Privet*, Mama."

She cut right to the chase, speaking a mile a minute in Russian. "Nik just called. Dimochka, you're getting *married*?"

Dimitri shut his eyes and pinched the bridge of his nose. "Mama, do you have bail money?"

"What? Why?"

"Because I'm going to murder my brother."

Chapter Sixteen

Natasha successfully managed to avoid Dimitri that night by going to bed before he got back from the restaurant. The next day, she hustled out the door before he woke up and spent the morning hanging out in the juice bar at the gym where she taught Pilates.

She'd brought her laptop with her, but a quick look at her bank account balance revealed she had no business scanning apartment listings. Instead, she pulled up the video from the day before. She had a little time before her first class, so she began to review the choreography she'd been working on.

She wanted to combine music from classical ballets with hip hop, pop, and Latin music, and create a routine that merged the multiple dance styles. It was the kind of thing she wished had existed when she'd been a teenager studying ballet in Manhattan, wondering how this beautiful, if rigid, technique could coexist alongside the dances she saw on TV and in the world around her. She dreamed of bringing a program like this to schools, to bridge the gap between classical and modern styles.

But those were bigger ideas. First, she had to nail the content of the dance.

As she watched the recording, she paused to make notes, jotting down what worked and what didn't.

When Dimitri walked into the video frame, she jolted in her seat. She'd completely forgotten that the camera had still been recording when he'd joined her.

She dropped her pencil, absorbed in watching the screen. Dimitri easily followed her choreography, improvising some of his own moves. He brought something edgier to it, and before she could examine that too much, she noted down his additions.

It was fascinating to watch herself with him. Her shoulders and neck had tensed when he surprised her, then relaxed as they continued to dance to the music.

She'd seen herself dancing with him before, of course. On her first season with *The Dance Off*, he'd chosen her as his partner for the opening dance of the premiere episode. That dance had thrust her into the spotlight, although she hadn't made it very far that season with her partner, an aging soap opera star. But that first dance, choreographed by Dimitri, had been a thing of beauty. It captured his magnetic presence, her infatuation with him, and the incredible sexual energy that had sparked between them the moment they'd met. No matter how many times she watched the footage, she still swooned, unable to believe her life had led her to a place where she got to dance with her former celebrity crush.

But this was different. There was no camera crew, no producers, no audience. It was just the two of them, alone, sleep-rumpled and unguarded. What she saw on her own face worried her, but what she saw on his…

Her finger hovered over the touchpad, ready to close the file, to hide from the raw vulnerability in his expression. The way his eyes followed her, like he couldn't get enough…it was the dance. It had to be. He was acting.

The vibe changed, then. It became hotter. Sexier. The camera picked up the sound of their breathing, louder and heavier. Even watching on a small screen with headphones on, Natasha's heart thumped harder.

Carajo, this was like the start of a sex tape. Her eyes followed his hands, noting the way his touch became stronger. Tighter. More possessive. And how she, unable to resist him, had leaned closer, lingered against his body for longer, and undulated more than was entirely necessary.

Her face burned, and she darted a glance around to make sure no one else could see her screen. She was getting turned on from watching herself dance with Dimitri! And she had to teach Pilates to a bunch of retired ladies in—she checked the time—twenty minutes.

She sipped her smoothie, but it did nothing to cool her down, especially when she saw the moment Dimitri decided to kiss her.

And the moment she decided to let him.

The camera's microphone had even picked up Nik's shouted greeting. The way they froze on screen, their eyes wide and horrified, was almost comical. Except she was so aroused right now, nothing was funny. A fantasy flashed through her mind, of jumping in her car, racing back to Dimitri's, and pouncing on him in his bed.

No, damn it. *No sex.* And she had *work.* So she could make money and get the hell out of his house.

Watching the shove, and his stricken expression when he'd realized what he'd done, she could see it was an accident. But she was grateful, both for Nik's interruption and the accidental push. The spell had been broken, and Nik's presence made it easier to hang out in the kitchen like everything was normal.

After packing up her stuff, Natasha headed to the reformer room early. This was the first of three classes today, followed by a private session and two auditions. She needed to stay focused. No more thinking about Dimitri and their almost-kiss.

Or how pleased he'd been by her latte art.

Kevin and Lori were blowing up her phone.

Natasha had never realized how often they used her apartment as their hangout spot until it was no longer available. They texted back and forth all day, suggesting potential plans. All involved meeting at Natasha's place first.

To get them off her back, she agreed to meet them for coffee in Culver City after her last audition, which she was sure she wouldn't get. The casting director had stared at her phone the whole time, looking bored, and the woman's "Thanks for coming in" had been cold.

Natasha almost texted Dimitri to let him know she'd be out, then stopped herself. Why bother? She wasn't his girlfriend or his roommate. She wasn't even a real houseguest, no matter what he said. She had a set of keys, a remote for the garage, and she knew the security code. There was no need to keep him apprised of her whereabouts. No reason to think he'd care.

On the way out of the parking structure, she received an email from her building's management company. They'd taken a dog through her apartment, and it was free and clear of bedbugs. They would still spray before she moved back in, but her stuff was okay.

That was a relief, but she'd already taken a ton of shit to the dry cleaners, not just items that had been damaged in the leak, but stuff that couldn't be washed normally. She was going to pay some hefty dry cleaning bills for nothing.

Kevin and Lori were already in front of the cafe when Natasha strolled up.

Kevin had the sort of look that magazines called "All-American" when what they really meant was "white." The faint freckles across his nose and cheekbones, along with his ready smile, made him more boyish than handsome. His build was lean but strong, and he was maybe a couple of inches taller than Natasha's five-foot-eight. He moved with a kind of barely-restrained energy that in some men, Natasha might have found unnerving, but Kevin was more likely to burst into a fast-paced jive than throw a punch.

Lori, on the other hand, was effortlessly cool, with a steadiness about her that belied her goofball personality. She'd risen to fame as a breakdancer, and her personal style combined brightly colored athletic wear with flashy accessories. She was Korean American and had grown up in San Diego before moving to LA.

Standing next to each other, they couldn't have been more different. Kevin, in a plain gray T-shirt, navy blue shorts, and white sneakers. And Lori, in a sleeveless red crop top, oversized yellow cargo pants, and black and silver high-tops.

Natasha had missed them terribly.

With a blue Dodgers cap covering his light brown waves, Kevin bounded over to her. He caught Natasha in an exuberant hug and gave her a smacking kiss on her temple. "Missed you, babe."

Lori's straight black hair was also covered by a hat, but hers was white with pointed silver spikes covering the bill, and it was turned backward. She caught Natasha around the waist for a hug, and Natasha had to lean down to complete the embrace. There was a good five-inch difference in their heights.

"This place is crowded," Lori said, jerking a thumb at the cafe behind them. Sure enough, all the outdoor tables were crammed with people, and the seating inside was similarly occupied.

"And I'm hungry for more than a soggy croissant," Kevin added. "We were talking about trying the new Mexican place that opened across the street."

He pointed, and Natasha turned. Yet another trendy—and expensive—restaurant had popped up since she'd last been in this area.

"We could try a different cafe," Natasha suggested. She was okay with meeting for coffee, but dinner was more than she could afford at the moment. When Kevin waved the idea away, she dropped it, in case one of them asked why.

Lori checked the menu on her phone. "Reviews say their guac is great, although I'm sure it has nothing on yours, Tash."

"I do make great guacamole." She held back from adding, *At a fraction of the price.*

Kevin snapped his fingers. "We should do a cast potluck again. Before the next season starts filming."

"It won't be the same without Gina," Lori mused as the three of them crossed the street to the restaurant. "How's she doing? Have you heard from her?"

The mention of Gina brought Natasha a pang of discomfort. "She sent a picture a couple days ago. She and Stone hiked a glacier or something."

"Whoa, really?" Kevin's pale eyebrows popped up. "I wonder if their Alaska house is ready for visitors."

They asked the hostess for a table for three. She told them it would be a twenty-minute wait, but one of the waiters recognized them and pushed them higher up in the queue. They only waited three minutes, during which time they snapped selfies with the restaurant staff.

"Fame has its advantages," Kevin muttered as they finally took their seats, but his tone was dark.

Lori kicked his foot under the table. "Don't complain. Besides, you're the one who said you were hungry."

The waiter arrived quickly. Lori and Kevin ordered margaritas. Since everyone else was drinking, Natasha ordered a mojito, even though it cost four times what her coffee would have.

Besides, she needed to relax. After dancing with Dimitri that morning and rewatching the footage on her laptop, she was wound up tight.

Once they'd placed their orders—and Kevin convinced them to try several items from the appetizer menu—conversation turned to industry gossip.

"Any idea who they're going to replace Gina with?" Lori asked.

Natasha shook her head. "I haven't heard anything. My

guess is one of the backup dancers—maybe Sienna? She's always smiling, and they gave her more airtime last season. But it wouldn't surprise me if they make some picks from *Everybody Dance Now.* It's been a while since they pulled someone from there. Gina and I were the last."

"Doubt it." Kevin leaned in. "*The Dance Off* pulls talent from *EDN* because they're on the same network and the showrunners used to be partners. But I heard they had a falling out."

The first round of dishes arrived—big plates with a tiny amount of food in the center of each one. They waited while a waiter made tableside guacamole. Natasha tasted it, and Lori was right—it was good, but not as good as her own.

When they were alone again, Lori nudged Kevin's elbow. "Tell me more."

"Before Muriel came to *The Dance Off* as showrunner, she helped launch *EDN.* Or, if you listen to the gossip, which I do, it was *her* idea. But Kristoff, her partner, took most of the credit. She didn't like how he was running things over there—or that he wouldn't leave his husband for her—so she left, joined *The Dance Off,* and took their best producer with her."

Lori frowned. "Who?"

But Natasha groaned. "I'm going to need another mojito if we're going to talk about *her.*"

Kevin's expression darkened. "Same." He flagged down their waiter, and they ordered another round of drinks.

"Which producer are you talking about?" Lori asked. "Obviously not Barry, otherwise I'd know this already."

"You mean Donna Alvarez, right?" Natasha said. "My producer. Fucking Donna."

"Nailed it." Kevin piled extra jalapeños on his side of the meager nachos platter and shoved a loaded tortilla chip into his mouth. Natasha eyed the nachos like they'd kicked her dog. Seriously, who made a small plate of nachos?

"Is Donna really as awful as everyone says she is?" Lori mused.

"Worse," Kevin said with a growl. "The woman is a soulless demon."

"I call her La Diabla," Natasha added.

Lori sipped her margarita. "And she used to work on *EDN*? Must have been before my time there."

"Me too." Natasha chased a bean around the plate with a chip. "She made the shift before I was on either show."

Kevin nodded. "Muriel took her because Donna has a well-earned reputation for being manipulative and ruthless."

Lori's eyes were wide, and she talked through a mouthful of carnitas taquitos. "What does she do?"

Natasha answered, since she had the inside scoop. "Did you see all the stuff that went down with Gina and Stone last season? That was Donna."

"Like that secret footage of them kissing?"

"Yep. Gina didn't know they were being filmed. Donna manipulated Stone into keeping it a secret, then aired the footage right before their semifinals dance." Donna's machinations had nearly been the end of Gina and Stone's budding romance, but the two of them had worked it out.

"That's horrible."

"She was really trying to turn them into the season's showmance, against Gina's wishes."

Kevin returned to the original thread of the conversation. "So, the reason they're not pulling from *EDN* anymore is that Muriel stole away another one of their producers, because Kristoff—who is still married, by the way—started dating someone else."

"In addition to Muriel?" Natasha asked.

Kevin nodded. "She wanted to be the only sidepiece."

"Lord, this is complicated." Lori munched on some chips.

But Kevin wasn't done. "Muriel is pissed, and after losing Gina, I heard they're cracking down on behind-the-scenes hookups."

Natasha froze with her fork stabbed into a grilled pepper popper. "What do you mean?"

"Some of the network execs are concerned it will affect performance and ratings. Muriel is just bitter that true love cost her the winning pro. So, no more backstage shenanigans for the rest of us."

Natasha wondered at that, since she'd never heard even a whiff of a rumor about Kevin fooling around with someone. Lori, on the other hand, was an open book. She didn't hide her search for true love.

Just then, Natasha caught Lori staring at her. Prickles raced up her spine, and the mojitos loosened her tongue. "What's that look for?"

"Nothing!" Lori squeaked. "I just—I mean, I know you and Jackson were kinda seeing each other. Since he was my partner, it was hard to miss it."

"'Seeing each other' makes it sound like more than it was," Natasha said easily, smothering her sigh of relief. She was worried they'd somehow heard about her and Dimitri. But then her defenses snapped into place. "Anyway, I wasn't the only one messing around last season. Joel was screwing Keiko Simon, and that *Future Fiancé* guy was—"

"Cool it, girl," Lori said, raising her hands. "I was just citing an example. I know you're not the only one. I was making out pretty regularly with one of the backup girls a couple seasons ago, until she claimed she was just drunk, not gay. I don't have time for that shit."

Kevin shrugged. "It's part of the industry. I don't think this will amount to anything, except people being sneakier and a higher incidence of DTD."

"Don't Tell Donna," Natasha clarified for Lori. "It's something all her dancers know."

Kevin shook his head. "Fucking Donna. After the second time I won, I told them I'd quit if they didn't assign me to a different producer."

Natasha rested her chin on her hands. "Maybe after I win a couple times, I'll be able to request a change. But I'd have to win once first."

Lori picked at her napkin. "I bet you would've won if you'd been paired with Jackson last year."

"You made it to the finals and came in third place," Natasha pointed out. "You two were great partners."

"I know, but the chemistry you guys had would've gotten you extra votes."

Natasha shrugged. Sex with Jackson had been fun, but that was it. And the last time she was supposed to meet him, she'd gone home with Dimitri instead. But all she said was, "Gina and Stone were really in love. Jackson and I weren't. Besides, *this* guy snagged second place." She flicked a finger against Kevin's forearm.

"Are you still in touch with Lauren?" Lori asked, and Natasha couldn't help bristling at the name.

"Nope." Kevin took off his hat and ran a hand through his hair. "Being her partner was *exhausting*."

Natasha believed him. Kevin and Lauren D'Angelo, an Olympic figure skater, had nearly won last season, but Lauren's technical perfection couldn't top Stone and Gina's emotional connection. In retaliation, Lauren had sought to sabotage the reality show Stone filmed with his family in Alaska.

Lori lowered her voice. "I heard Lauren made the rounds through most of the male cast—pros *and* stars."

Kevin held up both hands. "Not me."

Lori finished a chip. "Judges, too, come to think of it."

There was a loud screech as Natasha's fork skidded across her plate. "Sorry," she muttered, and used her hand to stuff the tiny taquito into her mouth before she could say something she'd regret.

But the flash of jealousy at hearing Lori reference what Lauren had done with Dimitri quickly faded as Natasha focused on the bigger picture. If the producers were cracking down on backstage hookups, how much worse would it be if they knew Natasha was shacking up with one of the judges?

Natasha cut into the conversation the others were having about a cute new camera woman. "Wait a second. How are Donna and the other producers going to know if we're messing around with anyone?"

Kevin shrugged. "Nothing stays secret. And you can bet Donna's stalking your social media and any news items that pop up about you. That's what she used to do to me."

Natasha sighed. Now she had to go on social media lockdown and be extra careful about coming and going from Dimitri's house. And with the gate broken, anyone could waltz up to the front door, including the braver among the paparazzi.

Lori held up her phone. "Hey, I just got an invite to a concert tomorrow night. We should go!"

"Looks good," Kevin said, glancing at the screen. "Hey Tash, we can pre-game at your place first. The venue's not too far from there."

Natasha shook her head, with perhaps a tad too much vehemence, because Kevin's brows drew together. "No. I mean, I have a full schedule tomorrow and work early the next day. You know I've got a ton of summer jobs, and I'm trying to cover the full rent, plus the new car..."

"I forgot about that." Kevin tapped his fingers on the table in thought. "What about dinner beforehand? Then Lori and I will go to the concert."

"My stove isn't working," Natasha blurted out.

"Oh, that sucks." Lori patted her arm. "You love to cook. How long has it been out?"

"A few days." The lies were getting out of hand. "The building is providing a new one, but things are kind of a mess, and you know...it's just one more thing." She gave a little laugh to imply it was a minor inconvenience, nothing they should worry about. "A new Korean restaurant opened down the street from me—why don't we try that?"

"Perfect, I've been craving tteokbokki." Lori seemed pleased, but Kevin's expression was unreadable. He opened his mouth, but the waiter appeared with the check, saving Natasha from further questions.

"Let's split three ways," Kevin suggested, tossing his credit card down on the tray. Lori added hers, and Natasha bit back a grimace as she placed her debit card on top of the pile. Living like this was going to clean her out. Why the hell hadn't she insisted on coffee? And why had she agreed to *another* dinner?

She took a deep breath. It would be okay. The dance classes she was teaching the next day paid immediately.

But unease roiled in her belly as she recalled what else was on her schedule.

Tomorrow would bring her face-to-face with La Diabla.

Chapter Seventeen

The next morning, Natasha pulled into the parking lot behind *The Dance Off*'s headquarters. Proximity to the building pushed her financial concerns from her mind and raised a different worry to the number-one position: she had to keep Donna and the others from finding out she was staying with Dimitri.

Not "living with." It was temporary. And they weren't sleeping together—literally or figuratively. It should be totally fine.

Somehow, she didn't think Muriel would see it that way.

The memory of dancing with Dimitri in his private studio, and watching the passion flare between them on video, flashed through her mind. She sucked in a breath and knocked the heel of her hand against the steering wheel. God, he was hot. When he put his hands on her, all her good sense flew out the window. Even her fingernails buzzed with need. It was killing her to stay away from him.

But after what Kevin had told her, it was more important than ever that she stick to her rule.

She grabbed her things and headed into the building. This line of thinking was only working her up, and she needed to stay cool around Donna. The woman was like a shark, scenting secrecy like it was fresh blood.

Natasha found Donna in her tiny, cramped office with the door halfway open. "Hi, Donna. You have something for me to sign?" Better to get to the point.

Donna looked up from her laptop. She would've been pretty, Natasha thought, if she weren't such a snake. Donna had straight black hair that fell midway down her back, and her skin, a sandy tan color with a smattering of light freckles, seemed like it had never even heard of pimples as a concept.

For a second, Donna's hazel-green eyes seemed distracted, but then her gaze sharpened on Natasha, and she smiled. "Oh, hey, Tash. Come on in. Thanks for agreeing to this at the last minute."

"No problem." There was a spare chair on the other side of Donna's desk. Natasha perched on the edge and hoped this would be a short meeting. Then she could stop by hair and makeup, get the shoot over with, and go on with her day. She still had classes to teach in the evening.

"Let me just find it." Donna opened and closed her desk drawers. "How's your summer going? I saw from your posts that you've been teaching classes all over LA."

Coño. Kevin was right. Donna *was* stalking her dancers' social media accounts.

Natasha kept her tone mild. "Just staying busy during the midseason."

Donna smirked. "That's all well and good, but don't hurt yourself. I need you in fighting shape. Hoping to go two for two."

Ohhh. Natasha got it now. Donna had also been Gina's producer, and Gina was the reigning champ. If Natasha won the upcoming season, Donna's dancers would win twice in a row. And if there was one thing that could be counted on, it was Donna's competitive streak.

It was a bad idea to joke around with Donna, but Natasha's

curiosity won out. "Does that mean you have a clue about who my next partner will be?" she asked coyly.

Donna laughed as she shuffled a stack of papers. "You know I can't tell you that, but I'm trying to secure someone who will get you on the right...*track*."

Natasha mulled that over. Track? Like...running? There'd been a Paralympian gold medalist in track and field last season, so she doubted the producers would bring on another runner so soon.

Maybe Donna had meant a music track, like on an album? A singer could be promising.

Singers who joined *The Dance Off* were either up-and-comers hoping to increase their fanbase or aging crooners aiming for a comeback. They often served as a musical guest, as well, and danced to one of their own songs at some point in the season. Some had pretty good rhythm, although it wasn't a sure bet.

Or maybe Donna had meant something else?

"Aha!" Donna held up a folder in triumph. "Here it is."

Natasha took the papers and scanned them quickly. They related to the promo segment she'd be filming that day. She selected a pen from a mug that read, "Trust Me, I'm a Producer."

Yeah, right, Natasha thought, eyeing the mug warily. As she signed the forms, she said, "Any other clues?"

"*If* I can get him, he'll be more your...speed...than Dwayne Alonzo was." But then Donna's expression turned serious. "I have to warn you, Tash. After Gina and Stone, there's going to be a crackdown on fraternizing with the celebs. Sexual chemistry is one thing, but don't do anything obvious." She raised her eyebrows and sent a meaningful look across the desk.

Heart pounding, it took all Natasha had to nod calmly. "Understood."

She didn't point out that it was Donna's own machinations and manipulations that had led to Gina leaving the show.

After Donna had aired secret footage of Gina and Stone kissing, Gina's response had drawn sympathy from fans, who'd taken to social media to lambaste the producers and editing team for throwing the dancers off their game in the final seconds before a pivotal dance.

Gina had crushed it, of course. She was a professional. But Natasha knew it had been her best friend's worst nightmare come to life.

Donna had done that to her.

But Natasha didn't mention any of that. Partly because Donna was her boss, and all of this talk about her next partner was just that, talk. And partly because it would be even worse for her if she were caught fucking one of the judges.

So she bit her tongue, handed over the forms, and left the office.

Once in the chair for hair and makeup, she idly scrolled through apartments in cheaper neighborhoods—not that anywhere in LA could be called *cheap*. Nothing jumped out at her, and the activity stressed her out, so Natasha was glad when it was time to don a sparkly purple halter dress with a ruffled skirt. Then she entered the largest rehearsal room, where the segment would be filmed.

A camera crew swarmed around a makeshift set with a full lighting setup and backdrop. Donna chatted with a woman Natasha recognized as Vita Schwartz, the host of a local morning news show. Natasha greeted the camera crew, stepped around a cluster of PAs, and froze.

Motherfucker!

She should have known.

Dimitri glanced over from the small craft services table set up on one side of the room, and his face lit with a grin. He ambled over to her, his outturned dancer's walk sexy as hell, his purple sequined suspenders looking anything but silly on him. They only served to highlight the strong lines of his body.

She gave him a warning glance. Donna was *right there.* "Hi, Dimitri," she said in an even tone. "It's been a while."

"Tasha." His gaze heated, and he leaned in to kiss her cheek. She was wearing heels, which made their heights almost even.

She caught a whiff of his cologne, the spicy, woodsy scent giving her flashbacks to the almost-kiss Nik had interrupted. She sucked on her lower lip, tasting lipstick, and his eyes widened.

"Tease," he whispered.

Damn it, he was going to get them in trouble, and so was she if she couldn't get her hormones under control. Natasha took a step back and aimed for light and impersonal. "So, what are you doing here?"

He shrugged. "Same as you, I guess. Pop culture piece for some morning show."

"Weird that they're doing this in the midseason," Natasha remarked, turning as a PA came over to hook up their lavalier mics.

Once the PA was gone, Dimitri dropped his voice. "It's because Gina and Stone have refused to do a lot of promo. People want the winners, but since they can't have them, they asked for the next best thing."

Natasha arched an eyebrow. "Kevin?"

Dimitri barked out a laugh, but when he leaned in, his grin turned wicked. "You're going to pay for that, Kroshka." His tone held a delicious mix of promise and threat.

Her pulse pounded in her throat, and she almost replied, *What are you gonna do, spank me?* But she was afraid it would come out eager instead of sassy.

Luckily, she didn't say anything, because at that moment, Donna approached them, followed by Vita and—shit, that was Muriel, the showrunner. Bitter Muriel, who was on the lookout for anything resembling fraternization between cast members.

Natasha took a step away from Dimitri as she faced them. Muriel, a bony woman in her mid-fifties with an expensively messy brown bob and perpetual stink-face, made introductions and outlined the scenario. Dimitri would explain a few basic ballroom dance steps, demonstrate them with Natasha, then teach them to Vita. It sounded simple enough, and Natasha wasn't expected to speak, just dance.

It would have made more sense for her to teach the woman's part to Vita, but Dimitri was the famous one here.

They began filming, and Natasha fulfilled her role, standing off to the side looking pretty while Dimitri chatted with Vita about the differences between the Argentine tango and Viennese waltz.

"The tango is a very passionate dance," he drawled, oozing sex appeal for the camera. Even knowing it was an act, Natasha fought the urge to fan herself. Then Dimitri turned to her, fire in his gaze, and held out a hand. "Let's show how it's done, Tasha."

She stepped forward, suppressing a shiver at the way he said her name. Lucky for her, these dances were ingrained in her muscle memory, and she could trust Dimitri to lead. She'd be fine.

Except Dimitri seemed to be doing all in his power to make her *not* fine. Yes, Argentine tango was a sexy dance to begin with, but coño. The press of his fingertips was just a little more forceful than the situation called for, his touches lingering a fraction of a second too long. He dipped her, his breath on her neck and his palm on her bare thigh, sliding, teasing, tantalizing…

Then she was upright, but she couldn't catch her breath. Her heartbeat pounded heavily in her veins, making her whole body throb.

And then Dimitri turned to Vita and pulled her into the dance like it was nothing.

Natasha struggled to get herself under control while she watched. Dimitri was perfectly respectful with Vita. All the sexiness was in his voice. His touch and posture were impersonal, teacher to student. Vita didn't seem to notice the difference. She was giggling and blushing by the time Dimitri released her.

And then they had the waltz. Most wouldn't consider it a sensual dance, but the way Dimitri did it, it was foreplay.

After the segment was over, and Dimitri's revenge was

complete, Natasha rushed to grab a bottle of cold water. Hot and bothered didn't even begin to describe the sensations racing through her body. She gulped down water like she was dying of thirst, and when she lowered the bottle, Donna was there.

Natasha jumped, splashing water on her chest. "Jeez, Donna, you scared me."

Donna's smile was razor sharp as she turned her head to look at Dimitri, who chatted charmingly with Vita.

Nothing like abject fear to douse the flames of desire. Natasha swallowed hard and wiped at the water on her sequin-covered boobs.

Donna turned back with her thin eyebrows raised. She searched Natasha's face for a moment before she spoke quietly, every word deliberate. "Don't ruin your life, Tash. He's not worth it."

"What?" The word came out more like a gasp, and Natasha tried to cover it with a nervous giggle and a shrug. "We were just dancing."

Donna only nodded, then walked over to Muriel. Natasha slipped out to change before Dimitri could get her fired on the spot.

Mission accomplished.

As Dimitri had danced with Natasha, he'd heard every catch of breath and felt every extra gyration beneath his hands. He recognized the glassy look in her dark eyes for what it was: *desire.* Of course, it had the same effect on him, but he could be patient. He was playing the long game.

Then Muriel approached with a smile that was too sweet to be true. He excused himself from his conversation with Vita and turned to speak to his boss.

"That was great, Dimitri," Muriel said. "We'd love to have you come in for more of these kinds of spots, if you're open to it.

It really keeps the viewers invested between seasons, and you know you have a rep as the mean judge. People love seeing the softer side of you."

His shoulders tightened. "No promises. I've got some other projects keeping me pretty busy at the moment."

Muriel was undeterred. "I also noticed we didn't get your contract for next season. Did you send that in?"

Pizdets. This wasn't going how he'd hoped. And Natasha had already disappeared, so there was no reason for him to stick around. "Not yet. Busy, like I said."

"Do you want us to get you a copy? You can sign it before you leave."

Under the collar of his costume shirt, he started to sweat. "I've actually got to get going right now," he said, edging toward the door. He snapped one of the sparkly suspenders. "I'll bring these back later. See you, Muriel."

He charged out the door. In the hallway, he untangled himself from the lav mic and slapped it into the hands of a passing production assistant. Still in costume and makeup, with his hair slicked down with industrial-strength gel, he dashed out to the parking lot and climbed into his Porsche. He looked for Natasha's Prius in the lot, but didn't see it. He didn't know how she'd gotten away so quickly, but he knew where to find her, at least.

When he checked his phone, he had two missed calls from Alex and five from the restaurant. Blyat. Was something on fire?

Everything else would have to wait. He got on the freeway and headed toward Krasavitsa, where he could put off thinking about Alex's deadline and *The Dance Off* contract for one more day.

Chapter Eighteen

As exhausted as Natasha was at the end of the day, her mind was still on that promo shoot. She took a cold shower and forced herself to go to bed early, the better to avoid Dimitri, who once again was out. But she tossed and turned, jumping at every little sound. When she heard him come home, her heart pounded so loud, she was sure he'd be able to hear it through the bedroom door.

Listening to him moving around the house didn't help her situation. Her body pulsed with need, and it took all her self-control to keep her ass in bed.

It would be so easy to stroll out and say, "Hey, wanna fuck?" Imagining the look of delight that would transform his features brought on an attack of the giggles, and she pressed her face into the pillow to stifle them.

Eventually, the house quieted, and she figured he'd gone to bed. She dozed a bit, but not for long. She tried deep breathing. She tried listening to a nighttime meditation recording. Nothing worked.

Disgusted with herself, she threw on her glasses and a thin, oversized sweatshirt and crept from the room.

On the other side of the house, she let herself into the TV

room and fumbled through the pile of remotes before she managed to turn on the TV. She searched the streaming services for a period drama, full of sweeping music, beautiful costumes, and perfectly manicured landscapes. Then she bit back a squeal when she found something much, much better.

The image she knew all too well from the cheesy movie poster filled the screen, and a younger version of Dimitri's dark, brooding eyes stared down at her. The title glowed below him in blue neon.

Aliens Don't Dance.

The movie that had taken Dimitri from ballroom dance competitions to Hollywood and made him a star.

After looking over her shoulder to confirm that the door was shut, she settled in to watch.

She'd seen *Aliens Don't Dance* countless times, of course. When it came out over a decade ago, she and Gina and all their dancer friends from high school had cut their last classes of the day and trooped over to the five-dollar movie theater. In that dark theater, Natasha had fallen in love.

Not with Dimitri, per se. She'd never admit to such a thing.

But Reygar?

That alien had possessed her mind, body, and soul.

The story of an alien crash-landing on Earth, taking the form of a super-hot human man, and stumbling upon 80s music videos for his Earth education had been silly, sure, but Dimitri made the character of Reygar endearing. The earnest way he used dance to connect with other humans—and eventually with one human woman in particular—warmed Natasha's heart, and embodied what dance was all about.

Like all creative arts, dance centered on connection. Dancers used their bodies to make the audience *feel* something. They interpreted music into physical form and thus gave it a shape. *Aliens Don't Dance* was everything Natasha loved about dance— the ability to use movement to express what you couldn't, or didn't dare, say in words. Dimitri didn't even talk until the halfway point of the movie, after he was able to repair his ship's translator device.

And once he could talk? Teenage Natasha had found his lines unbearably romantic.

Now, she wrapped a crocheted blanket around herself and snuggled further into the comfy leather sofa. It was super weird to watch a young Dimitri Kovalenko on TV *in his own house,* while he slept a few rooms away. But it also gave her a thrill. This was Dimitri as she'd first seen him, when she'd been a teenager, and he'd been in his early twenties. His Ukrainian - by - way - of - Brooklyn accent was slightly more pronounced than it was now, his voice not as deep or gravelly. His face was softer, his body leaner, but he still exuded enough charisma to power a small city—or a spaceship. He had incredible chemistry with Greta Marcus, the female lead, a once-popular actress who'd faded into obscurity after the movie became a hit, while Dimitri's career had taken off. Natasha had once looked her up online, and it seemed Greta had decided to settle down and have a family. It made sense. This business could be hard on relationships.

A smile curved Natasha's lips. Greta Marcus was actually an ideal candidate for *The Dance Off.*

Out of nowhere, a hand clasped her shoulder.

Natasha yelped and leapt a foot in the air. Heart pounding, she stared up at Dimitri. He stood behind the sofa, cloaked in shadows, his hair rumpled by sleep. His eyes flicked to the screen, and he made a sound of disgust.

"I can't believe you're watching this trash."

Natasha squished herself into a corner of the sofa as he came around and sat beside her. A rueful grin curved his lips as he watched his younger self on TV.

"I couldn't sleep."

He snorted. "This'll do the job."

"What are you talking about? This is a great movie."

"A great movie?" He gave her a sidelong glance. "You don't need to flatter me to get into my pants."

She rolled her eyes. "I'm not. Lord knows your ego is big enough already. But I'm serious. I love this movie."

"Okay, that's enough lies for one night." He reached for the remote on the coffee table.

"No!" Natasha flung herself across his lap and slapped the remote out of his hand. "I'm watching this."

His eyes sparked with interest. A warning sign, but she wasn't fast enough to scramble away.

And if she were being completely honest, she didn't want to.

"What do you like about this movie?" he asked in a low voice, leaning into her.

"Um…" At his nearness, her mind went blank. His warmth, the faded notes of his cologne, the sleepy rasp of his voice, scrambled her brains. What movie? The video on her laptop? Oh, wait, no. The movie on TV. Obviously. *Get it together, girl!* "Uh, the dancing."

His eyebrows rose, and she knew her answer had pleased him. "*My* dancing?"

"Just…in general. All the dancing. By everyone."

His eyes narrowed, like he could tell she was full of shit. "If you were that desperate for the real thing, you could have just asked. You didn't have to find me on TV." His grin was wicked, his eyes flickering with the reflected light of the television. She pressed herself back against the thick, cushioned arm of the sofa, but he crawled over her, blanketing her with his body. He wore only a pair of boxer briefs that did nothing to hide his arousal.

On screen, young Dimitri danced shirtless with Greta, larger than life with his six-pack abs and ability to dominate a scene. But the real Dimitri was so much more overwhelming, not to mention bigger, stronger, and older. Dark knowledge danced in his eyes as his hands molded over her hips, waist, ribs. In a split second, he'd divested her of her sweatshirt.

His chuckle was husky. "You're getting off on this, aren't you?"

Time to play stupid. "On what?" Carajo, her voice had gone breathy.

"Watching me seduce another woman."

"I like the story," she answered primly, earning a full-out laugh. Because he'd pushed her thighs apart, the vibrations of his belly pressed right against her most sensitive area, and she sucked in a gasp. His arms caged her in, but instead of feeling trapped, she felt safe. When she was in his arms, she almost believed everything would be all right, and she could have all the things she'd ever wanted but thought she'd never have.

Except it was all a lie. She lowered her lashes, unable to gaze upon either Dimitri—the real one, or the one on TV. This was the danger of being with him. He lured her into a false sense of security, but in the harsh light of day, she was still who she'd always been—a poor Puerto Rican girl from the Bronx whose own mother had never found it in her heart to love her.

Dimitri's lips on her arm were a welcome distraction. His mouth on her skin, his closeness, the warmth of his body, his scent seeping into hers, were all better than the road her thoughts wanted to go down. He shifted higher over her, bringing his heavy cock against her pelvis. She bit back a groan.

When he leaned in to kiss her, she'd already made up her mind that she would let him, but he stopped and tilted his head to peer at her in the light from the TV.

"You look tired, Kroshka."

He'd called her this a few times before, usually after sex or when he was drunk. She didn't know what it meant, but the term of endearment melted her heart a little every time he said it. She held those memories to her in the dark, when she was feeling weakest and most alone.

"I am tired," she admitted.

"So why are you sitting her in the middle of the night watching me on TV when you should be in bed?"

This line of questioning skirted too close to things she didn't want to discuss. She twined her arms around his neck and arched against him, hoping to sidetrack him. "It's nothing."

It worked—or so she thought. His lids drooped, and he rocked his hips against her, drawing a gasp from her lips. But then he growled, "Tell me."

She shook her head and rubbed her breasts on his chest, aching for the touch of his hands or his mouth. Why was he doing this? Why wasn't he distracting her the way he was so good at?

The movie's theme song, "Dance with Me," started playing on the TV.

Dimitri groaned and dropped his head onto her shoulder. "I hate this song."

Despite the desire incinerating her from the inside out, Natasha laughed. "I love it."

He scowled at her. "You would."

"Hey, I was the target audience when this came out."

His eyebrows rose. "You saw it when it came out?"

"Of course." Three times, but she'd never tell him that.

"How old were you?"

"Fifteen."

"That makes me feel ancient." His eyes roamed her face, his scrutiny so intense, she had to look away and watch the big dance number on Reygar's ship.

"Tell me why you're not sleeping even though you're tired."

She shut her eyes. Why was he pushing this? They never talked about real-life stuff. "You're so stubborn."

"I prefer tenacious or persistent."

"Try annoying."

He nudged her with his cock, and her eyes flew open. "Tell me."

"I'm stressed, okay?" she snapped. Seeking revenge, she clamped her thighs around his hips and did a body roll that had him moaning.

He nipped at her shoulder. "About the apartment? I told you, you can stay here as long as you need."

"The apartment, money—" She stopped short of saying "my mother." "And I can't stay here that long. I have to be out before *The Dance Off* starts filming. You know that."

He shrugged and pressed his face into the curve of her neck, nibbling along her collarbones. It was suspicious that he didn't answer, but with his mouth on her, she didn't give a shit about anything else.

"It's time for the sex scene," he murmured against her jaw.

"What?" The word was a gasp, a prayer, a plea.

His tone held amusement. "In the movie."

"Oh." Her gaze flew to the screen, where young Dimitri fisted his hand in the back of his T-shirt, pulled it over his head, and flexed his abs. The absurdity of the situation hit her. She'd seen him do that move at least a dozen times. And here he was now, years later, seducing her during the sex scene of his own movie.

She almost laughed. But then he kissed her, and she didn't care how ludicrous this all was.

His kiss was as domineering as the rest of him. His lips commanded obedience, yet his tongue soothed when his demands were met. His hands possessed her, traveling over every inch of her skin, stoking the flames and making her desperate for more.

Yes, touch me, she wanted to say. Touch me everywhere and never stop.

A litany of pleas and demands and requests played through Natasha's head. But she refused to let him know how much she wanted him, how much she craved his touch, his attention, his…

Don't go there.

She shut off her thoughts, sank into the moment with him. Her gasps matched Greta's on screen, and she wanted to know if they'd fucked off-screen, all those years ago, but didn't ask.

"Take these off," he said with a growl, tugging at her sleep shorts. It took some fancy maneuvering, since they were on the sofa, but he stripped her of her shorts—and panties—in record time.

This was going faster and further than she'd expected. "What are you—" His mouth cut off her question; one fingertip stroked between her folds, and she had her answer.

Yes.

When he broke the kiss to let her suck in air, he whispered in her ear. "What kind of host would I be if I didn't put you to sleep?"

Kind of him to offer. Except now she didn't feel sleepy. Sensation zinged through her body. With his thumb on her clit and two fingers plunging inside her, he plied her with skill and determination. The weight of his body pressing her into the sofa anchored her in the moment, and his kisses drove all thought from her mind.

And there was the dirty talk.

"Mmm, that's it, baby. Take it. Feel it. You work so hard. Let me help you relax."

Relax? How the hell was she supposed to relax when his touch was winding her tighter and tighter?

"Were you going to touch yourself during this scene? Isn't the real thing better than a movie? You're living the fantasy. Don't worry about anything but how good this feels."

When she snapped at him to shut up, he only laughed and shoved her tank top up to drag his tongue over her nipples. In retaliation, she stuck her hand down his underwear and grasped his hot length, wanting to feel his hardness as she came. He groaned and doubled his efforts.

It was too much and never enough. They stripped off their remaining clothing and rolled on the sofa, naked, their sweaty skin sticking to the leather and each other, their movements knocking cushions to the floor. He was like a man possessed, obsessed with stoking her desire, but every time she got close to coming, he backed off. When she whined, he laughed and returned to the task.

Through it all, the need to have him fill her taunted her from the edges of passion. Why the hell had she told him no sex? She begged with her whimpers, with her hand on his dick, trying to yank him closer to her slit.

The infernal man only laughed and pushed her hand away. Then he put his mouth between her legs and drove her even higher. With lips and tongue, he broke her apart and put her back together countless times until finally, *finally*, he let her explode.

The orgasm rolled through her, massive and all-consuming, wiping out her thoughts and satisfying everything except her need for *more*.

As she was coming down and thinking about how to shift her hips to get his cock inside her, the end credits rolled, along with the theme song. Dimitri's body rose over hers and his lips touched her ear.

"You see how well I treat my houseguests?"

She froze, trying to force her brain back online. Houseguests? Wait, was he referring to other women?

Her skin broke out in goosebumps. She pulled back and stared at him. He blinked, like he realized what he'd said was shitty, then covered it up with a smile and gestured at the TV.

"I mean, I can't have the ladies staying under my roof turning to cheap copies of the real thing."

Natasha stared at him as aftershocks from her explosive orgasm ravaged her body. Her heart pounded even as her limbs chilled at his words, at his smug, self-satisfied smile. Had she heard him correctly?

Normally, an orgasmic experience like that left her boneless and sleepy. But his words triggered a bolt of adrenaline, a fight-or-flight response, and she scrambled out from underneath him. Snatching up her clothes, she blurted out, "Thanks, I think I can sleep now," and ran naked from the room.

The shocked look on his face followed her all the way back to the guest room she dared not think of as *hers*.

Nothing about him or his home was hers. Playing house like this was a game to him, a pleasant diversion. She was one of many. Hell, maybe he'd even done this exact thing before—helped a desperate woman by letting her stay with him for a while. Maybe he got off on it, on having someone need him.

Her heart would be ruined if she ever allowed herself to expect anything more from him. She couldn't read deeper meaning into his actions, no matter how caring he seemed at times.

It was her mother all over again. Every time Natasha thought she was getting closer, catching a glimpse of real emotional connection, it was snatched away from her, and she was reminded of the truth.

Beyond an easy screw, Dimitri didn't care about her. He never would.

After pulling her pajamas back on, Natasha climbed underneath the covers again.

Tonight had sealed the deal. No sex, and she must avoid him at all costs.

Chapter Nineteen

Twelve years ago

Dimitri never would've guessed how much *Aliens Don't Dance* would change his life.

Practically overnight, he'd gone from a competitive ballroom dance champion who taught classes on the side to, of all things, a movie star.

And to think, he almost hadn't taken the job. But Alex had secured the audition and insisted Dimitri try out, so he had.

When Dimitri had gone in, they'd asked him to dance first. Fine, dancing he could do. The people sitting at the cheap folding table had seemed marginally impressed, and they'd asked him to come in again to read pages with an actress named Greta Marcus. Greta, who'd started out playing so-called "wholesome" characters in teen comedies, was looking to change her image with a more adult role.

The story was silly, to say the least. But if Dimitri were being honest, the role wasn't a huge stretch. The movie revolved around an alien dude named Reygar who crash landed on Earth and adopted an arrogant swagger to cover how lost he felt.

Yeah…Dimitri could identify with that.

When Reygar met the female lead, Hannah—played with spunk and compassion by Greta—he couldn't speak English. But he *could* dance.

Reygar and Hannah connected through dance first, and eventually, his spaceship was able to install a translator in his head. By that point, the two characters were already half in love.

Silly, but also not too far off from Dimitri's own experience.

Like Reygar, dance had helped him connect. At first with peers, later with friends, and now, with audiences.

Surprising everyone, including Dimitri, *Aliens Don't Dance* was a huge fucking hit. He was rich and famous overnight, thanks to a solid contract and his smoldering glare on the posters. Suddenly, everyone wanted a piece of him.

No lie, it felt great.

They were in talks for a sequel, but in the meantime, he'd filmed quick cameo roles on a handful of TV shows. Movie studios were throwing rom-com scripts at him left and right. He'd been invited to dance at major venues and with world-famous troupes.

And parties. Lots and lots of parties.

Nik thought it was the greatest thing ever. He told everyone at school about Dimitri's exploits and claimed all his high school friends were jealous. Somehow, Dimitri's success had boosted his younger brother's cred, along with the teenager's focus. Nik was taking dance more seriously now that he'd seen how it could be a career.

And best of all? Dimitri was dating the Oscar-winning actress Juliette Jacobs. Sure, she was almost twenty years older than he was—and secretly, he suspected it was a little more—and she'd been in the spotlight longer than he'd been alive, but that didn't bother him.

High on his own success, he couldn't get enough of all the good shit happening in his life. So he'd decided to take the next step. That night, he was going to ask Juliette to move in with him.

Unable to control his excitement, Dimitri pulled out his phone and called his cousin, Alex. Alex had graduated from college early and was now in law school. He was Dimitri's most trusted friend and unofficial manager.

Alex picked up after the third ring and, after exchanging greetings, got down to business. "How are the sequel discussions going? Is the screenwriter signed on?"

"Coming right along," Dimitri said. "But listen, I wanted to tell you something else."

"Another audition?"

"No, not about work." Dimitri took a deep breath and forged ahead. "I'm going to ask Juliette if she wants to move in together."

Absolute silence on the other end of the line.

Dimitri frowned. "You still there?"

Alex cleared his throat. "I'm here. Um, what does your mother have to say about it?"

"I haven't told her. You know she gets that look on her face whenever I bring up Juliette."

"Uh-huh. And your dad?"

"He just asks if I'm happy."

"I see. And are you?"

"I am, Sasha. So fucking happy." Dimitri paced back and forth in his tiny studio apartment in Hell's Kitchen. "Juliette's amazing. Funny, smart, and gorgeous. And she knows so much about this business."

"Mm-hmm." Alex was quiet for a stretch.

Dimitri stopped. "That's it?"

Alex sighed. "I'm glad you're happy, Dima."

"Thanks." It came out short. Alex's response, or lack thereof, had annoyed him. "I'll tell you how it goes."

"Please do," Alex said, and there was something ominous in his mild tone.

Dimitri closed the phone with a snap.

Chapter Twenty

Present day

It started with a bra.

Just one bra. Not even a super expensive one, because even after the boob job, Natasha was still only a C-cup.

"You should buy it," Lori said, peeking past the curtain into Natasha's dressing room. "It's pretty."

Natasha turned in the mirror, checking herself out from multiple angles. The lacy black demi-bra *was* pretty, and her cleavage looked phenomenal. Just wearing it made her feel better about life.

And, okay, she couldn't help imagining what Dimitri would think of it, too. Her plan to avoid him had been a success, and she hadn't seen him in three days.

What she hadn't counted on? Her own desire for him.

She missed his dark scowl and flashing grin, the woodsy, citrusy scent of his cologne, even his corny jokes. But especially his touch. Damn it.

She'd almost given in. But he'd reminded her why she needed to keep her distance, and it wasn't just because her job was at stake.

Although that was a big fucking reason to keep her panties on and her ass in her own bed.

Not her own bed. It wasn't hers. Nik's bed. Shit, that sounded worse. *The guest bed.* She was a guest. Sort of.

Not quite guest. Not quite roommate. Definitely not girlfriend.

"I would buy it if I had boobs," Lori added. She glanced down at her chest. "It's okay, though. It's easier to breakdance without them. And besides, our costume designers are experts at padding."

The subject of padding brought Natasha back to another conversation from years ago, before she'd bought her new breasts, but she pushed the memory away.

"That's why I got small implants." Natasha adjusted the straps on the black bra, looking for a reason to leave it behind. Nope, the damn thing fit perfectly.

Lori snickered. "For breakdancing?"

"No, that's all you, girl." Natasha pulled on the tank top provided by the store to see how the bra looked under fabric. Still fantastic. Ugh. "I got them for me, because I wanted them, and because I'm never going back to ballet."

"Why not?"

Natasha shrugged and took the shirt off. "I didn't *just* want to be a ballerina, and while things are getting better, ballet is still overwhelmingly white. Anyway, I'm twenty-seven now. That's like sixty-seven in ballerina years. And if I'd gotten implants any bigger than these"—she poked her chest—"they wouldn't look right on my body."

"Makes sense." Lori ducked out while Natasha changed back into the bra and shirt she'd worn to the store. "Are you going to buy it?"

Natasha stepped out of the fitting room, holding the bra in her hand. It really was pretty… "I'm thinking about it."

"It looked great on you." Lori waved the neon green bralette she held. "You can think about it while I wait to pay."

Shopping with Lori was a dangerous pastime. Lori was an enabler, and it wasn't like Natasha needed encouragement when it came to spending money. And since she'd lost so much in the great apartment disaster, and one of her direct deposit checks had come in, it only made sense to pick up an item or two…

She bought the bra.

And that one purchase proved to be a slippery slope.

By the time they left The Grove, Natasha was weighed down with shopping bags from five different stores, and her checking account was right back where it had started. But seeing the bags filling the trunk of her car gave her a thrill. The royal blue romper looked amazing on her, and the low-heeled ankle booties fit like a dream on her poor, battered dancer's feet.

Natasha said goodbye to Lori in the garage and sat in her car for a few minutes, drinking the coffee she'd picked up while validating her parking. The whole time, she ran through the reasons why her purchases had been a good idea.

She'd been working hard. Didn't she deserve nice things?

She was a celebrity. That meant she had an image to uphold.

After losing so many items in the ceiling leak, she needed to replenish her wardrobe.

They were the reasons she always gave herself when she splurged. She deserved, she needed, she wanted. All to shut up the voice that whispered, *No necesitas eso. No tienes el dinero. People like you don't get to have things like that.*

That stupid voice followed her everywhere and sounded just like her mother.

Then Kevin called. Kevin usually texted, so Natasha picked up immediately, worried that something bad had happened. "Kev? Is everything okay?"

"Hey, Tash," Kevin said. "I'm cool, but I just wanted to give you a heads-up. Donna's been asking around about you and Dimitri. Are you still seeing that guy?"

Crap. "I filmed some promo with him, and you know how it goes. Harmless flirting. Donna's just digging for dirt."

"That's what I figured, but I still wanted to let you know."

"I appreciate it, Kev. Talk to you later."

"Oh, are we still on for dinner with Lori tonight?"

Damn it. Why did she keep making plans to spend money? "Sorry, I have to back out. A work gig came up."

"Aww, we'll miss you. Next time?"

"Sure." They said their goodbyes and Natasha jumped out of the car and went to return everything that wasn't a final sale.

Except for the black demi bra. That, she kept.

She had to stop digging herself deeper into the hole. It was time to make smart financial choices. The sooner she saved enough money, the sooner she could get the hell out of Dimitri's house.

No one could know she was living there. That meant saving her coins and making dinner at home.

She headed to the supermarket and prayed Dimitri would be stuck at the restaurant so she could cook in peace.

Chapter Twenty-One

Five years ago

Natasha had been in Los Angeles for less than a month, and money was slipping through her fingers like water. She was getting auditions, but LA was different than New York, and she was having trouble finding her footing and scoring jobs. She was either too dark, too "ethnic," too young, too old, too tall, too skinny, not skinny enough, or not curvy enough.

Now? Her boobs weren't big enough for a chain restaurant where waitresses in short-shorts and low-cut tops served less-than-mediocre food.

The manager looked at her critically. She should've been used to it by now, but after so much rejection, she felt raw.

"If you pad your bra—a lot—and can make it look convincing—not real, mind you, because most of the girls here aren't real, but just convincing enough, maybe you could work. You're pretty, and you have New York City waitressing experience. Those are points in your favor. You're a bit tall, but you'll be in sneakers, so it should be okay. Just fix those tits."

What the hell was she supposed to say to that? Besides, she *was* wearing a padded bra.

"Come back tomorrow to show us your cleavage." The asshole turned back to his laptop, and she took that to mean she was dismissed.

Natasha nodded, because she couldn't bring herself to thank this cretin for his time, and left the office without a word.

In the hallway, she got turned around trying to find her way out, and almost ended up in the kitchen. She flagged down one of the waitresses, who wore the signature tiny white tank top with the restaurant name stretched across her large breasts.

"Excuse me," Natasha said. "Could you point me to the exit?"

"Sure thing." The other woman looked her up and down. "Were you interviewing?"

"Yeah." Natasha patted her chest, her mouth twisting into a self-deprecating smirk. "The girls don't make the cut. Not unless I pad even more."

The waitress rolled her eyes. "We all pad, mami. You don't get this kind of cleavage otherwise. But with your build...are you a dancer, by any chance?"

Natasha nodded. "Guilty as charged."

After a quick glance around, the woman leaned in. "I'm Delfina. Give me your number, and I'll hook you up with an interview at the other place where I work. The pay is better, and I guarantee your tits are good enough as is."

Natasha froze, and the back of her neck prickled as Delfina's meaning sank in.

Did she mean *stripping*?

It was on the tip of her tongue to say, "No, thank you," but Natasha paused, thinking of her bank account. Of her rent. Of the fact that her mother was right, and Natasha was failing to make it as a dancer in LA.

She thought of what her mother would say if she found out.

She thought of what her mother would say if Natasha came home broke, with her tail between her legs. It would just be the two of them in that apartment, now that Abuela was gone.

¡Te lo dije! Mami's voice rang in Natasha's ears. *I told you so!*

Natasha slid a business card out of her purse and passed it to Delfina, who accepted it and asked, "Can you pole dance?"

"I can learn *any* dance," Natasha told her, confident in that, at least. She'd be damned if she went home now, before Gina graduated from Lennox and moved out here to join her. Los Angeles was home now, and Natasha would do whatever it took to stay.

And at least this way, she'd still be dancing.

Chapter Twenty-Two

Present day

Three days. Dimitri hadn't seen Natasha for *three days*.

Now, stuck in LA traffic while trying to get home early enough to catch her, he had a lot of time to think about her.

Better than thinking about the past or his future. Alex had been texting him daily, asking about his plans. Dimitri hadn't replied, because what could he say? He didn't have any concrete plans, aside from getting through Natasha's defenses and learning more about the woman underneath.

But first, he had to *see* her.

When he'd offered to let her live in his home, he'd thought having her there would bring him a greater sense of security. *Ha.* The woman was as elusive as a nearly forgotten memory. She was gone when he woke up, asleep when he got home. He hadn't even had the opportunity to apologize to her for his thoughtless words, and he didn't want to do it via text or a sticky note on her bathroom mirror.

She was pissed at him, and rightfully so. The other night, when he'd woken up and gone to the kitchen for a glass of water, he'd seen her bedroom door open. Despite his earlier decision to give her space, he hadn't been able to resist looking for her. Coming across her in the TV room, watching his movie, had mixed up all his emotions. And then, after finally getting her right where he'd wanted her, he'd fucked it all up by blurting out a stupid, poorly-phrased joke meant to mask his own unsettlingly vulnerable feelings.

If anything, he felt even more insecure around her than he had in the past. At least then, he'd understood their dynamic. Now? He had no idea what they were doing or how to navigate it.

By the time he pulled into his driveway, he was starving. Despite being at the restaurant all day, he hadn't eaten much. He parked in the garage, his scowl clearing when he spotted Natasha's Prius.

She was home. And it was way too early for her to be asleep.

Dimitri crept into the house quietly, smothering the smile that threatened to take over his features. A melody of aromas greeted him, along with reggaeton playing loudly in the kitchen. As he got closer, he could hear Natasha singing along off-key.

He lost the battle against his grin. She was fucking adorable. And the music provided the perfect opportunity.

Every time they danced together, their connection deepened. It was the only time she didn't hold back. Even during sex, as open and giving as she was, she often avoided his gaze. She expressed her physical pleasure yet hoarded her emotional responses. It was hard not to take it personally. But when they danced? She couldn't hide the way he affected her.

He lurked in the doorway, watching her cook. She stirred something in a large pot, humming along with the lyrics. Her hips swayed and her bare feet shuffled on the floor.

The chorus started. Dimitri advanced. With one hand, he cupped her hip. With the other, he wrapped his fingers around the wooden spoon before she dropped it.

She opened her mouth, maybe to protest, but he nudged her into a close salsa step, New York style, adjusting for the beat of the music. As they shifted back and forth on the tiny rug in front of the stove, he caught her gaze and let her see how much he wanted her.

Her expression softened. Her dark, sexy eyes went liquid behind her glasses, and her full, wide lips parted.

Keeping his eyes on hers, Dimitri directed the spoon—still clasped in her hand—to his mouth and licked it.

She blinked, desire sparking in her eyes. "Sancocho," she whispered, and fuck if that wasn't the sexiest thing he'd ever heard.

It tasted delicious, the flavors of beef and onion, garlic and carrot, mixing with many others into something comforting that made him think of home. His stomach reminded him of its hunger, but he had a stronger need at this point. He tossed the spoon into the sink and swept her up in the dance.

Magic. As always, it was magic. She anticipated his every move as if they had a telepathic connection. No hesitation, no lag time. No thinking. Just feeling, just bodies, just movement. She was living fire in his arms. The music soared around them, flowed through them. The bubbling pot on the stove surrounded them in aromas that made his mouth water, but underlying the scent of sancocho was Natasha's own fig and ginger combo. Dimitri breathed in the scent of her hair, which was pulled up in a curly bun, as she did a tight spin under his arm.

When the song ended, he backed her up against the edge of the counter, their faces close.

She ducked her head, but he caught the smile curving her lips. "Um, I have to stir," she said, not pulling away.

Swallowing hard, he released her, then spotted the open Cabernet Sauvignon on the counter with one glass next to it.

"I hope you don't mind," she said, nodding at the bottle.

"I don't. But you didn't pour me a glass." He took one down from the cabinet.

"I didn't think you'd be home." She turned back to the stove, missing his triumphant grin. She thought of his house as home? Good.

He poured himself a glass of wine and topped off hers. "I've had some late nights at the restaurant."

"Putting out fires?"

He sighed. "Literal and figurative."

She took the glass he passed her and clinked it against his. "Salud. And I'm sorry to hear that."

"Today wasn't bad. I met with my lawyer most of the day. Not as much drama with him, if you can believe it." He sipped, savoring the rich, fruity flavor, knowing that if he kissed her right now, he'd taste it on her tongue, too. "Tell me about your day."

She rolled her eyes and knocked back a long swallow of wine. "Well, Kevin called to warn me about Donna. Apparently, she's been asking about you and me, thanks to your little show the other day."

Uh-oh, work stuff. Dimitri could already feel Natasha closing off. "Is that why you're making comfort food?"

Her face broke into a surprised smile. "How did you know?"

He shrugged. "I also turn to food from home when I'm stressed. There are items on the restaurant's menu specifically for when I need Ukrainian comfort food. Varenyky, of course, which are like pierogies. Holubtsi, the cabbage rolls. And nalysnyky, the crepes, which can be sweet or savory. One bite of any of those, and I'm instantly transported back to my grandmother's kitchen."

She smiled as she sliced green plantains. "I get that. My great-grandmother taught me to cook Puerto Rican food. My mom was too busy."

He settled against the counter and drank his wine. "And your grandmother?"

She shrugged. "Never met her."

There was more to that story. He waited to see if she'd elaborate. After checking the rice, she did.

"My mother got pregnant when she was sixteen. Swore she was going to marry the guy—who was older and a loser, by all accounts—so her mother sent her from Puerto Rico to New York. I was born in the Bronx, and I grew up with my great-grandparents and my mother, all in a two-bedroom apartment."

"Where did you sleep?"

"A section of the living room."

"When my family moved to Brooklyn from Odessa, we first lived with my dad's brother. I shared a room with Nik, who was still a baby, and two of my cousins."

She shrugged. "Whatever it takes, right? But look where you are now."

"You, too."

She snorted. "We both know I'm here out of desperation. Without Gina, I'm a fucking mess."

She was retreating again. Her shoulders hunched, and her eyebrows drew together in a scowl. He wanted to help her, to take away the stress in her posture and her voice. He was good with money. He could help her, teach her.

But first, he wanted her to relax.

The second she put the lid on the pot, he eased her into a slow and sensual bachata. They danced between sips of wine and taking turns at the stove. When the food was ready, they opened a second bottle of red and made their plates.

"What are we eating?" he asked, standing behind her at the counter.

"This is sancocho—it's like stew." She ladled the hearty, fragrant mixture of beef, corn, potatoes, carrots, and more into a bowl, then added a side of white rice, garnished with chopped cilantro. "And these are plátanos maduros—sweet fried plantains." She lifted one on a fork to give him a bite. "Like you said, it's comfort food."

He pressed a kiss to her hair. "Well, I feel comforted."

She leaned against him. "Damn it, D."

"What?" He tipped her chin up, forcing her to look at him.

Her voice trembled, and her dark eyes had gone liquid. "Why can't I ever say no to you?"

It was what he'd been waiting for. Natasha, soft and pliant in his arms. Her thoughts only on him, not on her money troubles, or her past, or her job. She'd opened up to him tonight, told him more about her life than she ever had before. It left him with more questions and an even deeper desire to know her. But now wasn't the time to follow those threads.

Now was the time for seduction.

Her face was already lifted toward his. Her lips parted, and her tongue darted out to swipe against that full lower lip.

With a groan, Dimitri closed the distance and kissed her.

Chapter Twenty-Three

S *weet Jesus*. Dimitri's knees locked to absorb the impact. Would he ever be prepared for Natasha's kiss?

She tasted like wine and spices, and her mouth was hot and ravenous under his. He cupped her face to hold her to him, then backed up until the edge of the granite counter hit his ass. Her slim fingers gripped the waistband of his pants, sliding between the fabric and his skin. He groaned, hardening as the backs of her nails teased his nerve endings.

Touch her. He had to touch her. *Needed* to. He skimmed his hands down her body, and on the way back up, he pulled off her yellow tank top. Underneath, she wore a lacy black bra that framed her tits to perfection.

He broke the kiss to run his fingertips along the frilly edges of the cups where they met her skin. "Is this new?"

"Uh-huh." Eyes heavy-lidded and full of heat, she grabbed the back of his neck to draw him down for another kiss.

Natasha kissed like she was drowning and he was the only one who could save her. She kissed with fire and teeth, and a hint of desperation. Her kiss hooked him every time. For a man who needed to be needed, it made him want to give her everything he had and more.

Sex was the only way she'd take it. Even now, she was only here in his kitchen because she had nowhere else to go.

He'd change that, though. He'd show her how good it could be between them if she stayed.

"We shouldn't," she whispered against his mouth.

He nipped at her chin, trailed his lips down the long, strong column of her neck, and sucked at the delicate skin. "Yes, we should."

She slipped out of his arms. He reached for her, but she wasn't going away. Instead, she slid down his body to kneel at his feet. Dimitri tipped his head back and groaned. His pants and boxers were down around his thighs in a matter of seconds. When it came to blow jobs, Natasha didn't waste time, and he loved her for it.

Shit. Love?

Too much. She was too goddamned much.

"There's a new rule at the show." Her breath puffed against his thigh, making his skin tingle, as she stroked his dick along her soft cheek.

"What show?" She was killing him. His brain was fried. What were they talking about?

"*The Dance Off.*" She licked along his length, curling her tongue around the head, and he gulped for air. Before he could ask her to elaborate, she sucked him into her mouth, and he didn't care about talking anymore.

Her cheeks hollowed out as she moved her mouth up and down his cock, using her hand to pump the base. He unclipped her hair and sank his hands into the alluring mass of spirals. Sensation zinged through him, his skin prickling, and he flexed his legs to keep his knees from buckling. This was going too fast, like always. If they didn't slow down, he was going to prop her up on the kitchen counter and take her here and now.

"Tasha," he panted out. "Kroshka."

"Mmm?" She looked up at him, mouth full, his dick making one of her cheeks poke out. So fucking sexy.

He gave a shaky laugh and stroked her face. "Bedroom."

Her gaze dropped to the floor, and she slid him out of her mouth. "We shouldn't."

There were those words again. He hauled her up from the floor and pulled her in for a searing kiss.

"We should," he whispered hotly against her mouth, and kissed her again, losing himself in the soft fullness of her lips.

When he pulled back and looked her in the eye, she nodded.

In that moment, they were closer than they'd ever been before. Vulnerability shone in her gaze, or maybe he was only seeing his own reflected there. Either way, he took a chance. "Because you can't say no to me?"

Another nod, and she closed her eyes.

"Why, Tasha?"

Her reply was a mumbled, "I don't know."

He was too fired up to question her further. With a muttered curse, he kicked off his shoes and pants, leaving them on the kitchen floor. He grabbed the wine bottle and threw an arm around Natasha's waist, hustling her into the bedroom.

They made quick work of their remaining clothing, then tumbled naked into his bed, kissing and drinking directly from the wine bottle until it was empty.

"This is a bad idea," Natasha said as he leaned away to set the bottle on the nightstand.

"Stop saying that." He scowled at her and crawled between her legs, pressing her into the pillows. "Sex is always a great idea."

She propped herself up on her elbows to look at him. "They're cracking down on backstage hookups."

"We're not backstage right now."

It was solid logic, but from her glare, it was clear she disagreed. He tried again. "Hasn't that always been an unspoken rule?"

"Yes, but now it's been spoken out loud *by my producer*. If she finds out I'm staying here..." Her finely arched brows drew together, and he wanted to smooth them. He tried logic again.

"That never stopped you before."

Her eyes went wide, and her mouth flattened into a thin line. With *me*, he meant, but she shot her retort at him before he could explain.

"It never stopped you, either!"

He narrowed his eyes. Yeah, it was true for him, too, but he had a bone to pick with her about the previous season. Maybe it was all the wine coursing through him, but now seemed like a *great* time to bring it up.

Running his hand along one of her strong thighs, he settled his thumb into the sensitive spot below her hip bone, where leg met torso. "You fucked Jackson García."

She tossed her hair, but he didn't miss the sharp intake of breath when his thumb rubbed gently, circling closer to her pussy. "You fucked Lauren D'Angelo," she shot back.

He lowered his head and teased the curve of her inner thigh with the tip of his tongue. "Not exactly."

"No?"

"She thought sucking my dick would help her scores."

Natasha's hips rocked as his mouth drew closer to her core. "Did it?"

He raised his head. "Did she win?"

"No." She scowled and shoved his head back down into her lap.

Smothering a grin, he parted her folds with his thumbs and gazed openly at her. The attention made her squirm with anticipation, as it always did.

"Besides," he said, leaning in. "It was only half a blow job. And only once. She bit me." He nipped her inner thigh with his teeth.

Natasha's head fell back, and she let out an unsteady chuckle. "You like a little biting sometimes."

"Only when you do it," he admitted softly.

And then he stroked her clit with his tongue, and she didn't ask any more questions.

Dimitri wasn't done, though. He had more he wanted to say, but he needed her pliant and desperate. He licked her seam, driving his tongue inside her, savoring her taste and her high-pitched little moans. He circled her clit with his tongue and teased her entrance with his fingers, but he didn't give her the penetration he knew she wanted, and held back on letting her shatter.

When she was gasping and sobbing, her nails scrabbling at his shoulders, he sheathed his dick in a condom and moved up her body, notching himself against her.

She wriggled beneath him, arching and trying to take him in, but he held her hips down. He had questions he wanted answered.

"Dima, *please*," she whispered.

He kissed her hard, nearly losing the battle of wills when she sucked on his tongue. He pulled back and demanded, "Why Jackson?"

She shook her head, her curls spilling out across the pillow, the sweet scent of figs threatening to overwhelm his resolve. "Why do you care?"

He slipped an arm beneath her and cupped the back of her neck. "Why, Tasha?"

When she didn't answer, he flexed his hips, teasing her. She moaned and clutched his ass, trying to pull him into her.

"Tell me." With her breasts pressed to his chest and her hot little body under his, his control was hanging by a thread. He had no right to ask. He'd had his fair share of women who weren't her, and he knew she'd fucked other men. But Jackson had been the most recent that he knew of, and the most often on his radar. "I was coming to the club that night to see you. When I got there, you were leaving with him. Why?"

With a groan, she finally cried out, "Because he wasn't *you*."

He blinked.

"Is that what you want to hear?" She glared fiercely. "He wasn't you. He was uncomplicated and easy and…goddammit, he never made me feel like this. *Never.*"

Dimitri's heart leaped. "Like what? Feel like what?"

"Like I'm going to fucking explode if you don't fuck me! Do it, Dimitri. For the love of God, just put your fucking cock inside me!"

With a powerful surge of his hips, he slammed into her.

She squeezed her eyes shut. "God, yes!"

They fucked until she was screaming his name, and he was grinding his teeth to keep from coming. Then he pulled out and flopped over.

"Your turn," he said, panting. "Climb on."

"We shouldn't be doing this," she said, even as she crawled over him. "I'm gonna lose my job."

He rolled his eyes. Again with this. He wasn't going to be able to convince her they were meant for each other if she was worrying about the stupid *Dance Off.*

"Stop thinking." He lifted her by the hips and drove into her. She moaned and arched to take him deeper. "Ride me."

She dug her nails into his chest, hard enough to leave marks, and took up the pounding rhythm.

Her long, lean body rose above him, her skin dewy with sweat, her cheeks flushed. Her hair was loose, the dark curls falling over her bouncing breasts and down her back. The scent of ginger surrounded him, and the way she bit her lower lip as she rode his cock captivated his attention.

She took his breath away. Having her here, in his home, in his bed…it was all he wanted. When she left…

If she left. He had to show her she had a place here. Interrogating her about her past lovers and making vague statements that could be about other women weren't going to help his case.

If he wanted her to stay, he had to put his heart on the line. For her, he could do it.

But not tonight. Tonight, he had her right where he wanted her, and he'd already pushed her enough.

He slid his hands up her torso and caressed her breasts, teasing the nipples with his thumbs, savoring her sigh of pleasure. He dropped one hand to where their bodies joined and repeated the motion on her clit.

"Yes," she said on a gasp. "Yes, touch me. Fuck, I'm *so close*…"

When her pussy squeezed him, when her body shuddered, when her cries rang through the room, he let go of his control.

He squeezed his eyes shut as he came, but she was with him. Blanketing his body with hers, clutching his shoulders in her strong hands, lips teasing his earlobe as she whispered his name.

"Dima…"

He wrapped his arms around her. It was the perfect moment. If he had the guts, he'd ask her to stay, to live with him, to *be* with him, forever.

Silence settled around them.

He sighed, limbs leaden with exhaustion, alcohol, and disappointment. He didn't have the strength to ask.

As much as he wanted Natasha, as much as he was sure his feelings for her were the real deal, hers were less clear. And until she stopped running away from him, he couldn't put his heart out there like that. Not again.

She stirred. "We should clean up and eat."

"Sure."

He opened his arms and let her go.

Chapter Twenty-Four

Twelve years ago

After dinner at a fancy French restaurant Dimitri never even would've considered visiting just a year before, he went back to Juliette's massive loft in SoHo. Juliette pulled him straight to her enormous bed, just as she always did, and demanded he fuck her. When they were done and lying side by side, Dimitri stared up at the exposed ductwork on the ceiling. Surrounded by the scent of expensive perfume he couldn't name, he mustered the nerve to ask her the question that had been on his tongue all night.

Rolling over, he pillowed his head on his arm and looked into Juliette's flushed, relaxed face. Her coppery red hair, which cost a small fortune to maintain, spread out in perfect waves. She had tiny lines fanning out from the corners of her eyes. She hated them and spent what seemed like hours coating her face in creams and lotions every night, but Dimitri liked them. They crinkled prettily when she grinned.

"Juliette."

She let out a long sigh and turned her head to face him. A soft smile played on her lips. "Yes, darling?"

Now or never.

"Let's move in together."

Her eyes widened, and her eyebrows shot up as much as they were able to after her recent Botox injection. Her jaw went slack. She stared at him as he waited, letting the idea sink in.

Then she blinked. "Wait, you're serious?" And she burst into laughter.

The harshness of the sound grated along Dimitri's skin. A pit opened in his stomach and spread to his chest, a black hole, like he was caving inward, falling into himself.

"Yes, I'm serious."

She laughed harder.

Fuck. He rolled over onto his back and stared at the ceiling again.

Slowly, her laughter quieted. She didn't touch him. "And where do you expect we'd live? Are you going to move in here?"

He shrugged. "If you like. Or we can find a place together." His tiny studio walkup wasn't anywhere big enough for two people, especially not with as much stuff as Juliette had.

But she shook her head. "Save your money, Dimitri. You think what you have coming in now will last forever, but it won't."

Nothing lasts forever. He'd heard his parents say it every time something came to an end, or one of them experienced a disappointment. *Nichto ne vechno.* Tonight, the words offered little comfort.

"Dimitri, what do you think is going on here?"

He didn't answer. Clearly, he'd thought something different than she had.

"This is fun, of course, but let's face it. I'm old enough to be your mother. This is just a mutually beneficial situation to boost both of our careers and have a little fun."

He froze. Well, his body did, but his heart pounded in his chest like it was trying to run away. The organ had the right idea.

"Both?" he asked, as if that was the most important part of what she'd just said.

"Sure." She fluffed her pillows and propped herself up. "The status of my career lends yours credibility. Your youth makes me seem younger, by extension, and puts me back in the tabloids for something juicy. It's a win-win situation all around."

His body was ice-cold, but his heart still pounded like a wild animal, raging to escape. He'd caged it in a scenario that it found disgusting, betraying it just as much as Juliette had.

"Sweetheart, you didn't think any of this was real, did you?"

Her tone had turned patronizing, and he couldn't take it anymore. He had two options. Give in to his feelings and storm out like a petulant child. Or play it off.

So he turned to her and smiled. "Not at all," he said. "Was just thinking of convenience."

Satisfied, she settled back on the pillows and shut her eyes. "Good. I like you—you're great in bed, and you're so busy with work, you don't bother me with other nonsense. But this is my space. I've worked too hard and too long to share it with anyone. You're welcome to be here when I want you here, but you're not moving in."

"Understood." He rolled out of the bed. "I've got to get going."

"I'm flying to Los Angeles for a few days. I'll see you when I get back."

"Okay." She wouldn't. His heart wouldn't allow it. Even now, it was begging him to get the hell out.

But she had taught him a valuable lesson.

Fame was a wild, irrational beast. It used people, chewing them up and spitting them out. It drew people to you, but they weren't really interested in you, only what you could do for them. And nothing lasted forever. Someday, you'd be without it. And when you lost it all, you'd be alone.

Dimitri vowed never to let himself get blindsided like this again. He knew the truth now. He'd be prepared.

Juliette had been right about one other thing—her work ethic. That was something he could learn from her. He'd work, he'd save, and he'd protect himself and his family from future losses.

From here on out, he was building toward his family's comfort and security. That was all. They'd given up everything to get him here. It was the least he could do.

And in the meantime?

He'd never risk his heart like this again.

Chapter Twenty-Five

Present day

In the grand scheme of things, waking up hungover in Dimitri's bed wasn't the biggest tragedy. After all, Natasha had done it plenty of times before. And despite the pressure in her temples and general queasiness, she couldn't bring herself to regret it. Sex with Dimitri was always amazing. His rough and demanding demeanor masked attentiveness and a single-minded devotion to her pleasure. He always made sure she came first, and usually multiple times. So, no, she never regretted having sex with him.

Still, they probably shouldn't have done it a second time. But she'd gotten cold in the middle of the night and snuggled closer to him. And then he'd rolled over to pull her into his arms. Dimitri cuddled with his entire body, as if he could consume her through skin contact alone.

For someone who loved to be touched, it was the perfect drug.

Natasha had clung to him the way she never let herself do during their waking hours. She soaked in the feel of his skin, the weight of his body, the deep, even rasp of his breath. The knowledge that, for this moment, at least, she wasn't alone.

She was all set to go back to sleep when his lips found her nipple. And then somehow her pussy found his dick, and they were at it again.

When her alarm went off in the pocket of her shorts on the floor, she leaped from the bed and muttered a prayer of thanks that she hadn't left the phone in the kitchen. Dimitri murmured and tried to pull her back into bed, but she found the strength to evade him.

That was about as far as her good sense went, because she was halfway through her shower before she realized she was in Dimitri's bathroom, using Dimitri's soap.

Fucking great. She was going to smell like him all day. She might as well dig out one of his many half-full bottles of the no-longer-manufactured Archangel by Rogelio cologne and roll around in it. But then he'd spend the rest of the day obsessively searching for more online, and she didn't want to do that to him.

It was a nice smell, though. Both on his skin and when it rubbed off on hers.

When she dashed through his bedroom in a towel, he rolled over in the bed. "Where are you going?" he mumbled sleepily.

"*Work.*" The hangover made it impossible to keep the bite out of her tone. She clutched the towel to her breasts in a tight grip. "I have *work*, Dimitri. Every day."

He blinked at her, his expression soft and sleepy. "I don't understand why you work so hard. Just come back to bed."

Her body went numb, stunned by his carelessness. It took a few tries to get the words out. "Are you serious?"

He shrugged his broad shoulders. "You've got a good gig on the show—"

"Dimitri, you of all people should understand. Our lives didn't start off that differently. Or did you forget what it was like in the beginning?"

He sat up and opened his mouth, but she held up a hand. "Never mind. I'm running late. See you later."

She ran down the hall to her own room.

No, *not* her room. The guest room.

She didn't see him again as she left the house, speeding through traffic on the 10 to get to her first job, an early morning beginner's pole dancing class.

From there, she had a packed day of teaching. By the time she got to her five-thirty "Soulsa" class—a workout that combined salsa moves and cardio—her head pounded, her feet dragged, and she was thoroughly sick of LA traffic.

California had a lot of advantages over New York City. Driving wasn't one of them. Days like this, Natasha actually missed the subway.

But the ladies who showed up to this class looked to her to perk them up after a full day of working in various offices around the city, and they paid well to work with a celebrity instructor at a fancy gym. Better than some of her other gigs, anyway.

Natasha chowed down on yet another protein bar—her fourth that day—as the women trickled in from the locker room. She waved and smiled, even though all she wanted to do was curl up on the floor and sleep.

She checked her phone one last time before connecting it to the sound system.

Nothing from Dimitri. Not a single text or call the entire day.

It shouldn't have bothered her, or surprised her, but each time she checked, her stomach sank a little further. It was currently somewhere near her ankles.

Sure, she would be back at his house tonight, and he wasn't great about texting, but she'd thought after last night…

Never mind. Any disappointment she felt was her own fault for getting her hopes up in the first place. And for breaking her "no sex" rule.

But seriously, would it have fucking killed him to send a text?

He'd fucked her brains out twice last night, and he knew she had a busy day. Was a simple "Hey, how's work going?" really that difficult?

Apparently so.

She swapped out her sneakers for dance shoes, then strode to the center of the room. Facing the mirror, she was met with her own grimace. Crap, she really had to get it together. She couldn't let the women in the class know she was exhausted and hungover. Fixing a brilliant smile on her face, she clapped her hands, signaling that the class was about to begin.

"Buenas tardes, ladies," she said, as she always did. "I hope you all had a good day."

She was met with the usual grumbles.

"I know, I know. Don't worry, we're going to turn this day around, starting right now. Ready for the warm-up?"

A chorus of affirmatives. She sidled over to her phone, turned on the playlist she'd queued up, and went back to the center of the room. A bumping rhythm poured out of the speakers. The mood instantly lifted, and smiles beamed at her in the mirror's reflection.

She smiled back. "Ready? Let's begin."

She stepped to the right—and kept going as her ankle rolled under her weight.

She started to fall.

Her body was finely attuned to its own movements, honed through years of practice and hard work. It knew when shit was going wrong. And now it was screaming at her.

Adrenaline flooded her system, and she stumbled to right herself. If she'd been firing on all cylinders, she would've been fine.

But she wasn't. She was barely operating on half power.

Gasps echoed through the room as she pitched forward and caught herself against the mirror, her palms making a smacking sound as she hit.

Natasha blinked at her own reflection. What the hell had just happened?

Someone turned off the music. Two ladies ran forward to support her arms.

"Are you okay?" one of them asked.

"That looked really bad," said the other.

"I'm fine." Natasha pushed off the mirror, her own voice sounding soft and far away, drowned out by the pounding of her heart in her ears. She put her right foot down to test her weight on it. "Just a stumble. It's—ay cabrón!"

Pain spiraled up her leg, blocking out her vision. She gritted her teeth and shifted all her weight to her left leg.

Motherfucker.

Her *ankle*. Her fucking *ankle*.

She couldn't stand on it. If she couldn't stand, she couldn't teach the class, if she couldn't teach the class, she wouldn't get paid…

Her thoughts swirled, jumping from *couldn't* to *couldn't*, all to avoid the one most important fact…

She. Couldn't. Dance.

Concerned murmurs filled the room. The women sat her down. An ice pack was draped over her ankle, and she grimaced at the pain. Someone packed her things for her. Someone else called an ambulance.

"It's fine," she tried to say, waving them all away. "I'm fine."

One of the women got in her face. "You are *not* fine. I'm a doctor, and you need to get this checked out."

"I'll drive—"

"You will *not* drive. Is there anyone we can call for you? Someone to meet you at the hospital?"

Too dazed to argue, Natasha unlocked her phone and handed it over. "Dimitri Kovalenko." Before she could think too much about why she'd named Dimitri and not Kevin or Lori, she tilted her head back and closed her eyes. God, she missed Gina. "No media. Please."

Someone patted her shoulder. "Cone of silence."

Chapter Twenty-Six

Five minutes into the ambulance ride, Natasha's ankle started to throb incessantly. By the time she was wheeled into the emergency room and transferred to a hospital bed surrounded by curtains, it had swelled to three times its normal size, and pain radiated up her leg.

After a nurse packed it in ice and assured her a doctor would be by "momentarily," Natasha settled in for a long wait. Her foot hurt like hell, but as it wasn't in danger of falling off, she would be low on the ER's priority list.

At least she had a bed. Exhaustion set in, overwhelming the anxiety. There was so much to worry about, but right then, sleep won, and she drifted off.

"Natasha!"

She startled awake at the sound of her name. Lori's worried face hovered inches above her own.

"Oh my god, are you okay?" Lori's brows drew together, and she gripped Natasha's hand.

"I don't know," Natasha mumbled, shaking Lori off so she could sit up. How long had she been asleep? "I haven't seen the doctor yet."

Kevin stood on the other side of the bed. "How do you feel?"

Terrified probably wasn't the answer he was looking for. "Um…" She glanced down at the ice pack on her ankle. "I don't know. It hurts. Wait, what are you guys doing here?"

Lori rested her hip against the side of the bed. "Gina called us."

Natasha blinked. Had she told Gina? Everything after the fall was a blur. "How does Gina know?"

"Dimitri called her." Kevin's voice was dark, and he stood with his arms crossed. "Why'd you call Dimitri and not us?"

Natasha didn't feel well enough to lie to her friends right now, but the truth would require even more explanation of her failure, and she didn't want to get into it. "Uh… I thought he'd be free."

Kevin's face said he wasn't buying it. "You've been acting strange lately. Putting us off, canceling plans. What's going on?"

Lori picked nervously at the pilling on the hospital sheet. "We just care, Tash. That's all."

Natasha swallowed. "I know, I—"

She broke off when, in a sudden burst of motion, Kevin grabbed the bedrail and leaned in. His voice dropped, and his green eyes were hard. "Did he do this to you? Did Dimitri hurt you?"

What the fuck? Natasha leaned away from his intensity. "*No*, Kev. I was teaching and I stepped wrong. That's it. Happens to the best of us."

He eased back, but his scowl remained.

"You're going to be okay," Lori said, patting Natasha's hand. "You're right. This stuff happens. And you still have a few weeks to recover before the next season starts."

Natasha bit her lip. She *didn't* have time to recover. She had classes to teach the very next day. Lori's words brought up the fears she'd shoved back after the accident, and her mind spiraled into panic.

If she didn't work, she wouldn't get paid. If she didn't get paid, she couldn't move out of Dimitri's house. If she didn't move out, she'd lose her job on *The Dance Off*. If she lost her job, she'd have to move back to the Bronx to live with her *mother…*

And underneath all of it?

If she couldn't dance, her career was over.

This would be it for her. Natasha hadn't yet established herself enough to book big jobs as a choreographer. She might be able to supplement with acting and modeling, but those gigs were few and far between, and again, she wasn't famous enough yet to command the big bucks.

Her ankle throbbed under the ice, mocking her, making her stare down the possibility of a future in which *she was not a dancer.*

If only she'd been paying more attention…

If she hadn't been so tired…

If she hadn't been hungover…

If she hadn't stayed up all night with Dimitri or opened that second bottle of wine…

If she'd stuck to her rule…

If she hadn't depleted her savings…

If she'd made better choices with money…

If, if, if. No amount of *ifs* would change the fact that right here, right now, her ankle was fucked up. And she still didn't know how bad it was. A fine trembling rocked her chest, tightened her throat, as worry and fear fought to overtake her.

Her friends were quiet. Before she could figure out what to say to them, the curtain behind Kevin was yanked back, and Dimitri's larger frame crowded into the space around the narrow hospital bed.

"Tasha!" Dimitri nearly knocked Kevin over in his rush to lean over the rail and press a hand to Natasha's cheek. His skin was warm, his dark hair in disarray. She closed her eyes for just a second, turning her face into his palm as if she could absorb some of his strength.

"I'm sorry I wasn't here sooner." He stroked her cheek. "Traffic is a nightmare."

In his other hand, he held a familiar bronze case.

Her breath caught. "Is that…?"

He handed it over to her. "Your glasses. And the stuff for your contacts. I didn't know how long you'd be here, so I stopped at home to pick them up. I thought you might need them."

"I…thank you." The sweetness of the gesture tore into her, giving the fear a sharper edge. She really was going to cry, right here in front of all of them. It was too much. Dimitri's creased brow, Kevin's glare, Lori gnawing at her fingernails… They *cared* about her. They were here because they cared. But all of it was too much.

Piece by piece, she was falling apart inside. And despite how much they cared about her, she'd be damned if she let them see her destruction.

Dimitri came to her rescue, his gaze darting to her ankle. "What happened, Kroshka? The woman who called me, she didn't say much." He skimmed his hand down her leg, stopping short of the ice pack.

Natasha cleared her throat. "Dimitri, did you call Gina?"

He nodded, his eyes still on her leg. His hand shook, like he wanted to examine her ankle further, but didn't dare. "I was in Malibu, otherwise I'd have been here sooner. I didn't want you to be alone."

She gritted her teeth against the tremble, hyper-aware of Lori and Kevin's interested stares.

"What did the doctor say?" Dimitri asked.

"I don't know. I haven't seen one yet."

"What?" Dimitri practically roared the word, and she winced. They were in a *hospital*, for god's sake.

"Keep it down," she whispered, catching Kevin's darkening glare. She didn't know what his problem was, but there was only so much she could worry about right now.

"This is unacceptable. I'm getting the doctor." Dimitri stormed away, and Natasha was left with her friends and her glasses case.

Exhaustion returned. Her eyes itched as the unshed tears receded. When she opened the case, she found her contact lens container inside.

Kevin sucked his teeth. "Home?"

This was the last thing she wanted to talk about with them. She played dumb, even though it was useless, as she swapped out her contacts for the glasses. "What?"

"Dimitri said, 'Home.' He ran home—his home, I'm guessing —to get *your* glasses."

Lori straightened. "Kevin, where Natasha sleeps at night is *her* business—"

"I know that. I'm not slut-shaming her."

"Then don't ask a lady to kiss and tell!"

"He said *home* like it was *their* home, not like it was *his*, so I just—"

"Maybe she doesn't want to tell us—"

"¡Basta! *Please*, that's enough." Natasha pressed her fingers to her temples. On top of the throbbing in her leg, her hangover headache had worsened, taking up residence behind her eyes.

Bless Dimitri for bringing her glasses.

Lori perched on the edge of the bed and looked contrite. "Sorry. We're just worried about you. And it seems like there's something you're not telling us."

Natasha was in too much pain to deny it anymore. "You're right." They both stayed quiet, waiting for her to continue, so she sighed and explained. "Last week, my apartment had an emergency. I had to move out immediately. So, I'm staying with Dimitri for the time being while the building makes repairs."

There, that sounded simple enough.

But from the stormy expression on Kevin's face, it wasn't. "Natasha, if he did this to you—"

She smacked her hands on her lap. "Kevin, oh my god! I already told you, Dimitri did *not*—"

The curtain was ripped back again. Everyone shut up as

Dimitri crowded in, along with a gray-haired man in a white doctor's coat and a pin that read "Dr. Ross."

The doctor's blue eyes twinkled behind his glasses as he greeted her. "So, you're on *The Dance Off*."

Natasha flinched. "Please don't tell anyone."

"Oh, I won't." Dr. Ross jerked a thumb over his shoulder at Dimitri. "This guy here promised to video chat my wife and kids. They're big fans."

Dimitri practically vibrated with nerves. "I'll come to your house and teach them to dance myself, if you want. Just fix my woman." He made wild gestures at Natasha's ice-packed foot.

His woman. That was new. Natasha didn't have time to think about it, though. Now that the doctor was here, she was subjected to a barrage of tests, expedited once the doctor and nurses found out she was a professional dancer and a minor celebrity.

Having four cast members of *The Dance Off* was a red-letter day for the ER. While Natasha was getting X-rays done, a nurse took Kevin and Lori to the pediatric floor to say hi to some of the kids. Dimitri stayed by Natasha's side and growled at anyone who tried to separate them.

Finally, Natasha was back in her bed, surrounded by Dimitri, Kevin, Lori, and Dr. Ross.

"The good news is nothing is broken," Dr. Ross began, consulting a tablet. "The bad news is, you have a pretty severe sprain. It doesn't look like you'll need surgery on the ligaments, but you'll have to stay off it."

Natasha blinked. She couldn't be hearing him correctly. "But I have to work."

"Does work involve resting with your ankle iced and propped up?"

The sarcasm was almost lost on her. "I'm a dancer—"

"And if you want to remain a dancer, you'll stay off the ankle." Dr. Ross gave her a sympathetic smile, but his tone was firm. "If you don't want the problem to worsen, give it a rest. If you push it and don't give it time to heal, you'll run into more problems later on. You know how it goes."

She did. She'd been injured before. But never when her livelihood was in such jeopardy.

"Tell me everything I need to do to take care of her," Dimitri demanded.

Dr. Ross gave him a measured look. "Are you her husband?"

"What? No. We live together."

Dr. Ross raised his hands. "Ah, my mistake. No judgment implied."

"It's temporary," she mumbled as Dimitri and Dr. Ross stepped out to get materials about treatment and rehab.

Kevin and Lori exchanged a look across the hospital bed. Kevin voiced the question written on both their faces. "Why didn't you ask to stay with one of us?"

Natasha pushed her glasses up and rubbed her eyes. "I didn't want to inconvenience either of you. Dimitri called while I was figuring it out, and he offered his guest room. But now with this new rule from the show…it'll look bad no matter who I'm staying with, so this falls under DTD territory."

"Don't tell Donna," Lori whispered.

"Right. I've also got all these side jobs right now, and it was just easiest to pack a few things and stay with Dimitri."

"Do you need help covering classes?" Lori asked. "I'm certified for a bunch of stuff."

"I can cover some, too," Kevin added.

Natasha opened her mouth to tell them no, it was too generous, then forced herself to shut it. They cared. They wanted to help. She searched their faces, looking for signs of obligation, but their offer seemed in earnest. "Really?"

"Of course." Kevin's usual grin had returned.

Natasha smiled at him. "The ladies in my Soulsa class will never want me to come back if you teach it."

He shrugged. "Text us your calendar. We'll work it out."

The trembling feeling was back. Natasha bit her lip to stop

the quiver and nodded. There were some classes she'd have to find specialized teachers for, but if Kevin and Lori could truly cover the majority of them…

She'd still lose out on the money, but at least she wouldn't have to quit the jobs entirely. Maybe this would be a quick recovery time. She'd stay in bed tomorrow and—

Dimitri returned, clutching a sheaf of green printouts.

"How many days?" she asked.

"At least seventy-two hours. Then we'll see how you're doing."

Natasha gaped at him. "That's three whole days!"

Lori rubbed her shoulder. "Don't worry, Tash. Kevin and I don't have any gigs right now. We'll cover for you, really."

Three days with no pay. *At least.* "Thanks, guys." She should sound more grateful, but reality was setting in. The longer she was out of work, the longer she'd have to stay with Dimitri. And the more people who knew she was living with him, the higher the chances of Donna finding out. Natasha had been careful not to let anyone photograph her in the hospital, but things always got out.

"They already called in your prescription," Dimitri said, helping her out of bed and into the wheelchair brought by a nurse. "We'll pick it up on the way home."

All Natasha could do was nod.

Chapter Twenty-Seven

"I switched out the Porsche when I stopped to get your glasses." Dimitri spoke over his shoulder to Natasha, who was propped up in the back seat of the SUV with her right leg stretched out on the bench to keep her ankle up.

"Mmm. Thanks for bringing them, by the way." Her eyes were closed now, and she'd taken the glasses off and was holding them in her lap.

"Your prescription should be waiting when we get to the pharmacy."

"Yes, I heard you the first time you said it."

At her snippy tone, his face cracked in a smile, the first since he'd received the call that she was injured.

Natasha. Ambulance. Hospital.

That was all he'd gotten from the call. He didn't know who'd made it, and he didn't care. He'd called Gina from the car, since she would be able to reach Natasha's other friends and family. Home had been on the way to the hospital, so he'd made a quick stop there, then broke all the speed limits to reach her.

Seeing her in the hospital bed like that, looking tired and wan, with bruises spreading over her swollen foot and up her leg… He'd wanted to gather her tight in his arms. Fuck whatever anyone else thought. The fear and worry had been tempered by crushing relief. She was awake. She was alert. She was mostly okay. The urge to touch her had been overwhelming, and he'd only held back by diving into action and harassing the staff.

Nothing broken, the doctor had said. Likely not even a ligament tear, but just in case, she had to stay off it.

She wasn't going to like that.

Dimitri grinned and shot a glance at her in the rearview mirror. Lucky for her, she had someone who would take very good care of her.

After a quick trip into the pharmacy, he opened the back door. "Hey."

Her eyelids fluttered. After a moment, she gave him a bleary-eyed stare. "¿Qué pasó?"

"Got your meds." He held up the container and shook it.

"Gracias a Dios." She stretched out a hand toward him, palm up. "Dame la medicina."

He laughed and shook out the pills, checking the instructions on the side. "When was the last time you ate a meal?"

At her bland stare, he cursed and wrestled a box of protein bars out of the brown paper bag. "I knew it. Here, eat this."

She scrunched up her face in a way that was really cute. "Ay, Machote, no los quiero. I've already had four of those today."

"Stick to Spanish, sweetheart. I'll manage." She had to be exhausted and in pain. It was easier at those times to slip into your first language. "And you're going to eat one, or you'll kill your stomach. These pills say to take them with food."

She grumbled but accepted the protein bar. He waited until she'd taken three bites, then handed her the pills and a large bottle of water.

"Keep eating that, and drink the water." He closed the back door and climbed into the driver's seat. When he looked back at her, her eyes were closed again.

"Tasha…"

"Hmm?"

"You're going back to sleep, aren't you?"

"Mm-hmm."

"Eat another bite. Please."

With a heavy sigh, she lifted the protein bar and shoved half of it in her mouth. "Only because you said please," she mumbled with her mouth full. Her eyes drifted shut again as she chewed. "Take me home?"

His heart squeezed. Damn, he was so in love with her. "Of course, Kroshka."

Her lips curved. "Gracias."

When he pulled up to his house, he parked in the driveway, angling the SUV so he could bring her in through the front door. First, he disabled the security system, then he went back and carefully opened the door she was propped up against.

He'd expected her to put up a fight when he attempted to carry her, but she poured into his arms, her body limp. He was carrying her through the living room before she managed to rouse herself enough to complain.

"I can walk," she said, slurring. From exhaustion, not the meds. The doctors had laughed when he'd demanded opioids for her sprained ankle, and told him she'd be fine with higher strength naproxen.

"Uh, no. Your ankle looks like a cantaloupe."

She made an effort to lift her head. "Everything's blurry."

"Your glasses are in the car."

"Where are my contacts?"

"You took them out."

"Oh. Right." Her head lolled on his shoulder. "Wait. Stop."

He paused. "What is it, Kroshka?"

She lifted a limp hand and pointed. "My room is that way. No, not my room." Her forehead scrunched, and she pouted. "Nik's room. *The* room. Guest room, I mean."

"You're so cute." Dimitri kissed her forehead and continued toward his own room.

"This is *your* room." Her sleepy mutter sounded accusatory.

"Oh, so you *can* see." He gently deposited her onto his bed.

"I can smell." She tapped the side of her nose and nearly poked herself in the eye. "It smells like you in here."

He quirked an eyebrow at her. "Yeah? What do I smell like?"

"Delicious." She rocked her head side to side on his pillow. "Like that stupid cologne you're always trawling the internet for."

He snorted, concentrating on making her comfortable in the bed. "It's my signature scent. I can't help it if it was discontinued. I've contacted Rogelio about it so many times, he's on the verge of getting a restraining order."

"You're so stubborn."

"I never said I wasn't. Sit tight." After grabbing extra pillows from the hall closet and ice packs from the freezer, he propped up her ankle, which had been bandaged tightly by the nurse.

"Stop it," she mumbled.

"Stop what?"

"Taking care of me."

His hands stilled. In a quiet voice, he said, "It's what I do."

She didn't realize it, but she'd just hit at the heart of who he was. It was all he wanted from life, to have the means to take care of those he loved most. His parents, his brother, some extended family, and now, Natasha. He would give her everything if she let him.

But he couldn't tell her that yet. Not until he was sure she felt the same.

"I'll take care of myself."

"You can barely keep your eyes open."

She opened them now, comically wide. "Yes, I can."

"You can't walk."

"I—" She shut her mouth. "Where are my crutches? I know they gave you some."

"They're in the car. You don't get them until you promise not to go hobbling around unnecessarily. The doctor said to rest and keep your ankle elevated."

She narrowed her eyes. "You're pissing me off."

Good. Maybe if he annoyed her enough, she'd let him past her walls. "I'm just looking out for you. Someone has to."

Her expression turned fierce. "No. I *need* to take care of myself."

Need to? That was interesting. He sat on the edge of the bed. "Why?"

"I just do. I have to do everything on my own." She turned her face away from him and covered it with her arm.

Dimitri stroked her good leg and waited, hoping she'd say something else. When she didn't, he got to his feet. "Stay here. I'm going to get the other things from the car."

Her voice was muffled. "What about my car? It's still at the gym."

"I sent a couple guys from the restaurant to get it. It should be here soon."

"Oh." Her voice was small. "Thanks."

"Anything you need, Tasha. I'll do it."

She sighed.

Dimitri went back out to the car and parked it in the garage, then just sat for a moment, scrubbing his hands over his face.

Okay, so she was still holding back. It was bad that she was injured, but at least now, she couldn't get away from him. Before she was back on her feet, he'd get to the bottom of her feelings for him.

And then he'd know, one way or the other.

Chapter Twenty-Eight

Twenty-five years ago

The small apartment was packed with relatives for Nikolai's second birthday, but the mood in the Kovalenko household was anything but festive.

Dimitri's parents had been tense for months. Glued to the radio, speaking in hushed tones over strong-smelling coffee. At every family gathering, the adults inevitably congregated in the kitchen—like they were doing now—for whispered arguments they thought the kids couldn't hear.

Dimitri always tried to listen, loitering outside the kitchen door and straining his ears over the raucous sounds of his cousins and his brother playing in the rest of the unit. Dima was the oldest, although his cousin Sasha was only four months behind him.

Something was coming. Dimitri didn't know what—his parents had told him not to ask—but it was happening soon.

He was nearly ten. He was old enough to know, old enough to understand.

But on some level, he also didn't want to know. He wanted

everything to stay the same. He didn't want whatever was coming to affect him. Maybe it wouldn't.

Nik crawled into sight as he ran a toy car over the pattern on the rug like it was a system of roads. He made zooming noises with his mouth.

Nik wasn't even speaking in full sentences yet. He didn't care what the grown-ups were saying.

Dimitri peered around the edge of the door.

Inside the kitchen, Dimitri's aunt shook her head. "It's a big risk." Her lips pressed together in a tight line.

"Nothing lasts forever," Dimitri's father, Mikhail, muttered ominously.

"I don't care if we have to leave everything behind," his mother, Oksana, declared, topping off the cups of coffee. "I want to go. As soon as possible."

Her words made Dimitri suck in a breath. *Go?* Go where? Leave *what* behind?

He glanced back at his brother. Surely, wherever his parents went, they would bring their children, too?

His uncle passed in front of the door, and Dimitri ducked out of sight, trying to ignore the fear clinging around his throat.

He didn't want to go anywhere. He liked his home, with its balcony and soft lighting, smelling of coffee and his mother's cooking. He liked the room he shared with his brother, even if Nik still had trouble sleeping through the night. He liked their neighborhood, his friends, his cousins, and aunts and uncles who lived so close by that he rarely went a day without seeing at least one member of his extended family.

He even liked his dance school. He didn't care what the other kids said about it. He was good at dancing, and it made his parents happy.

His mom used to be a dancer, but then she became a teacher instead. She said dance and sports were good for him because he had so much energy, and he needed a place to use it that wasn't the house, the classroom, or the street.

And if he had to use his fists sometimes to deal with the teasing, well…she didn't always find out about that.

"Spend it all," his mother said in a fierce voice. "We will work hard and make more."

The hiss of her words sent a chill up Dimitri's spine.

Things were changing.

He shook off the thought. No, nothing was changing. It couldn't. Right? Their life was here, in Odessa. They couldn't leave.

If he asked again, they'd tell him everything was fine, that there was nothing to worry about.

Except he'd picked up enough from whispered conversations and the kids at school to know that wasn't true. A *lot* had changed, and now, it seemed, change had finally come for him.

The questions swirling in his mind became too loud to ignore, so he screwed up his courage and swung open the kitchen door.

"Where?" he asked, breathless with worry. "Where are we going?"

And were they taking him, too?

The adults all looked up, startled at his sudden appearance. A couple of them exchanged guilty glances, like they hadn't known he could hear them.

Dimitri kept his gaze on his parents, who stood together by the small window. His father frowned and looked grim, but his mother raised her chin and announced, "We're moving to America."

Dimitri got a shaky feeling in his stomach.

So that was it.

America. They were moving to America.

And leaving everything behind.

Chapter Twenty-Nine

Present day

If Dimitri didn't stop coddling her, Natasha was going to scream.

After she fell asleep in his bed, he woke her up in the evening and demanded she eat leftover sancocho from the night before. He sat besides her to make sure she didn't go back to sleep until the plate was clean.

Shit, had it been only yesterday that Dimitri had seduced her in the kitchen? Only yesterday that she'd broken her "no sex" rule?

She stopped arguing about being in his room. He had a better mattress anyway. But when he insisted on carrying her into his bathroom, she balked and clung to the bedding.

"Dimitri, I've been injured before. I'm a dancer. It happens. I can take care of myself."

"Your version of taking care of yourself will land you back in the hospital," he shot back. "Let me help you."

"I draw the line at letting you watch me pee!"

He laughed long and loud at that, then gave her an indulgent look. "Tasha, if I got off on watching you urinate, you would've known about it long before now."

She rolled her eyes, but allowed him to transport her to the bathroom. True to his word, he waited outside the toilet stall. After she was done, she saw he'd retrieved her toothbrush from the hall bathroom, along with her collection of skincare products, and arranged them neatly around his sink.

And when she fell asleep that night, her ankle was so uncomfortable, she didn't even mind his presence in the bed beside her.

Despite Dimitri's wonderful mattress, she slept poorly, and the next morning, her ankle was *killing* her. She was in a foul mood when he carried her to the bathroom, and she kept up a running commentary of Spanish curse words.

He only laughed.

When she was back in bed, he rewrapped her ankle and packed it in new ice packs, clucking over it like una viejita. He brought her eggs and toast and would have fed her if she'd let him, but she was in a fighting mood and snatched the plate away from him. Chuckling, he left her to take a shower.

By the time she was done eating and the painkillers were kicking in, exhaustion had caught up to her. With her ankle propped up, she settled back into the pile of pillows at the head of the bed and began to drift off.

She didn't know how much time had passed before she heard Dimitri moving quietly around the room. His steps came closer, and then his lips touched her forehead in a light kiss. "I have to swing by the restaurant for a few hours. You should call Gina."

She shook her head, her eyes still closed, and she felt him lift her glasses off her face. From her left came a soft tap as he set them on the bedside table.

"Why not?" he asked.

"Why not what?" Talking was hard. She was so sleepy.

"Why not call Gina? She's your best friend. She said she hasn't heard from you in a while."

She opened her eyes a crack to glare at him. "Dima, did you tell Gina I'm living here?"

"I told her you're staying with me while you heal. She doesn't know you were already here."

Natasha groaned and snuggled into the pillow. "Gina's got her own life now. I can't keep leaning on her."

His fingers smoothed over the hair at her temple. The gesture was soothing and almost too sweet. She wanted to tell him to stop, but what came out instead was, "That feels nice."

He didn't say anything, just continued to stroke her hair. After a minute, he kissed her again, on the cheek this time, his lips lingering and his "signature scent" surrounding her.

As sleep drew her under, his voice was the last thing she was aware of.

"You can lean on me."

That was a lovely idea, but no. She couldn't. She had to prove she could make it on her own.

"I'm sorry," she whispered. And then she was out.

The phone ringing next to her head startled her out of a deep sleep. She swiped it on and held it to her ear, gritting her teeth at the pain that radiated up her leg. What the hell time was it? She felt around for her glasses.

"Natasha?"

Shit, it was her mother.

"Hola, Mami." She gave up on the glasses and closed her eyes. Where was Dimitri? Not that she wanted his help, but he knew where her pills were.

Esmeralda barreled on in Spanish. "Gina called. She said you're hurt?"

"Just a sprained ankle. I'll be fine." Madre de Dios, this was the last fucking thing she needed right now.

"Are you still going to be on the show? You can't dance if you're injured."

"It's not that bad, and I still have time before the show starts. Don't worry."

"Okay, because I haven't bought my plane tickets yet, and if you're not going to be in the show, I won't buy them."

Wait, was this woman for real? This was about her stupid trip? God, she was so selfish.

Natasha gritted her teeth in an attempt to keep her tone measured. "I'm *fine*. I just have to stay off it for a few days."

"Where are you? How are you going to do anything if you can't walk?"

"I'm staying with a friend."

"Who?"

Carajo. "Just a friend."

The silence was full of disapproval.

"You're staying with a man, aren't you?"

"Mami, please—"

"You never listen to anything I say, but I'll tell you anyway—this is a bad idea. Why do you think he's taking care of you? He wants one thing. That's all they ever want. You can't rely on men."

"This is temporary—"

"¿Oh, verdad? Well, what do I know? I'm just your mother. It's not like I've ever been lied to by a man before."

Natasha rolled her eyes and bit back a sigh. When her mother got sarcastic, she turned downright nasty.

"You've chosen a hard life. I tried to warn you away from it, but no, you insisted on being a dancer. What happened? It got too difficult, and now you're looking for a man to make it easier?"

"No, Mami." Natasha rubbed at the headache forming behind her brows. "You have it all wrong."

"We'll see about that. You always did look for the easy way out."

Natasha opened her mouth to dispute that she'd worked her ass off to get here, then shut it. To get where? Here in Dimitri's bed with a busted ankle and an embarrassingly low number of dollars in her bank account?

"Well, heal quickly. Let me know if I should cancel my trip."

Of course. Why should Esmeralda come to Los Angeles if she wasn't going to attend the premiere? Why would she come just to visit her daughter? "Seguro."

An awkward silence stretched between them. Before Esmeralda could say something else shitty, Natasha brought it to an end. "Ciao."

She hung up.

Natasha tossed the phone into the blankets and squeezed her eyes shut as the truth burned through her. Esmeralda was right. She was a failure. She'd ridden Gina's coattails through school, their troupe work afterward, and all the way to Los Angeles. The only reason Natasha had a place to stay now and someone to help her with her ankle was because she was fucking him.

Dimitri was being so sweet, though. Calling her friends, bringing her glasses to the hospital, taking care of her…

Well, shit, he wasn't a monster. Those were things any decent fuck buddy would do. It didn't amount to anything more than that, didn't equate to real feelings.

Natasha threw an arm over her face as tears threatened, hot and intrusive. She didn't have time to cry, to indulge in hurt feelings because her mommy didn't love her and the guy she adored would never commit. Yeah, her ankle throbbed like a motherfucker, but that wasn't a reason to cry, either. She should use this time wisely, like reaching out to people who could cover her other classes or lining up apartment visits. She was running out of time to find a new place to stay.

Turning her head to the side, a blurry orange shape caught her eye. She squinted dand just made out her bottle of meds on the nightstand, next to a water bottle, a collection of snacks, and her glasses. He'd left everything she needed within reach.

Her heart melted a little.

Slipping on her glasses, she picked up her phone and drafted a text.

Hey, I know it's been a while, but I have a favor to ask. I'm teaching a pole dancing class and I busted my ankle. Can you cover for me?

She added the necessary details and sent it.

And then, because it was all too much and her ankle throbbed mercilessly, she ate a handful of crackers, popped another pill, and went back to sleep.

Chapter Thirty

Two years ago

Natasha first met Rocky Lim at the premiere of *Speed Demons 3*, an action flick with lots of car races, explosions, and fight scenes. She'd walked the red carpet with Kevin, who was always getting invited to movie premieres, but at the after party she bonded with Rocky over a shared love of the soapy British historical drama *Carlton House.*

Rocky was tall and lean, with a light tan, dark hair, and serious eyes. He was British and Chinese, with a delicious accent and an aversion to wearing sleeves. On top of being gorgeous, he was also an expert in at least half a dozen styles of martial arts, and he'd studied Shakespearean theater in London. When Rocky asked if she wanted to leave the party early, she said yes.

After that, she met up with Rocky whenever he was in LA. They had sex first, then they sat around rewatching their favorite episodes of *Carlton House.* Rocky was able to add context to the upstairs-downstairs dynamic, and Natasha enjoyed scrutinizing the characters' outrageous antics with him.

It didn't hurt that he also had ridiculously defined muscles, and he liked to be touched.

So when Rocky asked her to be his date for Rogelio Hernandez's new cologne unveiling, she said yes. She had a good time with him, and there was no expectation of a deeper connection, which she appreciated. They were friends-with-benefits in every sense.

She also liked Rogelio's Angel Dust perfume and was hoping they'd be giving out samples of women's scents, too.

Gina helped her shop for a new outfit, and Natasha promised to bring back samples if they were available. Natasha wore a slinky silver sheath that managed to be loose and clingy at the same time, making the most of her few curves. It was held up by thin straps and dipped low in the front and even lower in the back, showing off her slim, muscular upper body and her perfectly perky tits.

Her credit card was crying, but it was worth it for the look on Rocky's face when he picked her up and the way the cameras turned toward her when they posed in front of the step and repeat. Beside her, Rocky looked dazzling in a sleeveless maroon suit that highlighted his mouth-watering delts and triceps.

The event was held at a big, industrial-looking loft, with exposed ducts and soft neon accent lighting in purple and pale blue. Banners depicting pretty men with angular faces hung over the concrete walls, and the high-end silver and navy blue design of the new Fallen Angel by Rogelio packaging was everywhere, clashing with the decor of the venue. The scent of cologne permeated the space in an overwhelming cloud. It was like walking into the perfume department at Macy's. Rocky coughed and rubbed his nose.

"It's a little strong, huh?" She gave his arm a comforting squeeze, or at least, she tried. His muscles were like granite.

"No kidding." He turned and let loose a violent sneeze. A woman at the bar gave him a dirty look, and Natasha steered him away.

"There's a vent," she said, pointing at the ceiling. "Maybe the smell won't be as strong there."

He sneezed again and let her lead him to a dark corner.

It was a little better under the vent, but Rocky still looked miserable. "Sorry about this." His posh accent sounded a touch nasal, and his dark eyes watered.

Natasha rubbed his back, feeling bad for the guy. "Why don't I get us drinks?"

He nodded and sniffled. "Good idea. I'm going to go blow my nose. I can't greet Rogelio like this." He gave her a small, utterly charming smile. "I'll meet you back here."

At the bar, she ordered two Jack and Cokes. It was an open bar, and remembering her bartender days, she left a nice tip and left to find Rocky.

She only made it two steps before she froze, her fingers tightening around the tumblers.

Six feet away, Dimitri walked in with his arm around the waist of a voluptuous blonde with a wide smile. Her face was vaguely familiar, although it took Natasha a moment to place her as the host on some entertainment news show.

Natasha let out a long exhale, battling the jealousy that rose up. This shouldn't matter to her. Sure, she'd had lots of amazing sex with Dimitri in the lead up to her first season of *The Dance Off*, but after she danced with him in the premiere—an amazing performance, if she did say so herself—it was like she'd ceased to exist in his eyes. She hadn't heard a word from him since the season ended. And that was *fine*. Dimitri was just a guy she'd hooked up with. Like Rocky. No big deal. She wouldn't care if she saw Rocky on a date with someone else.

Except, for reasons she didn't want to examine, seeing Dimitri cozying up to another woman felt like a *very* big deal, and she *did* care.

Get it together, girl. If there was one thing Natasha had learned when she was shaking her ass for cash tips, it was how to work with what she had to make her audience beg for more. Dropping her shoulders and cocking a hip, she prowled in the direction of the vent, where Rocky waited for her. Maybe it was petty, but she didn't care. She was feeling petty. She sailed straight past Dimitri and his date, strutting in her stilettos like she was on a motherfucking catwalk.

From the corner of her eye, she caught Dimitri's hard glare, and her nipples tightened in response.

As she approached Rocky, his expression lit with hunger, but the flash of heat spreading through her body was all because of Dimitri. She could feel those chocolate-brown eyes devouring her, his gaze as tangible as a hot stroke of hands.

By the time she reached her date, Natasha was flushed and flustered, and her skimpy little panties were damp. She passed Rocky his drink and took a sip of her own, hoping it would cool her down.

Rocky slipped his free arm around her waist and pulled her close. "You are by far the fittest woman here, you know that?"

"It isn't the first time, and it won't be the last." Pleased by how flippant and in control she sounded, Natasha knocked back another swallow.

Rocky's hand trailed up the bare skin of her back, then down to caress the top curve of her ass. His voice was a soft murmur in her ear. "We don't have to stay long."

"Good." She drained the glass, relishing the languid feeling that spread through her limbs. But she was still inflamed, her body crying out for a strong, sure touch.

Not Rocky's, though.

It was so fucking unfair. Here she had this man with an incredible body, crisp accent, and a shared interest in TV shows, who made no demands on her life or her heart. She enjoyed Rocky and his company, even if his kisses tended to be a little overenthusiastic.

And yet she was pining after an emotionally unavailable choreographer who liked to boss her around. What the hell was wrong with her? Really, she shouldn't be pining over *anyone.* That wasn't what she was about.

As for jealousy? Fuck that shit. Natasha didn't need any green-eyed monsters in her life.

Rocky's lips brushed her neck. "Why don't we say hello to Rogelio and then go back to my place?"

It irked her a little that he asked. Dimitri wouldn't have. No, the cocky bastard would already know she was itching to rip off this nine-hundred-dollar dress and have him inside her. He'd march her over to Rogelio, probably interrupting someone else in the process, and rush them through the social niceties before making some excuse for why they had to leave immediately. Then he'd take her home and rail her until she forgot her own name.

Maybe that was it. Dimitri knew what she wanted, what she needed, and he gave it to her without making her ask.

Rocky didn't have that confidence, that innate knowing. He was always asking her what she wanted, if things were okay, if it felt good. And while Natasha appreciated the concern, and his focus on consent, she just wanted him to fuck her. She wanted him to already know what would make her feel good, to have such a deep awareness of her body and her responses that he didn't have to ask. She wanted to sit back and enjoy the ride.

She wanted him to *lead*.

But Rocky wasn't a dancer. He was a martial artist who specialized in stage combat and stunt work. Those skills required a partnership, and Rocky worried about his partner's well-being.

Natasha didn't want him to worry about her. She was fine, and she'd tell him if she wasn't.

This was what awaited her if she went home with him. Questions that took her out of the moment and check-ins that felt rehearsed.

She covered her sigh with another sip of her drink, getting only the remnants of soda mixed with melted ice.

At least she knew where she stood with Rocky. He didn't

make her feel insecure or off-balance. She knew exactly what the parameters of their relationship were.

She nodded and said, "Let's go."

Rocky took her hand and led her toward the low stage where Rogelio chatted with a pair of male models. The designer was a Latino silver fox with a complexion like burnished gold, short curly hair, and an ebullient personality. Both of the models called him "Daddy" with a tone of reverence.

Natasha spotted Dimitri from the corner of her eye, forever attuned to his presence, even though she'd have been better off ignoring him. He was with his date at the bar, leaning his elbows back on it, watching Natasha as she crossed the space with Rocky. Dimitri's eyebrows were drawn together in a fierce scowl.

She bit her lip.

His eyes narrowed at her. She looked away.

The whole time Rocky spoke with Rogelio, Natasha resisted the urge to peek over her shoulder to look for Dimitri. She smiled, thanking Rogelio when he complimented her dress, and leaning into Rocky's touch when he rubbed her back. She did and said all the right things, but her attention was elsewhere. She was wet at the thought of Dimitri watching this display, wondering what he was thinking as Rocky touched her body with casual caresses.

Was he angry? Jealous? Turned on?

All of the above, hopefully.

She made eye contact with Dimitri once more as she and Rocky were leaving. Dimitri's nostrils flared, and the look he gave her was ferocious in its intensity. She still couldn't tell what he was thinking, but oh, she wanted to find out. She wanted to leave Rocky's side and stalk across the floor into Dimitri's hold. Not embrace; he didn't embrace. He held, like when they were dancing, making it clear that he was the one in charge. She wanted him to show her with his body what he was feeling, and let him slake the fire he'd ignited in hers.

But she didn't. Instead, she grabbed a couple of gift bags with

—score!—tiny bottles of Angel Dust, and followed Rocky out to his car, a flashy red thing with no legroom that probably cost him a small fortune in car insurance. He'd once told her that he'd rather drive a hybrid sedan, but he had a brand image to maintain.

They went to his house in Studio City. After he undressed her —slowly, tenderly—he stroked his fingers between her legs— again, slowly and tenderly—and marveled at how wet she was. She teasingly attributed it to the cologne. He fucked her—slowly and tenderly, of course—and then he put on their favorite episode of *Carlton House*, the season two finale where the manipulative mother-in-law finally received her comeuppance.

The next morning, Rocky drove her home. And since Gina wasn't there and Natasha was still feeling needy, she invited him upstairs and fucked him again in her own bed, for the hell of it.

It was fine. Good, even.

But Rocky wasn't Dimitri. And Natasha couldn't stop thinking about the arrogant bastard.

Part of her hoped Dimitri was thinking of her, too. Another part wanted him to forget her, so she could forget about *him*.

Rocky left, and after washing the lingering scent of Fallen Angel out of her hair, she spent the rest of the day catching up on errands. That night, as she was settling into bed, she got a text.

Come over. Now.

She dropped everything and drove to Dimitri's house.

Chapter Thirty-One

Present day

Natasha was cute when she was angry, and as cabin fever set in, she was plenty pissed. Dimitri had never seen this side of her, and he liked it. It meant she was getting more comfortable around him.

By the third day of her confinement, she was moving around easily with the crutches. He set her up in the living room so he could talk to her from the kitchen. She sat on the sofa with both feet propped on an ottoman, complaining about the state of the LA housing market.

"How the hell do they get away with charging this much? That isn't even a legal bedroom. It doesn't have windows." She muttered about greedy pendejos and went back to clicking.

Dimitri poured ice into the blender for virgin piña coladas. Even though Natasha had claimed her ankle didn't hurt as much and had downgraded to regular ibuprofen, he didn't think rum and crutches mixed well. "I told you, you don't need to look for a place right away."

"I do. I can't be living here when the show starts."

Before he could question her further, he heard a car pull up in front of the house. Damn, he really needed to fix the gate. He shot Natasha a quizzical look. "Expecting someone?"

"No." She moved to get up, but he gestured for her to stay and went to look out the front windows.

"It's a goddamn Lamborghini. Who do you know who drives a red Lambo?"

"Oh. That's Kevin."

Kevin Ray, *The Dance Off*'s number-one star dancer. Dimitri had known him for years, through the industry and through the show. They weren't friends, but Kevin was friendly with everyone, so his behavior at the hospital had been weird. Dimitri hadn't imagined Kevin's accusatory glares.

"Why is he here?"

Natasha shrugged and set her laptop aside. "I don't know. Checking on me, I guess. I've had my phone off."

"Really? Why?"

She avoided his gaze. "Too many texts and calls."

Making a mental note to ask about that later, Dimitri opened the front door and greeted Kevin as the other man walked up the front steps. "Hey, man. Welcome."

Kevin gave him a nod and an assessing glance. "Hey, D. How's it going? Is Tash here?"

"She is."

Kevin raised his eyebrows. "Can I see her?"

Dimitri's protective instinct flared, and for a second, he was tempted to block the doorway and question Kevin further. Instead, he stepped back. "Come in."

Kevin's face broke into his signature grin when he saw Natasha. "There's my girl." He kissed her on the cheek and dropped onto the sofa next to her. "How's the leg?"

Dimitri bristled. Who the fuck did this guy think he was? He closed the front door with more force than was necessary and stalked back into the kitchen. "You want a piña colada?" he tossed out as he passed.

"Huh? Oh, sure." Kevin gave him a thumbs-up.

Fake-ass bastard. Dimitri wasn't buying it. He pulled out a bottle of rum for himself. He'd need it to get through this "visit."

After passing out drinks—virgin for Natasha and Kevin, because fuck that guy—Dimitri leaned on the bar while the other two gossiped. Dimitri offered a few comments here and there, but otherwise just listened. When Kevin asked how Gina was doing, Natasha gave a general response and changed the subject.

Hmm. Something was going on there. Dimitri would bet money she hadn't called Gina, even though he'd suggested it. And her phone was off? That was weird, too. Natasha lived with her phone glued to her hand.

They were talking about auditions now. Kevin was up for a few roles, and he was regaling Natasha with the details.

Dimitri turned around so he could roll his eyes without being seen. This guy was such a blowhard. But he was Natasha's friend, and he'd stepped in to cover some of her jobs while she was injured. He couldn't hate him.

But he could be pissed that Kevin threw his arm over Natasha's shoulders, like it belonged there.

When Natasha yawned for the fifth time, Dimitri intervened. "Time to go," he told Kevin. "She's too polite to tell you she's tired."

Dimitri didn't miss the way Kevin's eyes narrowed at him, but his expression was full of genuine concern when he turned back to Natasha. "Are you gonna be okay, Tash?"

"Yeah." She gave Kevin a reassuring smile and patted his knee. "I've got the most overprotective nursemaid in Los Angeles watching over me. I'll be good."

"Let me know if you need anything." Kevin bussed her cheek and got to his feet. "Even if it's just to talk."

"I will. Thanks for coming by."

Dimitri had already opened the front door and was waiting for Kevin to leave. When Kevin walked past, he bumped Dimitri with his shoulder.

Oh, this fucker was asking for it. Instead of closing the door, Dimitri followed Kevin outside.

"You got a problem, man?" One didn't grow up in Brooklyn as a dancer without being able to fight. Dimitri had never had issues with Kevin before, but clearly, the guy had a bone to pick with him.

"Yeah, I do." Kevin's light eyes were hard as he rounded on Dimitri. "I don't think you're good for her, and I can't help but wonder why the hell she's staying here with you instead of with one of her friends."

"That's a damn good question, and one you should ask yourself while you look in the fucking mirror. But you sure that's the only reason you're getting up in my face?" Dimitri shot back. "Because she's your *friend*?"

"Yeah, asshole. Unlike you, I know how to be friends with women and respect them."

"What the fuck is that supposed to mean?"

"It means you use women and don't give a fuck about them. If you think Lauren didn't talk about you, you're an even bigger idiot than I already thought you were."

"Don't believe everything you're told."

Kevin shrugged. "Whatever, man. She's not the only one who talks. I care about Natasha—as a *friend*. And I don't like seeing anyone take advantage of my friends."

"I'm not taking advantage of her." Dimitri spoke through gritted teeth, clenching his fists and wrestling down the urge to punch Kevin's handsome mug. "I'm taking *care* of her because I care *about* her."

Kevin snorted. "Sure. Okay."

"I *do*."

"You have a weird way of showing it."

Dimitri shook his head. "I don't have to explain our relationship to you."

"Relationship?" The asshole had the nerve to laugh. "So, it's the kind of relationship where you both screw other people. Got it."

Fuck this guy, but he wasn't wrong. "That was before." The excuse rang hollow, even to Dimitri's own ears.

Kevin held up his hands and took a step back toward the car. "Whatever you say, dude. Just be straight with her, all right? Don't be a douche."

Dimitri seethed while Kevin climbed into the car. Part of him wanted to drag the guy back and have it out, right there in the driveway. The other part wanted to drill Kevin for details. Maybe Natasha had said something about him.

No. He wouldn't stoop so low as to ask her friends for dirt. It was time he grew a pair and got to the bottom of this himself.

Starting right the fuck now.

Chapter Thirty-Two

Dimitri stormed back into the house but when he reached the entrance to the living room, he stopped short.

Natasha was *crying*.

"What's wrong?" He flew to her side, nearly knocking over a standing lamp. "Are you hurt? Is it your ankle?"

Natasha pushed her glasses up on her forehead to wipe at her eyes. "No, it's not my ankle. I'm just…never mind. Go away."

"No." Settling on the sofa beside her, he lifted a hand and rubbed at the tear tracks on her cheeks. "Kroshka, please. Tell me what's wrong. Tell me so I can fix it."

When she shook her head, he jerked a thumb at the door. "Was it Kev? You want me to go after him and break his legs?"

"What? Of course not!" She gave him an incredulous look.

He leaned in close and cupped her cheek. "Forget him. Tell me why you're crying."

Her lower lip trembled, and desperation churned in his gut.

She sniffled. "I guess it kinda was Kevin."

Dimitri's jaw tightened. "I knew it. That guy's a dick."

"No, he's not. He's just so fucking *successful*." She spat the word out like it was a curse. "Did you hear what he said? He has three film roles coming up. Three!"

She let her head fall back against the couch, speaking and gesturing toward the ceiling.

"Jobs just fall into his fucking lap, and all he does is smile and laugh, and everyone loves him. If he weren't my friend, I'd hate him."

She was talking fast, which wasn't a problem, since Dimitri talked fast, too, but he was having trouble following her logic. "You're crying because Kevin's going to be in movies?"

Her chin quivered, but she scowled. "I guess so."

"Are you…happy for him?"

She glared at him. "Of course I am. But I'm also *pissed*."

Ah. He got it. "You're jealous," he said, proud that he'd figured it out.

Her eyebrows shot up. "Excuse me?"

Shit, he'd said the wrong thing. But she was off again before he could get a word in.

"I'm not *jealous*, I'm just…you know what, sure, fine, let's say I am. I'm not, but if I *were* jealous, I'd have every right to be." She ticked things off on her fingers. "Gina's living her dream, headlining a Broadway show, and she's got a hunky man along for the ride who worships the ground she walks on." She ticked another finger. "Kevin is getting job offers left and right, and yet he always seems to have free time. I don't understand it. I work my ass off, I'm always tired, and I never have any money."

Dimitri had a theory about that, but now wasn't the time to bring up her spending habits.

"Three, my life is falling the fuck apart."

He swung an arm around the back of the sofa and leaned in, trying for a boyish grin. "On the plus side, you get to spend more time with me."

Again, that glare. What did it say about him that he found it so sexy when she glared at him?

But the tears gathered again on her lashes. Before he could brush them away, she shook her head angrily.

"I'm a goddamn failure, and soon, everyone will know it."

Alarm made him sit up straight. "What do you mean?"

She gestured at her leg, then around the room. "Look at me. I'm a screw-up. The only times I've ever managed to take care of myself were when Gina was around. As soon as she's gone, I lost my car, my apartment, my money, and now..." Her breath hitched. "If I can't dance, it's all over."

Her words triggered his protective instinct, even though in this case, he was defending her from herself. "You're not a screw up. You've had some bad luck, exacerbated by the fact that you're working yourself into the ground." He pointed at her ankle. "This happened because you're overdoing it."

She sucked in a breath. "This happened because I was up all night with *you!*"

He shook his head. "That was probably the best sleep you've had in weeks. For once, you turned your brain off and let yourself be in the moment. This is your body's way of telling you to sit your ass down."

"I *need* to work," she said through her teeth. "If I don't work, I can't find a place to live, and if I can't move out of here, I lose my job at the show."

"Like I said, there's no rush to move out. No one needs to know—"

"Kevin and Lori know. Everyone who was in that emergency room knows. It's only a matter of time, and there's that stupid new rule—"

He waved it away. "I don't care about their rules."

"That's all well and good for you. You're a judge and a movie star. I'm just another dancer trying to make it in this town, and I will not go back to—" She clamped her mouth shut.

"To what?" he pressed.

She shook her head. "Nothing. I just...I have to be able to dance. That's all there is to it."

"Or what?"

That caught her off guard. She gave herself a shake.

"What do you mean, or what?"

He leaned back and spread his hands wide. "What if you can't dance?"

Her mouth fell open, and the expression on her face was so full of hurt, he wanted to take the words back. But it was something she had to deal with, something every dancer had to confront after an injury. He felt like an ass for saying it, but he added, "Who are you if you're not a dancer?"

She choked on a sob. "I...I don't know..."

He rubbed her arm. "It's okay, it's just something to think—"

"Nothing." She smacked her hands down on her thighs. Her lips were set in a tight line, like her fate was decided and there was no arguing it. "I'm nothing if I'm not a dancer. Just a giant idiot for thinking I could do this."

"Hey, stop it." He trailed his hand up to the base of her neck and tried to massage her there, but she shook him off. "You're not an idiot. You're not nothing."

"Dancing is all I've ever tried to do." She dashed at the tears falling from her eyes. "But I'm a complete failure."

"You're on one of the top ten network TV shows," he reminded her. "How is that failing?"

"I got it because of Gina. She found the audition for *EDN*. They liked us because we were friends, and we moved to *The Dance Off* together for the same reason. She found our apartment, she made sure our bills were paid, she—"

"Okay, so your friend helped you out, and you're bad at managing money. You can learn. I'll help you."

"No. I need to stop getting help from people. I have to do it on my own."

"Damn it, why won't you let anyone help you? Why won't you let *me* help you?"

Startled, she met his gaze. Her dark eyes sparkled, and he

wanted so badly to kiss her until she stopped crying and forgot all these ridiculous notions.

"I don't want your help," she whispered.

"For god's sake, why not?"

For a second, it seemed like she wouldn't answer. And then she blurted out, "Because I don't know why you're giving it! Or I do, and it's not a good enough reason. And I *need* to make it on my own. I have to prove I can do it, that I can be a success as a dancer. That's all that matters."

"Why the hell are you so stuck on this? It's not about the end result, Tasha—"

"That's really easy for someone in your position to say." She waved her arms. "Look at this house. You've done it. Kevin's done it. Now Gina's done it, and I'm the fuck-up who's been left behind."

"Stop saying that." He was done listening to her berate herself. "You're hard-working and you have incredible talent. You were born to dance. And I'm not going to listen to you call yourself an idiot just because no one ever taught you to manage your money."

She let out a shaky breath and ducked her head. "I'm so stupid for thinking I could do this on my own."

"No, you're only stupid for pushing away the people who want to help you."

She lifted her head and gave him an offended look. "Did you just call me stupid?"

"No." Except he had. Blyat. He rushed to explain. "I mean, you called yourself stupid first." Damn it, that was worse. "But you're not. You're amazing. And you're going to let me help you, because you're smart. I mean, what the hell, Tasha? If you were stupid, would I be in love with you?"

Her eyes grew round, the whites visible all around them, and her eyebrows shot up on her forehead.

He blinked. Shit. Had he just said that? Yes, he really had. Well, no taking it back now.

"Yeah, I said it." He shrugged. "Don't make a big deal about it. And don't try to change the subject."

She grabbed the crutches and struggled off the sofa.

"Whoa, where are you going?"

"Bed. I'm tired. Goodnight."

"Are you serious?" He put a hand on her arm before she could get up. "I just said I love you, and you're running away?"

"You said not to make a big deal about it. So, I'm not. Besides, it's not true."

He reared back. "What the hell do you mean, *it's not true*? It damn well fucking is."

She covered her face and shook her head. "No. It's not."

"Why did I say it, then?"

"To be nice. You're trying to make me feel better."

At that, he laughed. "When have you ever known me to say anything just to be *nice*?"

She side-eyed him and didn't answer.

"Natasha—"

"Stop. You don't love me. No one does. Maybe you think you do, because the sex is great, or you like having someone here you can bang whenever you want, but that's not love."

He shoved a hand through his hair, exasperated. "What is love, then?"

"I don't know. Not that."

Quiet fell between them. Dimitri pinched the bridge of his nose. It was happening again. He'd put his heart on the line and was being rejected. But it wasn't going how he'd feared. He'd imagined her laughing at him, assuring him that this was just another affair, no need to make things serious.

Tasha hadn't done that. Instead, she had outright doubted his feelings for her. Doubted her own worthiness of them.

How the hell did he combat that? Especially when he'd done everything in his power to maintain their no-strings relationship out of his own fear of being hurt. He'd cemented a situation where she couldn't believe in him.

Words weren't going to fix this. He had to prove his feelings to her.

Sliding one arm under her knees and the other around her back, he lifted her from the sofa.

"What are you doing?" Her voice was dull and tired.

"Putting you to bed."

"My bed?"

"No."

She sighed, but didn't argue.

After he got her settled in his bed with her foot propped up, he placed her phone on the nightstand beside her.

"Call Gina," he said.

She shook her head. "She's busy. I don't want to bother her."

"She's your best friend. She's not too busy for you."

Another sigh. "Tomorrow."

"Fine."

He shut the bedroom door behind him and headed for his office on the other side of the house. He needed time alone to sort out what had just happened, and he suspected she did, too.

The question he'd asked her had stuck with him. It was something one of his coaches had once confronted him with, back when he was on the ballroom dance circuit.

Who are you if you aren't a dancer?

Dimitri went to one of the shelves in the corner of the room and pulled down a large three-ring binder. "Idea Book" was written on the front in permanent black marker. Taking it to his desk, he sat and began to flip through the pages.

The binder was packed with printouts of mood boards, costume inspiration, and set design concepts. Stories, song lists, and choreography notes strained the rings. Alex laughed at him for it and had often said Dimitri should "go paperless" and make everything in the binder digital.

Dimitri didn't care. He'd had this binder since he was a teenager. Since before *Aliens Don't Dance*. Between these two peeling plastic covers lived all his ideas, no matter how big or small, organized by old-school dividers with brightly colored tabs.

Who was he if not a dancer?

A creator.

And someday he'd have the wealth, the reputation, the fame, and the clout to bring his ideas to life *his* way.

Chapter Thirty-Three

Eleven years ago

"We have to close the show."

Alex sounded apologetic, but Dimitri knew he wasn't wrong. They were losing money, and despite glowing reviews from critics, *Sem'ya* was a flop. Still, Dimitri resisted.

"It's only been three weeks."

Alex sighed. "We can finish out the month. But after that, we need to close."

Alex and Dimitri both looked like their fathers, who were brothers, which meant Alex and Dimitri looked like brothers, too. Dark hair, brown eyes, olive complexion, although Alex's features were a little sharper and made him look more serious. Alex was also about an inch taller than Dimitri, although leaner. When they were little, people had often mistaken them for twins, although not anymore, since Alex's face was always clean-shaven.

Now, Dimitri scrubbed his hands over his face, scratching at the thick beard on his cheeks. He'd let it grow out for the show—and honestly, because he hated shaving.

The sequel to *Aliens Don't Dance* had fallen through. His

costar, Greta Marcus, had refused to sign on, and the studio wouldn't consider replacing her. They didn't think audiences would accept someone else in the role of Hannah, or a story where her romance with Reygar hadn't lasted. Dimitri had turned down jobs to focus on producing and starring in *Sem'ya*, an intensely personal exploration of family and feeling. He had scraped and borrowed and begged for the money to bring the dance-intensive stage show to Broadway.

And now it was a failure.

He didn't know what to think. People loved him in the movie. They loved every silly TV cameo he'd done. He'd joined singers and musicians on tour to dance at their concerts. But when he created his own show, sank his blood, sweat, tears, and money into it, it was a fucking failure.

He'd put everything he had into *Sem'ya*, into the choreography and the story, the production and the marketing. He was exhausted, sick, stressed.

And what was it all for? A few good reviews and shitty ticket sales.

That was the thing about being a performer. It didn't fucking matter unless you had people to perform for. Sure, there were a few devoted fans who'd seen it multiple times. But it wasn't enough.

He'd thought his fame and name recognition would be enough of a draw. He'd been wrong. And that was humbling.

"Close the show now," Dimitri said in Russian.

Alex hesitated. "You're sure?"

Dimitri shrugged. "What choice do we have?"

Alex looked relieved, probably because Dimitri had stopped arguing. Dimitri had been arguing a lot over the last few months, with everyone. Between losing the sequel and watching *Sem'ya* fail, he was wound up tight. His temper, never well leashed, was ready to blow over at the slightest provocation.

But right now, there was no point. Alex was right. It was time to let go and return to doing work for other people. Other people's dreams and ideas, their words and their moves. At least those things carried little risk for him. Sure shots at money, easy ways to climb the steps of stardom.

"I'm positive," he said, when Alex continued to stare at him. Finally, his cousin nodded.

"I'll take care of it."

And then there was nothing left to say.

Chapter Thirty-Four

Present day

Natasha woke in the middle of the night from a dream—a nightmare, really—where she'd slept through all the next day's gigs. It didn't take a psychoanalyst to figure out she was stressed about missing so much work.

The room was dark and cool. Next to her, Dimitri's slow, even breathing and solid presence soothed her, even as her thoughts skittered away from the memory of his earlier words.

If you were stupid, would I be in love with you?

As far as romantic declarations went, it was pretty weak. Also, it was a hypothetical. He started with *if,* and continued with *would I.* So, to follow it to its logical conclusion, she *was* stupid, and Dimitri was *not* in love with her.

Right? He had to be kidding, or making some misguided attempt to cheer her up.

She scowled over at him in the dark. Why did he have to joke around so much? One night, when they'd both been dead-ass drunk and lounging in the hot tub, he'd turned to her and said, "Let's get married."

When he claimed he was serious and suggested they hop a

flight to Vegas, she took that to mean he was drunk enough to drown and dragged him out of the water. The asshole had laughed and laughed, then fallen into his bed with her, soaking wet, where he'd proceeded to screw her brains out.

It was easier when she knew the rules. Easier when she knew exactly where they stood, and what they were to each other. Most of the time, they got drunk at a club, or he showed up at her apartment, or invited her over here. They screwed, she left, and she didn't hear from him for a while.

She'd slept in this bed dozens of times. She trusted him—with her body, at least. But with her heart?

That was a whole other story.

Sometimes, it was like she got off on the tension, the difference between going so far with him physically, while completely hiding her emotions. It was like a game with high stakes, her very survival depending on how little she could reveal to him, how deeply she could conceal her desire for more.

It hadn't been a problem with other men. With Jackson, for instance, they'd had fun in bed and made small talk about their careers. Jackson wasn't a big star yet, but he was easy-going, and their connection hadn't progressed much beyond sex and laughing at internet memes.

Her dynamic with Rocky had been similar. They had a good time together, and she went with him to red carpet events, but when it came down to it, they were just friends. It was easy to keep their conversations on the surface and she never worried about revealing too much.

Rocky was in London now, but he still texted her sometimes. Whenever he passed a landmark she'd recognize from *Carlton House*, he snapped a picture and sent it to her. It was sweet, but love? No. And she hadn't wanted it to be. She hadn't cared enough to want that.

She *did* want more from Dimitri, though, and the admission was like a sickness inside her. Sure, he was acting the part of the caring companion now, but that was decency, not love. Hell, he probably felt bad for her. Poor Natasha, no money and nowhere to live. She'd made that rule about no sex, and he must have known she wasn't going to stick to it. He knew all her weaknesses.

She didn't know what to make of Dimitri's insistence on questioning her about Jackson, though. That had been weird, even for him. They never talked about the other people they saw, aside from oblique references to their latest STI testing results. Since her injury, the topic of Jackson hadn't come up again.

And what the hell was Dimitri's problem with Kevin? She'd heard the two of them shouting in the driveway, but couldn't make out what they'd said. She'd been desperate to peek out the window, but it wasn't worth the risk of hurting her ankle further.

One thing was sure—she had to get out of this "playing house" situation. At the beginning, at least, she'd convinced herself she was here as a guest. She had a different bedroom, even her own bathroom, and she and Dimitri weren't banging. Now?

She looked over at him again, barely able to make out the curve of his face where it was buried in the pillow.

Her mother's words drifted back to her. *No puedes confiar en los hombres.*

You can't rely on men.

Eventually, Dimitri would tire of her. His offer to let Natasha stay had been impulsive, because he'd witnessed her desperation firsthand. Nothing more. There was no chance in hell that what he'd said was true.

He didn't love her.

The certainty of the thought fell on her like a lead blanket. As long as she held on to that, she could keep her heart and her feelings locked up tight. She'd come out the other side intact and go back to her life as it was. This time, she'd take care of *herself*. She wouldn't rely on anyone. Not Gina, not Dimitri, and certainly not her mother.

With that settled, Natasha closed her eyes. The bed was comfortable, and the pain in her ankle had dulled. Dimitri was right, damn him. She did sleep better in his bed. There was nothing in the way of drifting off into a deep, restful sleep…

Except now she had to pee.

She breathed deeply and tried to drift off, but now that she was awake, her bladder wasn't having it. *Get up,* it urged her. *Now.*

Moving quietly so as not to wake Dimitri, she pushed the sheet off her and lowered her feet to the floor. She couldn't find her crutches in the dark, but she could lean on the wall and furniture while she hobbled to the en suite bathroom.

In the dark. Without her glasses.

This was a great fucking idea.

Still, it was fewer steps away than the hall bathroom.

She was wincing by the time she made it to the toilet stall and was grateful for the chance to sit down for a moment. After she was done, she opened the door to step out…and found Dimitri was waiting for her.

Because of course he was.

He squinted at her in the light from the stall, and looked sexy and sleep-rumpled in nothing but navy blue boxer briefs.

Her heart lurched. Her body burned for him. But self-preservation kicked in, and the walls around her heart slammed down.

You can't rely on him, a little voice whispered through her mind. *Resist.*

When he murmured her name and reached for her, she jerked back. And because it was the middle of the night and she was tired and emotionally strung out, she forgot all about her stupid ankle…

And put her full weight on it.

Chapter Thirty-Five

Natasha didn't scream, but from the way she gasped and grimaced, Dimitri knew it had to hurt. He quickly yanked her into his arms, taking the weight off her feet.

"What are you doing, Tasha?" He cradled her close. "Why are you walking around without crutches? You should have woken me up."

"Put me down," she demanded in a firm voice.

"Kroshka, I'm too tired to argue with you. Come back to bed." He carried her through the bathroom, holding her with care, but she struggled.

"Damn it, I don't need your help."

With a sigh, Dimitri set her on the edge of the jacuzzi and sat beside her, shifting her leg to keep her injured ankle elevated across his lap.

Ignoring her glare, he unwrapped the bandages and skimmed his fingers gently over the fading bruises. "Did you hurt yourself?"

She was breathing hard. "Dimitri, I need you to stop doing this."

"Doing what?" With slow, methodical movements, he wrapped her ankle again. They'd ramp up the light physical therapy exercises tomorrow to make sure her ankle healed right. "Caring about you?"

"Yes."

He shook his head. "Don't be silly." He was too tired for this conversation. He'd stayed up late, flipping through his binder, before sliding into bed next to her and falling into a deep sleep. When he'd rolled over and found her side of the bed empty, he'd gone looking for her. The crutches were still in the living room—his fault, for not thinking to bring them into the bedroom—and he'd worried she would hurt herself.

And then she had.

"There's no need for it," she continued.

"For what?" He yawned.

"For you to care about me. You never did before."

At that, he pinned her with a hard look. "I have *always* cared about you."

She shrugged. "You've never shown it."

Damn it. She was right. "I'm trying to show you *now*."

"It doesn't matter anyway," she muttered, looking away from him.

"Why not?"

And then, to his intense horror, her breathing hitched. His heart broke for her, and he crooned her name as he pulled her into his lap.

She gave a few half-hearted sounds of protest, but when he tightened his arms around her, she lay her head on his shoulder and let the tears come.

These weren't like before, when she had cried on the sofa. Those tears had been more of the feeling-sorry-for-myself variety. These spoke of deep inner pain and strummed answering vibrations of his own fears.

She wiped at her eyes. "Will you please just go back to bed and leave me alone?"

"No." He rested his cheek on her head and rocked her. "You're going to let me care about you."

"You shouldn't."

"Why not?"

She was quiet for a while. "Because I don't deserve it."

He sighed. "Bullshit."

She shook her head, her hair sliding against his chin. "It's true. I'm a mess." Her body shook harder, and she sobbed out the words. "I'm useless. I can't get my life in order. Can't take care of myself. I've failed at everything. It's all going to fall apart."

"That's not true," he murmured, dropping kisses onto her head. "You're going through a rough patch. It happens. We'll get through it."

"There's no *we*, Dimitri. It's just me. Alone. And this is it. The end."

He shifted her so he could look at her face. Her eyes were red and puffy, but even more alarming was the desolation in her expression. She was giving up.

"I'm going to lose my job, either because of my ankle or because I haven't been able to work enough to make the money to move out on my own. When that happens, I'll lose my main source of income, and that'll be it. I can't stick around LA imposing on people. I'll have to go back to New York. Back h-home."

Fresh sobs wracked her frame, and he held on, gritting his teeth against the onslaught. He wanted to make it right. He wanted to fix everything for her. But she wouldn't let him. So, he just held her and tried to show her, without words, that he was here for her, however she needed.

After a few minutes, she sniffled and struggled to speak, gasping the words out.

"And what if this gets worse?" She gestured at her ankle, now resting on the edge of the massive tub. "All I know how to do is dance, and who's going to hire me for choreography gigs? I'll be nadie—no one. And then she'll be right."

It was difficult to follow her rapid-fire verbal spiral into sadness, but he latched on to the last thing she said. "Who will be right?"

He almost missed it, so light were the words. But he was fully awake now, and listening closely.

"My mother."

Ah. He chewed that over, soothing her with soft caresses. When her sobs quieted, he asked, "What will she be right about?"

She hiccupped. "That I'm a failure."

"How, exactly?"

"Nothing I've done has ever been good enough for her. Most of the time, she couldn't even be bothered to come to my shows. And when I got into Lennox, she acted like it was no big deal. A waste of time and money. Why not get a real job or a real degree?"

That surprised Dimitri. Located near Lincoln Center in Manhattan, Lennox was the most prestigious college for the performing arts in the country and notoriously difficult to get into. He'd thought about going there himself, but with Alex's help, he'd already built a career for himself, and he hadn't wanted to get off track.

"Did you go?"

"Of course not." She rubbed her nose. "Gina did. I told her I didn't get in. Instead, I worked, and saved, and waited for Gina to graduate so we could move out here. But then my great-grandmother died, and I couldn't stay in that apartment another second. So, I came out here on my own, and that was a fucking disaster, too."

Everything she said was new to him. He'd known she was from New York, like he was, and he'd known she moved to Los Angeles with Gina and secured a gig on *Everybody Dance Now.* But he suspected there were holes in the story, so he asked, "What happened?"

She shook her head and buried her wet face in his neck. "I don't want to talk about it."

"Okay." There would be time later. He didn't need all her secrets now. But there was one thing he had to try to make clear to her. "You're not a failure, Natasha."

She sniffled hard. "My mother makes me feel like I am. Every step I took, every achievement—it was never good enough. I'm not like Gina. Gina wants to be the best, to be a huge success and a household name. I don't need that. I just want to make a living off being a dancer. To be able to pay my bills and buy nice things. If I can do that, I'll prove that I'm a success. And I was so close, until all this shit started happening."

"What about later, when you can't dance?"

"I don't know. I'll deal with that when I get to it. Maybe… maybe choreography. I don't know."

It was a short-sighted mentality, especially for a career that was so hard on the body. But it was interesting that she'd mentioned choreography again.

"Is this why you're so dead-set on doing everything yourself?"

She nodded. "It doesn't count if people help me, because when they're gone, I'll be nothing. You can't rely on others for help, or you're just asking to be disappointed."

That sounded like something she'd been told, rather than what she truly believed, but she was crying again, so he let it pass.

He held her through the fresh round of tears, murmuring sweet nothings to her in Russian, pressing kisses to her wet cheeks, and bringing tissues to blow her nose. When she was finally quiet, he whispered, "I'm putting you to bed."

She nodded and didn't argue when he picked her up. She didn't pull away when he tucked her into the bed and climbed in beside her, cuddling her close. She let him hold her, let him soothe her, as she drifted off to sleep.

Dimitri didn't rest so easily. He was overwhelmed by all she'd shared, both grateful that she'd trusted him and determined to help her, somehow.

Her mother had done a number on her. But if there was one thing he was good at—other than dancing—it was caring about people. At one point in his life, he'd had nothing but his family. Now, even though they were separated by an entire country, everything he did was for them.

If he'd loved Natasha before, it was nothing compared to the way he felt now. He admired the hell out of her—her quiet strength, her compassion, her work ethic. How could someone so amazing think she was unworthy of love? It was ridiculous to him, but they all had their own demons.

It was on him to show her the truth. By the time he was done, there'd be no doubt in her mind that she was lovable beyond belief.

Chapter Thirty-Six

Nine years ago

Natasha was ready to jump out of her skin with excitement. Why did it have to be Tuesday, Mami's late night at work?

"Cálmate, mija," Abuela said from her spot by the stove, where she stirred a pot of fragrant carne guisado. Why Abuela was making this in May was beyond Natasha, but no one could beat her great-grandmother's beef stew. Abuela refused to use a crockpot, and she was pushing eighty, but she still insisted on prepping dinner every night, even when it was just the two of them.

Natasha clutched the envelope in her hand and grinned.

"I can't calm down," she replied in Spanish.

"Are you going to tell me what that letter says or not?"

"Not yet. Not until Mami gets home."

"Muchacha!" Abuela flapped her hand in a dismissive gesture. "I'll be in bed by then."

It was true. Abuela went to bed early these days and rose before the sun.

"Okay, fine." Natasha pulled a letter from the envelope as her great-grandmother shuffled over in her chancletas to peer at the paper.

"Dear Ms. Díaz," Natasha read in English. "You have been accepted to the Lennox Institute of Performing Arts…"

Abuela let loose a cry of delight and crossed herself, whispering Spanish prayers in soft undertones while Natasha continued to read. When Natasha got to the part about being offered a half scholarship, Abuela whooped again and hugged her.

"This is wonderful news." Abuela held Natasha's face in her hands and pulled her down to lay a smacking kiss on her cheek. Natasha got her height and build from her unknown father, and in this house, she stood out like a tall, skinny scarecrow.

"You're going to be the first in our family to attend college."

"I know." Natasha shimmied her shoulders, vibrating with her excitement. "I can't wait to tell Mami."

"She's going to be very proud of you." Abuela moved back to the stove to check the stew. She sounded so sure, and Natasha wanted to believe her. Maybe this would finally be enough to make her mother proud. Maybe getting a scholarship to the most competitive, most prestigious performing arts college in the country, which would all but ensure her a spot in the Metropolitan Ballet Company, would finally be enough.

She hoped for it, but she'd been burned before. Still, she couldn't stop her heart from beating fast at the thought of presenting her mother with this letter.

Hours passed. Natasha ate dinner with Abuela and they watched an action movie on TV before Abuela went to bed. Natasha tried to do her homework, but she was too excited to focus. She watched a 90s rom-com instead, stretching out on the sofa positioned on the other side of the bookcase that separated her "room" from the rest of the living room.

Idly, she daydreamed about moving into the dorms at Lennox, but she knew that wouldn't happen. She already lived in New York City, even though the Bronx was a fair trek on the train to Lincoln Center. There was no reason to stay in the dorms.

But it would be so cool if she could.

The scrape of the key in the lock woke her. Natasha sat up and blinked at the TV. An old rerun of *Home Is Where the Heart Is* was playing, and she shut it off with a sneer. Once, she'd thought parents acted as perfectly as they did on that show. Life had shown her otherwise.

Waking up to that seemed like a bad sign. Abuela was always looking for omens, and Natasha couldn't help but do it too, even though she didn't believe in her great-grandmother's many superstitions.

Mami entered the apartment, her eyes puffy and shadowed, despite the full face of makeup she wore to the salon every day. This month, her hair was shoulder length, the roots black, and the ends streaked with magenta.

Then Natasha glanced at the clock. Her mother was two hours late.

"Where were you?" she asked.

Mami rolled her eyes and sighed. "The sink in the salon's bathroom flooded. Had to stay late to help clean up."

She headed into the kitchen, and Natasha followed. Mami dumped her bag on one of the kitchen chairs. They all ate at the small rectangular table in the kitchen, since the space that would have been a dining area was Natasha's bedroom. Most of the stew had been put away, but Abuela left some on the stove over low heat. Natasha hovered while her mother lifted the pot lid and sniffed the carne guisado.

"I got some good news today," Natasha said, unable to wait a second longer.

Her mother sat at the table and removed her heeled boots, uttering a soft groan as her stockinged feet were freed. She was petite, so she wore heels at work, and she soaked her feet almost every night. "At least one of us did," she finally replied.

Natasha sat across from her and produced the letter.

"I got into Lennox." She tried to hold back the excitement in her voice, but it was impossible.

Her mother's tired expression didn't change. "Wasn't it obvious that you'd get in? You took pre-college dance courses there."

Natasha had, through her performing arts high school, but that wasn't the point. "They have a seven-percent acceptance rate, and a lot of people apply from all over the world. And not only did I get accepted..." She brandished the paper. "They offered me a half scholarship!"

She waited, smiling, hoping, and praying her mother would smile back.

Esmeralda didn't, of course. She frowned instead.

"Half?" Mami took the paper and scowled at it. Flipping it over, she skimmed the tuition fees. "Holy shit, that's not enough. Look how expensive this place is."

Not enough. Her words rang in Natasha's ears.

Natasha's face fell, but before she could retreat to her "room," Mami kept going.

"Look, I don't care what you do. You're eighteen now, which means you're not my problem anymore. If you want to be thousands of dollars in debt, that's your choice." She flipped the paper again. "But I think you should get a real job or go to a real college, like one of the city schools. They're much cheaper. Don't waste your time and money on a dance school that's never going to earn you a living."

Mami slapped the paper onto the table and returned to the stove.

Natasha sat in silence, the smell of carne filling the kitchen. She wished Abuela were awake. She'd say the right thing and replace the silence with her love.

Mami, as always, had none to give. Natasha didn't know why she'd ever thought she would.

Without a word, Natasha picked up the letter and left the kitchen. Up on her twin-sized loft bed, she found her phone.

There was a text from Gina waiting for her.

Did you get in???

Natasha swallowed hard. It was a few minutes before she replied.

No.

Natasha set the phone aside and stretched out, staring at the ceiling in the dim light. Her eyes found a series of cracks that resembled a dragon's face. The lines had been there for as long as she could remember. And since her bed was so close to the ceiling, she'd spent a lot of time with that dragon.

When she was little, she'd imagined it as a sort of protector, watching over her.

She knew better than to believe in such things now.

Natasha rolled onto her side, unable to tolerate its gaze any longer.

Her mother was right. The student loans would bury her. But there was one thing Mami was wrong about: Natasha *would* make a living from dance.

And she was going to start immediately.

Chapter Thirty-Seven

Present day

Natasha woke the next morning and stared at Dimitri's ceiling for a long time. It had that popcorn stuff on it, but with her glasses on, she picked out faces here and there. Her eyes jumped from one to the next. There, a crooked smiley face. To the right, someone with a big nose and funny glasses. Above that, a sleepy bunny. Diagonal from there, an elf. And back to the beginning.

Her gaze had traced this path other mornings when she'd woken in his bed. Now, warring senses of comfort and awkwardness kept her pinned to the sheets. Should she cuddle with him? Or should she grab her stuff and run-slash-limp away?

Dimitri liked to cuddle, and he never made her feel like she had to get out of his hair, but…there was always the worry that he'd change his mind. Casual flings were nice in a lot of ways, but since there was no commitment, it was impossible to feel totally comfortable in the other person's space. Even now, having spent the last few days in his bed, the dual urges of *run* and *stay* paralyzed her.

Especially after last night.

She closed her eyes and sucked in a breath through her nose at the memory of her breakdown. She couldn't believe she'd unloaded all her fears and mommy issues onto him. Worse, she'd *wanted* to do it. All the worry, the pain, the toxic feelings she kept bottled up—like a dam breaking, the pressure had finally become too much, and it was easier to let it all spill out.

Maybe now he'd understand why she had to get out of here.

Not that she could go anywhere at the moment. Her crutches were still nowhere to be seen, and Dimitri had slung a heavy arm around her middle and buried his face in her shoulder. Rather than feeling trapped, his weight was a comfort. He was *here*. She wasn't alone.

She'd shown him her shadows, and he hadn't run screaming into the night. He'd stuck it out, holding her, soothing her, listening and murmuring endearments in Russian. It didn't matter that she hadn't known the exact words. The sentiment was clear, although her still-raw feelings wouldn't let her read too much into it. Love was a stretch. She didn't believe that was it. But maybe she didn't have to hold back so much. Maybe she could let him in.

After last night, the prospect didn't seem so scary.

Before she could talk herself out of it, she snuggled into his warmth. His eyes didn't open, but his chest rose on a deep inhale, and he shifted his arm to pull her closer.

With her face tucked into his chest, she breathed in the lingering notes of Archangel by Rogelio. She'd researched it once to tease out the scents she so closely associated with Dimitri. Most of them she didn't understand—what the hell were aldehydes? But the others she could pick up. Something woodsy, citrusy, with an overlying layer of what the color green would smell like, if colors had smells.

After a brief moment, his hand rubbed up and down her back, a hot, heavy pressure through the thin fabric of her sleep tank. Then his chin shifted against the top of her head before he laid a kiss on her temple. He was slowly waking up.

"Buenos días," she whispered against his skin.

"Dobroye utro," he replied. He leaned away so he could look at her face. "You slept okay?"

She nodded. "Yeah, I...I did. Thank you."

Instead of the joke she expected in response, he wrapped his arms around her. "Anything you need, Kroshka."

They fell into an easy rhythm after that. For the next few days, Dimitri was attentive without smothering her, and in return, Natasha made an effort to be more pleasant. She dutifully completed her physical therapy exercises for her ankle, and while Dimitri was at the restaurant, Lori and Kevin visited to keep her company and fill her in on gossip.

Natasha did not call her mother or Gina.

Miracle of miracles, her injury seemed to have escaped the notice of the gossip sites, and Kevin claimed no one at *The Dance Off* knew Natasha was living with Dimitri.

"Staying," she corrected him. "Temporarily."

Her bank account told a different story. As July ticked into August, all her bills were due, including rent on the apartment she couldn't currently live in. But since her stuff was there, she still had to pay. She had just enough to cover everything, but after missing so much work, she was back in financial jeopardy. On top of that, she couldn't find anyone to cover her children's ballet class.

The night before the class, she mentioned it during dinner—a meal provided by Krasavitsa.

"Will you be around in the morning?" she asked Dimitri. "I'm not sure I can drive yet, and I need to get to Santa Monica to teach."

His expression turned stormy, and he dropped his fork onto his steak. "No. You haven't healed enough."

"Relax, Macho." She sipped from her wine glass. The man

really did have an excellent selection of wine. "It's a ballet class for little kids. I won't have to do much."

He cut his meat with angry movements. "It's a bad idea."

"Doesn't matter. I can't cancel, and I can't find anyone to cover for me. I have to go in."

He chewed quickly. "I'll do it."

Her eyebrows shot up, and she held back a laugh because he looked perfectly serious. "You'll do what?"

"I'll help you. You sit on the side with your foot elevated, and I'll teach the class."

She shouldn't agree. Dimitri was big and bearded and gruff. Her students were tiny and high-spirited and giggly. It was going to be a disaster.

Or it would be *adorable*.

"Okay," she said, fighting a grin.

Dimitri nodded and went back to eating. It was settled.

DIMITRI WAS CLEANING up their dinner plates when Carlito called from the restaurant.

"Yeah, what?" Dimitri tucked the phone into the crook of his neck as he loaded the dishwasher.

"Your mother is here."

Dimitri exhaled heavily through his nose. "Put her on."

"Bueno. Here she is, jefe."

A moment later, his mother came on the line. "Privet, moy syn."

Dimitri bit back a sigh and switched over to Russian. "Allo, Mama. What are you doing in Los Angeles?"

"The weather is beautiful. Does one need a reason to visit?"

Okay, so that was how this was going to go. "Is Papa with you?"

"No, he went to Florida to visit Nik on his tour."

Divide and conquer, huh? "Why are you at the restaurant?"

"I was hungry. Come meet me."

He'd just left there a few hours earlier, and he'd already eaten, but Dimitri couldn't say no to his mother. "Fine. But I can't stay long. You have a hotel already?"

"Yes, a good one. Don't worry, I won't intrude on your love nest."

His *love nest*? Jesus. "Thanks. I appreciate it."

"Was that sarcasm?"

"Never. See you soon, Mama."

Since he'd already changed into sweats, Dimitri dashed into his room for slacks and one of the expensive polo shirts he wore when he wanted to wear a T-shirt and couldn't get away with it. Then he found Natasha in the living room with her laptop balanced on her outstretched legs.

Her eyebrows drew together when she saw him dressed to go out. "Where are you going?"

"Emergency at the restaurant."

"You were just there."

"This can't wait. I'm sorry. I'll be back soon."

Her lips pursed in a worried frown. "I have to leave early tomorrow for the dance class."

"I won't be out late." He kissed her forehead, paused because he wanted to do more, then thought better of it. If his mother got tired of waiting, she'd come here. "I promise."

Natasha shrugged and turned back to her laptop. "I hope it's only a minor emergency."

"Me too."

He hurried to the garage. As he climbed into the Porsche, he prayed for no traffic.

He felt bad leaving Natasha at home alone. She was used to working all the time and wasn't the kind of person who handled idleness or boredom well.

If he could convince her to move in, to let him take care of her, she wouldn't have to work so hard. Sure, she could still work as much or as little as she wanted, but he didn't think the constant cycle of quick-paying gigs made her happy. He got it, and he'd been in that position himself, but now he had enough sources of income that he could live comfortably and take care of the people he loved. Really, it was all he wanted out of life. He loved dance, loved being a dancer, but it was secondary to his love for his family and the desire to make them comfortable.

Natasha fell into that category now, whether she believed it or not.

She obviously didn't believe he loved her. Maybe he should have said more, been more convincing. After all, he'd kind of sprung it on her out of nowhere. But she hadn't pulled away from him, so he was trying to give her space, being there for her without pushing, because he'd noticed that when he pushed, she retreated.

Except now they were locked in this weird stalemate. She didn't seem like she was about to run away, which made him happy, but their relationship wasn't much closer to where he wanted it to be, and that worried him.

What if it never got to where he wanted it to be? What if she just didn't want that with him?

It was the fear that kept him from laying all his cards on the table. It was the same fear that had him avoiding Alex.

What if he put himself out there and was rejected?

Dimitri didn't know how to proceed with Natasha. Did she need *more* space? She seemed fine with sharing his room, but she'd made a really big deal about it in the beginning. Maybe she wanted her own space back but was scared to tell him.

Bringing his mother into the equation would *not* help matters, that he was sure of. Natasha had enough issues with her own mother. He didn't know what the woman was like, but he suspected Oksana Kovalenko was probably the opposite. He'd gotten his pushiness from his mother. If Oksana met Natasha and liked her, she'd be planning their wedding by the end of the week.

And while Dimitri sort of liked that idea, he'd bet Natasha

wouldn't, and it would ruin all the progress they'd made. As much as he wanted his mother to meet the woman of his dreams, it wasn't the right time. He had to find out how Natasha felt first.

So ask her, Alex would say.

In their family, Alex was the pragmatic one, while Dimitri was the *dramatic* one, although he preferred the word "passionate." This situation with Natasha was the kind of thing Dimitri would have asked Alex about if he weren't actively avoiding his cousin.

Stop running away from your dreams, Alex's most recent text had read. Perceptive asshole.

Dimitri pulled into the lot next to Krasavitsa and jumped out of the car, tossing the keys to Raul, the lead valet.

"Back again?" Raul asked.

"No rest for the wicked." Dimitri went in through the front, nodding at everyone as he passed.

His mother was seated at one of the best tables. It boasted both a full view of the restaurant and relative privacy.

"Mama." He leaned down to greet her.

"You walk in here like you own the place." She gave him a kiss on the cheek.

"I do." He sat across from her. "Now, you want to tell me why you're really here? I know it's not for the borscht."

"I told you, I'm having dinner." She spread her hands to indicate the assortment of plates on the table.

"What, did you order one of everything?"

She winked. "I know the owner. So, let's get to the real reason why I'm here."

He held his breath.

"I want to meet her."

He exhaled. There it was. "Not yet."

His mother's brows—waxed to within an inch of their life, since they were naturally as thick as his own—arched. "Why not?"

"She's…" He trailed off as Sergei, one of the waiters who was fluent in Russian, appeared with an extra wine glass and set it at his elbow. Dimitri waited until Sergei left, then poured from the open bottle of red on the table, just to have something to do. "Puglivaya." There. That was the perfect word for Natasha.

His mother frowned. "What does she have to be skittish about? You will make a great husband. I made sure of that."

"I know that. And you know that. But she doesn't trust me."

His mother frowned and munched on a French fry. They were her weakness, and he'd grown up with an appreciation for good fries. The ones at Krasavitsa were excellent, crafted to Dimitri's particular specifications—skinny, salty, slightly crunchy, and served in a cone with ketchup and garlic aioli on the side.

"Why doesn't she trust you?" His mother pinned him with a shrewd gaze. "Have you given her reason not to?"

Dimitri stole some of her fries and scooped up a healthy dollop of aioli with them. "I guess I have."

Her eyes rolled up to the ceiling. "I don't want to know."

"It's better that you don't."

"So, what are you doing now to show her that she *can* trust you?"

He finished chewing, lest she tell him not to talk with his mouth full. "I'm trying to show her."

"Odobreniye." She shrugged. "But *how*?"

"What, specifically?"

"Yes."

"Well, she sprained her ankle."

"Is she also a dancer?"

If he weren't careful, his mother would ask enough questions to guess Natasha's identity. Oksana watched every episode of *The Dance Off*. Lori Kim and Danny Johnson were her favorite pros, but she certainly knew who Natasha was and would likely have opinions about her. "Um, yes."

"Do I know her?"

Blyat. "Mama…"

She held up her hands. "Fine. You tell me when you're ready. Continue."

"Right. So, she sprained her ankle, and I'm taking care of her."

His mother's expression softened. "That's sweet of you."

"I'm trying to show her she doesn't have to be alone. But she thinks she does. She doesn't want my help."

"Women want to be independent, Dima. She's not going to want you because she needs you to make her life good, but because her life is already good and you make it better."

He sat back in his seat and mulled that over. "You're saying I shouldn't want her to need my help?"

"I'm saying, if she wants to prove she can do it on her own, she doesn't want you to prove that she *can't*."

Frustrated, he swirled the wine in his glass and scowled at the soft light reflecting through it. "So, what do I do? Nothing? Don't help her? She's in a bad situation. She needs help."

"Are you sure?"

When he blinked at her, she looked away and sipped her wine.

"Am I sure about what? That she needs help?" When his mother didn't answer, he leaned in. "She does need help. She's broke, her apartment is under construction, and she's injured. I'm doing everything I can to help her, short of giving her money, and that's only because I know she won't accept it. She needs my help."

His mother was immune to his stubbornness. After all, she was ten times more stubborn than he was. She only shrugged and said again, "Are you sure *that's* what she *needs*?"

He opened his mouth to argue, then shut it. "I'm…" He had been sure. But now that his mother had pointed it out, his brain started poking at the problem from different angles.

An uneasy feeling spread through his gut. What if he was going about this all wrong? Trying to anticipate and meet all of

Natasha's needs. She needed a home, he provided one. She needed a ride, he drove her. He was trying to show her he cared, but she wasn't buying it. What could he do differently? What did she *really* need?"

I don't want your help, she'd said. Okay, but what else? He thought back to her raw confession from the middle of the night.

You're going to let me care about you.

You shouldn't.

Why not?

Because I don't deserve it.

Those words had haunted him. And now they gave him his answer.

"I have to show her…that she deserves to be loved."

"Ah." His mother smiled and reached for his hand across the table. He clasped her small fingers in his big ones, stunned as always that his larger-than-life mother was, in reality, a small woman. Her eyes glistened, and she smiled like she was proud of him. "And how do you do that?"

This was the part he hadn't figured out yet. "I guess it's not by bullying her to do her physical therapy exercises."

Once again, Oksana looked to the ceiling for patience. It was something she did a lot around him. "Figure it out, Dima. I believe in you. Now, drop me off at my hotel and go back to your woman."

As they left the restaurant and waited for Raul to bring the car around, Dimitri gave his mother a sidelong glance. "Did you really fly all the way to California to ask me about this?"

She shrugged. "I had the miles. And besides, you've been ignoring your cousin, so why should I think you'd have this conversation unless I forced you into it?"

He shook his head and took the keys from Raul when he pulled up. After they climbed in and his mother buckled up, she said, "I still want to meet her."

Dimitri sighed. "Soon."

He hoped.

Chapter Thirty-Eight

Natasha briefed Dimitri on the class while he drove them to Little Lilac Dance Studio in Santa Monica.

"I met Lilah, the owner, after I moved to LA," she explained. "We were roommates for a little while before Gina got here, but we kept in touch. After I started working on *EDN*, Lilah asked me to teach a children's class during the summers. It's good promo for the school."

"So, she's using you?"

Natasha shook her head. "She pays me. Not a lot, but... This isn't a class for training the next ballet prodigies. It's about having fun through movement. And I...I can't explain it."

He gave her a quick glance. "Try?"

Staring out the window, Natasha tapped into the feeling of being at Little Lilac and let the words flow. "The kids are adorable and enthusiastic. I teach them the basics, but we also play games, sing songs, and do arts and crafts. In all the other classes I teach, the people are there with an agenda. These kids just want to have fun. And..." She swallowed hard. "They love me."

His gaze cut to hers, and his eyes were serious when he said, "Of course they do."

She ducked her head and looked out the window. Until his declaration in the living room a few days ago, she couldn't remember the last time someone had said they loved her, except for these children. Abuela used to say it, but Mami? Never.

And while Natasha knew she'd be better off staying quiet for the rest of the ride, he'd pulled the lid off her feelings, and she couldn't hold back what slipped out next. "With everything else I've done for work since moving to Los Angeles, Little Lilac is the one that feeds my soul. I can't give it up."

She expected him to argue with her about how financially irresponsible that was, but when he spoke, his tone was resonant with understanding. "It's important to have something like that. A reminder that dance is more than just a job, that we didn't initially get into this for the money."

"That's true," she agreed. "But I still want both. I want to dance *and* make money at it."

He shifted lanes and topics. "How young are the girls?"

"This is the three-four-five class. And they aren't all girls. There are two boys, although we call everyone 'friends,' as opposed to gendered terms."

He nodded and didn't question it.

Nerves fluttered in her belly as they parked in the tiny lot next to the building. Lilah had won a big chunk of cash through a talent competition, then used it to open the studio. It was Lilah's passion, in a way dancing professionally had never been.

Natasha envied her that a little. It was the same way that Gina's dreams and drive sometimes made Natasha feel inadequate for not being as ambitious.

"Don't you want more, Tash?" Gina used to ask. Natasha always gave a flippant shrug in reply and said something along the lines of, "More than paying my bills and living large? What else is there?"

Inside, though, she envied their dreams, their direction, their sense of hope.

Hope. Thanks to her mother, Natasha had locked that urge

away a long time ago. What was the use in hoping for more? In wanting more?

But as Dimitri came around and helped her out of the passenger seat, handing her the crutches one at a time, her heart fluttered with something suspiciously like longing.

Natasha slammed it back down. No use longing for something she'd never have. Sure, he wanted to help her *now*. How long would that last? It wasn't worth entertaining the idea.

And anyway, they had a ballet class to teach.

"Do you have any experience with this?" she asked, crutching over the gravel to the side entrance.

"You think I can't teach a kids' ballet class?"

"That's not what I said." She pointed to the side door, and he held it open so she could hobble in. "I didn't ask if you *could*, I asked if you have experience."

"Let's make a bet."

She rolled her eyes and pointed to the locker where he could stash her purse. "What kind of bet?"

"If this isn't an unmitigated success…you can go back to the guest room."

Her breath halted.

She'd still been sleeping in his bed. There'd been a lot of cuddling, but nothing more. As much as she'd first complained about the arrangement, she'd gotten used to sleeping beside him, and she didn't *want* to go back to the other room. But did *he* want her to?

"And if it *is* a complete success," he went on, "you'll have dinner with me tonight at Kras."

That made her pause.

It shouldn't bother her that he hadn't yet taken her to the place that consumed so much of his time and attention. They never went out together. They didn't go on *dates*. They were just two people who worked on the same TV show. Occasionally they went on group outings with the rest of the cast, and sometimes they screwed. But they weren't a couple, and this wasn't a *relationship*.

But if all that were true...

His words from the other night echoed in her head. *Would I be in love with you?*

If they were just fuck buddies, just roommates with benefits, why would he say that? And now, with this stupid bet, he was either going to kick her out of his bed or take her on a date.

None of it made sense.

"So, is it a bet?"

She blinked. They were about to enter the studio, and he was holding a hand out for her to shake.

"Um...whatever." She shook his hand. "Open the door. And remember, no cursing in front of the kids."

He shot her a wounded look. "What do you take me for?"

"You really want me to answer that?"

He laughed and held the door open for her.

As she crossed the threshold, Natasha switched into teacher mode. With a big smile on her face, she hobbled into the room on her crutches, noting the looks of surprise and worry on her students' small faces.

"Hi, friends!" she said brightly, hoping her tone would allay their fears.

Cara, a three-year-old in a purple tie-dye leotard, hopped up from her spot on the floor and touched Natasha's left hand where it gripped the crutch. "Miss Tasha, what's this for?"

"What happened, Miss Tasha?" Emiko, the oldest at five-and-a-half, came closer, and the others crowded in around them, asking more questions.

Mindful of the children gathered around her, Natasha made her way to the chairs Lilah's assistant had positioned next to the sound system. She took a seat and propped her foot on the second chair. "I tripped a little bit," she told them, giving an exaggerated shrug. "I'll be fine in a few days."

"Does it hurt?" Ryan, an energetic five-year-old boy, stared at the wrapping around Natasha's bare foot. His little hand crept closer.

"Not anymore," she told him. "But I still have bruises, so I have to be extra careful."

Ryan snatched his hand away, then shifted through the crowd of kids so she could give him a one-armed hug. He'd been in the class since he was three, and of all the kids, he was the most attached to her. He had already cried twice about not having Natasha as his teacher once he turned six.

As she assured them she was okay, their curious gazes drifted over to Dimitri, who stood off to one side.

"Who's that?" Sofia, at four, finally voiced the question that must have been on all their young minds. She pointed a finger straight at Dimitri and did not look impressed.

"That's Mr. Dima," Natasha told them. "My friend. Since I can't stand up for very long, he's here to help us."

Ryan looked skeptical. "Can he dance?"

Natasha stifled a chuckle. "Um, yes. He's a very good dancer." She clapped her hands. "All right, friends. Time to take your places."

The children scrambled to their spots on the brightly colored plastic circles spaced around the floor, already set out by Lilah's assistant, who sat in the front waiting area, watching the parents.

Dimitri sidled closer as the kids took their places. "Mr. Dima?"

"Dimitri has too many syllables," she said in a hushed tone. "You don't want to hear them mangle it."

"Actually, I did."

They shared a smile, and then she directed him to take her usual spot in the front of the room. She turned on the music and called out instructions from her chair. Dimitri demonstrated, and the kids followed his moves, sneaking looks at her periodically. Natasha kept a smile fixed to her face as she counted out loud.

When it came time to put the moves in order, Dimitri took over, leading the class. She manned the music, stopping and starting as necessary, and tried to close her heart to the scene before her.

Dimitri was a natural, damn him. His deep, booming voice, which had made some of the top dancers in the industry nearly shit their tights, managed to sound comforting and encouraging when he talked to the children. He did silly moves to make them laugh and he was attentive to each child, looking them in the eye as he listened, and speaking to them as equals.

There was something wrong with her. She'd never been the kind of woman to get all sappy about a guy interacting with kids. But these were *her* kids. She cared about them, and she cared about the work that was done at this school, how it fostered an appreciation of dance that had nothing to do with how well the children completed moves and everything to do with how much they loved what they were doing.

Once upon a time, when Natasha was their age, dance had saved her. It had provided her with a focus for her life and a community of people who understood her. Dance had given her value when her mother hadn't.

Her first dance teacher, Mr. Richie, had seen Natasha's promise. He'd nurtured her talent and interest. At the time, she'd hoped her mother would see her skill and be proud of her.

It had never happened.

So, Natasha did her part here, because she knew firsthand how much it meant to have an adult who wasn't a parent be invested in a child's well-being.

For her, it had been priceless. And she'd been blessed to have other dance teachers later who had also cared.

Who would she be now if not for them?

Who are you if you're not a dancer?

No, this wasn't the time to think about that. She *was* a dancer. She had to be.

It was all she had.

She glanced at her ankle. It was almost fully healed. She'd be back in fighting shape in a day or two, would probably be running around already if not for Nursemaid Dimitri.

He was singing a song with the kids while they waved their arms and acted out the lyrics. He was a terrible singer—not that she was one to talk—but his low, rich voice made up for being off-key. Normally, his voice gave her delicious chills, goosebumps, and a sweet tingle she craved. When he growled her name or called her Kroshka—hell, even when she overheard him backstage at *The Dance Off*—she came close to throwing herself at his feet.

But she never had. That would reveal how much she wanted him.

Today, though, his voice had a different effect. Rather than setting her on edge in a sensual way, keeping her in a state of suspended tension where she never knew what he'd do next, today his voice comforted her. All these days of living with him, hearing him call out to her from a different room, or muttering into the phone in Russian, she'd grown accustomed to his timbre. He'd twined his way into her consciousness and set up residence like he belonged there and had no intention of ever leaving.

And this definitely wasn't the moment to think about *that*, either.

"Time for the last song," she called out. "Will you all show Mr. Dima what we've been practicing?"

The kids ran to their places, and Dimitri stepped aside to watch. Natasha turned on their recital song, calling out the moves while the children went through them with uncharacteristic seriousness.

When they were done, she and Dimitri broke into applause. Dimitri stuck two fingers in his mouth and whistled.

The kids beamed and rushed them both, full of smiles and questions. Natasha fielded them one by one as the parents hovered by the doors.

Dimitri's hearty laugh made Natasha glance over. He had

two kids hanging from each bicep, their delighted squeals ringing through the air. His eyes met hers over the children's heads, and he shot her a smile full of...

She didn't know what. It scared her too much to put a name to it.

But at that look, her heart rolled over in her chest and woke the hell up.

Chapter Thirty-Nine

"You were really good with the kids," Natasha said in a quiet voice.

Dimitri cut her a quick look as he drove. After they'd left Little Lilac, she said she had to make a quick stop on the way home to hand something off to someone who was covering one of her classes.

"This isn't my first rodeo, Kroshka. My mother owned a dance school, and I used to help her teach."

She twisted in the seat to face him. "What does that word mean? Kroshka."

He raised his eyebrows. "You're just now asking this? I've been calling you that for years."

Her chin dipped. Half her face was covered by big, dark sunglasses. He wanted to slip them off her face so he could see her eyes but kept his attention on the road.

"I...didn't want to ask, I guess."

"Why not?"

She shrugged. "Just tell me what it means."

"It's the equivalent of 'baby' or 'sweetheart,' although the literal translation is 'crumb,' like a bread crumb."

"Huh." She turned her head to gaze out the window.

"Why do you call me Macho?"

She smirked. "Aside from the obvious, it's short for 'machote,' which is like a tough guy."

The urge to touch her was killing him. He gave in, dropping a hand to her bare knee and squeezing. "You should learn Russian."

She snorted. "I had a hard enough time learning English."

"Me, too. And I bet I was older than you were."

She shifted in the seat, and his hand slid further up her thigh. "How old were you when you moved here from Ukraine?"

"Ten."

"Wow. Yeah, you were older."

"You were born here." It wasn't a question. He already knew she'd been born in New York.

"Yes, but we only spoke Spanish at home. I learned English from TV and other kids, and it wasn't until preschool that I heard English from an adult. After that, my great-grandfather started speaking English to me at home." She fiddled with her glasses. "And books. Somehow, the language divide didn't seem so strong when it was written down. I learned a lot about how English was supposed to sound from reading, but since I was a terrible writer, I still got bad grades in school. It drove me crazy. I loved books so much, but I couldn't express my thoughts about them in a way the teachers could understand."

He gave her leg another light squeeze. "I get it."

"I bet." She rested her head against the back of the seat and turned her face toward him. "Tell me about little Dima."

He chewed his lower lip as he sorted through the feelings raging through him. Gratitude and love threatened to overwhelm him. The easy conversation, her willingness to tell him about herself, and her interest in him—those had to be signs they were growing closer. Right?

But she wanted to know about his childhood, and it was something he didn't talk about much.

"You don't have to tell me." She leaned back in the seat. "It's okay."

"No, I want to." In his rush to answer, his voice came out loud and gruff. He tried again. "I want you to know about me. I just...I don't think about that time a lot. I try to forget it, you know?"

"Dimitri, you don't have to—"

"I do." He took a deep breath and thumped the wheel with both hands. "You know how adults talk about politics in front of kids in this roundabout way, thinking they won't understand? As the government was collapsing, my parents and aunts and uncles did their best to keep us from worrying, but I knew something was up, and it freaked me out."

She nodded, and now she reached out and placed a hand on his knee, warm and comforting.

"When we arrived from Odessa, we had a slightly easier time of it than some, because my aunt and uncle and cousins had moved here first. They helped us get set up, but for a while we all lived in the same house." He flicked her a glance. "That's why my cousin Alex and I are so close. We grew up together, and we're close in age. Nik was still a toddler when all this was going on. He doesn't remember any of it."

"Do you think it affects him?" she asked softly.

He shifted in his seat. "I guess it does. Our experiences with the move were different. He can't stay in one place for long, but me? All I want is for everything to stay settled."

Her fingers rubbed his leg, and despite the serious conversation, he wanted her badly. He gripped the wheel hard.

"You're very close to your parents," she said.

"They were my rock. Stable, even though everything else was in upheaval."

Her lips twisted. "I'm glad you had that."

He dropped one hand to capture hers, bringing it to his lips. The words welled up in him, the need to tell her he could be that for her, that he loved her and would stand by her.

But his mother was correct. Right now, Tasha didn't think she deserved love. So it was on Dimitri to convince her that she did.

Chapter Forty

Natasha's nerves jitterbugged as Dimitri pulled up in front of the gym.

"I'll find a spot to park," he said, but she shook her head quickly.

"No need." She opened the door and climbed out awkwardly with the crutches. "Stay in the car. I'll just run in and hand this over, and then I'll be back." She maneuvered a tote bag over her neck.

His eyebrows drew together like he knew something was up, but he didn't say anything as she shut the car door and hobbled into the gym.

At least he hadn't insisted on following her.

Natasha greeted the woman at the front desk, exchanged small talk about her ankle and the minor repairs to the gym's locker room, then crutched her way toward the classroom where she usually taught.

Before leaving the reception area, Natasha checked over her shoulder once more. Dimitri hadn't come in. Good. No matter what, he could *not* meet Renee. Renee would lead to all sorts of questions that Natasha wasn't prepared to answer.

The classroom door was ajar, so Natasha stuck her head in. "Hello?"

Renee sat in the corner on a folding chair, typing on a tablet with one finger. When she looked up, her face brightened. "Tash!"

Natasha eased into the room as Renee set the tablet aside and strolled over to her, navigating around the series of poles set into the floor. Even barefoot, in boy shorts and a camisole, with no makeup on and her wine-red hair pulled into a ponytail, Renee walked like she was on a runway and every eye was on her.

Renee had taught Natasha that trick, and while Natasha had managed it on stage, if she wasn't thinking about it, she still walked with her feet turned out, like the ballerina she was.

Andas como una patita, her mother used to say. You walk like a little duck.

Renee gave Natasha a one-armed hug and took the tote bag full of grip aids from her. "How's the ankle?"

"Better. Being extra careful with it."

"Smart move." Renee gestured toward the chair. "Here, you should sit down."

"How's everything going at the Planet?" Natasha asked once she was seated, using the affectionate nickname for their old workplace.

Renee settled down on the floor with her legs folded under her. "Same old. They finally renovated the dressing room and the bathrooms."

"Good. They needed to."

As Renee gave a quick rundown of the workplace gossip, Natasha gazed around at the poles, and her earlier nerves transformed into unease.

Once, this had been her life. She'd been desperate then, and she was desperate now. In both cases, she'd entered into situations that, while not untenable to her, had forced her to lie to her friends and family. Hell, she'd still be lying to everyone about living with Dimitri if she hadn't sprained her ankle.

Both times, she'd been broke and in need of paid work. *Dance* work. Because it didn't count if she wasn't dancing.

Although that rule was starting to seem more and more ridiculous.

Renee stretched out her long legs and leaned back on her elbows. Her enormous, round breasts strained the stretchy fabric of her turquoise top. "By the way, Jeff says hi."

Jeff, one of the nicest bosses Natasha had ever had. "Thanks. Tell him hi for me."

"You could tell him yourself." Renee rummaged in her purse, then handed Natasha a postcard. "I'm hosting a burlesque show tonight. You should come by."

"There you are, Kroshka."

Natasha promptly dropped the card when Dimitri strode into the room, his typical hurricane-force charisma swirling around him.

Her voice came out tight. "I thought you were going to wait in the car."

He ignored that and turned his grin on Renee. "Dimitri Kovalenko. Pleasure to meet you."

"Red Hott, but you can call me Renee." Renee sent him a sultry smile from the floor. It wasn't personal, Natasha knew. All of Renee's smiles were some degree of sultry.

Dimitri reached down to shake Renee's hand, then he stooped to pick up the card. His eyes flicked over it. "Are we going to a show, Tasha?"

"Um…" She glanced at Renee, who wore her usual slightly amused expression. Full lips curved, bedroom eyes unreadable.

Natasha bit her lip, waiting for Dimitri to react. His brow creased as he read the card. "Babe Planet?"

"It's the name of the venue," Renee offered. "You're both welcome to come. I'll put your names on the guest list."

"What do you say, Tasha?" Dimitri raised an eyebrow, but Natasha couldn't read his expression either. Was he curious? Judgmental? Turned on?

She looked to Renee, who still wore her cat-with-cream smile. No help from that quarter.

Natasha's fluttering nerves picked up the pace. As much as she wanted to yell "No thanks!" and hustle Dimitri out of the room, something else bubbled up inside her.

The urge to tell him the truth.

Sharing with him on the drive here had left her feeling lighter. She had so many secrets, but she was unburdening them on him, one by one.

Why not one more?

In a faint voice, she said, "Sure, let's go."

Dimitri turned to Renee. "It's tonight?"

"Yes." Renee took the hand Dimitri gave her and rose to her feet. After he helped Natasha up and she was balanced on the crutches, Renee leaned in and kissed Natasha on the cheek, leaving behind the scent of rosewater.

"See you later, dear." Followed by a sassy wink. And then she added, "Until then, Mr. Judge."

Dimitri led the way out of the room, winding around the poles and making sure the door was open wide enough for Natasha to get through easily. Once they were in the hallway, she shot him a dark look.

"You were supposed to stay in the car."

"I found a parking spot." He lowered his voice. "What, I'm not allowed to take a piss?"

She huffed. "How did you even get in?"

"The lovely woman at the front desk is a fan."

Sure enough, as they were leaving, the lady behind the desk waved and called out, "Bye, Mr. Kovalenko!"

Dimitri sent her a charming smile and opened the door for Natasha to exit the gym.

Natasha kept her mouth shut as they got in the car and back on the freeway. By some miracle, he hadn't peppered her with questions yet, but he had to have figured it out. After meeting

Renee, seeing that card, and...shit, had she mentioned that Renee was a former coworker?

As her mind searched for ways to lie or get out of telling him the whole story, her heart made a decision.

She would tell him the truth. It was a secret she'd kept for years, but she wanted to talk about it with someone. No, more than that, she wanted to talk about it with *him*. Maybe he would understand. Maybe he wouldn't judge her.

Dimitri wasn't her mother.

When she'd first met him, Natasha had equated Esmeralda and Dimitri in her head, connecting them with her need for validation. If she couldn't get it from her mother, maybe she could get it from him, the guy who expected the best and was notorious for withholding praise. Even when they started sleeping together, it was with that same kind of longing. If the man who withheld commitment could give her a sign that this was more than just a fling…

Well, he'd given her a sign now. He'd said he *loved* her.

What if he meant it?

Her mother never said it. But Natasha was finally realizing that Dimitri was nothing like her mother. He was a natural caretaker, concerned about everyone around him. His family, his restaurant, *her*.

What if he did love her? What did that even mean? Natasha had so little experience with it that she didn't even know. Did he love having sex with her? Having her in his home? Eating her cooking? What were all the little things that added up to the bigger emotion of love?

Her heart pointed the way to the people who'd shown her their love. It was a short list. Abuela. Gina. Even Kevin and Lori. Just look at the way they'd stepped up to help her out after her injury.

Abuela had taken care of Natasha until the day she'd died. Beyond making sure Natasha was clean and fed, Abuela had valued Natasha's feelings and had given her space to explore them.

Dimitri did that, too. The night Natasha had broken down in his bathroom, he'd held her and listened.

And Gina. Gina had been taking care of Natasha since they'd met at fourteen years old. When Gina had applied for colleges and scholarships, she'd also made sure Natasha filled out all the same forms. When they moved to Los Angeles, Gina had lined up auditions for both of them. It had never been a competition. Everything they did, they did together. Gina had never left Natasha behind.

Even now, Gina had offered to pay her portion of the rent until the lease was up. But at the time, Natasha had stubbornly wanted to prove she could do it on her own.

But who was she proving this to? Her mother? Gina? Herself?

If Gina were here, she would have done everything Dimitri had done at the hospital. Badgered the doctors, taken notes on healing and recovery, and made a schedule for Natasha's meds, ice packs, and physical therapy.

Dimitri had done all of that and had even called her friends to ensure she wouldn't be alone. He'd brought her glasses to the hospital so she wouldn't be stuck wearing contacts. He carried her around the house and drove her wherever she needed to go.

What did it all mean? Was that love? Was that what it amounted to—listening and caring?

"You're thinking a lot over there."

She blinked at the sound of his deep voice, then checked the signs out the window. They were almost home.

Home. Dimitri's home.

"Got a lot on my mind," she said.

He made a noise of assent in the back of his throat. "Anything you want to share?"

A month ago, he would have demanded she tell him.

A month ago, she would have refused to answer.

Now, she took a deep breath and let it out slowly. "Yes, actually. When we get home."

Home. There was that word again.

He nodded, and when she looked at him from the corner of her eye, she thought she saw him smile.

Chapter Forty-One

Five years ago

The exterior of Babe Planet looked about how Natasha had expected: a plain concrete building with a neon sign out front, the name written in futuristic script with a small ringed planet worked through the letters.

Inside, it looked like a regular dive bar, albeit with a central stage and a catwalk outfitted with a few poles at regular intervals. The furniture was basic and cheap. So was the menu. But the cocktails were "out of this world," according to the sign out front.

Everything was dark blue or deep purple, with pink and green neon accents, although the effect of those was lost at the moment because the house lights were on.

The decor consisted of kitschy sci-fi movie and TV paraphernalia, creating a retro-futurism meets rock 'n roll vibe. There were framed pulp-style art prints of men with phallic-looking blasters, women falling out of the tops of their skin-tight spacesuits, and sexy aliens getting it on.

To Natasha's surprise, she didn't hate it. This was a place that didn't take itself too seriously and knew exactly what it was and wasn't. According to the website, the venue was known for its eclectic performances and hosted everything from album release parties to fashion shows. She wasn't sure if that was normal for a "bikini bar" or not, this being her first time in one.

Jeff, the manager, seemed impressed by her credentials. He was a white guy with sandy hair, in his late forties, if she had to guess. He looked her in the eye when he spoke to her and treated her like a human being. He asked questions and listened to her answers before commenting.

He was more respectful than many of the casting directors and producers she'd encountered. Still, she couldn't believe she was here.

"All right, Natasha. Let's see you dance."

In the main area of the bar, Natasha perched on one of the purple vinyl chairs and swapped her sandals for pointe shoes. She climbed up on the stage, which extended into the room like a runway, and did a few warm-up stretches. Since she'd never pole danced before, she was going to show what she *could* do.

Behind the bar, a young Asian woman with a faux hawk and lots of tattoos stacked clean glasses in the rack over her head. An older white man mopped the floor by the front door. At Natasha's nod, Jeff turned on the music, and she began to move. Arabesque, grand jete, plié, and so many spins. She arched and twirled, leaping across a stage that probably wasn't meant for such forceful jumps, but Jeff didn't stop her. When she came to the end of the runway, she struck a pose, eyes out at the imaginary audience. The woman at the bar and the man with the mop joined Jeff in clapping. Feeling lighter than she had when she arrived, Natasha bowed.

"Well, you're certainly good at ballet," Jeff said. "You were going to show us another dance style?"

She nodded, and after she changed her shoes, a new song came on, a salsa remix she'd danced to countless times.

To the sound of horns, she spun and flounced across the stage and down the catwalk, shaking her hips, shimmying her shoulders, and grinning widely for the imaginary audience. She displayed moves from a variety of Latin dances—salsa, samba, cha-cha-cha—moving seamlessly from one to the other.

When Jeff shut off the music, she curtseyed, and everyone clapped again. This time, Natasha noticed another woman had joined Jeff near the stage. She had a pale complexion, dyed red hair done in big tousled curls, and her voluptuous figure was encased in a tank top and bikini bottoms.

"You're clearly an accomplished dancer," Jeff said when Natasha climbed down from the stage. "You might want to work on your facial expression, to get somewhere in between a scowl and a giant grin, but that's easy. Ready to give the pole a shot?"

At Natasha's confident nod, he brought the other woman forward. "This is Renee. She'll give you some pointers."

Renee was barefoot, so Natasha took off her shoes and slid off the wrap dress she wore over a camisole and dance shorts.

"Do you have lotion on your skin?" Renee asked as they took the stage and stood next to two poles.

Natasha shook her head. Delfina had warned her not to wear moisturizer. It made it harder to stick to the pole.

"Good." Renee launched into an explanation of the basics and demonstrated some moves. Natasha watched carefully, noting hand placement, balance, and body lines. She followed along, and soon, she was getting the hang of it.

It felt good to be learning new moves. Natasha forgot about Jeff, the job, and her bank account, and threw herself into it.

She didn't know how much time had passed before the music clicked off. Natasha clung to the pole, blinking, as once again, everyone clapped. Jeff wore a big smile as she and Renee hopped down from the stage.

"Are you sure you've never done that before?" he asked.

Natasha shook her head. "Never."

"Well, that was amazing for your first time."

The praise soaked into her like the sun on a hot, humid beach day. After all the rejection she'd faced since arriving in LA, it was nice to be recognized for her talent.

But on the flipside, working at a bikini bar wasn't what she'd come to LA to do. Her mother could never know about this. Neither could Gina—she'd never understand.

And if Natasha couldn't rub it in her mother's face, what was the point?

She knew what was coming next. Part of her dreaded it, but another part wanted to get it over with. Natasha had been psyching herself up for this all week, since she'd met Delfina and gone on five more failed auditions.

Jeff was going to have to look at her tits and decide whether she was lacking or not.

But all he said was, "Let's see how you strut around in a bikini."

And with direction from Jeff and Renee about attitude and creating a character, Natasha found that it...wasn't all that bad. A surprising amount of stomping, plus a lot of posturing and flipping her hair around. She was playing a role and learning choreography, just like any other gig.

When Jeff and Renee had seen enough, Natasha got off the stage. The bartender brought her a bottle of water and gave her a thumbs-up.

"We'll start you off easy," Jeff said, "on weeknights. But I have a feeling that once you learn some tricks on the pole, you'll be on Friday nights in no time. Renee will teach you the basics, and you can learn about the rest from the other girls—hair, makeup, the rules, the clients. Play by the rules and you'll do fine. We take care of our own here."

He gave her a nod, said, "Welcome to the team, Natasha," and headed back to his office.

Renee sat on the edge of the stage while Natasha got dressed.

"How long have you worked here?" Natasha asked.

"Four years," Renee said, kicking her heels. "I've danced in a lot of different places, in three major cities, and the Planet is my favorite. It's clean, they don't let anyone touch you or take pictures, and Jeff is actually nice." Her lips curved in what would have been a smirk on anyone else, but on Renee, it managed to convey affection and warmth. "You're going to make a lot of money here. Not as much as you'd make nude, but the clientele here appreciates talent. Come back tomorrow at one and we'll start your lessons."

Natasha thanked her, waved goodbye to the bartender and the man with the mop, who'd both watched the whole thing, and headed out to her car.

A lot of money. Renee thought Natasha would make a lot of money.

The prospect worried her. If the money were bad, this would be easy to turn down, to leave if another opportunity came up. But if it made her enough to live on, and fueled her need for adoration...

She was getting ahead of herself. Maybe she'd hate it and quit on the first day.

Shit. Who was she kidding? She'd liked Jeff and Renee. She'd liked being on stage. Hell, she even liked the corny sci-fi décor, which reminded her of *Aliens Don't Dance.* This was going to be easy, and she was going to get off on it. As much as she told herself this was temporary, she was scared it wouldn't be.

She was also scared that her mother was right, and this was the only way she could make it as a dancer in this city.

As she drove away, she decided to set a deadline for herself. When Gina got to LA, Natasha would quit and say she'd been working as a bartender the whole time. Hell, it probably wasn't a bad idea to tend bar or wait tables a couple times a week, just to cement the illusion and bring in more cash.

For now, she was going to do this.

And no one would ever know.

Chapter Forty-Two

Present day

The questions were eating away at Dimitri. Between Little Lilac and the pole dancing classroom—and the woman he suspected might be a stripper—he wanted to bombard Natasha with inquiries until he'd unearthed everything there was to know about her.

But as antsy as her mysteries made him, he couldn't demand she spill her secrets. She had to offer them willingly. He had to show her he was worthy of them.

That meant giving her space, when all he wanted to do was wrap her in his arms and beg her to let him in.

For the past three years, all it had ever been between them was sex, because he'd been too scared to ask for more. No sense making a move until he was sure of the result.

Right?

It had been his guiding principle in business and relationships for many years. He didn't know how to put his heart, or his career, on the line. He couldn't chance failing. He couldn't chance losing everything he'd worked for.

While he was grateful to his family for making the choice,

moving to America had left a mark on him. He still carried the stress and fear of that time in his blood and in his bones.

But if he wanted this to work, he had to trust Natasha. He had to show her she was safe with him. Even if doing so left him feeling unsteady.

Once they were in the house, he stopped at the kitchen doorway to suggest they make coffee or a snack, but she kept going on her crutches, through the living room to the sliding glass doors.

"Where are you going?"

She shot him a shy look over her shoulder. "It's hot out. I was thinking it would be nice to use the pool."

The pool? He was nearly vibrating out of his skin with the force of all his unasked questions, and she wanted to go for a *swim*?

When she struggled to unlatch the sliding doors, he rushed to help her, but she got them open and was out before he could reach her.

"Tasha?" He followed her to the rectangular in-ground pool. She perched on the edge of a lounge chair and set down her crutches. He was about to offer to go back inside for her swimsuit when she said, "Can you pass me the sunscreen?"

He looked around, then grabbed a spray-on sunscreen from the bin of pool supplies by the patio table.

He walked over to hand it to her, but drew up short when she pulled her thin white t-shirt over her head and tossed it aside on the chair. He nearly swallowed his tongue when she reached behind her and unclipped the lacy bra, releasing her soft, round breasts with their dark, puckered points. And when she dropped her hands and undid the button and zipper of her denim shorts before sliding them—and her panties—down her long, shapely legs? He had to remind himself to breathe. Here she was, stripping off her clothes in his backyard in the middle of the day, like it was no big deal.

You perfect woman, he thought. And then he thanked God and the previous owners that the property had a high fence and foliage surrounding it.

Fully naked now, she gave him an expectant look. "Well?"

He swallowed hard. "Well, what?"

She held out her hand. "The sunscreen?"

"Oh. Right." He handed her the spray. She used it on her arms first, rubbing it into her skin with brisk strokes of her palms. Then she spritzed it across her chest in a way that had him groaning and growing hard. With a knowing smile, she watched him as she massaged the sunscreen onto her breasts, cupping and kneading the soft globes.

He watched, lips parted, nearly drooling. She had small, neat scars on the undersides of her breasts. They seemed to be especially sensitive, judging by the way she'd croon and sigh whenever he ran his tongue along them, as he imagined doing now.

She grinned wickedly, like she knew what he was thinking, and tweaked her own nipples. He groaned again and reached down to adjust himself. He loved her nipples. The areolas were small and brown, the nipples stiff and pliable. He loved curling his tongue around the hard peaks and knowing he could close his lips over her entire areola and suck it into the warm cavern of his mouth.

But most of all, he loved her responses. The way she arched into him for more, writhing under his ministrations and clutching his head to her chest.

She continued to apply the sunscreen, taking her time and missing not an inch of flesh. When she got to her ankle, she propped it on the lounger and unwrapped it, using more care as she smoothed the sunscreen over her right foot and leg. The bruising had lightened to a greenish-yellow and barely showed against her light brown skin.

When she sat up again, she met his eyes and shrugged. "Tan lines." Then she flipped over onto her stomach and stretched out on the lounge chair, giving him a great view of her tight ass and a quick peek at her labia. Raising her eyebrows, she held the spray can out to him.

"Do my back?"

The innocent tone wasn't fooling him.

"Goddamn tease," he growled, snatching the metal canister away from her and swatting her butt lightly with the flat of his hand. When she laughed, he sprayed sunscreen all over her back and ass and rubbed it in vigorously. "For the record, I know what you're trying to do."

"Do you?" When he was done, she sat up to twist her hair into a knot, looking for all the world like a goddess or a nymph about to bathe in a sacred lake. She was all lithe, lean limbs and graceful movements. Her eyes, when they flicked over to him, held the secrets of the universe, and the smirk playing on her wide mouth urged him to drop to his knees in worship.

"Uh, yes." What had he been saying? Oh, right. "You're trying to distract me."

She scrunched up her face cutely and held her thumb and index finger about a centimeter apart. "Maybe a little bit."

"Nothing little about it," he muttered, adjusting himself again, and she laughed.

Using one crutch, she got to her feet and stood before him. He was wearing sweats, which did nothing to hide his erection. She glanced down and gave a hum of appreciation. "Just trying to make an uncomfortable conversation a little more fun. Come on. Let's talk in the pool."

He shook his head. "Hold on. It isn't safe for you to use crutches out here."

He tossed aside his fitted cap—Mets, of course—and stripped out of his clothes. He didn't miss the way her gaze zeroed in on his dick. But when he reached for her, she held up the can of sunscreen and sent him a smile full of heat.

"Safety first."

Growling a string of his favorite Russian curses, he quickly sprayed his torso and threw the can onto the chair. "That's enough. I need to cool down so we can talk."

She eyed his cock appreciatively and then had the nerve—the nerve—to lick her lips. "Not too much, I hope."

He scooped her up, and her sunscreen-covered body slid against his chest, hot and slick. "If it weren't for your ankle, I'd toss you right into the deep end."

She locked her arms around his neck, pressing her luscious breasts against him in the process. "Don't you dare. I just straightened my hair this morning."

He knew, because he'd watched her do it. She'd sat on the stepladder in his bathroom with no fewer than three heating devices and a collection of bottles, converting her mane of long dark spirals into a smooth fall of waves.

When she was done, he'd run his fingers through it and said, "You're always beautiful, but I like your real hair." In the mirror, her reflection had flushed at the compliment.

He carried her over to the pool and carefully navigated the steps into the shallow end. She sucked in a breath when her ass hit the water first, then sighed as her body was submerged.

"Feels good," she murmured.

He tightened his arms around her. "Yeah, you do."

Rolling her eyes, she pushed off from his shoulders and swam a few feet away, leaving him hard and aching in water up to his chest.

"Careful with your ankle," he warned, as she frolicked and slid through the water like a mermaid, the light from the sun sparkling on her wet skin.

Instead of following her, he reached down and gripped the base of his cock in a tight grip.

She swam back and forth, her long arms cutting through the water in a modified breaststroke. "Are you jerking off over there?"

"No, but I should." He gave his cock another squeeze and

groaned, wishing it were her hand on him. "Then I'll be able to focus."

She stopped in front of him, treading water. "You want to know about Renee."

He did, but that was before Natasha's wet, naked body was within arm's reach. The water played with her image, distorting her lean curves. She was like a siren, calling him beneath the waves.

"Dimitri."

"Yeah?"

She laughed and put her arms around his neck, bringing their bodies together. Under the smells of chlorine and sunscreen, he caught the sweet scent of figs. Her flat belly pressed into his cock, pushing it up between them, and he groaned again. Unable to resist her, he cupped her butt and squeezed.

"You want this cock?" he growled, grinding against her.

"Yeah." She tilted her head and her lips parted, ready for his kiss. But now it was his turn to tease.

"What did it? Watching me with the kids this morning got you ovulating?"

She splashed him right in the face. He hadn't seen it coming, although he should have, after a shitty joke like that. Water went in his eyes and mouth. He tried to pinch her butt, but she was too quick, too slick, and she slipped away.

Wiping water out of his eyes, he grumbled, "You're going to pay for that."

She was over by the side of the pool now, near the steps. Stretching her arms out to grip the edge behind her, she gave him a wicked grin and spread her legs under the water. "Make me."

He dove under the water and swam along the bottom of the pool with quick, strong strokes until he was below her. On his way back up, he pressed his face between her legs, nuzzling her spread-open pussy with his lips, before he came up for air.

Her head was tipped back, resting against the edge of the pool, and she was gasping.

"Congratulations," he growled. "You've effectively distracted me."

"Good," she said, panting. "Now fuck me."

With a groan, he hauled himself out of the pool and lunged for his pants, which were just out of reach. With wet, shaking hands, he yanked his wallet out of the back pocket, probably ruining the leather in the process, but he didn't fucking care. He pulled out a condom, ripped open the package, and rolled it on. When he jumped back into the pool, he splashed her a little.

"Sorry," he muttered. "Your hair."

"Forget about my hair." She wrapped her legs around his waist and pulled him to her.

It took only a second for him to position himself, and with one push, he slid right in.

They both groaned, and he kissed her hard.

"How do you want it?" he whispered in her ear, reaching for her hands and gripping them tight.

Her lids were heavy with desire, but her eyes were bright and excited. "How we always do it. Hard and fast."

This wasn't what he'd wanted. He'd planned to talk to her, to get her to open up to him more. Or, barring that, to take things slow and use his body to show her how much he loved and cherished her. He didn't want to do things like they always did— that's what had gotten them into this messy situation to begin with. But with her sheath clamped tight and hot around him, and her breasts bobbing in the water with sunshine caressing her pointed nipples, he couldn't resist her.

She'd asked—no, *told* him to fuck her. So he would. Whatever she asked of him, he'd give.

Slipping an arm around her back to protect her skin from the wall, he gripped the edge of the pool with his other hand for leverage and gave it to her exactly how she'd asked for it.

Hard and *fast*.

She locked those long legs around his hips, rocking against him as he pounded into her. Water splashed around them, and the sun beat down on his back and shoulders.

"This is how you want it?" he rasped, needing to know, needing to understand her.

"Yes." Her voice was breathless, thready. "Yes, Machote. Así. Just like this."

He licked the curve of her ear and inhaled her sweetness. "Touch yourself, Tasha."

She let go of the pool with one hand. He felt her fingertips brush his cock and he groaned, pausing when she slipped her hand lower to cup his balls. He let her fondle them for a minute, then resumed his pace. A moment later, her fingers fluttered against her clit and his dick where they joined.

He kissed along her neck and jaw, tasting pool water and Natasha. Her eyes closed, and she bit her lip, little moans falling from her lips as her hand moved faster.

"What do you think about?" he demanded.

Her eyes cracked open a fraction, and her hand didn't stop. "What?"

"What do you think about when I'm fucking you?"

She closed her eyes and moaned. Her body gave a little jerk against him. She was close.

He put his mouth to her ear and sucked on the lobe. Then he breathed out, in a low, deep rumble, "*Natasha.*"

"Nothing!" The word burst out of her. Her body shivered again, and her legs tightened around him, her pelvis pumping to meet his thrusts. "Nothing. That's why…"

"Why what?" He slowed his pace, only giving her half thrusts. "Why what, Kroshka?"

She tried to pull him closer with her strong legs, but he resisted. Her voice was half-sob, half-gasp when she finally cried out, "That's why I love fucking you so much. You make my brain turn off."

It wasn't how he wanted to hear that word from her, but hell, he'd take it. He gritted his teeth and bent his knees, changing the angle as he slammed into her. She cried out, tightening around him.

"Make yourself come." He dipped his head to close his lips around one pert nipple, rolling it with his tongue. "Fuck, I could suck on these tits for hours."

"Duro," she moaned, arching her back. "Dame más."

He didn't know if she meant for him to go harder with his mouth or his cock, but he doubled his efforts on both counts, just in case. She rewarded him with a series of high-pitched moans that made his balls draw up tight.

When he switched to her other nipple and laved it with his tongue, her whole body jerked against him. Spasms rippled through her, and she squeezed his dick as she shattered. He gave himself over to her pleasure, pumping into her in short, hard thrusts until his own orgasm roared through him and threatened to bring him to his knees.

They leaned against the wall of the pool, catching their breath as they sank into the water up to their necks. Dimitri pressed his face into her throat, not caring that they were sticky with sweat and sunscreen. He just wanted to be close to her, to feel her pulse against his cheek.

Her shoulders lifted, and she let out a deep sigh.

"All right," she said in a small voice. "I'll tell you everything."

He tightened his hold on her, willing her to feel the truth of his words. "Nothing you say could change my feelings for you."

He felt her swallow before she whispered, "We'll see about that."

Chapter Forty-Three

Dimitri helped Natasha out of the pool, and they cleaned up. Then they slid naked into the hot tub and turned on the jets. Dimitri sat beside her but kept his distance.

Natasha was quiet for a while. He waited, giving her space to collect her thoughts. If he pulled her into his arms now, would she let him? He didn't try it. Instead, he rested a hand on her shoulder and caressed her gently. It seemed like a good compromise. He wanted to touch her, to let her know he was there, but he didn't want to crowd her. It was a hard balance for him to strike, but he was making an effort.

Finally, she lifted her chin and met his gaze. "No one else knows about any of this."

"But you're telling me."

She nodded.

Despite his resolve, he shifted closer. "Why?"

She turned away, looking out over the rest of the yard. No grass—too many droughts for that—but a multitude of plants that did well in the dry Southern California weather. Mostly succulents and other desert plants, like agave and cactus, with some avocado and orange trees. When he'd bought this place, he'd wanted a backyard, thinking of the big family parties his uncle had thrown once he'd moved to a bigger house in New Jersey.

Natasha cleared her throat. "Ever since I decided I wanted to be a dancer, I've been struggling to prove I could do it. Not the dancing part, but actually making a living off it."

The struggle of all creatives—to do the work and pay the bills. "That's the dream," he said.

She shook her head. "It wasn't about my dreams, though. It was about proving that dance is a valid, viable, realistic profession, and that I'm good enough to make it my career."

It sounded like she was having an argument with someone else, likely her mother, but he stayed quiet.

Natasha's eyes glimmered with sorrow and pain. "This is something I never wanted anyone to know about. But I'm starting to realize…maybe I don't have to hold it all in."

"You don't." He slid an arm around her. "You can let me carry some of it for you. With you," he corrected. "I can carry it with you. Together."

She flicked a glance at him, a grateful smile on her lips. Then she looked down at the water, bubbling around them. "I guess I should start at the beginning."

Please, he wanted to beg. Please, tell me everything about you. I love you, and I want to know anything you're willing to share. Instead, he just nodded.

"Remember how I told you I got into Lennox and didn't go? Well, Gina went. I worked as a waitress and a dance teacher, and I did a lot of dancing with a troupe we'd joined in high school. Our plan was to move out here together after Gina had graduated and saved some money. But then my great-grandmother passed away."

He gave her a light squeeze. "I'm sorry."

She sighed, like grief still weighed heavily on her. "Abuela was the best person in my life. Without her, it was just me and my mother in that apartment. Finally, I couldn't take it anymore, so I moved to LA on my own, before Gina was ready to go."

There was a lot she wasn't saying about her home life and her relationship with her mother, but he didn't dare interrupt, now that she was finally opening up to him.

"When I got here, I blew through the money I'd saved. Gina's better at the organizational stuff, like searching for the best prices on apartments. And even though I went on a ton of auditions, nothing panned out. Like, not a single thing."

He had a feeling he knew where this was going and his gut churned, imagining how desperate and sad she must have been. Alone, separated from her best friend and missing her great-grandmother.

"I got a job at a bikini bar," she said in a rush. "Because at least then I was making money as a dancer. It was at Babe Planet, where Renee works. She's the one who taught me how to pole dance."

There it was. As soon as he'd seen Natasha sitting with Renee, he'd suspected, and the postcard was another clue. Still, he hadn't wanted to jump to conclusions, and it meant the world to him that she'd revealed it on her own.

When he didn't respond, she shot him a glance, her brows slanted in worry.

"What?" he asked.

She blinked. "You don't have anything to say to that?"

He abandoned the idea of distance and shifted her into his lap. "What is there to say? This is a tough industry. But we're New Yorkers, and I don't know if you've heard, but we can make it anywhere. Even if it means doing things other people might balk at. We're strong enough to turn our low points into success."

She exhaled, and he felt the tension drain out of her body. Winding her arms around him, she relaxed against his chest. "You don't know what a huge relief it is to hear you say that."

"You were worried I was going to judge you."

"Of course. I mean, I'm not ashamed of having worked there. It was actually fun, most of the time. I learned a new skill set, and in reality, my costumes weren't that different from the stuff I wear on *The Dance Off* now. And it met my short-term goal of making enough money to stay in Los Angeles while working as a dancer." The dreamy nostalgia in her expression became troubled. "But it was a slippery slope, and I ended up doing a few nights at a topless club, too. I didn't like the vibe there at all, but I could feel how easy it would be to get addicted to the money, to the attention. And I knew I couldn't do that. Not because there's anything wrong with stripping, it's a totally valid job—but because it strayed from my long-term goal."

"Which was what?"

She released a heavy sigh. "To prove to my mom that she was wrong. Stripping wouldn't have sustained me in the long run, creatively, but it also wasn't something I could throw in my mother's face to show her I was a success as a dancer. Instead, I would've been handing her the biggest 'I told you so' ever. So I only worked at the Planet until Gina moved out here, and then I quit."

"And you never told Gina?"

"Ay Dios mío, no." She huffed out a laugh into his neck.

"Why not? She's a good friend."

"No way. Gina would never understand. She's so focused on integrity and busting Latina stereotypes, she wouldn't get how I could take my clothes off for money."

He tightened his arms around her. "I hope she'd see that you were sticking to your own integrity by continuing to work as a dancer even when it was difficult."

She tilted her head back to search his face, her dark eyes glassy and full of uncertainty. "That's...that's exactly why. Maybe it wasn't what I set out to do, but at least I was still dancing."

"Then why do you see it as a failure?"

She sighed and tucked her face back into his shoulder. "Because I couldn't tell anyone about it. I said I was a bartender, and then I had to get a bartending job, too, just so it wouldn't be a lie. I was working seven nights a week, which sucked, but coño, I was rolling in money."

"Hard to give that up."

"It was. But I told myself it was only temporary, until Gina got here. Then, I would quit, no matter how good the money was. And…no matter how much I loved the attention."

Her use of the word "temporary" stood out to him. Was she here with him for the same reason? Because she loved the attention he gave her?

While he mulled that over, she ran her fingers over his chest where it met the edge of the water. The hair was growing back from the last time he'd shaved. "Is it scratchy?" he asked.

"No." She scraped him lightly with her nails, sending shivers of sensation across his skin. "So, you're not…upset? Or, like, jealous?"

The wariness was back in her eyes, in the set of her shoulders. He recognized it easily. It was how she'd always been around him, until recently.

He leaned in close and nipped her chin. "Do you want me to be?"

"No."

Her tone was defensive. She was lying. And he was *thrilled*. Over-the-moon thrilled that he'd gotten to know her well enough to discern when she was lying or defensive. He'd finally seen the real Natasha, and now he knew when she was holding back. Grinning, he pressed a kiss to her ear.

"You're lying," he whispered.

"I'm not." She tried to move off his lap, but he held tight to her waist.

"You are. You want me to be jealous."

"I never said that."

"Are *you* jealous?"

"Of what?" she replied tartly. "The multitudes of other women you've fucked?"

"Multitudes" was a stretch, but he just nodded and waited

for an answer. Watching the emotions play over her face was a treat, from defensiveness to aloofness to finally anger as she slapped his chest with both hands and burst out, "Yes, you asshole, I'm jealous! Are you happy now?"

He couldn't have wiped the grin off his face if his life depended on it. "Yes."

She leaned back, her eyes wide and worried. "Is that why you did it? To hurt me?"

"Nyet, lyubimaya moya." He cuddled her closer and kissed the tip of her nose. "I did that because I didn't think you cared. And..." Fuck, this was hard to admit. "I don't like being alone."

"I..." She closed her mouth, and her eyebrows dipped. "I wanted you to think I didn't care."

"Aha." He gave her a smacking kiss, full on the mouth. "That means you *do* care."

She gave him a begrudging smile that warmed the very depths of his soul. "Maybe a little."

That smile gave him the courage to revisit an earlier conversation and finally tell her the full truth.

"Kroshka, I don't care if you gave lap dances to every person in West Hollywood."

She rolled her eyes. "I never actually did lap dances, you know. I probably would have, if I'd stuck with it longer, but the Planet didn't make us do that."

He shook his head. "None of that matters to me. You did what you had to do to survive this bullshit industry, and thank God, because I wouldn't have met you otherwise. But let me make one thing perfectly fucking clear."

Her expression turned wary again, and he knew it was in response to the way his voice had hardened, but he couldn't help it as he ground out, "Yes, damn it, *I was fucking jealous.*"

Her eyes widened, but he couldn't stop to see if she was going to reply, because everything poured out of him.

"Any time I saw you with another man, I lost my

goddamned mind, because I couldn't stand the thought that you were letting him closer than you let me."

She shook her head. "None of them were—"

He shushed her, stroking her arm with soothing swipes. "That's in the past, and I'll get over it. But you asked me something before, and I didn't give you a complete answer. Do you want to know the real reason I let Lauren get anywhere near me? I'm not proud of it. But I'll tell you."

Fire sparked in her eyes, and he imagined he saw a flash of green. "*Why?*"

He cupped her face in both hands and rasped, "Because I'd just seen you kissing Jackson, and I was either going to tear his pretty face off or revenge bomb his scores."

She sucked in a breath. "Wait, did you rig the final three?"

He shook his head. "Gina deserved to win. And I'd cooled down by then."

Her eyes narrowed. "Because I fucked you after the semifinals?"

His grin flashed as he remembered that night. "That certainly didn't hurt. But no, it wasn't that." He dropped his hands to her waist and let out an exasperated sigh. "The guy was just so fucking *likeable*. Always fucking smiling, even when he was kissing you. And I couldn't hate him for it, because I knew he'd be nice to you in a way I never was. In a way I can't be. So I told myself, for the thousandth time, the *millionth* time, to leave you the fuck alone. To let you be with someone nice." He caressed her cheek with the tips of his fingers. "I could see the way he touched you. Soft. Gentle. Like you're made of glass." He shifted his hand to grip the back of her neck firmly, and his next question came out as a growl. "But that's not what you want, is it?"

"No." Her reply was barely audible over the jets. "It's not."

His grin flashed, fierce and triumphant. "Of course not. Not when you're so fucking strong. You like it rough and a little mean, don't you, Kroshka? You need a way to work out all that aggression you hide." He pulled her face to his and pressed their foreheads together. "You can do that with me. I can take it. Let me see what's inside, Tasha. All of it. You won't scare me off. Nothing you say or do would ever make me want you less."

Her lower lip trembled, and her eyes were big and luminous with uncertainty. "Are you sure?"

"Fucking positive, baby. I want all of you."

Her lips parted. He pressed his mouth to hers in a searing kiss.

And then his fucking phone rang.

He squeezed his eyes shut and groaned. "That's the restaurant. We're having a new vent system installed, and they're all terrified of something going wrong."

She arched an eyebrow. "You mean they're terrified of what *you'll* do if something goes wrong."

He inclined his head. "Correct."

His hands flexed on her hips, and she smiled. "Go to work, Macho."

"I don't want to leave you."

She gave his cheek an indulgent pat. "I'll be fine by myself for a few hours. And I promise to use my crutches."

He set her on the edge of the hot tub, then got out and picked her up.

"Don't slip," she warned.

"Trust me."

Her expression softened, and her fingers played in his hair, teasing the nape of his neck. "I do."

He wanted to stay, to explore this further, but work awaited him. They dried off and showered quickly, and once she was settled, he picked up his car keys from the table by the door that led to the garage. Anticipation for the evening ahead lightened his step.

"You sure you'll be okay without me?"

She gave him a bright smile from the kitchen counter. "Of course. I'm going to look for apartments."

His neck muscles tensed. Again with that damned apartment

search. After everything they'd shared and done, she was still looking for a way out? Hurt sharpened his tone. "Don't forget, we have plans tonight."

She ducked her head. "You still want to go?"

"Of course. It looks like a good show." Mostly, he wanted to go with *her*, to see the place where she'd worked, a place from her past.

She pressed her hands to her cheeks like she was embarrassed. "You want to go to what is essentially a strip club. Tonight."

"What's wrong with tonight?" When she didn't answer, he went back to the counter and leaned on it across from her. "Natasha." He waited until she raised her eyes to meet his. "I'm sorry. If you don't want to go, we don't have to. I don't want it to bring up bad memories or make you uncomfortable."

She shook her head. "It's not that. I just don't know why you want to go there."

"Don't worry, it's not for the women. I have all I need right here." He wiggled his eyebrows at her, hoping it would make her laugh.

She looked down at her laptop again, but her lips pressed together like she was hiding a smile.

"Besides," he added. "I owe you dinner." At her puzzled look, he explained. "The kids said I was 'awesome,' so I think it's obvious that I won the bet. That means you have to go to dinner with me tonight at Krasavitsa." He placed a hand on her laptop and pushed it shut. "Stop looking for apartments. You deserve to relax. Watch some TV, take a nap in our bed, whatever. I'll text when I'm on my way back. Okay?"

She nodded, but her eyes were troubled, and he couldn't figure out why. With his mind full of Natasha, Dimitri left for the restaurant.

Chapter Forty-Four

Our bed.

Dimitri's words stayed with Natasha the rest of the day, even as she tried to take his advice. She watched TV—while looking at apartments. She tried to nap—in *their* bed—but couldn't get the day's events out of her mind.

From the way he'd charmed the children at Little Lilac to his response at finding out she'd worked at a bikini bar and as a topless dancer, and then his revelations about his behavior during the last season, Dimitri was surprising her left and right.

And then, to hear that *he* thought *she* hadn't cared? Eye-opening. Was it possible he'd held back all this time for the same reasons she had? Her mind flashed to the times she'd flirted with other men while Dimitri was around. Rocky Lim, Jackson García, maybe a handful of others. Yes, she'd wanted to make him as twisted up inside as she'd felt. But she'd never known it had *worked.*

To get her mind off everything, she closed the rental websites and pulled up her video files to work on the piece she was choreographing.

As she watched herself move on screen and jotted her thoughts in a notebook, she had a hard time tapping into the emotions that had originally led her to choreograph this piece. The haunting melody and lyrics, describing a modern love that had been betrayed, no longer compelled her.

You burned me, the singer crooned in her smoky voice. *You burned me down, and all that's left are ashes.*

When she'd chosen this song, she'd identified with the lyrics. She'd felt empty and hollowed out, like the husk of a house after a fire. Exhausted, drained, devastated. But she didn't feel that way anymore. Now, she felt...*seen.*

She'd told Dimitri things she'd never told anyone, not even Gina, and he hadn't looked at her any differently.

Hell, the man had said he *loved* her. Nothing she knew of Dimitri indicated that he was someone who threw that word around. It had certainly never come up any of the other times they'd been together. Sure, he'd said the L word while yelling at her, but he'd seemed just as surprised by the admission as she was.

Still, trust didn't come easily. Telling Dimitri her secrets had left her emotions muddled and raw, like an exposed wound. Those months at Babe Planet had been her most desperate, and here she was, back in a similar situation: broke and doing something she knew wasn't good for her in the long run. The longer she stayed with Dimitri, the more she was tempted to believe that they could...

She shut down that line of thinking before she could dream too big or too bold. Survival came first. Dreaming was a luxury for other people.

She pulled up her music library and skipped through songs, looking for something that fit how she felt now. She spent hours every week listening to music and thinking about mood, story, tone, and movement. She'd even taken a music engineering class last year, so that she could make her own mixes.

An hour and many notebook pages later, she finally found a song. It had more of a pop beat, but it was undercut by dramatic violins. *I am a masterpiece,* the singer repeated throughout the song. *You ain't seen nothing yet. Just watch me fly.*

Natasha listened, jotting down the lyrics, which gave her chills. This was the song. From burning to flying, it was a phoenix story. She could adapt the existing choreography to tell a story of triumph, of personal faith and trust.

Flexing the toes of her right foot, she was tempted to jump up and move. Her best choreography ideas came to her this way, inspired by feeling and a song that hit all the right emotional notes. The dance came through her like a download. It was happening now, but she couldn't dance.

Except that wasn't true. She simply couldn't put weight on her right ankle, and suddenly, that didn't seem like such an insurmountable obstacle.

It took some back and forth, but she got her laptop, speakers, and camera set up in Dimitri's studio. In addition to those, she dragged in the desk chair from his office. She cast a worried glance at the shiny floor, but something told her he wouldn't mind. Once everything was ready, she sat in the chair and propped her crutches against the barre. Keeping her phone in her lap to control the sound, she started the camera and the music and rolled into the center of the room.

When Dimitri appeared in the doorway a while later, she wasn't even surprised.

She stopped spinning in the chair and turned off the music. "Hi."

A small smile played on his lips, and his eyes were full of... something. Affection, maybe. "Hi."

She rolled back over to her equipment and turned off the camera. "I took your chair," she said.

"So I see." He walked into the room, his hands in his pockets.

She focused on the laptop screen. She'd just been naked with this man in broad daylight. It was ridiculous to feel nervous now. He wasn't even doing anything.

But she was starting to believe he might be telling the truth about his feelings. And it was a dangerous thing for someone who'd never thought she'd ever have something like what he offered.

Hope. That was it. That was the thing fluttering in her chest like a bird trying to escape from a cage.

He stood over her, perusing her setup. "Trying to dance without using your feet?"

"I can use my left foot just fine."

To prove it, she dug into the floor with her bare left foot and sent the chair spinning in a circle.

He grabbed the armrests, bringing it to a stop. Leaning down, he brought his face close to hers. Natasha swallowed. He still wore that unreadable smile, and his chocolate-brown eyes had grown even more intense.

God, he was handsome. Her skin itched to be touched by him, to feel his strong hands skimming over her. His hot mouth, the rasp of his beard, his tongue…

She cleared her throat. "Sorry. I said I wouldn't go into your office."

His brows drew together like he was annoyed. "And I told you it was fine. You're allowed anywhere in this house."

"I still should have asked."

"Tasha."

"Uh-huh?" Her pulse pounded in her throat.

His eyes bored into her, and the smile was gone from his lips, now set in a stern line. "Every time I walked away from you in the past, it killed me. I don't intend to do it again. I love you. So, you can have my desk chair. You can have my studio and my pool and my bed and my body and anything that's in my power to give. Got it?"

She nodded, struggling to breathe.

"Good." He stepped back. "Let's get ready for our date."

"Date?" She let out a nervous giggle to cover how much his words had affected her. "That's a first."

Frowning, he paused in gathering her equipment. "We haven't been on a date?"

"No."

"Why not?"

Her cheeks grew hot. "You've never asked me."

He put the laptop back on the stool she was using as a table and took her hand. "I'm asking now. Natasha Díaz, will you go on a date with me tonight? I thought we'd see some naked women, then eat a meal I don't have to pay for."

She swatted his hand away, laughing. "No wonder we've never been on a date. You're terrible at it."

He shrugged. "Don't worry, I'll make up for it with the good-night kiss."

She raised her chin haughtily. "Who says you're getting one?"

He laughed and rolled her into the hallway.

Despite her trepidation, she couldn't wait to go out with him, and she was dying to see the restaurant.

But a little voice in the back of her mind refused to be silent. You'll get caught. And then what? You think he'll stand by you? You'll never be good enough for him.

It was an echo of the phrase that had haunted her for her whole life. *Not good enough.*

No. Inner doubt be damned. Donna and *The Dance Off* be damned.

Natasha was going on a date with Dimitri Kovalenko, and fuck anyone or anything that tried to get in her way.

Chapter Forty-Five

Nerves made Natasha antsy as Dimitri drove them to Babe Planet. It was one thing to joke about it at home, but actually going there was something else entirely.

She fiddled with her bracelet and watched cars streak past on the freeway. What the hell was she thinking, bringing Dimitri there? It wasn't the worst, as far as strip clubs and bikini bars went, but it wasn't the best, either. It looked exactly like what it was—a dive bar with poles. The thing that set it apart, according to some of the other women she'd worked with, was Jeff, the manager.

Despite Natasha being up front about her plans to move on after a few months, Jeff and the girls had invested time and attention in her, teaching her and giving her room to adjust. For a short time, they'd been like family to her, certainly more than her own relatives back in New York and Puerto Rico, but that might have had something to do with her mother alienating everyone else with her bitterness.

"You okay?" Dimitri glanced over at her as he drove.

"Yeah. Sure."

"You've chewed off all your lipstick."

She flipped down the visor mirror, and sure enough, the red

she'd painted on before they left the house was nearly gone. She rummaged in her bag for the tube, then reapplied.

By the time they parked, Natasha was ready to jump out of her skin. This was a terrible idea. She shouldn't be here at all, let alone with Dimitri.

What would he think of her? Yeah, he'd been all sweet and accepting in the hot tub, lulled by sex and bubbles, but he might not be so nonchalant when faced with the reality. And, god forbid, what if they were *recognized*? She'd gotten caught up in his passionate words, in the idea that Donna and *The Dance Off* weren't a threat to her very survival. They should turn around *right now* and go straight to the restaurant. Or home. Or literally anywhere other than here.

But then Dimitri was at her door, helping her out. "Let's go."

Taking hold of his hand, she swallowed back her doubts and exited the car.

They'd debated whether it looked worse to walk with a cane or crutches. Natasha felt like crutches indicated a temporary injury, but Dimitri argued that a cane would be better for navigating tight, dark spaces.

In the end, after a lot of testing, she'd worn the boot he'd picked up for her. He wasn't happy about her walking on her ankle yet, but she couldn't sit around forever. And besides, she pointed out, he was there to help her if she needed anything.

She hadn't missed the way his chest puffed out at that.

Entering the Planet was like the weirdest kind of flashback. The bouncer didn't recognize her, and he didn't bat an eye at her boot as he checked their IDs. Inside, it smelled the same, a combo of beer and fries, floor cleaner and perfume. The décor was the same, too. It was dark inside, with cool lighting, and tiny lights twinkled on the ceiling like stars. A club remix of a pop hit played over the speakers.

The clientele was always a mix of men and women, and a large group in the corner was clearly a bachelorette party, if the matching T-shirts were anything to go by.

Natasha had expected to see a familiar face or for someone to remember her, but she didn't recognize the bartender or either of the waitresses making the rounds. Then again, it had been over five years since she'd worked here.

It was honestly kind of a letdown. She'd amped herself up for it, and now the nerves and adrenaline had nowhere to go.

Dimitri led her to a small, round café table with two chairs. It wasn't super close to the stage but it had a good view. When she was settled, he stood with his hands on his hips and gazed across the room at the bar. "Are you going to be all right while I get drinks?"

She shook her head at his overprotectiveness. "I used to work here, remember? I'll be fine. Besides, no one will mistake me for the talent in this." She plucked at the modest neckline of her simple black mini dress, the nicest of the few wash-and-wear dresses she'd brought with her. "Go get us drinks. I'll have a Cosmos-politan."

At his puzzled look, she added, "You heard that right. And I think you'd like the Dark Matter Martini." She lowered her voice and said, "The 'dark matter' is just espresso, not the stuff holding the universe together."

Chuckling, Dimitri headed for the bar. Natasha let out a breath and peered around the familiar space, remembering the first time she'd been here. Part of her did want to leave, but the part that loved dance was curious about what Renee had in store. Renee had been an excellent teacher, and she was good at curating talent.

Natasha turned her attention to the stage, where a pink-haired woman, clad in a yellow tiger-striped bikini and glittery silver platform stilettos, executed an advanced spinning combo around the center pole that ended in an effortless inside leg hang. The dancer's body was strong and flexible, her ghostly pale skin covered in video game tattoos, and her tits seemed to defy the laws of physics.

Natasha glanced down at the fairly modest amount of cleavage showing above the neckline of her own dress. The irony was, she'd gotten the implants *after* working here, using money earned on this very stage. Despite the kitschy dive bar atmosphere, Babe Planet's clientele appreciated a good show and they rewarded talent. While Natasha hadn't been curvy, she'd quickly mastered the basic pole dancing moves and used the grace and control honed from years of ballet training to score lots of tips.

Once Dimitri returned with their drinks, she gestured toward the stage with her glass.

"That used to be me," she said, and joined the crowd in cheering as the dancer completed another complicated spin.

Dimitri sent Natasha a sidelong glance. "If I got a pole installed at home, would you…"

Heat flooded through her at the suggestion. The performative aspect of striptease had made her feel powerful, and while she wasn't an expert by any means—there was a reason she only taught the beginner class—she found she wanted to do this for him. But since they were in public, she only flashed him a coy smile and said, "For you? Maybe."

He groaned and shifted in his seat.

"Pants suddenly a little tight?"

"Yes, damn it."

Before the act ended, Natasha sent Dimitri over to tip the dancer on stage, and she was pretty sure she saw him pull a few hundreds out of his wallet.

For some reason, that made her melt a little inside.

Finally, the lights went down, the music lowered, and the pole dancer collected her tips and swept offstage amid whoops and cheers.

Dimitri leaned in to whisper in her ear. "Sit on my lap."

Natasha wanted to do it, to feel his strong thighs underneath her, his cock pressing up against her ass. But anyone could be watching.

"Don't be a perv," she said primly, and he let out a low chuckle.

The show began. There was an emcee, a Black nonbinary drag performer who went by Catnip, and they had the audience cracking up. The first two acts were fun and flirty, using the classic feathers and fans. Then Renee came out and blew them all away, doing a burlesque and pole routine that mimicked rhythmic gymnastics, but with whips, leather, and chains.

Natasha kept her eyes on the stage but watched Dimitri in the periphery. His gaze drifted from the stage to her and back again. Knowing he was there with her, watching the performance, maybe thinking about her doing these things, made her senses sizzle with awareness. She sucked on her lower lip, wishing it were his mouth, his teeth, scraping against the sensitive flesh. Her body throbbed with need.

Renee's act finished. Natasha cheered louder than anyone, and Dimitri threw a handful of hundreds onto the stage. Renee winked at them as she tucked the bills into the string of her thong, then sauntered away, her fabulous ass and hips swaying.

The next act involved two women, who interspersed their striptease with making out, and Natasha couldn't take it anymore.

"Fine, I'll sit on your lap." She said it like she was doing Dimitri some great favor, like she wasn't about to jump out of her own skin with the need to be touched. "But promise me that we can still go to dinner afterward. I don't need you getting all worked up and depriving me of food."

His grin flashed in the dark, wicked and full of anticipation. "I promise. Now get that sweet ass over here."

Chapter Forty-Six

The burlesque show was the best and worst kind of tease. Not because of any of the action happening on stage—though Renee and the other performers were shaking and shimmying like champs.

No, Dimitri's current source of discomfort came from Natasha's reaction.

On stage, two women kissed hungrily and ran their hands over each other's bodies. On his lap, Natasha whined and wriggled against his growing erection.

"Touch me," she whimpered, and he was only too happy to oblige. The space was dark, and the table blocked them from view. He kept one arm around her waist and slipped his other hand under her dress.

"Fuck," he ground out, noting the dampness of her panties. "You like this, Kroshka? You like watching beautiful women together?"

She twisted to kiss him, her tongue delving deep into his mouth. Her dark eyes seemed luminous, reflecting the stage lights, and her voice held a hushed tone of confession. "Yeah. I do."

His cock surged at her admission, and with a muttered curse, he grabbed her hips and plopped her back onto her own chair. "Keep that up and we won't make it to dinner."

She gave him a petulant look, but she behaved for the rest of the show.

Once it was over, and Dimitri's wallet was a few thousand dollars lighter, he helped Natasha to her feet. "Ready to eat?"

"Sorry, we have to go backstage first." She sounded almost apologetic. "I can't leave without saying goodbye to Renee and Jeff."

Dimitri raised his eyebrows. "You think I'm going to complain about going backstage after a burlesque show? Or maybe you're the one who wants to sneak a peek."

She pinched his arm.

The dressing room was small, but clean and brightly lit, and filled with warm, sweet smells—hair spray, perfume, makeup, and whatever else the performers used before going onstage. It reminded him of the way his bathroom smelled after Natasha finished blow-drying her hair. Rows of vanity tables lined both walls, each mirror surrounded by round light bulbs. Another wall held framed black and white photos of classic movie stars, visible over a rack full of costumes.

Renee bustled over to them, wearing a short robe of ice-blue silk. She kissed Natasha's cheek and shot Dimitri a teasing grin. "Glad you both could make it. What did you think?"

While Natasha launched into a discussion of the dance quality of the routines, punctuated by effusive praise, Dimitri put a hand on her shoulder and tried to keep his gaze at eye level.

He had years of backstage experience with dancers and actors. Seeing people in various stages of undress was normal for him. But this was different. Despite the joke he'd made to Natasha, he was aware of being a man in a mostly feminine space, and he'd be damned if he made anyone feel ogled.

Then another man walked in, medium height and build with sandy brown hair, holding a clipboard. "Alicia and Delfina, you're up," he called out.

Two women, touching up their makeup, slipped off their robes and headed out. One of them, a slim brunette, spotted Natasha and let out a gasp of surprise.

"Tash? Is that you?"

Natasha turned and squealed. "Delfi! I didn't know you were still here."

Delfina gave Natasha a squeeze. "I came back to do one night a week, to pad my savings."

The man with the clipboard stepped closer and nodded at Natasha. "Hey, Tash. Good to see you. Renee told me you might come by."

With a wave, Delfina headed out, and Natasha made introductions.

"Dimitri, this is Jeff, the manager here. Jeff, Dimitri is a…a friend of mine."

Jeff grinned and shook Dimitri's hand. "How'd you like the show?"

Renee patted Dimitri's arm. "You don't have to answer that. He only wants your opinion because he knows you're a judge."

Some of the others were watching, so Dimitri gave a thumbs-up and used the scoring language from *The Dance Off*. "Everybody gets a hundred percent."

At his side, Natasha snickered and muttered, "You're so corny." But then she slipped her hand around his arm, like she was staking a claim, and he loved that.

"Delfina is the one who got me the interview," Natasha explained. "And Jeff hired me. Even though I didn't have boobs back then."

Jeff tapped the clipboard against his thigh. "Your audition blew us away, and you picked up the pole technique faster than most. I only wish you'd stayed longer."

Natasha turned a grateful smile on Jeff and Renee. "I always said it would be temporary."

Dimitri stiffened. There was that word again. *Temporary.*

Jeff nodded and sounded wistful. "I know. And I get that this place wasn't your dream job. But you were such a pro."

Renee leaned in. "We all vote for you on *The Dance Off.* Any hints as to who you're paired with next season?"

Natasha pressed a finger to her lips. "You know I can't tell. Besides, I haven't met him yet. We're still a few weeks away from filming."

Renee heaved an exaggerated sigh. "Fine." Then she sent Dimitri a wink. "Nice meeting you, Mr. Judge."

They said their goodbyes and left, getting in the car to head to Krasavitsa.

The word *temporary* still rattled around in Dimitri's thoughts as he drove. Was that how Natasha felt about his place in her life? Something that was here now, gone tomorrow?

That had been the nature of their relationship for all these years. But he didn't think of her that way. Even when he'd kept his distance, she'd been a constant—in his thoughts, in his heart. An eventuality. What if he'd waited too long?

"Have you ever been to Krasavitsa?" he asked, just to break the silence.

She shook her head. "What does that word mean?"

"Beauty. My mother named it."

The restaurant was where he spent most of his time. How was it possible she'd never been there?

Because until a few weeks ago, he'd never been close enough to a woman to show her this place. Not even Natasha. Maybe Babe Planet was the same for her. A secret she kept close, because she didn't trust other people with it.

Now that he'd been there, he couldn't remember why he'd felt so adamant that she tell him about her past. He'd wanted to know everything about her, sure, but why?

When he dug deep, the answer was rooted in security, not

trust. If he knew everything there was to know, if he could shine a light in all the dark recesses, maybe then he'd feel comfortable enough to take the next step with her. To risk putting his heart on the line.

But this secret hadn't done that. Yes, he was grateful she'd trusted him with it, especially since she hadn't told anyone else, not even her best friend. She'd trusted him not to judge her or make her feel ashamed. He valued that trust and didn't take it for granted.

But it hadn't made him feel any more or less secure. She'd lived a life before she met him. She'd made decisions, and while he was curious about her motives so he could learn more about what made her tick, knowing every piece of her past didn't change how he felt about her. He loved her for who she was now, and all those decisions had led her to this point. He wouldn't change them, although he did want to be part of her decisions going forward.

He thought of the contract burning a hole in his desk drawer. Of the Idea Book. Of Alex's voicemails and texts. He had his own things he was holding close.

Still, she'd shared part of her life with him, and it was only right that he do the same.

She was everything he'd ever wanted in a woman, in a partner. Everything he ever would want. He loved her, and whether she accepted it, returned it, or…some other outcome, he wanted to show her Krasavitsa. And he wanted everyone there to meet her.

Although he still wasn't ready for his mother to get involved yet.

Besides, it was ridiculous to be nervous. He'd dated tons of women. Well, not *tons*. Dozens? Anyway, he'd gone on dates. Taken women to dinner, movie premieres, live shows, and fancy parties. It was part of the lifestyle. You got a plus one, and there was no shortage of women eager to fill that role.

Not because of him. He wasn't quite *that* egotistical. But for the fame. The chance to brush elbows and maybe get a leg up. He knew people and, thanks to the diversification of his interests, he got invited to a lot of places.

But he'd never taken Natasha to any of those events, and he'd never brought *any* woman to Krasavitsa. It was the equivalent of introducing her to his family.

He cleared his throat. "Remember that time I ran into you at Rogelio Hernandez's launch party?"

She glanced at him from the corner of her eye. "Yeah…"

"That guy you were with—what was his name again?"

She pursed her lips and looked out the window. "Rocky Lim."

"He's a martial artist, right? In those car racing movies?"

"Yes."

"Where is he now?"

"London." She let out an exasperated sigh and glared at him from the passenger seat. "Why are you asking about Rocky?"

"I'm curious about the people you've dated."

She snorted and turned away. "Rocky and I weren't *dating*, no more than Jackson and I were *dating*."

"And like how you and I weren't dating."

She didn't answer.

"*This* is a date, Tasha."

She made a noncommittal sound. "Does that mean *we're* dating now?"

"If you're asking me to be your boyfriend, the answer is yes."

She snorted again. "I didn't ask. Anyway, it's against the rules."

"We're way past your rule, Kroshka."

"Not *my* rule. *The Dance Off*'s rule. We can't date. It's the only defense I have for living with you."

He drove in silence. He'd forgotten about that stupid rule. He was a judge, so it didn't quite apply to him, but only because he was more famous. He wouldn't be the one to be penalized. If they were discovered, Natasha would take all the blame and the consequences. Their relationship had the potential to ruin her career.

He wanted to give her everything. But even he couldn't gift her a career, especially when his own felt so unsteady.

He'd find a way around it. But not tonight. Tonight, his only goal was to make this the perfect first date.

Chapter Forty-Seven

Two years ago

Watching Natasha leave the Fallen Angel by Rogelio event with that fucking prick from *Speed Demons* made Dimitri see red.

Okay, maybe calling Rocky Lim a prick wasn't fair. He was an impressive martial artist, and those stupid movies were actually fun. But that didn't stop Dimitri from wanting to punch the guy in his pretty face for being with Natasha.

The rest of the night was a haze. Dimitri brought his date back to her place, but he barely remembered anything about what followed. He was distracted, more like a rutting machine than a man. She didn't seem to notice, and afterward, he left immediately.

The next day, Dimitri was in such a foul mood that Nik didn't even dare tease him about it. Instead of subjecting everyone at Krasavitsa to his ire, Dimitri stayed home, opting for a long swim and a brutal workout. He started drinking vodka in the early afternoon, and when he couldn't take it anymore, he called Natasha. He had no idea what he said to her, but she came over. Like she always did.

He met her on the front steps and pulled her inside, slamming the door shut and shoving her against it. Without a word, he kissed her like he was going to eat her alive, pouring into her all the rage and confusion the night before had stirred up in him.

And maybe Natasha was harboring some conflicting feelings of her own, because she was rougher than usual, scraping her teeth up his neck and scoring her nails up the backs of his thighs and ass through his pants.

Dimitri yanked down her skirt, leaving her in some kind of stretchy black lace bodysuit. "Take this off," he demanded, bunching his hand in it. "Take this fucking thing off."

She wrapped her arms around his neck, arching her body into him. "Do it your goddamn self," she purred against his mouth. With a harsh groan, he clutched the fabric in both hands and tore it to pieces.

The sound of rending cloth broke something in him, and he filled his hands with her bare skin, unable to get enough. He kneaded her breasts with his left hand and shoved two fingers of his right into her mouth. She sucked them with a moan, her tongue sliding between the digits, but he didn't let himself imagine it was his cock buried in that hot, wet cavern. Like a man possessed, he yanked aside her panties and drove those saliva-slick fingers into her.

"Look how fucking wet you are," he hissed. "Been here five seconds and you're already drenched. Were you thinking about what I'd do when I saw you dressed like this? Were you thinking about how I'm going to take such *good fucking care* of this needy pussy?"

He didn't know why he'd emphasized "good fucking care" with deliberate thrusts of his hand. And now wasn't the time to think about it.

"*Yes!*" She clutched his shoulders as her knees buckled. He slid his free arm around her and hoisted her up against him as he continued to pound her soft flesh with his fingers, stroking her inside in the way he knew would make her shatter.

"Come on my hand, Kroshka. Do it. Do it now."

"Oh, God," she moaned. "Don't stop, Dima. I'm coming—*ahh!*"

He groaned at the feel of her inner walls clenching his fingers and yanked his hand out to drag his tongue over them, tasting her release. Without giving her a second to catch her breath, he gripped her waist, trying to kiss her while he hustled her through the house. Her clothing hung from her in tatters and she still wore those super sexy heels that made them the same height. In the back of his mind, he worried he was going too far, pushing her too hard, but it made him want to go further, harder, to see when, if ever, she told him to stop. He wanted everything she had and more. He wanted to consume her down to her very essence and know she was *his.*

Except she wasn't. Last night had shown him that. And he wasn't hers.

He didn't know which truth hurt more.

That hurt drove him to bend her over the closest surface, which happened to be the dining table.

"Show me that ass," he growled, slapping one of her butt cheeks. She let out a startled yelp, followed immediately by the breathy moan he heard in his favorite dreams. She plastered her front to the shiny surface of the table and wiggled her butt at him, welcoming another swat. He gave it to her, smacking the other cheek, then filled his hands with her taut flesh, kneading away the sting. She was panting, and he knew she liked this, but he was too overwrought to drag it out.

After grabbing a condom from his pocket, he undid his pants and boxers and shoved them down. Lifting one leg out of the pile of fabric, he propped his bare foot on one of the dining chairs. He licked his hand, tasting her, and groaned as he spread his spit over her swollen folds. He gave his cock a few pumps with his fist, but he was already on edge and hard as steel. Rolling the latex down his length, he gripped the base and slid his shaft through her wetness, letting her drench him before he rubbed the head over her clit.

She reacted like he'd electrocuted her, bucking and moaning and trying to chase the crown of his cock with her entrance.

"Fuck me," she murmured, desperation thickening her voice. "Fuck me, fuck me, fuck *me*."

As if he could resist her. Notching the head, he pushed into her in one long, inexorable slide. She was practically screaming by the time his hips met her firm ass, and he paused to catch his breath. Sinking into her like this was as close to heaven on earth as he would ever come.

Why didn't you come home with me last night? he wanted to ask. *Why didn't we ditch our dates so we could do* this?

But he already knew the answer. She might come whenever he called, but he had to do the asking.

Every. Single. Fucking. Time.

It took him a second to realize he was thrusting into her as he thought each word. That she was groaning underneath him. That his hands were digging into her hips and her ass was a slightly warmer shade than usual from the slaps he'd delivered. He watched his dick disappear inside of her and knew he wanted this woman more than he'd ever wanted anything, which was saying a lot. Too much, really.

Hold back, asshole, he told himself. *She's not yours.*

But his cock didn't seem to know that. And from the growl rising in his chest as he leaned over her and pounded into her willing body, there was at least another part of him that didn't know it either.

The way he took her on that table was dirty and rough, and it would likely leave both of them with bruises. He'd toppled the chair at some point and heard the sound of cracking wood, but he didn't stop to investigate. He just planted one knee on the table's surface, rising above her for leverage. The table alone cost five thousand dollars, and he didn't care if it collapsed into splinters beneath them, so long as they both came first.

Speaking of…

He stuck his fingers in her mouth again. Her moans turned briefly into the sound he recognized from when she deep-throated his cock, but she didn't pull away. Lowering his hand, he swirled his wet fingertips in circles over her clit, pinching and releasing, while continuing to fuck her. Before long, she was screaming as her pussy clamped down on him. She was so tight, he had to grit his teeth and wait, pumping slowly, and when her moans died down, he let loose.

"Take it," he growled. "Take this cock. Every inch. And know that it's *me* fucking you, *me* making you feel this way."

Some bit of self-preservation had him biting back the last words he wanted to say. *Only me.*

The need to claim her was riding him hard, and just before the orgasm hit, he pulled out. Yanking off the condom, he pumped his erection in his fist. Pleasure raced through him like lightning. He heaved a guttural groan as ropes of pearly semen spurted all over her beautiful ass and onto the table beneath them.

An incredible climax like that should have cooled the fire in his blood, but it didn't. Fierce possessiveness took hold of him as he rubbed his spend into her skin. Then he leaped off the table and pulled her with him into the bathroom, where he dragged her into the shower stall and took her again standing up.

They fucked so many times that night, Dimitri didn't know which way was up anymore, and still, that hot, tormented feeling inside him wasn't assuaged.

It scared the shit out of him.

So when she slipped from the bed the next morning, he pretended to be sleeping. After she left, he got up and threw his phone into the pool so he wouldn't be tempted to call her and tell her to come right back.

"That was a bit dramatic," a sarcastic voice said from behind him, and Dimitri turned to see his brother watching him through the sliding screen door.

"When did you get back?" Dimitri demanded.

Nik scratched his stubble as his face scrunched in thought. "I'd say it was sometime after one of you broke the chair, but before the last time you two…how do I put this delicately? Took a trip to pound town." Nik speared Dimitri with an unexpectedly serious look. "Honestly, I wasn't sure if I should make popcorn or call the police."

"We had something to work out," Dimitri muttered, and instantly regretted it. This was already more than he'd meant to reveal.

"And did you?"

"No," he said curtly, sliding open the door and shoving past Nik to get into the house. Dimitri's shoulders tensed, waiting for his brother to make some smart remark, but all Nik did was sigh.

Dimitri hated that Nik had heard him with Natasha the last time. That he might have heard Dimitri demanding she tell him she was his.

And if Nik *had* heard, he might know that Natasha had refused to respond.

Days later, Dimitri finally got a new phone and changed her first name from "Kroshka" to "She Doesn't Want You," and her last name to "Don't You Fucking Call Her."

And for a long time, he didn't.

He told himself he didn't need her. That he had no feelings toward her, and therefore, there was nothing to get over. He was fine.

But then season ten of *The Dance Off* began filming, and he had to face the truth.

He *wasn't* over her. He *did* need her.

And he was not fucking fine.

He changed her name in his phone to "Tasha" and texted her a single word.

Tonight.

Chapter Forty-Eight

Present day

I n the parking lot at Krasavitsa, Raul's eyes nearly fell out of his head when Natasha climbed out of the car. Dimitri bit back a grin at the young valet's stunned expression. Even in the boot, Natasha was a gorgeous woman, and her tight black dress showed off her long, lean curves. While she'd complained about the loss of her wardrobe and her inability to shop for something new, the woman could make a garbage bag look like high fashion, and Dimitri couldn't figure out why she needed so many over-the-top outfits. She'd done her hair in sexy, tousled waves, and her eyes looked dark and mysterious. The lipstick she'd reapplied in the car was a bright, slick red.

Dimitri thought she was just as beautiful in her pajamas and glasses, especially when she smiled sleepily at him in their bed.

When Dimitri walked through the doors with his arm slung around Natasha's waist, every eye turned their way.

Well, not *every* eye. But all the eyes belonging to the staff. He caught the bartenders exchanging grins, and one of the waitresses actually stopped in her tracks before bouncing on her toes and giving a squeal of delight.

Lord. Why had he hired a bunch of sentimental fools?

Carlito, his manager, bustled over to them. He took Natasha's hand and beamed at her. "Señorita, encantado."

"Es mi placer," she replied, smiling.

Dimitri bit back a sigh. "Natasha, this is Carlito, the manager. He keeps this place in order and knows all the gossip."

Carlito led them to the table that was always kept empty for Dimitri, chattering with Natasha in Spanish the whole time.

When Natasha drew back a step and raised her eyebrows, Dimitri tuned in.

"¿De verdad?" She sounded surprised. "¿Nadie?"

"¡Lo juro!" Carlito placed a hand to his chest, as if making a solemn vow. "Nadie."

Dimitri rolled his eyes.

Once they were seated and Carlito had left them alone, Dimitri pinned Natasha with a look. "What did he tell you?"

Her smile was smug. "You'll never know."

"I can make him tell me. I pay him."

"He'll lie through his teeth. His grandmother was Puerto Rican. We have a bond."

Dimitri shook his head and sat back as Mariska, one of the waitresses, poured their wine. "I knew I was going to regret bringing you here."

At Mariska's gasp, Dimitri threw his hands in the air. "I didn't—come on, you know I didn't mean it like that. It's because you're all going to switch your loyalties over to her instead of me."

Mariska turned up her nose at him. "And now you know why," she replied in Russian, and patted Natasha on the shoulder before walking off.

He reached across the table and took Natasha's hand in his. "You know I didn't mean it like that, right?"

Natasha shrugged. "You've said worse."

He winced. "I have, haven't I?" Unable to look at her now, he stroked her knuckles with his thumb and said quietly, "I said something to you once, not long after we first met. About calling first—"

"To make sure you didn't have another woman over?"

He winced at her arch tone. "I don't think I phrased it like that exactly, but yes. That's what I'm referring to."

"What about it?"

"I meant Nik."

She blinked. "Your brother?"

"Yeah. I meant that you should call first so I could tell my brother to get lost, but it came out wrong. And when I realized how it sounded…I didn't clarify."

"Why the hell not?"

"Because it seemed like you didn't care, one way or the other. And that…shit, Tasha, it stung."

Her eyes narrowed. "And the other night? After we, um, watched your movie."

"Is that what the kids are calling it now?"

She rolled her eyes. "Ay Dios mío. You know what I mean. You said something that made it sound like you had lots of women staying over all the time."

He shook his head. "I was…overwhelmed. It was a bad joke. And really, there haven't been as many other women as I might have implied."

"So, what were you doing then?"

"What I've been trying to do since the moment I laid eyes on you."

"And that is?"

He exhaled heavily. Just because it was getting easier to tell her how he felt didn't mean it was *easy*. But he had to try. "Prevent you from finding out how fucking gone I was for you?"

A moment of silence passed between them before she asked, "Why did you phrase that like a question?"

"Because when I told you I loved you, you didn't believe me," he said in a low voice. "And once, in the past, I asked a woman I was involved with to move in with me and she laughed in my face."

Natasha's eyes dipped in sympathy. "Oh, Dima. I'm sorry."

He shrugged. "I was twenty-three and stupid. She was right to turn me down. It would have been a disaster."

"I meant I was sorry for *my* response," Natasha grated out, her voice full of exasperation. "You caught me off guard when you said…that."

"Surprised myself, too," he admitted. "But with you, everything I want to say comes out wrong. Probably because I've been hiding so much." He took a sip of his wine. "So I guess I should stop doing that."

Her hand tightened on his. "I do it, too."

"I've noticed."

Her lips curved, but the smile disappeared as her shoulders slumped. "You are right about one thing, though."

"Finally." He took another sip. "What's that?"

Her fingers toyed with the stem of her own wine glass. "I should call Gina. And probably tell her about…what I did before she moved here."

"Only if you want to. It's yours to tell. Nobody needs to know everything you've ever done."

Not even him, he was starting to realize.

"How do you feel?" he asked. "After going there again."

She gave a vague shrug. "I'm glad we went. It's part of me and my journey as a dancer. I can't forget about it or lock it away."

"It would be okay if you did. You're entitled to your secrets."

"Says the guy who was practically drooling with curiosity after meeting Renee." She rolled her eyes. "You're a big ol' chismoso, Macho. A gossip."

He snorted. "You think I'm bad? You should meet the rest of my family."

Shit. Why had he said that? It was what he was actively trying to avoid. He quickly changed the subject. "I'll admit, I was surprised by how good the show was. And Renee? That woman can move."

"I know, right? She's like a snake. Everything I can do on a pole, I owe to her."

"I'm definitely getting one installed. And then I'm sending her a thank-you present."

Her smile dimmed, and the look in her eyes was sad. "Dimitri, I can't stay. They'll fire me."

"Who said the pole was for you?" he said lightly, because he was worried she was right. "It looks like a good workout."

He was saved from having to elaborate on that when the appetizers arrived. He knew what Natasha liked from the nights he'd brought food home from the restaurant. Krasavitsa's signature beet salad, derived from his grandmother's borscht recipe. The seasonal varenyky option—this month featured summer corn and basil with the traditional sweet cheese. And of course, fries.

"The fries here are fucking fantastic," she said, digging right in. "Even when you bring them home and we have to reheat them."

She shoved a few in her mouth, and her eyelids fluttered in pleasure. "And fresh? They're heavenly."

"They're my mom's favorite, too," he said, then kicked himself. Why was he still talking about his family? "I had to make sure we had fries on the menu, just the way she likes them."

Natasha dipped one in ketchup and used it to point. "Your mom has good taste."

And she wants to meet you. The words were on the tip of his tongue, but Dimitri held them back. It was enough that the staff were meeting her tonight. He'd hold off on subjecting her to his loud and pushy Ukrainian family for a while longer.

He reached across the table and took her free hand again. She smiled at him as she chewed and the moment was sweeter than any other he could remember.

And ruined by Carlito, who chose that moment to zip over to them.

"¿Todo está bien?" *Carlito asked.*

Even though the words were directed at Natasha, Dimitri answered, shooing away his nosy manager. "Everything's fine. Go away."

Natasha shook her head as Carlito left. "Are you always so mean to your staff?"

"Wait until you hear how they talk to *me*."

"You know, I used to think you were scary."

"You don't think I'm scary anymore? I need to try harder."

She snorted into her wine glass, then glared at him as she wiped her mouth with a napkin. "Aside from your reputation, I was a fan. I *loved Aliens Don't Dance*. When I met you, it was like a fantasy come to life."

Uneasiness filtered through him as her words brought to mind the first time they'd met. It had been an accident. He realized it later, but when she walked into the rehearsal room, he'd been going through some new choreography on his own, and suddenly, there was someone to test it out with. But he hadn't known she was a fan then. Had it contributed to her interest in him? A month ago, he wouldn't have asked. Now, they were too close for him not to, even as he dreaded the answer.

"Why did you go home with me? That first time." He paused and forced himself to voice the thing he'd always feared. "Was it because I was a judge?"

She rolled her eyes. "No, you dummy. It was because you were Dimitri Kovalenko, the physical embodiment of all my teenage sexual fantasies."

He winced. "Honestly, I'm not sure that's better. How old were you when that movie came out?"

"Fifteen."

"Christ. I don't think I want to know this." He scrubbed a hand over his face. "So that's why you went home with me? Because of a childhood crush?"

"Oh, no." She shook her head and waved a hand like that was silly. "I mean, it helped that I already knew who you were. It didn't feel like you were a stranger, so I wasn't worried you were going to murder me and bury my body in your backyard. But you were all intense and sexy and commanding, and dancing with you was like foreplay. I went because I wanted to."

"I don't even know how to respond to all that." He paused. "Wait, bury you in my backyard?"

"A girl can't be too careful."

The entrees arrived, and Natasha beamed when Mariska set down the oven-baked chicken kiev in front of her.

"That's your favorite, right?" Dimitri tucked into his steak. "You've asked for it a couple times when I've brought food home."

Her expression softened. "Yeah, it is."

"Good. Well, enjoy."

She started on the chicken, but after a few bites, she gestured with her fork. "I've gotta ask. Why do you work here? You're a literal movie star and world-famous dancer, but you spend all your time at a restaurant."

He took another bite and thought about her question. "There's the easy answer."

"Which is?"

"It's smart to diversify your interests and have multiple streams of income."

"Especially for us." She poked at the remaining beet salad. "Dance careers don't last forever."

"Right. But that's still the easy answer."

She turned her full attention on him, her dark eyes serious. "So, what's the real reason?"

He could tell her that it was a low-risk venture. That Alex had done most of the legwork. That it turned out he liked owning a restaurant. But he went with the deepest reason. "My uncle owned a bakery in Brooklyn. I spent a lot of time there, and the employees and customers were like family. I wanted to recreate that out here, since all my real family—my parents, grandmothers, aunts, uncles, cousins—are all back on the East Coast."

"But on a more extravagant scale than a neighborhood bakery," she said, glancing over her shoulders at the other diners.

He grinned. "You know I don't do things by halves, and I can't help it if celebrities like our fusion varenyky. But we have a lot of regular customers, and the employees stick around."

"I don't know what that's like." She picked at her napkin. "The family part, I mean. I barely know my extended family. Every so often, I think about hopping a plane to Puerto Rico to try to form a connection with my grandparents, maybe even try to find my father, but what's the point? They'd be strangers. I'm not even close with the relatives I have in New York."

"Have you ever been to Puerto Rico?"

She shook her head. "Can you believe that? I was almost born there, and I've never even visited."

"I haven't been back. To Ukraine." He shrugged. "Everyone left and never looked back. There's nothing there for me."

She squeezed his hand. "That's how I feel, too. I don't even go to New York, except for work. My great-grandmother died, and Gina moved out here with me. My mother is the only one left there, and we…well, we don't get along."

And now Gina was gone, leaving Natasha alone. He cupped her hand in both of his and rubbed. They'd both lost the people closest to them in this city when Gina and Nik's careers took them away from Los Angeles.

But they'd found each other. And finally, after all this time, they were getting out of their own way and coming together.

He'd make it work. He didn't know how yet, but he was determined. For now, he just had to show her she deserved love. Once she accepted that, they could take the next step, whatever that might be.

Chapter Forty-Nine

By the time they had finished eating, the restaurant had cleared out significantly. It was late, and as Natasha finished her dessert, she noticed that the staff were prepping to close.

"Do you want a tour?" Dimitri asked. His eyes followed the movements of her tongue as she licked molten chocolate off a spoon.

Yeah, she was teasing him. Who could blame her? She was still wound up tight after the burlesque show, and seeing him so at home in this space he'd created from the ground up was sexy as hell. But she kept her tone sweet as she said, "I'd love a tour. Unlike your house, I've never actually been here before."

He pressed a hand to his chest and whistled. "Ouch. Direct hit."

"Tell me I'm wrong."

"You're not." He got to his feet and held out a hand for her. Before spraining her ankle, it was something that would have driven her crazy. But the fact that he offered assistance now, every single time she got up from a chair or exited the car... well, his attentiveness didn't annoy her anymore. "Considerate" wasn't a word she would have previously associated with

Dimitri, but here he was, anticipating her every whim and need.

If she weren't careful, she'd get used to it.

She took his hand and let him lead her through the door marked "Employees Only."

"This better not be a ploy to bend me over your desk and play out some kind of boss-and-employee fantasy," she warned.

He bit back a laugh. "Don't give me any ideas."

He took her through the kitchen, where he introduced her to the sous-chef and the kitchen staff. A number of them spoke Spanish, and she chatted with them about the menu, praising the food. Even though she was full, she sampled everything they pressed on her, because it would have been rude not to, and also stupid. Only an idiot would turn down a private tasting at one of LA's hottest restaurants.

The waitresses asked her dozens of questions about working on *The Dance Off*. Apparently, Dimitri refused to talk about the show with them, and they were hungry for backstage gossip. Natasha assured them that any rivalries among the pros were good-natured and gently reminded them not to believe everything they read online.

Carlito joined the tour, and his pride for Krasavitsa and his admiration for Dimitri's restaurateur skills were evident in the way he spoke.

As they were finally leaving, Carlito reiterated his earlier message to Natasha, that Dimitri had never brought another woman to Krasavitsa.

Natasha mulled over his words as baby-faced Raul brought them the car. She came to one conclusion.

Maybe Dimitri's feelings for her *were* real.

He'd gone with her to Babe Planet, seen what it was like, and didn't judge her for her choices.

He'd brought her to the restaurant, subjecting them to scrutiny by his staff. From the way everyone had smiled at her and watched her interactions with Dimitri closely, as if they were all

hoping for something, made Natasha sure she'd passed whatever tests they'd devised with flying colors.

As far as first dates went, it was pretty perfect.

Which sucked, because it *couldn't* be a date.

Natasha didn't even want to picture Donna's reaction: the
cold smile, the flat eyes. Donna would start with an apology, but
she'd be eating it up, thriving on the drama. Or, worse, she'd
hold it over Natasha's head, using it as leverage to twist
Natasha's onscreen storylines, like she'd done to Gina a few
months earlier.

Or—shit—what if they didn't fire her outright, but knocked
her down to backup dancer? She'd bypassed it before, because
she'd proven her skills on *EDN*. The backup dancers were fresh-
faced hopefuls, happy to be on TV but aching for the chance to
be partnered with the celebrities. They danced during group
numbers and commercial breaks, but they got paid less and
didn't receive as much press or attention. Getting demoted
would look terrible to future job prospects. So terrible, Natasha
would probably have to quit to save face.

God, this was a nightmare.

She should leave Dimitri's house immediately. Pack her
things and go crash on Lori's couch. Find a hotel. Or just give up
and put the last of her money toward a one-way plane ticket to
New York.

But as she looked over at Dimitri, she couldn't do it. Even if
what was growing between them was impossible, she couldn't
deny that *something* was there. Something real. At the very least,
she deserved to indulge it for one night, if only to quiet the
stupid hope clamoring inside her.

What was one more mistake? She'd already made so many.

"What are you thinking about so hard over there, Kroshka?"

Taking a deep breath, she decided to tell him the truth.

"You."

Chapter Fifty

<hr>

Three months ago

After the semi-finals, Natasha joined a bunch of her castmates from *The Dance Off* at Club Picante. As usual, they got on the guest list thanks to Lori's ex-girlfriend, Mimi, who worked at the bar, but Lori and Jackson had told her they were going to be late. Natasha ran home first to change, and she would have chilled there until Jackson arrived, but she knew Gina was bringing Stone back to their place, and the two of them needed privacy.

Natasha sat at the end of the bar in the VIP section, sipping a vodka cranberry while the others joked and flirted. It was a weird night, and she felt off-balance. She was pissed at Stone for upsetting Gina, but she was also a little jealous, which sucked to admit.

Gina had every right to be upset. But she also had a guy who would move mountains for her, and Natasha didn't think her friend saw it yet. Stone *loved* Gina. It was plain as day, but Gina could sometimes be oblivious to this stuff.

Not her fault, really. Gina wasn't the only one with daddy issues. Natasha hadn't even known her father. When she was eighteen, her mom finally revealed that Natasha's maternal grandparents had told him that Mami had an abortion. The man literally didn't know Natasha existed.

Probably for the best. This way, she only had one parent to disappoint her.

She was scowling into her drink when a hand landed on her shoulder.

"Hey, Tash!" It was Kevin, who'd just arrived with his celebrity partner, Lauren D'Angelo. He slid his arm around Natasha for a friendly squeeze. "What's up? You okay?"

She shook off thoughts of her parents and flashed him a smile. It was almost impossible to be in a bad mood around Kevin. "Just tired. Congratulations on making it to the top three."

"Thank you, thank you." He took the seat next to her at the bar. "How'd you get here? Did you drive?"

"Nah, I took a car." She figured Jackson would probably drive directly from the studio, and they'd take his car back to his apartment. Natasha would use a rideshare app to get home from there.

"Awesome. I'll buy you a drink. Whatcha having?" Kev waved to Mimi, who nodded and headed in their direction.

Natasha drained her glass, hoping it would help her push thoughts of Gina and Stone from her mind. Kevin chatted with Mimi while she mixed their drinks.

Natasha was happy for Gina. Really, she was. Gina deserved the best, including true love.

Because as much as she was a cynic, Natasha still believed in true love. Well, she believed it existed, anyway. For other people. Not her.

Kevin kept his arm around her, like he could tell she wasn't feeling like herself. Natasha didn't know how he sensed that stuff, but he always looked out for the women on the cast. But since he was also the only finalist at the bar, everyone wanted to talk to him.

During a break in the conversation, Natasha bumped Kevin's ribs with her elbow.

When he peered down at her, she gave him a little smile. "Hey. Thanks."

The light in his green eyes dimmed, his premature smile lines disappearing into a seriousness she didn't often see from him. "Don't mention it," he said softly.

There was a commotion near the entrance to the VIP section, which was really just an area at one end of the bar cordoned off with rope. Natasha turned her head with a grin, expecting to see Jackson.

Only it wasn't him.

The smile slid off her face as she watched Dimitri walk into the space like he owned it. Hell, maybe he did. He was part-owner of at least two restaurants, as far as she knew. But really, that was how he always walked. With total arrogance, like he had a big dick and he knew it.

Fuck. He *did* have a big dick, and *she* knew it. The asshole had every reason to walk with a swagger.

She sucked in a breath, and her body tensed. Kevin must have noticed, because his arm tightened around her protectively.

"All right there?" Kevin murmured in her ear. She nodded, but she wasn't all right. Not even a little bit.

Lauren sashayed over to Dimitri and wound her arms around his waist. She said something in his ear that made him laugh.

A hot spike of possessive jealousy lodged itself in Natasha's gut, but all she did was roll her eyes and mutter, "Mira esta comemierda."

Kevin snorted. "You talking about him or her?"

Good question. She'd meant Lauren, but... "Both of them. They're both comemierdas."

"What's that mean?"

She turned back to the bar and leaned her elbows on it. Mimi plunked another drink in front of her, and Natasha murmured her thanks. To Kevin, she said, "It's like a snob, but literally translates to 'shit-eater.'"

She sipped her drink while Kevin fell over himself laughing.

A hand slid up her spine—not Kevin's. Natasha instinctively leaned into it, sucking in a breath through her nose. A deliciously woodsy scent consumed her, and desire flooded her body as Dimitri leaned against the bar beside her. She'd know his touch, his scent, anywhere.

A smile played on his lips, more visible since he'd shaved recently. But this was a guy who had a five o'clock shadow by noon. The beard would be back soon, making him look like the bad guy in an action movie.

Good. She liked his beard.

"What's so funny?" Dimitri asked, sparing Kevin a glance.

"Huh?" Kevin wiped his eyes. "Oh, nothing, man. Just talking shit about the producers. You know how it is."

As Kevin got to his feet, he caught Natasha's eye and raised an eyebrow. She gave him a short nod, indicating that she was fine. She wasn't sure where Kevin's hyper-protective streak came from, but he had nothing to worry about. She trusted Dimitri completely.

With her body, anyway. Her heart was another story.

Dimitri took the seat Kevin vacated and picked up Natasha's drink. After taking a sip, he grimaced.

"What is this, Kool-Aid?" he asked.

She shrugged. "Nobody told you to drink it."

"How many of these have you had tonight?"

Shit. "Um…four?" Maybe it was five. Shit.

He raked her with his gaze. "How do you feel?"

Better, now that you're here. Luckily, no amount of alcohol in the world would get her to admit that.

It was true, though. Arousal speared through her, mixing with the vodka. Her body pulsed in time to her heartbeat, which had sped up since he'd touched her. No, before that. Since he'd walked in and she'd set eyes on him. Her skin prickled as she waited for him to touch her again.

He would. There was no other reason why he'd come over. She knew this dance. They'd done it before, too many times now. And she'd always been a fast learner when it came to choreography.

At the beginning of the season, she'd sworn she was done with him. He twisted her up too much. But she was a big fucking liar. When it came to Dimitri, she always wanted more.

And she was really bad at saying no to him.

"Tasha."

He breathed her name in that deep, husky voice, the *T* sound thick in his mouth.

She loved the way he said her name.

"Huh?" She blinked.

His lips curved, not quite a smile, but the sensual lilt matched the heat in his eyes. "I said, 'How do you feel?'"

Oh. He wanted to know if she was drunk. She glanced at her drink, his hand still curled around the glass. "I'm fine."

His eyes were on her mouth. "I guess I have to catch up then." He raised her glass to his lips and chugged it, his throat working as he swallowed down the red liquid. When he lowered it, he made a face. "Blyat. How can you drink that?"

When he turned to order something else, he dropped his hand onto her thigh. Casually, as if it were no big deal. His fingers gave a gentle squeeze. Natasha's mouth trembled open, and her pulse pounded between her legs. He wasn't even looking at her. He was smiling at Mimi, chatting easily, and turning Natasha into a sloppy mess of hormones and desire with one touch.

It was honestly kind of impressive, the power this man had over her.

Mimi brought over a handful of shot glasses and poured something into them. When they were full, Dimitri nudged one toward Natasha. He took another, and Mimi took one as well. There were still two more on the bar.

Mimi counted—*three, two, one*—and they knocked them back. Dimitri slammed his empty glass down, then consumed the two remaining shots in rapid succession.

Whatever Natasha drank burned as it went down, and she watched Dimitri blink and take a deep breath.

Mimi laughed at his reaction and collected the glasses. "That'll put hair on your chest."

It was funny because the neck of Dimitri's open shirt revealed his dark chest hair. He waxed and shaved before performances, but like his face, his body hair grew back fast, too.

Natasha loved that she knew this about him.

The shot coursed through her, molten and thick, and Dimitri's grin seemed extra bright when he took her hand and said, "Let's dance."

She followed him onto the dance floor, and it was a relief. When they danced, she didn't have to think. Her muscles knew the moves, and Dimitri was a master—at both dancing and commanding her body. They danced salsa, in the flashy LA-style that Dimitri loved. He swirled her into spins and pulled her into lifts. Years of training took over, along with a complete awareness of Dimitri's touch. Natasha was like a radio tuned only to his frequency, and the signal was loud and clear.

They were sweaty and flushed by the time the band took a break and the DJ started his set. Natasha had hoped the physical exertion would burn through the hunger in her blood, but it hadn't. She was still ravenous.

Mimi had drinks waiting for them when they returned. A beer for Dimitri, water for Natasha. They guzzled them down, and then he pressed his body against Natasha's back, trapping her against the bar. Her breaths were short and shallow, and not just from dancing. She wanted him, she wanted him so fucking bad, but she wouldn't ask, she wouldn't…

"Kroshka." He breathed the word into her ear while pushing

his erection against her ass. He'd said this word before. She didn't know what it translated to, only that it meant he was getting drunk. Mimi pointedly ignored them.

His hands clutched Natasha's hips, and he rocked, grinding against her, and she must have made some kind of sound because he leaned in. "Come home with me."

One of his hands snaked around, and he pressed his palm low on her belly, his warmth seeping into her skin through her purple mini-dress. The fingers on his other hand dug into her hip, anchoring her to him, and an image of them fucking against the bar in this crowded club flashed through her mind. She gasped and nodded, before tilting her head back to rest on his shoulder.

He spun her around and leaned in to kiss her, right there in the bar, something he'd never done before. A breath away from her mouth, he stopped and squeezed his eyes shut.

"Fuck." He shook his head and pulled back enough to dig his wallet out of his pants pocket. He threw a few hundreds onto the bar, grabbed Natasha's hand, and pulled her through the crowd and out of the club.

It was only as Dimitri was summoning a car on his phone that she remembered she'd been there to meet Jackson.

"Two minutes," Dimitri said, slipping his phone into his pocket. Then he caught Natasha's face in his hands and laid a passionate, vodka-spiked kiss on her.

Something settled within her as she opened her mouth for him, and one last thought flittered through her mind.

Jackson would get over it.

Chapter Fifty-One

Present day

"**M**e?" Dimitri couldn't hide the pleased note in his voice, even if he'd wanted to. "What about me?"

The freeway lights skittered over Natasha's face, casting her in bands of light and shadow. Her lips curled in a slow, sexy smile. "I'm thinking about all the things I'm going to do to you when we get home."

The steering wheel creaked as his fingers tightened on it. The speedometer ticked past eighty.

Home. It meant everything to him that she thought of his house as *home.* When really, she was the one who made it feel that way.

Her sweet, playful presence filled the open spaces to every corner, making it feel lived in and loved. She brought new scents and new music, conversation and laughter. She gave him a reason to dance in his own house, something he'd never seemed to do before now.

God, he was desperate for her to stay.

After he pulled into the garage, he rounded the hood to open the passenger door and help her out. She stepped close to him and put her hands on his cheeks. Her eyes were dark and hot, her smile tempting beyond belief. When she pulled him down to kiss her, he would have given her the world.

His hands settled on her waist, and she kept the kiss light and soft. Just the warm press of lips and the tease of tongue. When they broke apart, she whispered against his mouth, "Take me inside and make love to me?"

"Da, lyubimaya." As if the answer would ever be no.

Hooking his hands under her thighs, he boosted her up so she could lock her legs around his hips and her arms around his shoulders. She punched in the security code while he gripped her ass. Then he carried her to the bedroom and gently set her on the edge of the bed.

She turned her back to him. "Unzip me?"

He set the lights on low before he sat beside her, skimming his hands up her bare arms. Her skin was cool. Smooth. Soft, despite the strength of her dancer's body. He ran a finger down the elegant column of her neck, down the center of her back, tracing over the bumps of her spine. The buzz of the zipper parting was loud in the quiet room. Goosebumps rose on her back, and when he touched his lips to her shoulder, she shivered.

"Cold?"

"No." Her chest rose and fell with quick, shallow breaths. "I just want you."

He turned her toward him and kissed her like they had all the time in the world. Just kissing, just his lips exploring and cherishing every centimeter of hers, just hints of tongue and the light press of teeth. When she tried to increase the intensity, pressing closer and sucking on his lower lip, he only caressed her body in soothing, languid strokes.

When her eyes were clouded with passion and her lips wet and swollen from his attention, he pulled back.

"You've never said you wanted me before."

She pressed her face into his chest, as if hiding her expression. "Wasn't it obvious?"

He craned his neck to look into her face. "It was obvious that I wanted *you*. Not the other way around."

"Why do you think I never said no?"

"Never saying no isn't the same as always saying yes."

She bit her lip and toyed with his shirt buttons. He waited, his heart on the line, his mind running through all her possible responses.

Finally, she looked him square in the eye. Her eyebrows tilted like she was scared, but her voice was firm. "Dimitri, I have wanted you since the second I saw you. Even when I wished I didn't, I couldn't make myself stop. Wanting you is in my blood, and it terrifies me because I don't think I'll ever get enough."

His chest swelled at her admission, and he kissed her again. Deeper this time, but still slow. Tonight was about her, about showing her she deserved to be loved. His hands slid down her arms and up her legs before finally thrusting into her hair. "What do you want, Tasha? Tell me, and I'll give it to you. I'll give you everything."

"Get undressed." Her hands made quick work of his shirt buttons.

"I can do that." While he shucked off his pants and boxers, she shimmied out of her dress. Clad only in a black and red bra-and-thong combo, she straddled his thighs, her cool fingers roaming over his chest.

He leaned back on his hands, sucking in a breath as his cock rubbed against the inside of her leg. "Enjoying yourself?"

"Inmensamente." She caressed his arms, and he flexed, just because he could.

"Let me touch you." His tone was more pleading than demanding.

"God, yes."

He leaned forward, wrapping his arms around her and palming her butt. The skinny frill framing the globes of her ass teased his fingertips and drove him crazy. "You always wear the sexiest underwear." He breathed the words into her neck, his lips trailing along her collarbone and down, where he pressed a kiss into her cleavage. "Is it for me?"

"No." When he lifted his head, she grinned and struck a pose that pushed her tits up. "It's for me."

He groaned and filled his hands with her breasts. "That's even sexier."

"Just wait until I take it off." With a saucy wink, she settled back on his lap.

Eyes on his, she undulated her spine, rolling her shoulders and reaching up to slide one skinny bra strap down. When she pulled her arm free, she waved it seductively in the air before bringing it to her opposite shoulder. She pinched the other strap between thumb and index finger, and when he thought she'd pull it down, she instead leaned forward and shook her tits at him.

The surprise of it made him blink, but it was her sexy little smile that had his cock straining between them. Groaning, he dug his fingers into her hips. She had the teasing part of strip-tease mastered. "You're killing me, Kroshka."

She didn't answer. Arching her back, she writhed on his lap, trusting him to keep her anchored. Flipping her hair, she somehow got her other arm free of the bra strap. Now, she cupped her breasts in her own hands, kneading them as she pursed her lips and blew him a kiss.

"Ah, fuck." Wrapping one arm around her hips to keep her steady, he reached between them and took hold of his dick, giving it a few pumps before squeezing the base. "You're so hot. So unbelievably fucking hot."

"You ain't seen nothin' yet," she sang softly. Then she rolled her hips, bringing her warm cleft closer to his cock. She'd always been playful in the bedroom, but now, he could see she'd still been reserved. This Natasha, the one who taunted and teased, flirted and played, wasn't holding back anymore.

If he hadn't already been in love with her, he would have fallen then and there.

While she held her bra with one hand and reached behind herself to unhook it with the other, he licked his fingertips and pulled the fabric of her panties aside. She hissed on an intake of breath as his fingers slid through her folds.

"Sí, tócame más," she whined, writhing sinuously on his lap. "Touch me."

"Anything you want." He dipped into her entrance, gathering her wetness, then swirled his fingertips over her clit. Her beautiful face, transformed by passion, drew his attention even as her breasts were bared centimeter by centimeter. But when her fingers flexed, plumping her soft flesh, his eyes became glued to her movements. Bit by bit, her bra shivered down, closer to revealing her nipples. He licked his parted lips, ready to swoop in and capture one, when she suddenly whipped off the bra. Before he could catch more than a glimpse, she covered herself with her arm.

He groaned in disappointment. "You're such a fucking tease."

She laughed out loud and dropped her arm, baring herself to him. "That's the point."

"Speaking of points." He closed his lips around one of her dark nipples, rolling it with his tongue, as he rubbed his thumb over her clit.

She clung to his shoulders, sighing. He tumbled them both onto the bed, worshipping her body with his hands and mouth. She tried to rush, pulling at him and whimpering, but he resisted.

"Shh. Ne speshi, Tasha. Slow down." Tonight, he would take his time, and by the end of it, she would know how special she was.

She whimpered and pulled at his shoulders. "Dimitri..." Her voice held a note of pleading.

"Tell me what you want."

She panted and twisted her hands in the bedsheets. "Why do you keep asking me?"

"Because this is all for you." He kissed a line up the inside of her leg, adoring the strength of her. "You're a goddess. You deserve to be cherished and given all you desire."

She pressed a hand to her cheek and looked away. Amazing that sweet words embarrassed her more than anything else they'd done together in this bed.

"I'm just a regular woman, Dimitri. Not a goddess."

"To me, you are. It's about time I started treating you how you deserve."

"Don't be too good to me, or I'll get used to it." Her voice was shy. Wistful.

"I want you to get used to it. Now, tell me what you want."

She swallowed, and it took her a few moments to speak. "Hold me close."

He felt a pang in his chest, and sensed how much it had cost her to make that simple request. Without a word, he crawled up her body and settled next to her, wrapping her in his arms. "Like this?"

"Just like this." She snuggled against him, tucking her head under his chin. "Today was kind of an emotional roller coaster."

He nodded, rubbing his face in her hair, inhaling the scent of figs. It had felt that way for him, too, but this moment was all about comforting her, not him.

She raised her chin. "¿Bésame?"

"You never have to ask." He pressed his lips to hers, sweeping her tongue into a dance. *Slow, slow, quick-quick, slow.* His cock pulsed against her firm belly, but the sweetness of her mouth and the little noises she made as she squirmed against him were all he needed.

He broke the kiss to whisper against her lips, "What else do you want, Tasha?"

In answer, she took his hand and brought it between her legs. He stroked her in a slow, steady rhythm until she was gasping and quivering with need.

Again, the same question. "What do you want now?"

And when she answered, "Your mouth," he shifted down and tongued her clit until she was sobbing.

When he asked her again, her eyelids fluttered, but she met his gaze directly. "*You.*"

Heart racing, he slipped on one of the condoms he kept in the nightstand and covered her with his body.

Now, more than ever, he wanted to tell her he loved her. He wanted to say it again and hear her response, to beg her to accept him and love him back.

But tonight was about her. *He* knew he loved her. She didn't. So, he had to show her.

Pushing between her thighs, he pressed against her entrance. She was open and so, so soft. He sank right in.

"Moe serdtse prinadlezhit tebe," he murmured, then stilled. He hadn't meant to say it, hadn't meant to say anything as he slid inside her, but the words just tumbled out. They came from the truest part of him, and he wouldn't take them back.

But nor would he tell her what they meant.

"Dimitri." As she whispered his name, something shifted in him and settled into place. The word flitting through his thoughts was *home.*

The scent of figs and ginger on his pillow, and espresso in the morning. High, surprised laughter, and muttered curses in a mix of Spanish and Russian. A bed warmed by two bodies, long legs and arms entwined. Dancing, fighting, kissing, teasing.

Home.

He hitched her uninjured leg over his hip and rolled onto his side, taking her with him and keeping his heavy length lodged within her. With his eyes on hers and their breaths mingling, he set the pace. Slow and steady, deep and close. Their gazes locked, and he read her pleasure there, along with something else. There was something in the way she clung to him, in her voice when she'd said, "You." They'd been here so many times before, yet this time was unlike any other.

Open. She was open, hiding nothing. Her heart was in her

eyes. Maybe it always had been, and he'd been too scared of his own feelings to see hers.

She held onto him, pumping her hips to the rhythm he set. Every time they danced, every time they fucked, she followed his lead. Whatever he wanted, she gave, without question or hesitation.

Maybe that was the sign. Maybe he'd been oblivious to it all along, taking her silence and reservation for disinterest, when really, she'd been protecting her own heart.

It no longer mattered that she'd never made the first move or asked for more. Why should she have? He should have willingly given it. That first day, in the rehearsal room, he should have fallen at her feet and offered her everything.

There had been countless opportunities to remedy the situation since then, but he'd been too scared to take the risk. Too uncertain of her. But this was a woman who'd never known deep love. Of *course* she was hiding her heart.

And still, she'd given him whatever he asked. Every time. He'd just never asked for more, because *he* had been the one holding back.

Where else in his life was he doing that?

Gritting his teeth, he increased the pace of his thrusts. "I'm sorry, Kroshka."

Her eyes rolled back, and she dug her nails into his shoulder. "For what?"

"I should've been better." He slipped his hand between them to rub her clit. "You deserved better."

She let out a high moan. "What the hell are you talking about?"

"I'll make it up to you. I promise. From now on." He captured her mouth as he pumped into her with shallow thrusts, keeping the focus on her clit.

Her body clenched, then spasmed. Against his lips, she cried out. He held on to her, even as her pussy squeezed his dick, even as she shook and trembled. He held her, kissed her, stroked her, and then it was too much.

Too much, and exactly perfect.

His own body tightened. His skin prickled as pleasure zinged through him. A ragged groan tore from his throat as he pressed his face into her hair and pounded his hips, setting off his own orgasm.

It swept through him, leaving his defenses shattered and his heart raw. There was only him, her, and how he felt about her.

And really, what else did he need?

Natasha held him, rubbing his sweat-slicked back as his body ceased shuddering.

"What did you say?" Her voice was quiet. "Earlier."

He didn't lift his head, using her hair to hide his face. Like a damn coward.

"I said you deserve better."

"No. Before that. In Russian."

Oh. *That.* He hesitated, but why not tell her?

"My heart, uh, belongs to you."

She was quiet for a moment. Her hands still slid lazily up and down his back. Then she scooted down and pressed her lips to his chest, right where his heart pounded from exertion and pleasure.

He closed his eyes. How the hell had he ever found it in him to let this woman go?

One thing was for sure. He wasn't making that mistake ever again.

Chapter Fifty-Two

Dimitri convinced Natasha to join him for a quick shower —for safety's sake, because of her ankle—but before they got back in the bed, he cleared his throat.

"I want to show you something."

Natasha's gaze flicked down to his crotch. They were both still naked. "I've already seen it."

"Not *that*. Something I've never shown anybody else before."

She snorted out a laugh. "Okay, because we both know a lot of people have already seen your dick."

He glared at her. "You're a mean woman."

Her smug smirk challenged him and turned him on. "Tell me I'm wrong."

Nerves made his voice gruff, and he snapped, "Not as many as you think. Now, do you want to see it or not?"

"You haven't told me what it is yet!"

Embarrassed and out of patience, he grabbed her boot and gently slipped it over her foot, taking care to adjust the straps. "Come on." He took her hand and pulled her out of the room, ignoring her giggles.

He was about to show her his most prized possession, the

compendium of his life's work, and she was laughing about his sexual history.

Well, it was better that she laugh about it. When he thought of where they could be now if he'd had the guts to pursue her earlier, he was hit with a sense of loss and regret so profound, it was like a punch to the chest.

He brought her to his office. The sight of his desk chair reminded him of coming home and finding her twirling around in it, choreographing even with an injured ankle. Both times he'd come across her in the studio, she'd seemed peaceful. At ease. Her shoulders weren't tense, her brow unclouded by worry. When she danced, or more specifically, when she designed dances, the weight of the world fell away. She loved what she did.

It was why he'd dragged her in here now. She would understand. And after the night they'd had, he was done hiding from her.

Maybe his nerves were obvious, because she stopped laughing. Beautiful and distracting, she hovered near the door, arms crossed under her naked breasts. Fuck, he should have grabbed robes for them first. It wasn't enough to strip his emotions bare, he had to do this while physically naked, too?

"What do you want to show me, Macho?"

Her voice was soft and reassuring. She gave him a small smile, which bolstered his confidence.

He pulled out the binder and set it on his desk. "This."

She wandered over and her gaze dropped to the bold letters on the cover.

"Idea Book," she said, reading aloud. Her curious gaze met his. "What is it?"

He took a breath and placed a hand flat on the cover. "This contains detailed notes for all the personal projects I've ever conceived, going back to when I was a teenager. I want to tell stories through dance that express universal emotions through the lens of the immigrant experience."

Her eyes widened, and she touched the edge of the cover with her fingertips. "Dimitri, this is…full. Practically bursting."

"Twenty years' worth of concepts." He smiled ruefully. "Only one ever made it to the stage."

She covered his hand with hers and shifted closer, until their bodies were touching. "Will you show me?"

Shit, he hadn't even opened it yet. "Ah, yeah. Sure. Let's sit over here."

He picked up the book and carried it to the narrow pullout sofa at one end of the room. Natasha spread out the throw blanket so they could sit without putting their bare asses on the cushions. Dimitri balanced the book on his knees and Natasha cozied up beside him to look.

"Don't laugh," he warned her.

She gave him an offended look. "I wouldn't laugh about this."

"You were literally laughing at me a minute ago."

"Because I was *teasing* you. I wouldn't tease you about something this important." She nudged him with her hip. "Ábrelo. I'm dying of anticipation over here."

Now or never. He opened the cover, revealing pages he knew by heart. Each sheet lived in a plastic sleeve, connected to the three-ring binder. Flipping one by one, she stopped him four pages in.

"Esperate." She tapped a finger on a sketch of a dancer. "Did you draw these?"

He scratched the back of his head. "Yeah."

"D, these are great."

"They're just rough gesture drawings."

She pulled the binder onto her own lap and took over flipping the pages. She stopped, then went back a couple, then flipped ahead. Leaning closer, she trailed her finger along the faint handwritten notes, jotted down in pencil so many years ago. Finding the song list on the next page, she hummed one of them, slightly off-tune, and her shoulders moved as if of their own volition as she read through his notes.

"I can totally see this," she murmured as she moved to the next page, which detailed the third act.

He swallowed hard, holding very still as she read the notes, her fingertips stroking the pictures he'd pasted around the text. Some were there to evoke mood, others for color palettes or costumes.

When she reached the end of that section, she pressed a hand to her chest. "Oh."

Nerves frayed, he jumped on the word. "Oh? Oh, what? What does 'oh' mean?"

When she raised her head, her eyes swam with emotion. "This one. It's about losing everything, isn't it?"

He closed his eyes for a second. "Yes."

She nodded and turned back to the book.

Page by page, she absorbed the physical representation of everything that lived in his heart and mind. Everything he felt about family, fear, life, loss...love. He didn't look at the pages—didn't need to. Instead, he lived it all again through her reactions. A surprised laugh, a gasp, a sigh. Eyebrows lifted, then lowered as she pressed her lips together against some deep emotion.

Everything that made him who he was existed in this book, and he'd just given her the keys to unlocking his heart and soul.

He leaned back against the sofa, stretching an arm out behind her. Their thighs pressed together, and it took all his control not to resort to old nervous tics—bouncing his leg or chewing at his cuticles. He'd broken those habits long ago, but sitting beside her while she looked through this book was the most excruciating kind of stress. He'd never even shown this to Alex. Sure, his cousin had seen a few pages and was aware of some of the concepts, but Dimitri had never let Alex flip through the whole binder.

Moe serdtse prinadlezhit tebe, he'd told her. She had his heart in every possible way. Who could've guessed love would be so terrifying?

Sometime toward the end, her hair had fallen to cover her face from his view. He'd lifted a hand to brush it aside, then chickened out. Better that he not see. He'd wait until she was done, and then...well, he didn't know what would happen. She might just say, "That was nice, now let's go to sleep." She might say it was stupid or trite.

When she reached the last page, she closed the book and placed her hands flat on the back cover, which still held the address of his parents' house in Brooklyn, in case it had gotten lost. Her back rose and fell with her breaths, each one stretching his nerves further.

She set the binder aside and turned to him.

Her eyes were wet and spilling over. She wiped the tears away with her fingertips. "Dimitri."

Just his name, quiet and slow, every syllable enunciated.

She reached for him, and he sank into her embrace, needing to touch her, needing to feel her skin and hold her and—shit, needing to be *held*. Her arms went around his shoulders, and her tears wet his neck.

"My heart feels so full," she whispered. "Thank you for showing me."

Relief washed through him, leaving exhaustion in its wake.

"You get it?" he asked. Not the most articulate of questions, but she nodded and eased back.

"I do. It was like...watching you grow up and evolve as a creator. You've got everything in there. I had no idea you could make these kinds of stories."

He shrugged. "This stuff pops into my head. Sometimes it starts with a song, sometimes an emotion that sends me searching for the music. It bugs me until I put it in the book."

Even then, the book still haunted him. Stories and characters and ideas that wanted to be brought into the world beyond the pages of a three-ring binder.

"You said only one of them ever made it to stage," she said.

Here it goes. "Yeah. This one. *Sem'ya.*" He took the binder and flipped to one of the concepts in the first half of the book. It was about a family consisting not of people, but emotions, and how they all worked together to create a harmonious whole.

She smiled at the page he pointed at. "Oh, I loved this. It has so much depth. What does that word mean?"

His chest swelled to hear her compliment, but the memories dragged him back down. "It means 'family.' Alex and I brought it to Broadway. It wasn't long after the alien movie, so I rode the fame wave to get it greenlit."

"I remember seeing ads for it. I wanted to go, but it closed before I could save up for the ticket."

"You wanted to see it?"

"I had a giant crush on you, remember?"

They'd been so close, growing up in the same city. "Where in the Bronx did you live?"

"Castle Hill. The 6 train. You were in Brooklyn, right?"

"Bay Ridge. R train."

She shook her head and studied the images on the page. "Might as well have been a different planet, as far as the subway is concerned."

"We could have passed each other on the street and never known it."

She gave him a sidelong glance. "I would have recognized you, for sure. But you never would have given me a second look. I was a tall, skinny teenager with glasses who hadn't grown into her features." She cupped her breasts. "And I hadn't bought these yet."

His cock twitched, ready for another round. "Your age would've been a deterrent, but I like to think I'd have looked past all the rest. Now stop fondling yourself, or we'll never get to sleep." Collecting the binder, he returned it to the shelf.

"I have another question."

His shoulders tensed. "What?"

"*Sem'ya* was a long time ago. Why haven't you produced any of the other ideas in there?"

He busied himself with the stuff on his desk so he wouldn't have to look at her, despite the weirdness of sorting junk mail while completely naked. "Like you said, the show closed before you could buy a ticket. It flopped."

"A couple of my classmates went to see it, and they said it was really good."

He jerked a shoulder, gathering all the loose pens into a pottery cup. "Doesn't matter how good it is if most of the seats are empty. My name wasn't a big enough draw."

Her features twisted into a puzzled scowl.

He sat in the desk chair, the fabric rough against his butt, and looked for another distraction. He started opening and closing drawers.

"That was over a decade ago. You're even more famous now. Why don't you try again?"

"I did." He slammed his hand on the desk to emphasize his words and instantly regretted the outburst.

Natasha just gave him a mild stare and raised a single eyebrow. It reminded him of the face his mother made when he was being an ass.

"Would you like to try answering that again?" she said, her voice bland.

He propped his elbows on the desk and rested his face in his hands. "I'm sorry. This is kind of, uh…"

"A touchy subject for you? Yeah, I got that." She went to him, smoothing her hands over his shoulders and kneading the tension in his muscles. "I'm here, Machote. You can talk to me about this." She leaned closer, her breasts rubbing his arm, and kissed the back of his left hand where it covered his cheek. "If anyone understands, it's me."

He dropped his hands and looked up at her open, smiling face. She was right. It was why he'd brought this up with her in the first place.

"I did try again," he admitted. "I took more TV and movie roles, more investment opportunities—like the restaurant—so I wouldn't be as broke as I was after the show flopped. I worked my ass off as a choreographer and producer for other people. But they were always other people's projects, other people's names on the line. Even with the restaurant, I didn't come out as the owner until it started doing well."

Her hand smoothed up and down his spine, but she didn't speak, giving him space to continue.

"Then my cousin Alex and I approached some investors. Alex is my partner in all this stuff. He handles the logistics, I do the creative work. Anyway, we pitched one of the last ones in the binder. *Raz i Navsegda*."

Her face scrunching in thought. "The one with the hoops?"

"That's it."

"What does the title mean?"

He exhaled, knowing it would reveal too much. "The phrase is like 'once and for all,' which is probably what I'll call it if I'm forced to give the show an English title. It's the concept of permanence, of something lasting always and forever. That's what navsegda means."

"It's the search for a forever home," she said, her hands stilling on his shoulders. "The person in the story is jumping through all these hoops, into all these different worlds, searching for home, for permanence, for security."

He nodded. Odessa would always be the place of his birth. He had memories there from his most formative years. But he didn't want to return. He wanted to find a home where he was, here. He should have felt relieved that she understood, but instead, his skin itched with the urge to hide.

Was this how she'd felt visiting the bar with him? Raw, revealed, exposed?

He'd thought love would make it easier to bare your heart. It was still just as difficult, even when you trusted the other person not to stomp all over it.

When he didn't answer, she slipped into his lap, and he filled his arms with warm, naked woman, taking solace in the feel of her skin against his. It wasn't sexual, not like it might have been in the past, when he'd treated every second they were together as if it would be the last one. Now, holding her steadied him.

"It's you, isn't it?" She petted his cheek, smoothing down his beard. "The man in the story, looking for home. He's you."

When he nodded, she lowered her hand and pressed it to his chest. "It must have been hard to leave Ukraine."

"*Yes.*" The word tore from his throat, expelling all the air in his lungs with it.

Everything inside him tensed, and he closed his eyes and leaned into her, dropping his forehead to her chest. Her arms wound around him, holding on tight.

If someone had told him that being understood by the person you loved was akin to physical pain, he never would have believed it. But to have her see him so clearly, just from reviewing the book... Either he wasn't doing a good job of hiding it, or she got him in a way no one else ever had, except maybe his cousin.

Nik didn't understand. He'd been too young when they moved. Alex did, because they'd been closer in age. Dimitri's parents did, of course, but they'd been around the age he was now, and he couldn't imagine having to make that kind of decision.

"We dropped everything to move to America." His voice sounded like it was being pressed between rocks. "Start fresh, my mom said. No looking back. We lost everything. *Left* everything."

"I think you had it right the first time," she murmured, stroking his hair. "It was a loss. At least, in terms of how you felt about it."

His breath shuddered out of him, almost painful in its release. "Yeah. And we never talk about it. Everyone wants to forget. I understand, I do, but..."

"Were you scared?"

He huffed out a nervous laugh. "Hell yeah, I was scared. No one would tell me what was happening. And then one day, I overheard them talking about leaving. And then my cousins and aunts and uncles were *gone*. For months. America, they said, but I barely knew what that meant, or what it meant for us that we were going next. And Nik was so little, always trying to run away, so I was responsible for him a lot of the time. Sledi za svoim bratom, my parents always said. Watch your brother."

"And you were how old? Ten?"

"Ten when we moved, yes."

Her voice was quiet, her eyes soft as she ducked her head to look at him. "At least you had each other."

His heart broke for her. She hadn't had anyone. She'd been an only child with a mother who sounded like a real piece of work.

"We did. And we had it easier than some. Some of my relatives were already here. My father spoke a little English. It could have been worse."

"That doesn't mean it wasn't still traumatic," she said gently, and he acknowledged that with a nod.

"My parents had this attitude about it, like sometimes this stuff just happens. Nichto ne vechno. Nothing lasts forever. Sometimes you just lose everything and have to start over. It's normal, even expected." He shook his head. "Anytime something bad or disappointing happened, like when I had to close my show: Nichto ne vechno. Oh, well. Move on."

"Is that what you did when you tried to produce…let me try it…*Raz i Navsegda*?"

"Good pronunciation." He patted her hip. "And not exactly. The investors basically told me I wasn't famous enough."

She reared back, eyes wide. "Do they live under a rock?"

Her outrage warmed his heart. "They said I hadn't done anything mainstream in a while, and since the last show was a failure, they wouldn't go along with it until I was back in the public eye."

Her jaw dropped. "Is that why you joined *The Dance Off*?"

"Bingo." He bopped her on the nose with his finger. "You really have been following my career."

She scrunched her face up and looked embarrassed. "It's why a lot of people come on the show. To get famous, or get famous again."

"And it works."

"But that was years ago. Why haven't you tried since then?"

And there it was—the question he really didn't want to answer, mainly because there was no good reason.

"Busy." He toyed with a rubber band on the desk. "Between *The Dance Off*, the restaurant, my other investments—"

"Dimitri." She caught his face in her hands and forced him to look at her. "Why haven't you done your *own* show yet?"

"I need to think about it." Even to him, that sounded weak.

She rolled her eyes. Apparently, it sounded weak to her, too. "Are you going to make me spell it out?"

"Go ahead." Shit, he shouldn't have said that.

She shook her hair back and sat up a little straighter on his lap, a move that pushed her breasts into his face. He raised a hand to pinch her nipple, and she slapped his fingers away.

"Don't try to distract me." She pinned him with a direct look. "You're worried they'll turn you down again."

Her words triggered the fear, and excuses rose to his lips, the same ones he'd been telling himself—and now Alex—for ages. "I just want to be sure they'll go along with it before I start this whole process again. It's a lot of work, and—"

"Shut up." She pressed a finger to his lips. "Once a week, for six months out of the year, millions of people watch you on TV. As a judge, you get more screen time than any of the dancers, while doing a fraction of the work. You're famous, Dimitri. A fucking household name. You don't want to be *sure*. You, papi chulo, are *stalling*."

He scowled. She wasn't wrong. Hell, he'd done the same thing with her, stalling for three years, convincing himself it was because he wanted to be *sure* she felt the same way about him. But really? He'd just been scared she'd turn him down.

Looking back at himself, it was fucking pathetic.

"So, the question becomes," she continued, "why are you stalling?"

He opened his mouth, but she covered it with her hand.

"*I* think," she said. "You're scared of *failing*. I get it, because I worry about that, too. But you're worried about failing at something that has *your* name on it."

He sucked in a breath.

"Did I get it right?" she asked, looking pleased.

He pulled her against him and rained kisses on her neck. "Nail on the head," he growled.

She sighed and melted against him. "Just do it, Macho."

"Here?" His dick jumped, pressing against the underside of her thigh. If he shifted her just a little, he could slip right in.

Laughing, she pushed at his shoulders. "Not me. *Raz i Navsegda.* Make it happen. You have everything you need. Stop holding back. You can't wait for everything to be certain before you make a move."

Stop holding back. He'd been holding back in so many areas of his life. He was thirty-five years old. Wasn't it time he stopped waiting for the rug to be pulled out from under him?

Natasha yawned so hard her jaw cracked.

"You're right. But you're also tired. Come on." He stood, cradling her in his arms.

"I'm wearing the boot. I can walk."

"I don't care. I want to carry you."

She smiled and twined her arms around his neck as he carried her through the living room and down the hall to his bedroom, where he settled her into the bed.

"You're not coming to sleep?" she asked, snuggling into her pillow while he gently removed the boot from her foot.

"I will in a minute. Just have to send a quick text."

He sifted through their discarded clothing until he found his phone.

Opening his texts with Alex, Dimitri typed, *Let's do it*, and hit send. Just as he was plugging it in by the bed, it buzzed in his hand with a response.

About damn time.

Dimitri frowned and typed back, *Why are you up?*

Alex's reply came two seconds later. *I'm at the airport. Since you wouldn't answer my calls, I'm coming to knock some sense into your hard head. Pick me up at LAX in the morning and be ready to work on the pitch.*

Dimitri froze with the phone in his hand. Shit, this was really happening. Just like that.

Alex's flight info appeared on the screen. His plane was arriving at LAX in less than eight hours.

"Dima?" Natasha's head poked out of the covers. "Come to bed."

Dimitri texted back one word. *Yes.*

Then he scooted under the covers, spooning the woman he loved. Her ability to see him so clearly had chased away the lingering fears.

He could do this. He and Alex would get the funding and produce the show. He and Natasha would sort things out, and she would live here with him.

Everything would be perfect. Steady. Stable. Secure.

What else could a man ask for?

A profound feeling of peace settled over him, and Dimitri easily drifted off to sleep.

Chapter Fifty-Three

Five years ago

When Dimitri was nervous, he tended to get brusque.

It had been brought to his attention many times throughout his life, although others used words like "mean," "rude," or in Nik's case, "pissy."

Even knowing this about himself, Dimitri couldn't help it. And he was definitely nervous about this meeting. A lot was riding on the result.

"So, what do you think?" he asked, even though he probably should have let them consider his pitch longer.

To his right, Alex pressed his lips together like he was biting back a sigh. He did that whenever Dimitri couldn't keep his mouth shut.

One of the crusty old white guys sitting across the table raised his eyebrows. Dimitri had wanted to have the meeting at Krasavitsa, but these guys had insisted on using a conference room at their office. Since Dimitri was asking them for money, Alex said they had to comply.

After Dimitri had sunk so much of his own funds into his

first—and only—production, Alex had refused to let him take those kinds of risks anymore.

So Dimitri steered clear of anything that wasn't a safe bet and only involved himself in ventures that wouldn't reflect poorly on him if they failed.

Or he used someone else's money, like he was trying to do now.

The other crusty old guy, the one with glasses, tapped his fingers on the desk. "Mr. Kovalenko," he began, sounding apologetic.

And there it is, Dimitri thought.

"While this all sounds very…entertaining…"

The man didn't finish the sentence. And why should he? They'd already decided. Dimitri suspected they'd made their decision before he'd even arrived, otherwise they would have asked for time to think and discuss.

"We'd *like* to help," the first guy added, even though it seemed like the opposite was true. "We're big fans of your work. But the fact is, your previous effort in this arena didn't go so well for your investors, and we have to take that into account."

Dimitri had started to say something, but that stopped him in his tracks. All these years later, and *Sem'ya*'s failure was still following him around. His gut burned.

"It's also been a while since you've done something that hit mainstream audiences," the one with glasses pointed out, digging the knife deeper. "Maybe if you were about to do a blockbuster movie or secured a regular role on a TV show, we could justify a national tour. But at this point, we have to pass."

Alex thanked them for their time and hustled Dimitri out of the conference room. Good thing too, because Dimitri was going to explode. Fiery hot rage simmered just below the surface. He wanted to go to the gym and punch something until his knuckles bled.

But today, that fury was encased in ice, frozen solid by the reminder of his failed show. As long and as hard as he'd worked, it still wasn't enough for anyone to see his ideas as a viable bet. He was just a dancer to them, not a creator, or a producer, or a businessman.

He left the building with his cousin at his side. Alex put a hand on Dimitri's shoulder and squeezed.

"Dima," he began, but Dimitri didn't want to hear it.

"That was the twentieth 'no,' Sasha."

"It's okay. We'll try—"

"Call that TV show," Dimitri said, cutting Alex off.

Alex screwed up his face in thought. "You mean *The Dance Off*?"

"Yeah, that one."

"Why?"

"They've been asking me to join as a judge."

"And if I remember correctly, your reply was, 'over my dead body.'"

Dimitri gritted his teeth. "I've changed my mind."

Alex hesitated. "Are you sure?"

No. "Yes."

They wanted fame? He'd fucking give them fame.

Chapter Fifty-Four

Present day

"There you are."

Natasha lifted her head at Dimitri's sleepy grumble. He entered the kitchen and ambled over to where she sat at the counter with her laptop.

"Morning." She lifted her chin and accepted the kiss he placed on her lips. Then he straightened and sniffed the air.

"I made you a latte." She pointed to the small white mug by the sink. "I'm still in the habit of getting up at the crack of dawn to teach yoga to people who are about to undo all that relaxation during their work day."

He grunted and, after admiring the elaborate swan she'd made in the foam, took a sip. Breathing deeply, he opened his eyes fully and gestured at the crutches leaning against the counter. "How's your ankle today?"

"A little achy," she admitted. "I think I overdid it yesterday."

He scowled. "And you were thinking about going back to work tomorrow?"

She sighed and rested her chin on her fist. "I need to work so

I can find somewhere else to live before *The Dance Off* starts filming. We're only a couple of weeks away."

His scowl deepened. "You can live here."

"You know I can't." She sipped from her own cup.

He came up behind her. "What are you doing?"

"Looking at apartments." She scrolled through more listings she couldn't afford the security deposit on.

He made a frustrated sound in his throat. "Let me ask you something."

"Shoot." She clicked on a studio apartment that claimed to be near Santa Monica.

"If Gina's such a good friend, why did she leave you in the lurch? With your rent, I mean."

"She wanted to pay through the end of the lease, but I told her there was no need."

His mug clicked on the counter as he set it down. "Well, that wasn't too smart."

Natasha shot him a glare. "Excuse me?"

"How were you planning to cover the entire rent on your own?"

"I had money when she left." Even she could hear the defensive note in her tone.

He leaned his elbows on the counter next to her, getting in her space. "So, where did all the money go?"

She cringed away from him. "I was trying to be a responsible adult, so I paid all my credit cards down and closed them."

"You *closed* them?" His eyes nearly popped out of his head. He looked wide awake now. "Why?"

"So I wouldn't be tempted to end up back in debt."

"But that's damaging to your credit score."

"It is?"

He shook his head like he couldn't believe what she was saying. "Tasha, I know how much money you make. Why were you in debt?"

"I...I don't know." She turned back to the computer, but his questions and the prospect of not being able to afford any of the apartments she was looking at made her stomach burn. "I like shopping. That's what credit cards are for, right? Buy now, pay it off later. So, I paid them all off. But I wasn't expecting my car to die. Or Gina to move. The car cleaned me out, so I took all these extra jobs to cover the rent and bills for the summer. I just never thought I'd have to move out, too."

He exhaled slowly, then dropped a kiss to the top of her head. "I'm trying not to be pushy, but I strongly suggest you talk to someone about building your credit score and savings. I have a financial adviser who can help. I know it sounds like a lot at first, but if I could learn it, so can you. Are you open to that?"

Swallowing hard, Natasha kept her gaze on the screen and struggled to regulate her breathing. Thinking about managing her money made her hyperventilate, which was why she didn't think about it much. "Why are you so fixated on this?"

"Because I'm worried about you."

At those words, she turned to look at him. He didn't seem angry or judgmental. Just concerned.

"If you don't address it, you're going to end up back in the same situation the next time something unexpected happens. And your solution to work so hard that you run yourself into the ground isn't sustainable. Please, Tasha. I care about you. Let me help."

His plea touched her heart, but didn't dispel the fear. She shook her head. "I can't afford to speak to your adviser."

He snorted. "With what I pay him, he'll talk to anyone I ask him to." He stroked a hand down her back and his voice gentled. "Will you do it? Just start with a conversation. He's good at answering questions."

Her stomach twisted in knots. When was the last time someone had cared about her this much? Enough to not just help her do something, but to make sure she had the skills to do it again on her own?

She switched to a different tab and checked her dismal bank

account balance. Maybe he was right. "All right, I'll talk to him. But that still doesn't solve my immediate problem."

"Look, I know it's easy to focus on the immediate when you're in survival mode, but I want to help you manage your money for the long term. Don't worry about an apartment right now. No one knows you're here."

She counted on her fingers. "Kevin and Lori know. Nik knows. Gina and my mom know. Hell, *your* mom probably knows. I'm sure your brother told her."

"He did." Dimitri's phone buzzed in the pocket of his sweatpants, and he pulled it out to check the screen. "I need to run to the airport to pick up my cousin. Don't worry, he's staying in a hotel." He pressed his lips to hers for a quick, espresso-flavored kiss. "Just chill, all right? I'll be back soon, and we'll figure it out."

He sounded so confident. And the apartment search was stressing her out. She minimized the browser window full of open tabs. "Fine. Go get ready."

Twenty minutes later, he rushed back into the kitchen and rummaged in the pantry.

"What are you doing now?" he asked, emerging with a handful of protein bars.

"Working on a video."

He paused by her shoulder on his way out. "You're good at that, huh?"

"I bought the editing programs and equipment and took an online class. Sometimes I post videos of myself dancing to popular songs or explaining different styles, stuff like that."

He grinned. "I'll check them out." He kissed her again, this time with a flash of tongue and the taste of minty toothpaste, then he was gone.

The domesticity of the scene left her with a warm, hopeful feeling, and for once, she didn't try to push it away.

She continued scanning through a few of the videos she'd made recently, including the one where she'd rolled around in

Dimitri's desk chair. That one made her smile, and she started thinking about a group dance in rolling chairs…

And that was an idea for another time. She jotted it down in her trusty notebook, then went back to her existing videos. She ran through the piece she'd changed the music for, noting what she could tweak. It was really coming together, and she was anxious for her ankle to heal so she could try it out. Maybe she could get Dimitri to dance parts of it, so she could see how it looked.

He would do it if she asked. She was starting to believe he'd do anything, simply because she wanted it. That knowledge both thrilled and terrified her. Living with a single mother and two seniors, money had been tight. She'd learned early that the toys she'd seen on TV weren't things she could have, just like she would never have supportive, loving parents like the ones on her favorite sitcom. She'd been following Gina since they were fourteen, not just because they were friends, but because Gina had done the work to include Natasha in everything she did, from auditions, to college applications, to managing their apartment in Los Angeles.

Shit. Gina was the most amazing friend anyone could ever hope for. And Natasha had been too scared to call her.

What could she say, though? Hi Gina. Yeah, I've been doing really great since you left. I'm broke, injured, living with the guy I told you I wasn't going to see anymore—oh, and once upon a time, I worked as a topless dancer and decided not to tell you about it. How are you?

That would go over brilliantly, and Gina would have a million questions about Dimitri. No easy answers there, either. He said he loved her, and Natasha was starting to believe him. But what did it matter if loving him cost her everything—her job, her independence, her ability to prove to her mother that she was good enough?

The doorbell rang, interrupting her troubling thoughts.

Natasha yanked off her headphones and grabbed the

crutches. It was going to take her three times as long to get to the front door with these things.

On the way, the rubber bottom on one of the crutches got caught on a throw rug, and she nearly knocked over a lamp. Whatever was being delivered better be worth the trouble. Cursing under her breath, she hobbled over to the door and wrenched it open.

Her heart leaped into her throat.

La Diabla stood on the front steps, her smile thin and evil. "Morning, Natasha."

Natasha swallowed hard. "Hi, Donna."

Chapter Fifty-Five

There was a surprising lack of traffic around LAX that morning, and Dimitri made good time. Alex texted that there was a problem with the luggage carousel, so Dimitri parked the Porsche in the lot. While he waited, he pulled up Natasha's latest video on his phone.

Her face appeared on the screen with full makeup and her hair pulled back into a tight ballerina bun. Her image waved and blew kisses at the camera before she stepped back.

Dimitri couldn't hold back his smile. She was too adorable, too beautiful…and holy shit, *too talented*. His smile faded as he watched her move.

He'd seen her dance before, of course. Countless times. But it was always to someone else's choreography—including his own —or while paired with an unskilled partner.

This was something else. Her classical ballet training was evident in her strength and the lines of her body, the way she completed each movement. She incorporated other dance styles seamlessly, in a way that fit the music and the story being told. When a text from Alex popped up, Dimitri cursed and snapped the phone to the car's dashboard. Keeping Natasha's videos playing, he drove over to the arrivals terminal, his eyes darting to the screen every time he stopped in the long line of cars winding around to the curbside pickup spot. He was on the fourth, where she was dancing to a sexy R&B song, when Alex knocked on the car window.

Dimitri popped the trunk and finished watching the video while Alex stowed his suitcase. When his cousin slid into the passenger seat wearing a scowl very much like the one Dimitri often sported, Dimitri picked up the second coffee from the cup holder and passed it to him.

Alex gulped down half the cup before speaking. "So, you finally pulled that stick out of your ass and decided this was a good idea?"

"Posmotri na eto." Dimitri switched to Russian and thrust the phone at his cousin. "Look at this choreography."

With a sigh, Alex took the phone and sipped his coffee. Dimitri leaned over to watch it again. When the video ended, Alex passed the phone back.

"So?"

"So?" Dimitri shook the phone at him. "She's amazing. She's even better than I am."

Alex raised an eyebrow. "Is that the woman who's living with you?" He glanced back at the phone, then squinted. "Isn't that Natasha Díaz?"

"How do you know she's living with me?"

Alex rolled his eyes. "You just answered my question, and now I know why you've been ignoring my messages. Your mother told mine that Nik said you're living with a woman, but he wouldn't say who she was." He tipped his cup toward the phone. "Now I know. Isn't that a conflict of interest, since you're a judge?"

"Zamolchi." Dimitri started the car. "I got you a room at a hotel."

Alex snickered. "Good. I don't want to intrude on your little love nest."

Blyat. Why did everyone keep calling it that? "Did you fly all the way across the country to make fun of me or to talk about producing a show?"

Alex rubbed his eyes. "Didn't sleep much last night."

"I'll drop you off at the hotel. Drink more coffee, take a nap, whatever. Then take a car to the restaurant. I'll meet you there and we'll talk about the pitch."

Alex yawned. "Why not now?"

"I forgot the binder."

That was met with a long sigh. "When are you going to start doing this digitally?"

Dimitri shrugged. "I think better on paper. Easier to sketch out my ideas."

"You know you can draw on a tablet."

"It's not the same."

"Whatever you say." Alex pushed the seat back into a reclining position and popped on his sunglasses. "So, tell me what's going on with Natasha."

And because it was Alex, who was more like a brother than a cousin, Dimitri told him everything. There was an accident on the freeway, so they had a lot of time to talk while sitting in traffic.

By the time they pulled up to the hotel, Alex was rubbing his forehead.

"Let me get this straight." They'd switched back to English. "You've been messing around with Natasha—and other women—for three years, when you really wanted her the whole time?"

Put like that, it sounded terrible, but Dimitri couldn't dispute it. "Basically."

Alex gave him a bland stare and continued. "Because you were too chickenshit to tell her—what? That you want to be her boyfriend?"

Scowling, Dimitri stopped the car in front of the entrance. "She was seeing other people, too." Fuck, he sounded defensive.

"And now, because you work together, you have to keep it

quiet that she's living with you, and she's still trying to move out."

"Correct."

"Have you even told her how you feel?"

"I told her I love her."

"And what did she say to that?"

"She didn't believe me!"

"I don't think I'd believe you either." Alex squinted at him. "How exactly did you tell her?"

Dimitri rubbed a hand over his face. "That's private."

Hooting with laughter, Alex smacked his arm. "That means you fucked it up. Come on, tell me. Please. I flew all this way, and you've made me listen to this whole stupid story for forty-five minutes."

"I'm not telling you."

"Fine. But take it from someone who's married—words are shit. You've got to back it up with action."

"I'm trying," Dimitri said through gritted teeth.

"Action *she* sees as loving, not your dumbass version of it. Pop the trunk." With those parting words, Alex climbed out of the car.

Chapter Fifty-Six

Donna raised her thin eyebrows. "Can I come in?"

Puñeta. Natasha's fingers clenched on the edge of the door, itching to slam it in Donna's smug face. But this pendeja was sort of her boss, and besides, Abuela had taught Natasha better than that. Without a word, Natasha shifted to the side and held the door open.

Donna strolled into Dimitri's living room and took a seat on the sofa, like she belonged there. "Nice place."

Natasha shut the door. "Dimitri's not here."

"That's fine. I came to see you."

Of course, she had. It had been obvious the second the door opened. Donna hadn't seemed the slightest bit surprised to see Natasha answering Dimitri's front door while propped up by a pair of crutches.

La Diabla knew. That's why she was here.

Still, no need to play all her cards yet. Natasha maneuvered around the furniture and carefully lowered herself into the brown leather armchair. It would have been easier to sit on the sofa, but she didn't want to be too close to Donna.

Once Natasha was settled, she tried for a pleasant smile. "How can I help you?"

What she really meant was, *What the fuck do you want?*

Donna leaned into the cushions and rested her arm on the back of the sofa. Just making herself right the fuck at home. Her gaze flicked toward Natasha's wrapped ankle, and she sighed. "Didn't I tell you not to get hurt?"

"I'm fine." Natasha kept her breath even, her face carefully blank. "I'll be back on my feet soon."

"You're probably wondering why I'm here."

"I'd be lying if I said I wasn't." Flippant wasn't the right move with Donna, but Natasha tended to get mouthy when she was on edge.

"I heard a rumor you were injured, so I stopped by your apartment to check on you. Since Gina's gone, I wanted to make sure you had help." Donna raised an eyebrow. "Seems like someone else is offering assistance, according to your building's super."

Coño. Manny had spilled the beans.

Donna kept going. "He said your 'gran novio ucraniano' was picking up your mail, so I figured I would find you here, in the home of your *big Ukrainian boyfriend.*" She spread her hands. "And here you are."

Natasha blurted out the first question that popped into her head. "You speak Spanish?"

"Yes."

Natasha narrowed her eyes. "Why didn't I ever know that?"

"It's more convenient to have people think I don't. You know how it is. Some people look at you differently when they know. Or it becomes a weapon they can use against you."

"Maybe you're around the wrong people."

Donna only shrugged. "We all make our own choices for how we go about being Latina in this industry. You, apparently, have made yours."

Natasha sucked in a breath. "What's that supposed to mean?"

Raising a hand, Donna swirled it to indicate the space around them. "I get it. It's a hard life, and an uncertain one. One bad injury, and it's all gone. Or you age out. It's easier to shack up with a rich guy, especially one who's at that settling-down age, with family on his mind."

"¿Cómo?" Was this bitch for real?

"That will give you an out, if you want it." Donna nodded at Natasha's ankle. "Blame it on the injury, say it's worse than it is. That'll give you a reason not to do the next season, and you can keep on playing house with Dimitri."

"That's not what I want." This conversation wasn't going at all how Natasha thought it would, and Donna's implications were beyond offensive.

Worse, they mirrored what her mother had said when she found out Natasha was living here. *What happened? It got too difficult, and now you're looking for a man to make it easier?*

"Figure it out," Donna said. "Otherwise, there won't be a next season for you."

Fuck. Natasha struggled to keep her tone calm. "This is only temporary. I'll be healed soon and back in my own place before season fifteen begins." Whether that was the apartment she was currently paying rent on or not, that remained to be seen.

"See that you are." Donna got to her feet. "Screwing one of the judges is way worse than sleeping with your celebrity partner. With Gina and Stone, people could tell they were into each other. Even with Jackson, viewers would've understood. But Dimitri? You know what they'll say. At best, they'll call you a slut. At worst, they'll say you're jealous of Gina and will do anything to win."

Natasha's voice hardened. "That is a fucked up thing to say, and you know it's not true."

Donna's expression was unrepentant. "Being able to predict audience reactions is how I've made it this far. I'm just warning you."

And by manipulating people to achieve those reactions, Natasha thought, but kept it to herself.

"Don't get up. I'll see myself out." Donna headed to the front door and paused. "A word of advice, Tash. I've known Dimitri longer than you have. The men in this industry...they're not worth it. You're a great dancer and choreographer. You have the potential to build a bigger career. Don't throw it away for a guy who will never commit."

To Natasha's eternal shame, the words, *But he loves me,* flitted through her brain. God, she was so stupid.

Maybe he did love her. Who cared? Love was transient, unreliable. She had to think about herself. She couldn't rely on him to fix everything for her.

"Bye, Donna," she gritted out, instead of *Adiós, puta.*

"Make the right decision, Tash." The front door clicked shut.

Natasha sat for a minute, replaying the conversation in her head. Then, after locking the front door, she hobbled back to the spare room, which still held most of her stuff, and opened her suitcase on the floor.

It was time to go.

Chapter Fifty-Seven

Traffic had cleared by the time Dimitri got back on the freeway.

Show her with action, huh? He thought that's what he'd been doing. Helping her with physical therapy exercises, taking her to the restaurant, showing her with his body how much he cherished her—short of stepping in to solve all her problems, what else was he supposed to do?

Maybe...romance? They'd completely bypassed that part. Hell, they'd only been on one date, and it hardly counted. They should go on a real date. Dinner, at a place he didn't own. Or maybe a movie premiere, or a launch party, or—

Shit, those weren't the kinds of dates real people went on. Had he become so removed that he no longer knew how to date a woman he wanted to spend the rest of his life with?

Yep. He had. It was time to remember how to be a real person.

Dimitri called his brother and put him on speaker through the car's Bluetooth.

"Yeah?"

Nik had never learned the proper way to answer the phone. "It's me."

"I know, fool. What do you want?"

"Where do you go on a date with someone you really like?"

There was a pause, followed by hooting laughter. Dimitri gritted his teeth and decided to make a detour on the way home. "Just tell me."

"Are we talking about Natasha?"

"Of course we are."

"Bro, isn't it a little late for this? You guys have been…you know…for years now."

"Never too late." Dimitri parked in the lot and popped in his earpiece so he could continue the call outside the car. "What's wrong? You don't go on dates?"

"Oh, I go on dates. You're the one who doesn't go on dates. Too busy living that celebrity life."

It grated, because Nik was right.

While Dimitri surveyed the selection at the supermarket, Nik spelled it out for him. "You live in LA. There's tons of shit you can do with Tash. Go to a museum, the beach, hiking, a couples' spa. It's all about spending time together and sharing experiences. Doesn't really matter what you do. Hell, you could take her to a movie and share a giant tub of popcorn. Go see something scary so she has to cuddle up next to you."

"Cuddling?" Dimitri made his choice and ran to pay.

"Yeah, have you ever heard of it? It's supposed to be a precursor to sex, but you guys skipped over that step. You gotta show her you're not afraid of creepy dolls or haunted houses, shit like that."

"Wait, dolls? You've lost me." Clutching his purchase, Dimitri jogged through the lot back to his car. "Okay, movies, outdoor shit, sharing experiences. Got it."

"Why do I get the feeling you're going to fuck this up?"

"I'm not."

"You are. And it'll be glorious to watch. Except Ma will be upset."

"Nobody's gonna be upset. Call me if you think of any other dates."

"No. You're on your own. Don't blow it."

"I won't—"

The line went dead. Dimitri tossed his purchase onto the passenger seat and raced back to his house.

Anticipation built as he got closer. Not to home, but to her. The two had become synonymous. *Home. Natasha. Home. Tasha.* A longing in his gut, pulling him toward her.

He wanted to spend forever showing her how much he loved her.

Last night, they'd crossed a threshold. He'd revealed everything he was—his hopes, his dreams, his fears—and she'd accepted all of it. When he'd approached her about her own challenges—namely, managing her finances—she seemed more open to letting him help. As much as he wanted to swoop in and fix everything for her, she wouldn't welcome it, and it wouldn't help her in the long run. Just because she let him get away with being pushy didn't mean he had to be that way all the time.

Compromise. That was a couple thing, right? They were on their way.

He parked in the driveway, too anxious to even use the garage, and besides, he had to leave soon to meet Alex. Going in through the front door with his gift, he paused, listening for her. Rustling noises came from the spare bedroom. Smiling, he strode through the living room to greet her.

And froze the second he reached the doorway.

What. The. Fuck.

Instead of Natasha's sassy grin, he was met with chaos. She sat on the floor, her right foot stuck out straight, surrounded by everything she had brought with her from her apartment. At the moment, she was cramming those things into her suitcase and duffle bags.

He blinked. "What are you doing?"

He hadn't meant to say it out loud, but she turned. Behind

her red-framed glasses, her eyes were wide and wild. He had a flashback to a few weeks earlier, when he'd surprised her at her apartment. She'd had the same look on her face then.

"Packing." She said it like it should have been obvious, then returned to her task.

The floor no longer felt steady under his feet, and he leaned on the doorjamb, balling his hands into fists. It wasn't an earthquake—just abject panic. He sucked in a breath, and when he released it, the words flowed out of him in something close to a roar. "You're *leaving*?"

Natasha didn't even flinch. "Donna said she'll fire me if I don't."

Since she hadn't turned to look at him when she spoke, he strode into the room and stood in front of her so he could see her face.

She glanced up at him, then stilled when she saw the flowers crushed in his hand. It had once been a large bouquet with roses, lilies, baby's breath, and some other shit he didn't know. Now it was mangled. Her eyebrows dipped, and her mouth fell open. Before she could say a word, he tossed the flowers onto the bed and crouched down.

"I'm sorry, Kroshka." He placed his hands over hers, keeping them still. "I'm sorry I yelled, and I'm sorry I ruined the flowers. I was trying to surprise you."

"You're fine. I know you yell. I don't care. I'm Puerto Rican. We yell all the time. And you know who surprised me? Donna. Donna surprised the fuck out of me when she showed up here and threatened to *fire me*. But the flowers are nice. I love getting flowers."

She was babbling, speaking a mile a minute. He leaned in and kissed her, a long, closed-mouth press of lips. But when he drew back, she had tears in her eyes.

"Dimitri, I can't." Her voice was hoarse, and she refused to look at him. Her hands fluttered under his, and she gave a helpless shrug that broke his heart.

"We'll figure this out," he told her, striving to sound more confident than desperate. Because if he gave voice to the panicked refrain of *she's leaving, she's leaving, she's leaving,* running through his head, she'd never believe he was the kind of guy who wasn't afraid of haunted dolls, or whatever the hell Nik had been talking about. Dimitri held her hands in his and ducked his head until she looked him in the eye.

"We *will* figure this out," he repeated, more forcefully this time. "All right?"

Her eyes were still round, but she nodded.

"I have to meet Alex at Kras, but when I get back, we'll make a plan. Together. Trust me, okay?"

Her gaze fell to the clothing spilling out of her suitcase. "Dimitri, I—"

"Please. Trust me." He kissed her forehead and sent up a silent prayer. *Please, God, let her be here when I get back.* "I'll buy you new flowers."

Heart in his throat, he ran to his office for the Idea Book. While opening and closing drawers, looking for the binder, he caught sight of the plain folder that housed his contract for the upcoming season of *The Dance Off.*

The solution was staring him in the face. If he quit, Natasha could keep her job, and they could stay together.

But if he did that, how would he get his show off the ground? It was the whole reason why he'd joined *The Dance Off* in the first place. He needed the fame to make his next solo project happen. If he quit, he'd be right back at square one, unable to secure funding for his own work.

He slammed the drawer shut. They would find another way.

After unearthing the binder, he ran out to the car and drove to meet Alex.

Chapter Fifty-Eight

The second Dimitri's Porsche drove off, Natasha resumed packing. After finding her phone under a pile of socks, she called Kevin.

He picked up on the second ring. "Tash! What's up, girl?"

"I need a favor." She shoved the rolled-up socks into the corners of her suitcase.

"What do you need?"

"A ride to the bank."

A beat of silence. When he spoke again, his jovial tone had disappeared. "Yeah, of course. Everything okay?"

"Just please come get me?" Her voice broke, and Kevin's turned instantly alarmed.

"I'll be right there."

When Kevin showed up, he didn't ring the bell. He banged on the front door and hollered Natasha's name until she made her way over on the crutches to let him in.

"Why are you screaming?" She scowled as he entered the house. "Are you trying to make the neighbors call the cops? And how'd you get here so fast?"

"Are you hurt?" Kevin's normally carefree demeanor had been replaced by intense concern. He gripped her shoulders, and his pale green eyes lingered on the crutches. "You scared me. It sounded like you were crying, and I was worried—"

She shook him off. "I'm fine. Just overdid it walking around on my ankle yesterday, so I'm not taking chances. I need to be fully healed by the time the show starts up." She pointed to the bedroom. "I have to get out of here. Can you help me get my stuff out to your car?"

Kevin's face transformed into a dark scowl. "What did he do to you?"

"Nothing! Carajo, Kev. I was going to explain in the car, but I guess I'd better tell you so you don't think Dimitri's some kind of monster." She pushed up her glasses and rubbed her eyes. This was all too fucking much. The stress had her permanently on the verge of tears, and her armpits were sore from the crutches. But Kevin was going to be an overprotective pain in the ass unless she explained. "Donna came by today. If I don't get out of here, I can kiss my job at *The Dance Off* goodbye."

Kevin ground his jaw. "I swear, she lives to torment people."

"Exactly. Can you please help me with my stuff?"

Luckily, she hadn't brought much with her to Dimitri's, since Kevin's Lambo only featured a miniscule front trunk. Why the hell did all the guys in her life drive around in these totally impractical vehicles?

"Maybe we should take my car," she said. "There are thousands of dollars' worth of beauty products in that tote bag you're manhandling."

"I'm not leaving my car here." Kevin gave the bag one last shove, then closed the trunk's lid. "What do you think Dimitri will do to it when he comes home and finds you gone?"

Her palms started to sweat. She didn't want to think about Dimitri's reaction. "Just get me to the bank. Please."

Kevin helped her into the passenger seat, then climbed in on his side. They roared down the driveway, and Kevin drove like the hounds of Hell were nipping at his heels. Natasha scrambled to put on her seatbelt.

"What are you going to do at the bank?" he asked, as she set up the GPS on his phone.

"Ask for a loan or a credit card."

He shot her a pained look. "Tash. Come on. Why won't you let us help you? Lori's worried. She texts me about it all the time."

"I know. She texts me, too." On her own phone, Natasha did a quick search for hotels and sublets. There had to be *something* she could afford without going into overdraft.

Kevin banged a hand on the wheel as his phone called out the freeway exit. "This is ridiculous. Just stay with one of us until you get back on your feet. Literally and figuratively. We want to help."

"You guys have been incredibly helpful. More than I ever would have asked for, and I really appreciate everything you both have done. But this is something I have to figure out on my own. I can't keep leaning on other people. And if I stay with you or Lori, Donna will accuse me of the same thing—sleeping with you guys for the convenience of having someone take care of me. She basically called me a slut and Dimitri a sugar daddy."

Kevin shook his head, glaring darkly at the road. "I can't stand that woman. Manipulative people make me…" He trailed off, but his hands tightened on the wheel and his knuckles turned white.

It was on the tip of her tongue to ask him more, but the topic clearly wasn't up for discussion. Either way, Natasha was the last person who had any right to pry. Let Kevin keep his secrets.

At the bank, Natasha limped inside, wearing the boot. Twenty minutes later, she was back in the car, her mouth pressed into a thin line.

Kevin glanced over at her. "What happened?"

She didn't want to tell him. Didn't want to admit how fucked up her life had become, or how much of a failure she was. She'd never wanted her friends to know. But she'd dragged Kevin into this now, and he deserved the truth.

Besides, what did it matter anymore?

"My credit is terrible. A new card will need to be approved, and I haven't updated my latest tax and income info, so all of it will take time. Same for the loan. Dimitri was right. I do need to get my finances in order. Fuck." She shoved her glasses up and pressed her hands to her eyes. "I'm screwed."

Helplessness surged in her, a hot wave that threatened to spill out through her tear ducts. "I don't know what to do."

Kevin gave her shoulder an awkward pat. "If you won't stay with me, at least crash with Lori."

"Lori's roommates are horrible to her. I'm not going to sleep on their sofa and cause more tension."

"What about one of the others? Rhianne or Jess or—"

"I don't want to impose on anyone more than I already have." The tears started, and she wiped them away. "I'm stuck. I'm going to have to go home."

"To West Hollywood?"

"To the Bronx." She let out a shuddering sigh and dug a tissue out of her purse. "To my mother's apartment. I'm still injured, so I can't work. Can't work, can't make money, can't get my own place before *The Dance Off* starts. I'm a failure, and everyone was right. I can't make it on my own as a dancer. Without Gina keeping me on track, I'm just a fuck-up on my own."

"Slow down. Who said that to you? Dimitri?"

"No." Natasha blew her nose. "My mother. And Donna."

"Tash—"

Her phone rang, cutting him off. She frowned at the screen. "Hold on. It's my super."

She picked up and held the phone to her ear. "Hola, Manny. ¿Qué pasó?"

He said something, but it was so outrageous, she put the phone on speaker and asked him to repeat it.

Manny's voice filled the sportscar. "Tu apartamento está listo.

Debido a los problemas, no tienes que pagar el alquiler durante dos meses."

"Gracias, Manny. Un momentito." Natasha tapped the mute button and stared at Kevin. "Did you understand any of that?"

He scrunched up his face in thought. "Your apartment is…"

"Ready." She punched a fist in the air. "My apartment is motherfuckin' ready *and* they're giving me two months free rent!"

She brought the phone to her ear again and clarified the details with Manny. When she hung up, relief flooded through her, and she heaved a huge sigh.

"Where to?" Kevin asked, starting the car.

"Home. *My* home."

"What about Dimitri and your car?"

"I'll figure it out later."

She leaned back in her seat and closed her eyes.

Finally, things were starting to look up.

Chapter Fifty-Nine

Dimitri chewed on his fingers while Alex pored over the pages for *Raz i Navsegda*. Even though they'd pitched it before, Dimitri had completely reworked it since then. Alex hadn't seen the new version, and he now made notes on his laptop while he reviewed the ideas.

The suspense was driving Dimitri crazy. In his mind, he got up and paced, running his hands along the walls. It was something he'd done as a kid when he was anxious or impatient. Walking up and down the hallway, catching his palms on the doorjambs, until his mother handed him a soapy sponge and told him to wash off his dirty fingerprints.

Dance and sports had been perfect outlets for a kid with too much energy. And when he did have to sit still, he resorted to other nervous tics, like chewing on his fingers and nails. It was a habit he'd finally broken years before. He'd managed to refrain last night only by keeping his hands full of Natasha's lean body, but she wasn't here now, and there was no stopping him from destroying his cuticles. His manicurist was going to scold him at his next appointment.

Finally, Alex closed the binder. "Get your hands out of your mouth."

Dimitri slammed his hand on the table. "That's really all you have to say?"

Alex stared at him a moment longer. He had the best poker face of everyone in the Kovalenko family. No one else could hide their feelings for long. But then Alex's face broke into a smile, and he reached across the table to slap Dimitri on the arm.

"This is *great*," Alex said. "Really fucking great."

A tidal wave of relief roared through Dimitri. "Yeah? You think so?"

Alex flipped open the binder again, made a note of something on his laptop, then nodded. "I do. *Sem'ya* was good, but you were too worried about appealing to a broader audience back then. This one is more focused, with a stronger metaphor for the immigrant experience, and it's way better than when we tried to pitch it the first time. It's going to be a hit."

"*If* we can get the funding," Dimitri added. It was the thing that had hung over him for years. Back then, he'd begged and borrowed from everyone he knew, sinking all of his own savings and earnings from *Aliens Don't Dance* into the project. They hadn't even come close to breaking even, but over time, and thanks to Alex's meticulous financial records, Dimitri had repaid every single one of his family members who'd believed in him. But when he'd approached backers in LA a few years ago, they'd all turned him down, and he vowed he'd be damned if he let that happen again.

So he hadn't tried. Natasha had cut right to the heart of it. He hadn't even put himself in the position of having anyone say no to him.

"We'll get funding." Alex sounded confident as he began typing again. "Only an idiot would turn this down. It has that 'same but different' quality the execs always claim they're looking for, and it has your stamp all over it. If we get the pitch together immediately, we can line up some meetings before I head home. Where's your assistant?"

"I fired him."

Alex scowled. "I interviewed two dozen people to find him for you."

"He was scared of me."

"That means he was smart."

"I can't have someone around all the time who's scared of me." Dimitri gestured around the restaurant. "No one here is scared of me. Sometimes I wish they were, but it's easier to work with people who don't shake like a leaf when they have to ask me a question."

And then it hit him. *Natasha* had never done that. Even when they'd first met, she hadn't cowered before him. She was quiet, but it wasn't out of fear. She'd seen him yell and slam things, but she responded the way Alex did, being completely unfazed.

And she still stuck around.

Alex just shook his head. "We'll need a team if we're going to get this started before my kid is born."

"Right. My godchild. How's Marina?"

"She's good. No more nausea, which is why I felt okay flying out here. Her sister is visiting, and they're planning the baby shower."

Dimitri nodded. Marina was good for Alex, who tended toward more serious moods, although his sarcastic side came out with Dimitri. Marina, with her bright laughter and sweet demeanor, brought out a softness in Alex and pulled him out of his shell. They would make wonderful parents.

It got Dimitri thinking. What did others see when he and Natasha were together? There weren't many people he could ask. But his brother and the Krasavitsa staff seemed to think they'd be good together. They saw something even he hadn't been able to see, or had been too scared to admit for a long time.

Natasha was right for him. And he was right for her, too.

But she was probably still at home packing. Real life had intruded on the bubble they'd created over the last few weeks, and she was fleeing like a scared rabbit. Again.

Alex was typing with one hand while flipping through the binder with the other.

"You really think we can do this?" Dimitri asked.

His cousin stared at him over the laptop screen, eyes dark and intense like they got when he was working. "Yes. Don't be stupid." He went back to typing.

"I just mean—"

"Dima, cut it out. We're doing the show. It's brilliant."

"Really?"

"I'm not going to sit here inflating your ego. It's too big as it is. And if you make a 'that's what she said' joke, I'll murder you right here in your own restaurant and then Nik will be my child's godfather."

"But don't you think—"

Alex shut the laptop with a snap. "Stop making excuses. What the hell is wrong with you? None of the things that stood in our way before are here now. This is the best idea you've ever had, and you're more famous than you've ever been, thanks to that dumb show. What's the problem?"

Dimitri sucked his teeth. Maybe if he told Alex the problem, his cousin would have a solution. "It's that dumb show. That's what's in the way."

"Why?" Alex frowned. "Didn't you turn in your contract? I looked it over for you weeks ago. It's good to go."

"I haven't turned it in yet."

Alex rolled his eyes. "For god's sake, why?"

Because it felt like failure? Because they couldn't do what they were about to do without it, and Dimitri hated to admit how much he needed it?

Those had been the reasons before, but now, he had a whole new reason that outweighed all the others.

And Alex's faith scared him. What if they failed again? What if they couldn't do it before Marina gave birth, and Dimitri lost his biggest supporter? It would all fall apart without Alex.

Dimitri came up with the ideas, but Alex worked tirelessly behind the scenes to make them happen.

Alex had helped him since the beginning. Lining up ballroom dance competitions and making sure Dimitri had transportation and costumes. Securing auditions, including the one that led to *Aliens Don't Dance*. Every step of the way, Alex had been there, pushing him, cursing him, believing in him.

Shit, Alex was right. They needed a team. It wasn't fair to keep using his cousin this way.

Instead of answering Alex's question, Dimitri asked one of his own. "Why do you do all this?" He gestured at the laptop, the Idea Book. "Why do you help me?"

Alex's face settled into his signature unimpressed stare. "Because you're family, durak. And you're more talented than I'll ever be. Our parents brought us here to make a difference. That's what my dad used to say, remember? 'The Kovalenkos in America. People are going to know our name.' I hate the spotlight, but you eat that shit up. So, if I can help you, that's just as good."

"You don't do this for Nik, though." Dimitri didn't know why he was harping on this, but suddenly it seemed important to know why Alex was here, why he had always been here whenever Dimitri needed him. "Nik's a performer, too."

Alex shrugged and opened the laptop again. "Nik's not as serious about it. He doesn't remember what it was like before we moved here. He doesn't know how good he has it. If he were serious, I'd help him, too. But he doesn't want help. He doesn't see how much more we can be and do when we work together. He's stuck on doing it himself. At least, for now. If that changes, I'll help him, too."

Alex could have been talking about Natasha, and it was only then that Dimitri noticed the similarities between Tasha and Nik. They were even the same age.

And just like that, he *got* her. She wasn't ever going to be okay with him trying to fix things for her. But he could help her do it herself.

And then he had a plan.

"*The Dance Off* threatened to fire Natasha for living with me."

Alex's eyebrows raised. "That's messed up."

"She's trying to move out. I was thinking, if we can get this show going, we can hire her as choreographer."

"I thought you were going to choreograph it."

Dimitri shook her head. "She's better than I am. And she *gets* the story."

Alex smirked. "This is the first time I've heard you admit someone is better than you are at something. Must be true love."

"Zamolchi." He punctuated the mild "shut up" with a half-hearted middle finger. "But I'm thinking…if we can get this started soon, we can hire her, and she can quit *The Dance Off*."

Eyes narrowed, Alex leaned in. "And you don't think it'll be a conflict of interest that she's living with her boss?"

"It'll be different. We'll be a team."

"And what about you? You'd stay on *The Dance Off*?"

"Yeah. It'll build publicity for *Raz i Navsegda,* and make it a bigger hit, and she and I will both be successful from the new show."

"Hmm." Alex pressed his lips together and turned back to the computer.

"What? It's a good plan, right?" Dimitri didn't want to quit. Well, he did, but not now. One more season, maybe two, while he got *Raz i Navsegda* off the ground. He needed it. Without *The Dance Off,* everything would be too uncertain. How would they get the financial backing otherwise?

"Sure, cuz. Good plan."

Alex's face had settled back to its impassive lines, and Dimitri was sure he was lying. But he couldn't think of a better plan.

Dimitri got to his feet. "You good here? I'm going home to

tell her she can quit and do this instead. I want her involved in the pitch process."

Alex didn't look up. "Yeah, you do that."

As Dimitri walked away, he was pretty sure he heard Alex mutter "durak" behind his back. He didn't ask why Alex was calling him an idiot. His attention was attuned to Natasha. He couldn't wait to see her and tell her he'd found a solution for their dilemma.

And to make sure she was still there.

Chapter Sixty

The first thing Natasha noticed was the smell. Her apartment no longer smelled like *hers*. The scents of adobo, coconut oil, and ginger had faded from the air, replaced or overpowered by the impersonal smells of fresh paint, plaster, and the lingering odor of whatever had been used to fumigate.

This apartment had been her home for years. It was the place where she could relax, the place she could navigate in the dark. But now, it looked foreign to her. Plastic covered the floors and all her furniture, and nothing was in the right spot. Most of her belongings were still here, but the things that had once been so important to her were all just…stuff. She'd been fine without all of it for weeks.

Uneasiness slowed her steps as she ventured further inside, her footsteps crinkling the huge sheets of brown paper covering the carpet. A fine layer of plaster dust coated all of the plastic-covered furniture and hung thickly in the air. Natasha opened Gina's door first, where she'd stashed all her shit before leaving with Dimitri. It, too, had been painted, her things moved to the center of the room, and a giant tarp thrown over the pile.

Not Gina's room anymore. Not even Gina's *apartment* anymore. Her roommate, her best friend, wasn't ever coming back. Gina was gone, off in New York City, or Alaska, or wherever she and Stone found themselves at the moment. Natasha would know if she were a better friend.

A sinking sensation weighed her down, but Natasha pushed through, maneuvering in her boot around the now unfamiliar living room toward her own bedroom.

The door was ajar. Natasha nudged it open further and stepped inside.

Her room, her haven, was barren and white. A fresh coat of paint masked the repairs, and the smell was stronger in here. Without her tall lamps, it was dark, but enough light poured in from the curtainless window to show they'd done a good job on the ceiling, fixing the hole and smoothing over the damage from the leak. They'd even installed fresh wall-to-wall carpeting. It would be like moving into a brand new apartment.

Once, the thought would have filled her with excitement. Getting the whole place painted mid-lease without having to do it herself? It was a renter's dream. But the thought of filling this cold, alien space with her things no longer appealed. Organizing her closet would be exhausting, just from the sheer volume of her wardrobe. Why on earth did she own so much clothing?

Dimitri was right. She had to take a good, hard look at her spending and figure out *why* she was buying so much and living beyond her means.

But that was a problem for another day, and she didn't want to think about Dimitri now.

She had her apartment back. Calling it "home" at the moment didn't feel right. But she had a place to live that was hers and hers alone. No one could accuse her of awful things now.

And she could live here rent-free for the next two months. She'd be able to recover before the season began without having to hustle so hard. She could teach a few of the less strenuous classes so she could pay her other bills and buy food, and in the meantime, she'd take a look at her expenses and pare down. She probably didn't need *all* the streaming services, no matter how difficult they made it to cancel a subscription.

And best of all, when her mother came to visit for the premiere, Natasha could show her that she had her own place with a guest room for Mami and her friend to stay in. *A guest room.* For a family that had to section off the living room to make a bedroom, a guest room was the height of luxury. When Natasha unpacked, she'd decorate and make this place look even nicer than before. Maybe then Esmeralda would see how well she was doing and finally offer some praise.

Natasha limped into the kitchen, which was going to need a full scrub down. White footprints from the workers' boots covered the tiles, and the dust had gotten everywhere.

Maybe this didn't feel like home anymore, but Natasha would damn well make it look like it was before her mother arrived.

Sliding her phone out of her back pocket, she sent Kevin a text. *All looks good. You can bring everything up.*

Kevin was chilling in the garage. She'd pointed out the luggage cart, so he could unload her bags onto it and bring them up in the elevator.

Before he arrived, she sent one more text, even though her muscles locked with tension, as if trying to stop her.

I need this job. I'm sorry.

Chapter Sixty-One

Halfway up the stairs to Natasha's apartment, Dimitri remembered her building had an elevator.

Didn't matter. Blood pounded in his veins as he kept climbing, amped by anger.

Anger was easier. Easier than fear, easier than betrayal, easier than loneliness. The phrase *nichto ne vechno* ran through his mind. *Nothing lasts forever.*

No, damn it. He wouldn't let it happen again. He wouldn't lose her. Fuck *The Dance Off* and her producer for their meddling. Whatever had happened, he would fix it, and he'd bring Natasha home.

He was convinced now. Home was what his house had become over the days she'd lived there, something they'd created together. All these years, he'd been looking for a sense of home again, and he'd found it—with her. *She* was home to him. He finally glimpsed the stability that had been missing from his life for the past twenty-five years. And he hoped that he'd been able to do the same for her, that his efforts to show her that she was worthy and deserving of love had succeeded.

Regardless, he wasn't giving up without a fight.

When he got to her apartment, his chest heaved with exertion and emotion. The door was open, but he pounded a fist on it anyway as he entered.

Five heads whipped around in his direction. Natasha sat on the floor in the center of the living room, flanked by Kevin Ray and Lori Kim. In the kitchen stood two other pros from *The Dance Off,* Rhianne Davis and Mila Ivanova.

No fucking way was he doing this with an audience.

"Everybody out!" he barked.

Kevin's brow lowered, and he opened his mouth to reply, but Natasha laid a hand on his arm.

"I'll be fine. Just give us a few minutes, please."

Lori got to her feet. "Let's go to the overpriced ice cream place on the corner," she suggested in a nervous voice, and sidled past Dimitri without looking at him.

The other dancers followed her out into the hallway. As they passed Dimitri, Kevin stared him down, Rhianne seemed unconcerned, and Mila muttered in Russian, "Don't be an asshole."

Dimitri shut the apartment door behind them, then went to pull Natasha to her feet. "Tasha, what the hell is going on?"

The words tumbled from her lips in a nervous rush. "They finished the repairs and gave me two months rent-free. Thank you for everything you've done, but I need this job, and I need this apartment. I'll pick up my car soon."

"You can get the car when you come back—"

"Stop." She held up a hand. "Don't ask me." She wouldn't even look at him, keeping her face turned away. "If you ask, I won't be strong enough to say no, so please, if you love me, don't ask."

Betrayal and confusion warred with him, making his muscles tense. *If* he loved her? "I don't understand."

"We can't keep doing this. *I* can't. It's too big of a risk. Every time I've tried to stay away from you, you pull me back in, so this time, you have to let me go."

"I don't want to let you go."

"I need you to. Don't you get it? I have to do this myself. I have to prove that I can live on my own like a responsible adult, fix my finances, and get my life back on track."

"I can help you. If you won't come home with me, I'll get you an apartment, somewhere closer, and—"

"What, like a kept woman? I don't think so."

"Fine, then. Let's get married." The words came out of nowhere, surprising him, and as she stared, open-mouthed, he repeated them back to himself. They actually didn't sound half bad.

Before he could follow it up with anything, she snapped her mouth shut and shook her head. "You're out of your mind. We've been on *one* date. And how do you think it will look if I suddenly *elope* with one of the judges?"

"Stop worrying. I'll take care of you."

"Aren't you listening? I need to take care of *myself*." She rubbed her eyes. "You don't think it's tempting to let you fix everything? It fucking is. But I need to know, for my own sake, that I can do it on my own."

There was nothing he could say to that. He wanted her to accept his help, his *love*, but he couldn't force her to. And if this was what it took for her to build her self-worth, he had to let her do it.

Just when he was starting to feel like things were settled, at least in this area of his life, she was gone.

He was alone.

He took a step back, because it was what she wanted.

"You are asking me to let you go. Again. Do you know how fucking hard that is for me?"

"I'm sorry. But this is what I need."

"I know, Kroshka. I know. And for you, I'll do it. Because I love you that much. I love you enough to give you space. But this time, I want you to know that even though we're apart, I still love you. That's not changing. I'm letting you go because I love you and because you asked this of me, and no other reason in the world could get me to leave you right now. I see that you need this. But we're not over, all right? We're not."

He said it like he could make it true through sheer force of will.

He wanted to kiss her, to hold her, but his resolve was thin, and he got the feeling hers was, too.

If it was this hard to pull away from each other, wasn't that a sign they should give in and be together?

But this wasn't the time to push. He understood now. And he'd told her he'd give her anything she asked of him.

She wanted space? She wanted to fix things on her own? He'd give her that space.

And in the meantime, there was one more thing he could do.

Leaving the apartment, he took the stairs again, needing to burn off the restless energy. He didn't have time to be depressed or lonely. He had too much to do.

He called Alex and told him to come over, ready to work. Then Dimitri raced home and headed straight for his office. Once there, he yanked the folder containing his contract for *The Dance Off* out of the desk.

With great satisfaction, he fed it into the paper shredder.

Chapter Sixty-Two

After her friends helped make the apartment livable again, Natasha worked out an agreement with the management company. After the two months were up, they would allow her to break the lease and move into a one-bedroom apartment elsewhere in the building, applying her existing security deposit to the new place. In the meantime, since her ankle was still too sore to risk dancing on it, she got a head start on packing and purging.

For the first time in a while, she had free time where she wasn't worrying about survival. It was amazing how much energy stress used up. With Lori and Kevin's help, Natasha sold off her collection of clothes and shoes. To her surprise, it was a lot easier than she'd thought it would be.

Once, just owning them made her feel successful, even the items she'd never worn. Being able to buy them, to select an outfit from a closet full of beautiful pieces, had made her happy.

It seemed so silly now. They were just clothes. Overpriced and totally impractical. She lived in leggings and sweats most of the time, and when she performed, costumes were provided. Having a wardrobe like this was a status thing, so she could feel good about herself when she went out. And since she'd had the nice clothes, she'd gone out a lot, creating a vicious cycle of spending. And what did she have to show for it? Nothing. A bunch of "outfit of the day" posts. No wonder she was broke.

And now she was keeping her job on *The Dance Off* for the financial security. Why? So she could buy more clothes she didn't need?

And at what cost?

She shut down that line of thinking. The cost was painfully obvious every time she went to bed alone, struggled through her budgeting spreadsheet, or made a single latte in the morning.

At least she'd be prepared for her mother's arrival in a few weeks. Esmeralda wasn't as awful when other people were around. Maybe if the friend she was bringing appeared to be impressed, Esmeralda would find it in her to bestow praise as well.

Yeah, and maybe Donna would turn out to be a decent human being.

Natasha wasn't going to hold her breath waiting for either outcome. For the first time in her life, she was living on her own terms.

And if she wasn't all that happy about it, well, that was life.

To thank Kevin and Lori for all they'd done, Natasha hosted dinners at her apartment. They brought the groceries, and she cooked up huge meals for them, experimenting with different cuisines and dishes. Sometimes they invited the other dancers, too, but most of the time, it was just the three of them.

A week before Natasha was set to meet her new partner for the upcoming season, she invited Lori and Kevin over to try out an array of summer salads.

Kevin arrived first, with five bottles of wine. Natasha gave him a stern look. "Kev, you know I'm cutting back on drinking."

"I know, I know. Just stocking up for the next time." He stuck two bottles of rosé in the fridge and popped the other three into the small wine rack on top. Then he hovered over the large bowls on the counter. "What do we have here?"

Natasha pointed to each one. "Watermelon with feta and mint. Salmon with mango and avocado. Shrimp and nectarine. And orzo with veggies."

"You're the best." Kevin made himself at home, pulling down wine glasses and opening the bottle of Chardonnay she had chilling in the fridge.

Natasha's phone rang on the counter while she was setting out dishes and utensils. She thought it would be Lori, and was surprised to see her agent's name flash on the screen. She answered, and Kevin took over the task of setting out the flatware.

"Hi, Penelope."

Penelope jumped right in, speaking fast. "Hey, Tash. I was approached about a big choreography opportunity for you. They've seen your videos, and they want you to come in for a meeting in two days."

"That sounds amazing. When would it start?"

"Immediately."

Natasha frowned. "Pen, I already have a job. I'm meeting my celebrity partner next week."

"I know, but we could use your ankle injury to get you out of it. This is a really good opportunity."

The intercom buzzed, and Kevin went to answer it.

"I don't know, Pen. I'll think about it."

"Think fast. I *really* think you should at least meet with them. Maybe it could lead to something else. *The Dance Off* doesn't have to be forever. Talk soon."

Kevin came back from unlocking the front door for Lori, who was on her way up. "What was that about?"

"My agent. Someone reached out to her about a choreography job."

"Isn't that what you want to do? I mean, yeah, we choreograph dances every week for the show, but making up short routines for non-dancers is totally different than a job as a choreographer."

Natasha pressed her fingers to her forehead, which suddenly throbbed with pressure. "It's too much change all at once. Anyway, I said I'll think about it."

Lori bustled in. "You will not *believe* what I heard today."

"I'll get the wine." Kevin ducked into the kitchen.

Lori kicked off her turquoise and silver high tops by the door and ran over to Natasha. Her dark eyes were wide, her mouth pinched in a serious frown. "Tash, I know who your next partner is."

"Really?" Natasha perked up. "Donna hinted a while ago that he was a musician."

Lori shook her head slowly.

Kevin pushed full wine glasses into both of their hands. "Don't drag it out, Lor."

Lori blew out a deep breath, then the words tumbled out in a rush. "Tash, don't be mad at me. I'm just the messenger. But as soon as I heard, I knew I had to tell—"

"Lori!" Natasha and Kevin both yelled her name in unison.

"Spit it out." The longer Lori stalled, the more Natasha's nerves high-kicked into gear. She took a sip of wine to soothe them.

Lori's hands flapped by her sides, but she nodded and said, "It's Rocky. Rocky Lim."

Natasha froze with her lips on the rim of the glass.

Kevin spoke first. "Rocky Lim, from those car movies? Is he —oh, shit." He turned to Natasha, a hand covering his mouth. "Didn't you and he...?"

"Yeah." Natasha knocked back the wine, barely tasting the cool, crisp flavor. "And I'd bet anything that Donna knows it."

Lori shook her fist in the air. "Fucking Donna! Why would she even do that?"

Kevin glowered into his glass. "She's keeping Tash in line, showing her how much she can mess with her life, and trying to destroy her connection to Dimitri."

Lori's eyebrows shot up. "Does Dimitri know about you and Rocky?"

Natasha shut her eyes. "Oh yeah. He knows."

"How'd you find out?" Kevin asked Lori.

"The Hollywood AAPI gossip network. News travels fast." Lori's lips pursed. "But maybe I'm wrong?"

Natasha grabbed her phone and opened her texts. "You're not wrong. Look."

Kevin scrolled through the messages from Rocky, most of them general greetings with photos taken around London and commentary about British TV shows.

But the latest one, from just two days ago, read: *Hey there, darling. Give me a call when you're free.* It was punctuated with an emoji blowing a kiss.

Kevin pointed at the phone. "That's a booty call right there."

"It means he's in town." Natasha took the phone back. "I didn't call him. Didn't even think of it. But that means he's here. And if he's here, then there's a good chance you're right, Lori."

Lori squinted up at Natasha's head. "Is Rocky even tall enough to be your partner?"

"Barely." Natasha hit Penelope's number and put the phone to her ear. "Pen? Hi. Can you set up that meeting and email me the details? Thanks."

When she put the phone down, she turned to the counter to find Kevin and Lori wearing identical guilty expressions. Their hands were in the bowl of watermelon, mint, and feta salad, and they were eating it with their fingers.

"Sorry," Lori mumbled around a mouthful of watermelon. "All this drama makes me hungry. You got any popcorn?"

Natasha handed them forks. "Just eat out of the bowl. How is it?"

"Delicious," Kevin said. Watermelon juice dripped down his chin.

Natasha sat at the counter and covered her face with her hands. "I have to quit."

A full glass of rosé appeared by her elbow. She sent Kevin a grateful smile.

"Will it really be that bad if you partner with Rocky?" Lori asked, scooping forkfuls of orzo salad into her mouth. "By the way, this could use a little more lemon, if you have it."

"In the fridge." Natasha lifted the wine glass. The first had gone straight to her head, but she no longer cared about her resolution to drink less.

Kevin answered Lori's original question. "It'll be bad. Dimitri will lose his shit when he sees her dancing with Rocky, and I bet you anything Donna thinks sticking Rocky and Tash together will cause some fireworks with the fans or the execs, and maybe even give them cause not to bring you back after this season."

Someone knocked on the door, and Natasha groaned. "Now what?"

Lori gasped. "What if it's Rocky?"

Natasha shook her head and slid off the high barstool. "It's Manny. He's supposed to come by to scrape one of the electrical outlets that got painted over."

"If this were a movie, it would be Rocky." Lori tasted the shrimp salad and her eyes rolled back in her head. "Oh, my god. This is to die for."

"Let me try." Kevin approached with his fork.

Natasha went to open the door, her thoughts buzzing. If she could film the final piece she'd been working on and get it edited before the meeting, she'd be in good shape. With her mind on her choreography reel, she pulled open the door and froze.

It wasn't Manny.

Gina threw her arms in the air and yelled, "Surprise!"

Chapter Sixty-Three

A flood of emotions kept Natasha's feet rooted to the floor.

Surprise? Absolutely. Gina was supposed to be in Alaska or New York, not Los Angeles.

Shock, since Natasha had expected Manny.

Shame, because everything in Natasha's life had fallen apart since Gina had left.

But overwhelming all of those was *joy*.

That last one propelled Natasha's feet across the threshold, and then she and Gina were crushing each other in a tight bear hug.

It wasn't until her breath hitched that Natasha let herself feel just how much she'd missed her friend. Gina's familiar embrace, the scent of her shampoo, the way she squeezed before letting go, grounded Natasha in a way nothing else had in the past few months.

When they eased back, they were both wiping the corners of their eyes.

"So, what's been going on?" Gina asked, rolling her suitcase into the apartment.

"Ha!" From the kitchen, Kevin barked out a laugh, echoed by Lori. "What *hasn't* been going on?"

At Gina's curious look, Natasha beckoned her inside. "I guess I should fill you in."

"You *guess*?" The further Gina moved into the apartment, the more her eyes widened, taking in the boxes and the remaining tarp. "Did you repaint the walls?"

"It's…kind of a long story."

"Give me a minute, and then I want to hear all of it. You've been tight-lipped since I left." Gina took off her shoes by the door, then went into the kitchen to hug Lori and Kevin. After scooping a bit of each salad onto a plate, Gina gave Natasha an expectant look. "Well?"

"Let's talk in my room." Natasha led the way into her bedroom.

Gina stopped just inside the door and gazed around. "Where's all your stuff?"

"That's part of the story."

They sat on the edge of the bed. Natasha's stomach fluttered with nerves.

"I need a minute."

Gina shrugged and tucked into the food. "Take your time."

Natasha didn't want to admit how much she'd fucked up since Gina had left. How incapable she was of handling her life on her own. It was different with Lori and Kevin. They still didn't know the full story—Lori didn't know about her bad credit, and neither of them knew about Babe Planet.

And while no one *needed* to know every bit of her life, Natasha was holding back out of fear of judgment. She wasn't trusting Gina not to judge her. And that was a shitty way to think about your best friend. Of anyone, Gina deserved to know everything.

All along, Dimitri had been pushing her to reach out to Gina. He'd seen how Natasha was struggling, how unmoored she'd felt, and while he'd tried to help her himself, he'd also understood the need to connect with the one person who knew you better than anyone else, and who still loved you.

Her mother didn't accept her life choices, but Gina always had, even when she didn't agree with them. Despite the evidence, Natasha still hadn't seen fit to open up to her.

Now or never.

It was hard, but Natasha told Gina everything. Closing out her credit cards, buying a new car, the extra jobs, the leak in the ceiling, moving in with Dimitri, her sprained ankle, and Dimitri's confession of love. She told Gina about Lennox and Babe Planet and Donna's threat, all the way to breaking up with Dimitri and getting denied a loan. She even included the most recent developments—Donna's revenge through Rocky Lim and Penelope's call.

Through it all, Gina was quiet. She'd set her empty plate on the floor and leaned back on her elbows to listen.

When Natasha finished, the relief left her weak, but she anxiously awaited Gina's response.

Finally, Gina spoke. "Why didn't you tell me?"

Natasha could have asked, "About what?" She'd revealed so much tonight. But she knew what Gina meant. Why hadn't Natasha told her any or all of it? Why hadn't she asked for help?

"I'd been leaning on you for so long, I figured it was time I stood on my own two feet." She lifted her right foot, a simple bandage pulled over the ankle like a sock. "Guess that didn't turn out so well."

Gina hugged her around the neck, and Natasha's breath hitched again. It was what Abuela would have done. Maybe that was why they were friends. Maybe that's why she loved Gina so much.

"You're doing great," Gina whispered. "Get your mom's voice out of your head."

That did it. To have someone know her so well and still love her… The tears came, and Gina rubbed Natasha's back. Again, just like Abuela would have.

"I missed the hell out of you," Natasha admitted, clinging to her.

"I was worried about you. But I figured if things were bad, you'd tell me."

"I'm sorry I didn't. I didn't want to bother you."

Now, Gina gave her a light punch in the arm. "You're my best friend. You're never a bother. That's part of the best friend pact. Didn't you know?"

"Now I do."

"You were there for me when all that shit went down a few months ago."

Natasha narrowed her eyes. "Yeah, but you also tried to hide your relationship with Stone from me."

"Well, I didn't want to admit it was a relationship. If it was just a hookup, why did I need to tell?" She sighed. "I get it, though. Sometimes things feel too raw to share. And if I'd known you were struggling when you first moved here, I would have come out sooner. I wouldn't have left you alone for that. And I would have made you take rent money this summer."

"That's exactly why I didn't tell you. I'm not your responsibility, Gina. I've made mistakes, but…I'm learning."

Gina was quiet for a moment. "I'm sorry if I've been pushy or overbearing in any way. It's just—you're my best friend, you know? I don't want to see you struggle, especially if I'm able to help. But I hear you, and you're right. We have to make mistakes so we can learn from them."

They lapsed into companionable silence. Natasha looked around her room; the bed and a standing lamp were the only items in it. The walls were bare. She'd put the curtains back up, only so she didn't have to worry about the people in the neighboring building looking in on her. The closet was mostly empty, aside from a few items that would wrinkle if folded into the drawers. Most had been sold, and the rest were packed. Turned out, clothes didn't make the woman, and she didn't need that much after all.

This wasn't her home anymore. This apartment, this symbol of her independence, her success, no longer held any meaning to her. She had been so determined to come back here, to prove to herself, to her mother, and hell, even to the show's producers, that she could make it as a dancer.

Who was she kidding? Paying rent on a basic-ass apartment in WeHo wasn't a measure of success. Lots of people managed to do it. Yeah, it was great to be able to pay her own bills, but now it seemed like such a silly, capitalist thing to stake her entire identity on. The apartment didn't define her. The stuff she'd filled it with didn't say anything about her skill as a dancer or choreographer.

She glanced at her ankle. Being a dancer didn't even define her anymore.

Who was she, if she wasn't a dancer? Who was she, if she couldn't pay her own bills, pay rent on her own apartment, and support herself from her craft?

She was Natasha. Still, now, and always.

Compulsive spending and the need for external markers of success had kept her locked into a lifestyle and a job that didn't respect her. She didn't owe Fucking Donna any loyalty. And Donna had said it herself, Natasha could use her ankle as a way out.

"I think I'm going to quit *The Dance Off*," Natasha said out loud, mostly to hear how it sounded.

It sounded *right*.

Gina raised an eyebrow. "You think?"

Natasha shrugged. "It's just a job."

And if she got a different one, a better one, she could explore more of who she was without it.

And maybe she and Dimitri could explore who they were together.

Gina patted her leg. "Glad you see the light."

Natasha smiled. And for the first time in a long time, the future looked bright.

Chapter Sixty-Four

Since Natasha had an apartment full of dancers, she dragged Kevin and Lori away from the salads—everyone had chosen a different one as their favorite—and hustled them all outside to the building's tiny courtyard. It mostly held a few giant trash bins and some potted plants, but it caught the late afternoon light, and it had space.

Kevin stood at one end with Natasha's camera on a tripod. Gina and Lori recorded on their phones to catch different angles.

"You're sure you're okay to do this?" Lori asked.

"The doctor cleared me," Natasha said.

Thanks to Dimitri. If left to her own devices, she would have pushed it too hard, too soon, and likely injured herself again. Now, she felt stronger than ever, thanks to physical therapy and a break from her soul-crushing work schedule. Sitting on a bench off to the side, Natasha powdered and tied on her oldest pair of pointe shoes, then popped in her wireless headphones.

Gina gaped in horror. "You're wearing *pointe shoes* on *concrete*?"

"It'll be worth it."

Gina pursed her lips like she wasn't convinced, then glanced at the sky. "I think we only have enough light for one take."

"Aww shit, Gina, look at you," Kevin teased. "Spend a little while in nature and now you can tell time by the sun."

Gina stuck her tongue out at him.

Natasha took her mark.

"How does your ankle feel?" Lori called out. Lori was in charge of controlling the music on Natasha's phone, which she held in one hand, her own phone in the other.

"It's fine." Natasha tuned them out, wrapping her head around the choreography she'd been tweaking for months. Of course, she would have loved more time to perfect it, to fine-tune each turn and leap. Or better yet, to work on it with Dimitri and get his unique perspective. But there wasn't time. The meeting was in two days.

She nodded to Lori. A second later, the music pumped into her ears, starting with dramatic violins. Natasha launched into the dance, starting with classical ballet moves. The pop beat joined in. Natasha picked up the tempo. *I am a masterpiece*, the singer declared. Natasha spun, her arms outstretched. The chorus came to an end, and the singer cried out, *You ain't seen nothing yet. Just watch me fly.*

And just like the lyrics, Natasha flew.

A flurry of leaps and spins she'd learned in ballet, body rolls she'd picked up from the pole, elements of paso doble from the ballroom, and when the music paused for a beat, a perfectly executed arabesque that felt like coming home.

Natasha put everything she was into this routine. All of *who* she was. She'd never done well in school, but she'd studied dance forever, collecting different styles every step of the way.

Even if Natasha never danced again, she would still be a dancer. In her mind and body, in her heart and soul. Her muscles held a lifetime's worth of training. Her history and worldview informed the pieces she created. Dance was part of her at a molecular level.

No one could take that away from her. No injury, no disapproving mother, no asshole producers. Dance was *hers*. And it always would be.

You ain't seen nothing yet. Just watch me fly.

Fuck failure. Fuck other people's standards. It was time to do things her own way.

The song came to an end. In the last spears of light from the setting sun, Natasha untied her ruined pointe shoes and hurled them across the courtyard as hard as she could. They hit the fence with a clang and dropped to the floor, finally still.

And Kevin, Lori, and Gina, because they were good friends who followed instructions, kept the cameras rolling until she gave them the slashing hand signal to cut.

When the cameras were off, Lori and Gina screeched, and Kevin clapped his hands over his ears.

"Oh my god, that was *amazing*," Lori gushed.

Gina passed Natasha a pair of flip-flops. "You have this choreography job in the bag."

"Killer routine, babe." Kevin gave her a thumbs-up and began to fold the tripod.

Their praise warmed her, but even better, Natasha *knew* she'd killed it. Her thoughts drifted to Dimitri. Once, she'd wanted his praise like she'd wanted her mother's. Now, she just wished she could share this moment with him. And all moments. Damn it, she *loved* him. She loved dancing with him, fighting with him, *being* with him. The man was infuriating at times, but his passion for life stirred her up and made her want *more*.

For once, she wondered if wanting more wasn't a bad thing like she'd been raised to believe. Maybe it just meant that she knew she deserved better.

"I quit," she whispered.

Kevin glanced over at her. "What'd you say?"

Natasha shook her head and grinned. "Just practicing."

Chapter Sixty-Five

Dimitri raced around, getting ready for the meeting. Alex was already at the conference room they'd rented, but Dimitri had stayed up all night working on the pitch. His nerves were shot, and he was running late.

This had every possibility of blowing up in his face. After all, Natasha had specifically asked him *not* to fix things for her, but that was like asking him not to breathe. So here he was, preparing for a business meeting with the love of his life, when she had no clue he was the one behind it.

Alex thought it was a bad idea, but Dimitri didn't know what else to do. He was trying to give her space, but she was also the best choreographer for *Raz i Navsegda*, and if he had to build a team, he wanted her to be the first one on it.

He was in his living room, searching the couch cushions for his watch, when the front door opened. He expected it to be one of his relatives—Mama, Nik, even Alex. They all had keys and knew the security code. So when Natasha appeared in the entryway, all Dimitri could do was stare at her, open-mouthed.

She looked cool and professional in a slate blue blouse, trim black pants, and silver heels. Her hair was pulled back in a high ponytail, and her eyes looked dark and dramatic.

The sight of her stunned him. It wasn't just her beauty, although to him, she was the most gorgeous woman to ever walk the planet. No, the thing that struck him speechless was that she was *here*, not simply a hallucination borne from his hopes and dreams, but here, in his home, of her own accord.

Right where she belonged.

When her gaze landed on him, her face lit up. She hurried forward, her heels clacking, and she threw herself right into his arms.

Dimitri caught her and held on like he'd never let go. Closing his eyes, he breathed in the familiar scent of her shampoo, which had started to fade from his pillow. "Radost' moya," he whispered.

"What does that mean?" Her breath was warm against his neck.

He answered without hesitation. "My joy."

She pulled back just far enough to see his face. Her expressive eyes shone with determination.

"I can't stay long," she said in a rush. "I have a big meeting today. But I had to see you. To tell you."

"Tasha, I—"

"I'm quitting *The Dance Off.*"

That brought him up short. "You're what?" He'd thought she'd found out somehow that he was behind the meeting and had come over to confront him. This was...not what he'd expected.

"I'm quitting. It's too toxic there, and I can't take it anymore. And the person Donna paired me with for this season..." She shook her head as she trailed off. "I can't do that to you. To me. To *us.* I won't keep playing her games, and I don't want us to hide anymore. I want us to go on dates and make out in public until even the paps are sick of us. I even told Gina—about everything. You were right, D. I should've talked to her sooner, but we're good now. Oh, and I sold my clothes!" She gave a little laugh, and his heart soared to see her so light, so happy. He couldn't bring himself to interrupt her rambling update, and he soaked in every new piece of information she shared. This was what he'd wanted for so long—the real Natasha, coming to him of her own volition and opening up to him.

"It was actually really freeing?" She said it like it had been a surprise, and kept going. "I realized the clothes were just this arbitrary marker of success, and I don't need that anymore. Success is however you define it. I *am* a dancer, whether I'm dancing on TV, in a bikini bar, or in my kitchen. But I'm also more than that. And I want to start exploring the rest of me and see what it might look like if I..." She broke off and her expression became uncertain, but only for a moment, before she forged on. "If I let you love me. And if I let myself love you back. Because I *do* love you, Dimitri. I've loved you for a very long time."

He hadn't expected that, either, and it was on the tip of his tongue to make a joke referencing her teenage crush on him, but all that came out was a hoarse and hopeful, "Really?"

She bit her lip and nodded. "You've given me the kind of love that I never thought I deserved. I want to love you the same way, and to let you see me. *All* of me." She let out a breath. "Anyway, I wanted to tell you that. And see your face. God, I've missed your face." She lifted a hand and stroked his beard, and he could've died a happy man just from the wealth of affection in her tone.

He pulled her close and gave a ragged exhale. "I want to recite poetry to you, or sing, or say something clever or funny, but all I've got is: Ya khochu byt' s toboy vsegda."

She tipped her head back to look at him. "What does that mean?"

He swallowed hard and took the plunge. "I want to be with you forever."

Hope shimmered in her eyes, and he thought he saw them

glimmer with tears. Then she wrapped her arms around his waist and squeezed. "I'll take it," she whispered fiercely. After a beat, she asked, "What poetry would you recite?"

He huffed out a laugh. "The only one I can think of at the moment is by Pushkin."

"Is it a love poem?"

"Yes, but it ends tragically."

She snickered. "Maybe you should find a different one, then."

"I will. I promise. Even if I have to write it myself. I'll write you so many sappy love poems, you won't know what to do with them."

She let out a happy sigh. "I can't wait." But then her arms dropped to her sides and she stepped back abruptly. "Except I have to go or I'll be late for my meeting."

"Hold on."

When he reached for her, she winced apologetically and backed away. "Sorry, I know that was a lot to drop on you, but I hit traffic on the way here. I just wanted to tell you that I'm quitting the show. And I love you. I'll come back tonight, okay?"

She started to rush to the door, but he lunged and caught her wrist. "Wait a second. About the meeting…"

She turned back to him, puzzled, and he knew then that his cousin had been right. This had been a stupid idea.

There was no way around it. With a sinking sensation, he told her the truth. "It's me. I'm the one you're meeting with."

Her brows slowly dipped down while she stared at him. "I don't understand."

"Your meeting? The one your agent arranged for this afternoon? It's with me and my cousin, Alex. He's my business partner."

Her eyes narrowed in disbelief, and outrage colored her tone. "What is this, a joke? Some kind of trick to get me to talk to you?"

"*No.*" It came out too loud, too forceful, but she didn't so much as flinch. He got his desperation and his voice under control and tried again. "No, lyubimaya. It's a real meeting for a real job. *Raz i Navsegda* needs a choreographer. I want it to be you."

Her expression shuttered. "Why?"

He rushed to explain, praying that he hadn't just destroyed his chance at pure happiness.

"Because you're the best choreographer I know," he said honestly. "You're better than I am, and I don't say that lightly. And you're better than Kevin, even though people seem to think the sun shines out of that guy's ass."

Her lips twitched like she was fighting back a smile.

"The truth is, I want you to be part of this project. I don't trust anyone else to understand the story the way you do. And maybe I also wanted you to know that *The Dance Off* isn't your only option. Oh shit." He snapped his fingers. "I meant to lead with that—I'm *also* quitting *The Dance Off.*"

Her eyes widened. "You are?"

"You were right. I was stalling, and the only thing keeping me there was fear. Also, anyone who tells me I can't be with you can go fuck themselves." He chanced stepping closer and was relieved when she didn't move away. "I'm sorry if you feel like I tricked you. Alex said I should just talk to you, but I was trying to give you space."

She raised an eyebrow. "You should definitely listen to Alex more often, but I can see how, to you, it made a twisted sort of sense." Her tone softened, and she no longer held herself so rigidly. "The fact is, whether you're attached or not, I'd still want to be part of this project. I fell in love with the story when you showed it to me, and I haven't been able to stop thinking about it since. Not to mention, I'd do crime for the chance to choreograph an original show by *the* Dimitri Kovalenko." She sent him a sly smirk.

"I can't tell you how relieved I am to hear that. You're so talented, Tasha. It blows me away."

A smile played on her mouth. "I thought you didn't give compliments."

"Because I'm stupid. I should have told you how I felt the moment I met you. We wouldn't have wasted so much time if I had." His words were tinged with regret.

She closed the distance between them and took his hand. "We're here now."

"Finally." He slid his arms around her waist. "I want you, Tasha. In every way that exists. Love is a risk. So is creativity. But they're both worth it. And so are you."

He could tell, from the way her expression softened, that his words had made an impact. But then the side of her mouth quirked and she said, "So you're asking me to be your choreographer and your—what? Your girlfriend?"

He made a face. "I hate that word." Pressing his forehead to hers, he looked her in the eye. "Just be mine. And I'll be yours."

"I like the sound of that," she murmured. "And I know you want to take care of me, because it's how you show love. But you have to let me take care of you, too."

"That's all I want, Kroshka. For us to take care of each other. Raz i navsegda."

"Always and forever," she repeated in English, and kissed him.

Falling into her mouth, surrounded by the sweetness of figs and ginger, was like coming home. She was soft and hot, and her tongue went after his in a way that made him groan. He slid his hands around to cup her ass, pulling her flush against him and rocking his hips side to side to press his hardening cock against her.

She moaned into his mouth and hitched her thigh on his hip, like she'd climb him if she could.

They were both panting when she pulled back. "Don't we have a meeting to attend?"

"Alex will understand." He gave her ass a light swat. "Get in the dining room."

She shot him a puzzled look, but she was already heading in that direction. "Why?"

"We're about to break another chair."

With a wicked grin, she grabbed his hand and pulled him toward the table.

Chapter Sixty-Six

The look on Donna's face made up for all the stress Natasha had endured over the past few weeks. The whites of Donna's eyes were visible all around, and her jaw fell slack. She blinked hard and gave her head a little shake. "I'm sorry, you what?"

Pressing her lips together to hold back a smile, Natasha repeated the words she'd just said. "I quit."

God, that felt so fucking good. It took all her control not to add "bitch" to the end, but losing her temper might screw up Penelope's plans for getting Natasha out of her contract.

Donna scowled. "You can't *quit.*"

Penelope cut in. "The way you've treated Natasha could be considered harassment, and don't think I've forgotten what you did to Gina." Penelope consulted her tablet. "In this case, we have threats, showing up at my client's place of residence—"

"Hold on." Donna held up a finger. "Technically, I encountered Natasha at a different cast member's residence." Her voice was forceful, but her eyes showed fear.

Penelope shook her head. "Doesn't matter. We also have a witness who will attest to the fact that you first went to Natasha's home address, which could constitute stalking."

"*Stalking?*" Donna fell back in her chair. "I wasn't stalking her. I'd heard she was injured."

"There's a thing called a phone. And then, when you didn't find her, you tracked her down to where she was currently residing and trespassed on private property."

"The gate was open!"

"Were you working on your own or under orders from your higher-ups?" Penelope sent Donna a bland smile. "Just want to be clear on what names to include in the lawsuit."

Donna's eyes went wide, then her brows snapped down. She met Natasha's gaze with an angry glare. "This isn't necessary. You want to date the hot judge? Fine. Just keep it quiet, and you can stay on the show."

Natasha smiled. "I do want to date Dimitri, but I don't want to hide it. And I don't want to stay. Oh, and neither does he."

Donna's tan complexion paled. "You're *both* quitting?"

Natasha folded her hands in her lap. Check and mate. "Your behavior in this meeting will determine how Dimitri breaks the news to Muriel."

At the mention of the showrunner's name, Donna licked her lips, a sign of nerves. "Natasha, they'll kill me if we lose Gina, you, *and* Dimitri before the next season. We're only a few weeks out from the premiere, and Kevin—" She snapped her mouth shut, but something close to panic lurked in her dark eyes.

Ignoring the comment about Kevin—she'd ask him about it later—Natasha leaned forward in her chair, pinning Donna with a hard look. "Why do you want me to stay? So you can sabotage my relationship with Dimitri by pairing me with Rocky Lim?"

The guilty expression on Donna's face said it all. Natasha sat back.

"Yes, I heard about Rocky. You're not as slick as you think you are."

Penelope got to her feet and slipped her purse strap over her shoulder. "Well, I believe we're done here. Donna, you'll accept Natasha's resignation?"

Staring at her desk, Donna nodded. Penelope left the tiny office.

Natasha stood, then hesitated. Donna looked pitiful, although it was her own doing. And maybe it was petty, but Natasha couldn't resist a parting shot. "You don't have to be as awful as you are."

Donna didn't move, but her gaze lifted to meet Natasha's. "Actually, I do," she said in a hollow voice. "Don't you understand this industry at all?"

All too well. "Bye, Donna," she said, then added in a mocking tone, "Vaya con Dios."

Natasha was halfway out the door when Donna spoke again.

"You could've won this season."

Natasha turned back. "You can't know that."

Donna made a sour face. "Of course I can. I know who everyone is paired with, and I understand this show inside and out. Better than anyone. You and Rocky would have made it to the finals and won."

Natasha let that sink in for a moment, to see if she cared.

It turned out she didn't.

"Oh, well," she said, and left.

<h2 style="text-align:center">Chapter Sixty-Seven</h2>

For once, Natasha had options, and she was making choices based on what she wanted, rather than out of desperation.

While Dimitri was more than ready for her to move back in with him immediately, she chose to stay in her apartment for a little longer. Deep down, she knew that when she finally moved into his house, it would be for good. So she took the opportunity to sort through everything she owned, getting rid of what the myth of consumerism had told her to buy and keeping only what she truly wanted. She also made an appointment with Dimitri's financial advisor and had started using budgeting software to track her income and spending.

She thought she'd miss all the pre-season excitement of *The Dance Off*, and while she was sad not to see her friends on the cast and crew, this summer had shown her that she could continue the part she most enjoyed—namely, teaching others to appreciate dance and movement—in other ways. She dropped all the fitness classes, but kept Little Lilac, the teenage ballerinas, and some of her one-on-one clients.

When she'd made an offhand comment to Dimitri about her plan to combine classical and modern styles of dance, with the eventual goal of creating a program for high school students, his face had lit up, and he'd shot off a text to Alex about starting a nonprofit organization to make it happen. Then he'd calmed down, apologized for jumping ahead, and asked if she wanted his help.

She said yes and thanked him for supporting her dreams.

And then there was *Raz i Navsegda*. They were still in the early stages, but Alex assured her things were moving quickly and heading in a promising direction. She was excited for the project, and she had lots of thoughts on how they could bring more of the concepts in Dimitri's Idea Book to life. Every time she brought it up, Dimitri got this weird, awestruck look on his face. When she finally asked him about it—because their communication had improved to the point where she felt comfortable asking him questions, and he felt secure enough to give her a straightforward answer—he told her he just couldn't believe she was real.

He always said stuff like that now. It was like her acceptance of his love had unlocked a door, and Dimitri's own inner romantic had leaped out. The man had no chill where she was concerned, and she fucking loved it.

He hadn't been kidding about writing her poems, and she found one stuck to the fridge every single day. The ones he wrote in English were terrible, full of dirty puns and rhymes that didn't quite work. They never failed to make her laugh, which she suspected was the point. But the ones in Russian, when he translated them for her, made her heart feel like it would burst and often brought her to tears.

She cherished every single one, even the awful ones.

But they weren't alone in the world, and as much as Natasha tried to ignore her own mother, Dimitri could not do the same with his. Which was why, not two weeks after Natasha had finally gone to Dimitri and declared her love for him, they were flying across the country to see his family.

By the time they landed at Newark Airport, Natasha was a mess of nerves.

"What if she doesn't like me?" she whispered to him in the backseat of the car that was driving them to his parents' house. "What if she doesn't think I'm good enough for you?"

"That's the fifth time you've asked me that," he told her in a mild voice.

"No, it isn't."

"It is. I've been keeping count."

She scowled, then fixed her face as the car rolled to a stop.

"Relax. She's going to love you. Just like I do." He kissed her before opening the door and climbing out.

The corners of her mouth tugged upward in a smile. Hearing that he loved her never got old.

Natasha had expected to have a moment to collect herself before meeting Oksana Kovalenko. No such luck. Dimitri's mother awaited them on the curb in front of Alex's house, flanked by Alex and his wife, Marina, on one side, and Dimitri's dad, Mikhail, on the other.

Oksana, a former dancer, was still lean and willowy, with perfect posture. And *fast.* She swooped in the second Natasha was out of the car.

"There you are!" She went to throw her arms around Natasha, then froze. "Wait, can I hug you? I feel like I already know you."

Natasha laughed, a combination of nerves and giddiness. Had anyone ever been this excited to see her? Gina, Abuela…it was a short list. "You can hug me," she said, and Oksana clasped her in a tight embrace.

Oksana smelled like floral perfume. Maybe jasmine. But her hug…her hug felt *motherly.* Comforting. Warm. *Unconditional.*

Natasha pressed her lips together. Coño, she was going to cry if she didn't get ahold of herself. She'd have to blame it on jet lag.

Oksana pulled back but didn't release her. "Natasha, I'm so happy to finally meet you."

"Thank you, Mrs. Kovalenko."

"No, no!" Oksana pressed a hand to her chest, scandalized. "Shusha. You must call me Shusha."

"It's a nickname for Oksana," Dimitri explained. "We never use full names with family. Unless someone's in trouble."

Natasha grinned. "I get it. Puerto Ricans love nicknames, too." Her great-grandfather had called her Nati until the day he died. Funny, she hadn't thought about that in years.

Oksana slid an arm around Natasha's waist and walked her toward the house. "What do you call Dima?"

"I call him Macho."

Oksana let out a peal of laughter. "Perfect. And I'll call you Natka, if you'll let me."

Natasha's cheeks warmed. Did being granted a nickname mean she was part of the family? "I'd like that," she said, smiling shyly.

Inside the house, Dimitri made the rest of the introductions. Natasha had already met Alex, but she congratulated Marina and hugged Dimitri's father, who was less gregarious than his wife but smiled just as much. He insisted Natasha call him Misha.

Shusha and Misha. These were the people who'd raised Dimitri, who'd given up everything to protect their sons. Their love had shaped Dimitri into the man he was today, a man who was by turns stubborn and sweet, creative and cocky.

And so, so loving.

Natasha finally had a moment to breathe when she and Dimitri took their bags up to the guest room.

"They're a lot to take in," he said in a low voice as he set their suitcases in one corner of the room. A colorful quilt covered the bed, and a print of the Eiffel Tower hung on the wall.

"I like them." Natasha dropped her purse on the dresser and sat on the edge of the bed to catch her bearings.

"My mother has been *extremely* excited to meet you." Dimitri's tone was ominous as he hung their shared garment bag in the closet. "If you think *I'm* overbearing, just wait. I get it all from her."

"I thought she was very welcoming."

"Exactly. Don't be surprised if she tries to take you ring shopping."

"*Ring* shopping?" Natasha's eyes widened. "No me digas."

"I wouldn't put it past her."

Natasha let the implication of that sink in as she traced the embroidered designs on the bedspread with her fingers. The flippant way he discussed such a serious topic didn't send her running for the hills as it would have once upon a time, but the idea that his mother would be so heavily invested touched on some deeply buried wounds, and she wasn't sure how to proceed.

"Dima?"

Something in her tone must have given her away, because he stopped fiddling with the luggage and sat next to her. "What is it?" he asked, cupping her cheek. "After that display, you can't possibly be worried that she doesn't like you."

"It's not that." She smiled, but suddenly, and to her great embarrassment, tears welled in her eyes and her throat squeezed. If she tried to speak, she was going to start sobbing.

Dimitri's features pinched in alarm as he gripped her shoulders. "Talk to me, Kroshka. Please. What's going on?"

"I just..." She trailed off as tears spilled down her cheeks, and she struggled to convey what she was feeling. "I just want to thank you."

His brow furrowed. "For what? Making you cry?"

"No, you goofball," She huffed out a watery laugh, but it helped her regain control. "For bringing me here. For sharing your family with me. They're wonderful. And I..."

She had to stop and take a deep breath. He waited with his eyes glued to hers, nearly vibrating with intensity.

"It's something I never expected to have," she finished, with some difficulty.

He stared at her for a second, his warm brown eyes searching her face. And then he kissed her, his mouth tasting of passion, tenderness, and above all, love. The woodsy, green scent of him swirled around her, soothing her nerves. When their lips parted, he rested his forehead against hers and breathed hard.

"Do you remember what I told you?" he rasped, but he didn't wait for her to answer, which was good, because he'd said a lot of things over the past few weeks. "Anything you want, I will give you. Anything I have, is yours."

"I didn't think—"

"Anything means *anything*. And family is everything. *You* are my family, lyubimaya moya, and I am yours." His expression was fierce, but tender—a perfect encapsulation of him. "I'm done jumping through hoops, looking for somewhere to land. You're my home. Raz i navsegda."

Always and forever.

The love she felt for him threatened to overwhelm her, and fresh tears sprang to her eyes. "Cada día te quiero más," she whispered. "Every day—"

"I love you more," he finished. When she gaped at him, he winked. "AP Spanish, baby."

Her jaw fell open. "You mean every time I've cursed your ass from here to next Sunday in Spanish…"

He flashed her a shit-eating grin. "Don't worry. I won't tell my mother all the things you've said about her."

Natasha covered her face, but she was laughing. With a chuckle of his own, Dimitri enfolded her in his arms and pulled her down onto the mattress.

As her mirth subsided, Natasha closed her eyes and inhaled the scent of him. Snuggling into his warmth, she knew, with a bone-deep certainty, that she too had found a safe space to land.

Epilogue

Esmeralda frowned while Natasha showed her around Dimitri's house, but she didn't say anything. Which, if Natasha were being honest, was the best reaction she could have hoped for.

If anything, it showed that if her mother couldn't be dazzled by Dimitri's Beverly Hills home with the three-car garage, swimming pool, and private dance studio—now complete with a pole—Esmeralda never would have been impressed by Natasha's little two-bedroom apartment.

Good thing Natasha wasn't trying to earn her mother's validation anymore. Downsizing the sheer amount of stuff she owned had sparked an internal shift that allowed Natasha to release her attachment to the apartment and finally accept Dimitri's offer to move in with him permanently.

When Esmeralda's friend announced that she wouldn't be able to make it to Los Angeles, Esmeralda had threatened to cancel her flight, too. For once, Natasha let Dimitri step in and fix the problem. He insisted on paying for Esmeralda's hotel, so she had no excuse not to come, although he said it was because he didn't think it would be good for Natasha's mental health to be under the same roof with her mother. He wasn't wrong.

In the living room, Natasha let out a sigh of relief at the sound of Dimitri's SUV rolling up the driveway.

"Dimitri's here," Natasha said, grabbing her clutch from the chair. "We're meeting his parents at the premiere, since their flight is delayed."

Esmeralda shrugged and slung her bag over her shoulder.

Natasha offered her mother the passenger seat, but Esmeralda refused and sat in the back.

When Natasha met Dimitri's eye, a measure of tension eased. He was here. She wasn't in this alone.

The ride to the studio was mostly silent. Natasha spoke to Dimitri about logistics—his parents' hotel room, dinner plans for later at Kras—but her mother didn't say a word.

The silent treatment had been a big part of Natasha's childhood. When Esmeralda was pissed, she didn't speak and often acted like Natasha wasn't even in the room. For an active child who thrived on company, it had been the worst kind of punishment, and Esmeralda knew it. That she was doing it now meant she was trying to chastise Natasha for something.

And for the first time in her life, Natasha didn't give a shit.

Not caring what her mother thought of her, or why she was in a snit, was the most liberating feeling in the world. She should have tried it a lot earlier.

It was weird attending the premiere of *The Dance Off* as a guest. She and Dimitri had seats right at one of the VIP dinner-club-style tables on the edge of the dance floor, but their families had to sit further back.

Even stranger was how similar this felt to their trip to Babe Planet. Maybe it was always weird to visit a former job after quitting. It might feel the same if Natasha stopped by Corazón restaurant in the Bronx, where she had waitressed when she was a teenager.

Dimitri leaned in and spoke in a low voice. "You okay?"

"Yeah. Thank you again for arranging everything."

"Of course. Nothing makes me happier than taking care of our family."

Our family. He'd accepted that Esmeralda was difficult and had approached her with impersonal good cheer that bordered on dismissive. He didn't try to charm her out of her sulk, but he also didn't stoop to her bad mood. It was probably the best approach to take with her. Natasha wished she'd figured that out years ago.

Natasha slipped her hand into his and squeezed. Openly touching him in public was also weird, but in a good way.

They found Dimitri's parents standing near their table. When Oksana set eyes on Natasha, she rushed forward to kiss her on both cheeks.

"Beautiful girl!" she trilled, pulling Natasha in for a hug. "Look how stunning you look. That color is perfect on you. But of course, you always wear everything so well."

Natasha couldn't help but grin. "Spasibo, Shusha." Oksana was warm, giving, and effusive with praise. The opposite of Esmeralda.

Natasha made introductions. Oksana dialed back the enthusiasm, and Misha, Dimitri's father, was quiet but sweet. Esmeralda was polite, but kept her lips pressed together, as if releasing anything resembling a smile would bring about the end of the world. Oksana peppered Esmeralda with questions about being a hairstylist, and Esmeralda finally opened up a bit.

Dimitri kept his arm around Natasha's waist while he spoke with his father in Russian. It was a beautiful language, but so different from Spanish. Natasha had mentioned she might like to learn it, and he'd surprised her with a subscription to a language-learning app. When she commented on it, he'd said simply, "You wanted it."

Oksana turned to her new favorite topic—praising Natasha. As Dimitri's mother raved about Natasha's past performances on *The Dance Off*, Esmeralda's lips flattened into a line.

Before Natasha could jump in to change the subject, Esmeralda opened her mouth and said in a curt tone, "I know. She *is* my daughter."

Oksana blinked, but they were all saved from responding when Kevin bounded over, dressed in a sparkly costume tux for the opening number.

"Hey, what's good?" He threw an arm over Natasha's shoulder, earning him a dark look from Dimitri. "Are y'all ready for an incredible show?"

"Kevin, I'd like you to meet my…" Natasha trailed off when she caught sight of her mother's face.

Esmeralda's lips parted, her jaw fell slack, and her eyes rounded, as if transfixed. "Kevin Ray," she whispered.

Natasha blinked. Her mother knew Kevin?

Mami shuffled forward and took the hand Kevin offered her, clasping it between both of her own. "Kevin, you are *amazing*. I always vote for you."

Natasha stared at Esmeralda. *Everyone* stared at Esmeralda.

Kevin spoke first. "You don't vote for Natasha?"

"I vote for both of you. And Gina. Every single week."

"Mami, you watch the show?" Natasha couldn't keep the surprise out of her voice. All these years, her mother had bitched about *The Dance Off*, claiming she didn't have the time or inclination to watch a bunch of so-called celebrities tottering around like clowns.

"Of course I watch the show," Esmeralda scoffed.

Natasha raised her eyebrows. Well, that was news to her.

Oksana pulled Dimitri away, and Natasha listened with half an ear while Kevin charmed Esmeralda. They took a selfie together, and he pulled her into a quick salsa step. Natasha heard her mother say, "You're my favorite guy on the show. Not like that judge. He grades too harshly."

Oh, lord. Natasha barely resisted rolling her eyes. No wonder Mami was acting cold toward Dimitri—she'd fallen for his TV persona as the cranky judge.

Kevin leaned in close and whispered, "Dimitri's not so bad. I mean, he wouldn't know a perfect paso doble if it bit him on the ass, but he loves Tash, so…I guess he's not the worst."

Natasha turned her back on them to hide her smile.

Kevin said goodbye to the group, gave Esmeralda a kiss on the cheek, then slipped away backstage.

When Reggie Kong, one of the show's hosts, stopped by to greet them, Oksana and Esmeralda bonded over their love of Reggie's blue-streaked hair and edgy gowns.

"Look," Esmeralda said, shaking out her dark locks. "I added some blue to the underside, in your honor."

Natasha couldn't stay quiet a second longer. "Wow, Mami, you really are a fan." Lord knew where she found the courage to tease her mother, but to Natasha's surprise, Esmeralda's tan cheeks flushed and the corner of her mouth lifted.

Huh. Maybe there were other ways to deal with the woman.

Dimitri slipped an arm around Natasha's waist, and she bumped him with her hip.

"It's nice being here as guests," she murmured. "We get to watch Lori make history."

"The first pair of female partners on *The Dance Off*," he mused. "It's a huge deal. I almost wish I were still judging, so I could give them a hundred."

"Pssh. Like you would ever give someone a perfect score in the first episode."

He grinned. "I guess we'll never know."

She pointed to their mothers, who had pulled out their phones and were looking up videos of their favorite dance routines from past seasons. "Maybe this Ukrainian-Puerto Rican mix will work out after all."

"We'll make it work. No matter what comes our way, we'll make it work. Together."

He kissed her temple and she felt the warmth of it down to the tips of her toes, along with an illicit little thrill.

For years, her interactions with him in this very space had

been marked by tension and secrecy. Now, there was no reason to hold back.

She grabbed the lapels of his jacket and gave him a sultry pout. "Come on, Machote. You can do better than that."

With a wicked grin, he yanked her against him. "Challenge accepted."

———

WITHIN A FEW HOURS, footage of their kiss had gone viral. By the next morning, everyone was talking about the dance world's new power couple. *Aliens Don't Dance* hit the top ten list of most streamed movies that day, and Natasha's follower count soared. Natasha's agent and Dimitri's management team were fielding requests left and right.

Natasha sat at Dimitri's kitchen counter, sipping her latte as he spoke on the phone with Alex.

"Da. Do svidaniya." Dimitri hung up and scrubbed a hand down his face.

She leaned forward, nearly breathless with anticipation. "Well? Is it happening?"

He dropped his hand and appeared dazed. "I mean, it's still early, and things could go wrong, but...yeah. It's happening." A brilliant smile lit his face as he turned to her. "*Raz i Navsegda* is happening."

Natasha let out a screech like a pterodactyl. He grabbed for her mug, setting it aside a split second before she threw her arms around his neck.

And then she just held him while he clung to her.

"I'm so proud of you," she whispered, and he squeezed her tighter.

"I couldn't have done it without you."

Smiling, she rested her head on his shoulder.

She wasn't alone anymore. And neither was he.

Always and forever.

Author's Note

Dear Reader,

Dance with Me was my second novel, and was originally released as an ebook in 2017. It was only available for a few short years before the rights reverted back to me, and I'm happy to present this expanded edition that delves more deeply into Natasha and Dimitri's past. If you enjoyed it, I hope you'll consider leaving a review!

You can see more of Natasha and Dimitri in *Dance All Night: A Dance Off Holiday Novella*, which centers around Dimitri's brother, Nik!

The best way to stay up to date with future book news is to subscribe to my newsletter at alexisdaria.com/newsletter.

All the best,
Alexis

Want more of The Dance Off?

Take the Lead
Book One in The Dance Off

From Alexis Daria, *USA Today* bestselling author of *You Had Me at Hola*, comes a "very spicy" (*Cosmopolitan*) romance set against the backdrop of a reality dance competition.

After four lackluster seasons on *The Dance Off*, Gina Morales is determined to make it to the finals. When she's whisked off to the wilds of Alaska to meet her new celebrity partner, she prays for a winter Olympian. Instead, she gets Stone Nielson, a strong, silent, and ridiculously sexy survivalist. Which is a problem, because the only thing Gina won't do to win is fake a show-mance for the cameras...and that's exactly what her producers want.

Stone dreads relocating to Los Angeles almost as much as he fears revealing the truth behind his family's own hit show, *Living Wild*. Little by little, though, his vivacious dance partner drags him out of his shell, and soon, he'll do anything to help Gina reach her goals – even burlesque. But as much as they try to hide their developing romance, Gina and Stone's explosive chemistry on and off the dance floor is unmistakable. With the spotlight threatening to expose all their secrets, they'll have to decide if the real prize is the trophy, or a shot at true love.

Dance All Night
A Dance Off Holiday Novella

From Alexis Daria, *USA Today* bestselling author of *You Had Me at Hola*, comes a festive and flirty holiday romance set in the world of *The Dance Off*.

On New Year's Eve, Broadway dancer Nik Kovalenko and ballroom champion Jess Davenport shared an impulsive midnight kiss. Jess hoped it would be the start of something more, but when Nik left on a national tour the very next day, it confirmed all of Jess's cynical views on love.

Nearly a year later, Nik returns to Los Angeles, ready to prove to Jess that he'll stick around this time. Jess isn't convinced, but she agrees to three holiday-themed dates. If Nik can make a Scrooge like her believe in the magic of the holiday season, she'll give their relationship a chance. But he won't know until New Year's Eve. If she kisses him at midnight, he'll have his answer…

About the Author

Photo by Chandra Wicke

Alexis Daria is the award-winning and *USA Today* bestselling author of *You Had Me at Hola, Along Came Amor, Take the Lead,* and more. Her books have been featured on several "Best of" lists and have received starred reviews from multiple trade publications. A former visual artist, Alexis is a life-long New Yorker who loves Broadway musicals and pizza.